REVELATION IN THE CAVE

Nancy Flinchbaugh

ISBN-13: 978-0985524401
ISBN-10: 0985524405

Printed in USA by Spiritual Seedlings
Springfield, Ohio

The scripture quotations in this book are from the New Revised Standard Version Bible, copyright © 1989, 1995 by the Division of Christian Education of the National Council of the Churches of Christ in the United States of America. Used by permission. All rights re-served.

Taize Songs used with permission from Brother Christoph. Copyright © Ateliers et Presses de Taizé, 71250 Taizé, France.

All characters appearing in this work are fictitious. Any resemblance to real persons, living or dead, is purely coincidental.

The story of Thecla appearing in this book is adapted from *The Acts of Paul and Thecla*, an apocryphal story in the public domain.
View at http://www.christianscience.org/thecla.htm.

Cover design by Hebner Design Solutions, courtesy of the Small Business Development Center, Springfield, Ohio. Art: Tissue Paper Collage by Nancy Flinchbaugh.

Dedication

This book is dedicated to the memory of my spiritual mentors and relatives who call me to creatively love and serve God and people with my life:

To Rev. Charles Sheldon, a third cousin of my maternal grandmother, who wrote *In His Steps*.[i] From his book, has come the popular phrase, "What Would Jesus Do?" His work inspired me to write this novel, calling our generation to seriously rethink the book of Revelation and what it has to do with a man who preached a path of suffering love.

To my mother, Jean Turner Flinchbaugh, who loved me with all her heart through gestation and 51 years of my life and who called me to a deep faith in a loving God.

To my mother's sister, Aunt Ginger (Mary) Turner Ralston, who delighted in me and encouraged me to finish my book from her death bed,

To Ruth Turner, my grandfather's cousin, who spirits me as a fellow artist, through her watercolors, Persian carpet and encouraging spirit, and

To my father, Rev. Dr. James E. Flinchbaugh, who devoted his life to the service of others in Christian ministry and challenged me to do likewise.

Table of Contents

Foreword

Nancy Flinchbaugh is a passionate woman. Her passion focuses on interesting matters. For Nancy, poverty is an unacceptable reality. Injustice haunts her. Diversity fascinates her, and she has worked powerfully since the events of 9-11-2001 to combat the religious and racial intolerance that feeds oppression and justifies terrorism.

Nancy is passionate about getting religion right, but not "far right." The calculating misrepresentation of the Bible and deliberate distortion of the gospels sit high on her list of acts of injustice. No one understands life and religion completely. All of us have a framework of assumptions that serves as a lens to focus what we see, read, and understand about things that matter. Learning to see through a different lens of assumptions challenges everyone.

Feeling strongly about one way of reading the Bible over an alternative reading is not enough for Nancy. As the Bible is a collection of powerful stories, Nancy has chosen to create a powerful story of her own as an alternative framework for reading and understanding the New Testament Apocalypse known as the book of Revelation.

Nancy has written an interesting story about interesting people. You will be glad to know the "MAMs" and often wonder if they are for real. If you let them guide you on their own journey of discovery, you will have an opportunity to challenge your own assumptions about the things that matter so much to Nancy and her MAMs. If even you disagree, you will still have a good story. I do recommend it to you.

Dr. Bill Salyers, Hillsborough, NC
Retired American Baptist Pastor
February 2012

Acknowledgement

I would like to thank the many people who helped me write and publish this book. First and foremost, my husband, Steve Schlather, who has traveled to Greece and Turkey with me twice in the process of writing this book, and lent encouragement, love and support throughout the process, as well as providing copy editing services for the final edition. Thanks to my sons, Jacob Flinchbaugh Schlather for encouraging me and giving me an early hard back version of my unpublished book for Mothers' Day and to Luke Flinchbaugh Schlather for serving as webmaster. This book could not have happened without my friend, Mary Jane Salyers, who started a writing group and read and re-read my manuscript over several years with careful notations and recommendations, along with her husband, Rev. Dr. Bill Salyers, who offered his theological expertise in the group, and other group members over the years: Mildred Archie, Peggy Hanna, Mabel Jackson, Marva Riley, Steve Schlather, Geoff Steele and Holly Wolfe. Thanks to Dr. Barbara Kaiser for introducing me to St. Thecla at a women's retreat and assisting with my initial research. I also want to thank my other friends who read the book and gave suggestions, including Chris Parli and David Horne, Gundula and Larry Houff, and Dr. Ken Whitt. I am also indebted to Dr. Renate Pillinger of Vienna, Austria who corresponded with me concerning my project and Dr. Sabine Ladstaeeter who asked her Austrian and Italian archaeological crew that oversee excavation and restoration of the Cave of St. Paul at Ephesus, Turkey to welcome me and my husband to the cave to visit, practicing Turkish hospitality offering tea and a wonderful tour. I also would want to thank my friends at the Antioch Writer's Workshop who helped in early days of writing, including workshop leaders Elizabeth Strout and Carrie Bebris.

And finally, this book would not have been possible without divine intervention. From the beginning, I sought the direction of our Great Creator who loved me, blessed me and helped me write this book at every step. And so I say, "Thank you, thank you, thank you, God."

Prologue

September 18, 2006.

The brilliant sun streamed into the Ephesus amphitheater. Blue domed the heavens above, while the September heat settled dust on the earth below. Even now, after centuries of earthquakes and empires, the concrete steps and perfect acoustics offered a suitable forum for the day.

From the platform, Emily glanced out at people gathering for the press conference. In the front row, her grandmother's friends chatted like ladies on an afternoon excursion. A vested man cradled a heavy telephoto lens in his hands, aiming at the stage and the others getting ready to speak. A small man in a cowboy hat and blonde hair jotted notes on a long pad, nodding to his subject. She recognized the man being interviewed as an archaeologist from Istanbul. Lining the aisles and the top row, young Turkish soldiers stood erect with machine guns held diagonally across their chests.

Emily mentally rehearsed her script, choosing tone inflections and animations to bring the words from the first century alive. Looking up to the tree-covered hill, she focused on the red flag signaling the Grotto of St. Paul. Suddenly, Emily could imagine Thecilla there, looking down into the amphitheater. Draped in a blue robe, she cradled the scrolls in her hands. Protecting her uncle's revelation? Emily sensed Thecilla's excitement and... her fear. The girl turned, tucked the scrolls under her arm, and began to run, disappearing into the woods.

A moment later, Emily imagined yet another image. A red-cloaked man stopped his black horse in the same clearing. Light sparkled on his armor and caught the gleaming point of his spear. Emily shivered. The man pointed the horse toward the woods and charged on.

Halim's warm voice rang out and brought her back to the present. "Good afternoon, ladies and gentlemen."

Emily focused her attention back to the stage, the microphone, and her new friend, the Turkish archaeologist. Again, she rehearsed her lines, preparing to stand when Ursula called on her. Taking deep breaths, she knew she could calm her heart.

Ursula stood and began to explain the archaeological expedition. Emily listened, even while she kept reading her own lines. Any moment now, she knew it would be her turn.

And then, a shot rang out. The MAMs scrambled. What happened?

Another explosion knocked her back, collapsing her chair. Sprawled out on the stage behind the others, she looked up and saw Brother Gabriel. The familiar monk helped her up, shielded her under his brown robe, and ushered her off the stage.

Instinctively, her hand patted her breastbone. A dull ache spread down toward her heart. Blood seeped out onto her hand. Pulling up the small necklace Josh had given her many years earlier, she gasped at a deep gouge. The imprint of a bullet? A small abrasion oozed red where the metal lamb had been pushed against her chest.

Later on the boat, she reviewed the afternoon in her mind and tried to understand. What happened at that press conference? Who wants to kill her and why?

1. A Dig is Born

January, 2006

Katharine Long climbed out of bed, leaving her husband snoring on their king-sized mattress. Insomnia again. Sometimes her best ideas came at this hour. A crazy idea, perhaps, but it kept hanging there. Like the roll of fat camping out in her belly since menopause, this thought would not go away.

Downstairs, she signed in to her email account and began to compose a letter to her college roommate, Ursula. How long had it been? Had she called when her students voted her professor of the year last Spring? What will Ursula think? If nothing else, perhaps she could sleep if she pushed the thought out of her head and into cyberspace. Typing now, Katharine entered the idea to her favorite University of Michigan archaeology professor, the best friend of her college years, the buddy who was always there for her, who would at least find some humor in the thought.

***

Ursula Goodtree dusted the snow off her feet as she clicked open the door to her new Camry. Why am I in Michigan? Why am I here for another winter? She questioned herself and then answered: Where else would I go? And here I come for another exciting day with Generation "Y" and the frickin' male egos in the university.

An associate professor of archaeology, Ursula had watched her career grow and then stagnate in the throes of the Michigan public university system. She knew it was no one's fault but her own. She could blame it on the male-dominated profession, the lack of opportunity, the grind of the daily teaching process, but in the end, she was the one who wasn't going anywhere because she had forgotten how to dream.

The snowflakes swirled around her. At another time of her life, she might have enjoyed the beauty of this winter day. But now the flying ice bits only signaled three months of barren weather ahead, and a reminder to pick up her Prozac prescription on the way home from work. She wondered why she felt like a robot with frozen parts.

10

For many months, Ursula's fall sabbatical had been looming like a phantom on the horizon. Never before had she faced a quarter off with such dread. Her shrink kept bringing it up every week. The issue was a symbol of the state of her life. Only 48, but she felt like an Eskimo ready to wander off to die. Her enthusiasm had burned out somewhere along the path of 25 years of college teaching and archaeological digs.

If you were a fly on the wall, when Ursula drove onto campus this day, you would never guess what was going on inside her head. The custodian who greeted her at the door to her department building, though, could tell you about her beauty. Her black hair radiated out in curls framing a fashionable floppy hat of mink. Wool flaps covered her ears, and a ribbon pulled them together against her rounded chin. Her sable brown wool coat reached down to high heeled-black leather boots. Ursula's olive complexion, long slender body, beautiful face and dancing eyes still turned many heads. The leather furniture in her tidy office formed a cozy circle looking out onto the snow-covered campus. Warm reds, oranges and yellows created a place of quiet beauty and welcome. The place where Ursula hung her hat at the University of Michigan was a place of distinction she had achieved by years of hard work.

Ursula flipped on her computer to print out her lecture outline for the day and opened her email. A Pavlovian response, one she needed to unlearn with so much junk mail and faculty stuff cluttering her life. Scanning the new emails her eyes focused on something good: Katharine Long. Without thinking or looking at the clock, she opened the mail and began to read.

Dear Ursula,

Greetings from your old buddy in Ohio. It has been too long, girlfriend. We have got to plan a weekend trip sometime this spring. In the meantime, I have a very strange idea. I can't sleep. Ah, the change of life!

I think I told you that I've been in a book club for several years. Tonight, we discussed In Search of Paul[ii] *by John Dominic Crossan and Jonathan Reed. Our group was focused on cave paintings found in the Cave of St. Paul on the side of BülBül Dag in Ephesus by an Austrian archaeologist in 1906. Are you familiar with the picture of Thecla and Paul, side by side?*

Our group had the idea that they wanted to go search for Thecla. I know it's a long shot, but maybe to plan some further excavations in that cave? There are six of us ready to go.

11

You're our ticket to Turkey. What do you think? Am I just
some crazy old crone who can't sleep or is this a great idea?

Love, Katharine.

Suddenly, Ursula's sabbatical problem poked its head front and center, and she laughed. A cave dig in Ephesus with a group of Katharine's crazy romance readers? It had been a long time since Ursula was so amused. A few minutes later, Ursula headed for class with a smile on her face and a new spring in her step.

Yes, Katharine, you are crazy. But just maybe...

***

Three weeks later, Ursula felt like the master of her own destiny for the first time in years. She literally skipped to her counselor's office to share the good news.

"Don't you think it's perfect, Meredith? Don't you agree, it's exactly what I need? My department will fund the dig. Those wonderful men I'm always complaining about bent all the rules for me! The Turkish government has given me a green light. Tourism is big business there these days, you know. They've poured millions into excavating the tier houses in Ephesus, restoring some of them to their first century glory. Two-story condos! The Austrian archaeological team welcomes our help. The Austrians have been driving the work for years on the site, and the head of the Grotto of St. Paul dig is actually a woman! She wants us to put some extra attention to an area of the cave where there are no frescoes, and also to open a square or two outside the cave."

"You go, girl," Meredith sent her off, cutting the session short. "Make an appointment for next month to give me an update."

2. The Blessing of the MAMs

September 9, 2006

And so it happened that this unusual assortment of women formerly known as the "Romance Readers Anonymous," now calling themselves the "MAMs" (The Magnificent and Marvelous Book Club) descended on Chicago O'Hare on a September day to catch a plane for a cruise originating in Venice, with a final destination of Kusadasi, Turkey, for an archaeological dig at the Grotto of St. Paul, on the hill of BûlBûl Dag above the ancient Roman site of Ephesus.

The MAMs arrived on the first flight of the morning from Dayton, Ohio. The flight attendant's voice broke into the plane cabin, "Ladies and Gentlemen, welcome to Chicago. The temperature is 60 degrees and sunny. Enjoy your visit."

Katharine Long, 51-year-old religion professor whose email had started the ball rolling, flipped open her cell phone and pushed Ursula's number. "We're here, Ursula!" Where are you?"

"I just arrived. I'm on my way to Terminal 5."

"I can't wait to see you!" Katharine tucked her cell phone into her purse, combed her light brown hair into place, grabbed her carry-on and followed her friends down the aisle and into O'Hare.

Jane Masters gathered the group together. She towered over the others, with short dishwater blonde hair, lanky frame, button-down white shirt and khakis for the trip. With her always ready smile, she took command. "OK, we have 45 minutes to get to Terminal 5, Gate M23. Are you ready? We're going to sprint."

Sallie Quisenberry, a chubby retired kindergarten teacher whose laughter and delightful ways kept the group's spirit light, challenged Masters' order. "Sprint is not in my vocabulary. Hey money bags, why don't you hire one of those golf carts for us?"

"Not a bad idea," Jane replied. "I'll place the order, but we've gotta catch the People Mover to Terminal 5 first. Ladies, let's go."

"People mover?" Priscilla Johnson shook her head. The five-foot-tall, petite blonde secretary, dressed fashionably with a short black skirt, pink gathered top and long spiked heels came new to the travel arena, with her first time in O'Hare and her first trip across the Atlantic about to happen.

13

"Airport Transportation System. It's like a train that connects all the terminals," veteran traveler, Jane explained.

The group of six obediently followed Jane toward the train for the international terminal. Behind their leader, recent college graduate Emily Jean Turner pumped her short legs, perky as the pixie hairs standing on her head. Her fiancé had broken off their engagement because she'd chosen the trip over a fall wedding, yet excitement beamed out of Emily's bright blue eyes. Priscilla, an avid jogger, kept pace with Emily, despite the spiked heels. Katharine strolled slightly behind the two small women, long legs easily keeping pace. Bringing up the rear were Sallie and Molly Mabra, the short and heavier ones. Molly wore her favorite African dress, of gold with brown drums, showing off her plump behind, which kept a smile on her husband's face. Wrinkle lines emanating from her eyes carried years of laughter and tears.

Jane stopped at the information desk to order the motorized golf cart, while gesturing the others on. Hurrying to catch up, she bumped shoulders with a handsome man in khakis and a white button-down shirt and tie. Jane enjoyed people. She read the jolt as a come on and was quick with a retort. "Well, excuse you, Mr. Politician. Just who do you think you are, bumping into me that way?"

"I'm always distracted when I see beautiful women. I'm sorry, you took my breath away." The tall man, dressed almost identically to Jane, but for a dark blue blazer over his white shirt and khakis, threw back his head and laughed. "Yes ma'am, I forgot to watch where I was going."

A smile played on Jane's lips. She felt the intensity of his deep brown eyes probing hers. "Just a little accident, accidentally ran into the beautiful woman you were looking at?"

"I noticed you on the flight, but had no idea I'd actually get to talk with you. Dan Parks is my name." He extended his hand to Jane, who returned a firm shake and laughed.

"Men never cease to amaze me. Very smooth, Mr. Parks."

"Could I borrow that Wall Street Journal when you're done? I haven't checked my stocks yet today."

"Well, sure. As a matter of fact, you can have it." Jane handed the newspaper to him, walking quickly to catch up with her gang of six now a few paces ahead.

Molly turned around to look for Jane. She waited, then whispered, "What are you doing talking to a MAN? Didn't you know this is a women only tour?"

Jane gave Molly a side hug. "OK, OK. I didn't start that. I'll be good from here on out."

But Dan Parks had other ideas. Jane stretched her long legs out into a brisk walk. Parks matched her stride.

14

"Jane, we seem to be walking in the same direction. Where are you headed next?"

"Amsterdam, then Venice. What about you?"

"What a coincidence."

"You're scaring me. I think I better stick with my friends here, but maybe I'll see you around."

"Wait, Jane. No need to be afraid." Mr. Parks opened his jacket and held out his I.D. Jane read "Private Detective" engraved under "Daniel Parks" on the gold badge.

"No fear, OK. I'll see you around." Jane turned toward her group, walking over to the opposite side of the concourse.

Molly grabbed Jane's arm. "Now behave. No more picking up strange men in the airport. He could be a terrorist!"

"No actually, he's a private detective!"

"We haven't even left American soil and already I'm being followed. They don't trust Black people anywhere, you know. What now? Do they think I'm a terrorist?"

"You're paranoid. That man isn't following you."

"OK. I hope you're right. Do you have the hats and shirts for the ceremony? We thought we could crown Ursula at the gate."

Jane patted her carry-on luggage. "It's all right here."

Molly's brainchild would soon unfold. She loved ceremony of any kind and had created such an event for the MAMs before they boarded the trans-Atlantic flight. Jane's contribution of hats would cap off the event at their departure gate. Although she was very excited about the ceremony, sadness camped out in her spirit, too. She retreated into her own thoughts and took quick jogging steps while trying to keep up with Jane's long strides. Jane had no idea what it was like to be Black in America. And that was only the beginning of the differences. Talk about politics! Smack in the middle of George W. and six years of hell. Jane, she knew, had a completely different perspective.

Whether you look down from the ivory tower with a portfolio of stocks tucked under your arm or you look up from the Black slums, shuffling credit cards to put food on the table, hard to believe the United States of America was the same place. Jane didn't get it. In fact, she had made Jane mad trying to explain. Molly learned to keep her mouth shut, but that didn't keep her mind from racing.

From every angle she could find it seemed to her that the grand old U.S. of A. was heading for destruction. The family has fallen apart, the Black men in prisons, jobs leaving the country, a mistake of a war in Iraq, and now it had all scuttled Mark away. Her youngest son who should be in college, front and center in harm's way: Baghdad.

15

While Jane's stock portfolio had done very well in the past year under George W., Molly couldn't shake the persistent feeling that a crash was on the horizon. From her view in a small city government, she saw fewer jobs, fewer resources, persons living on the edge, an underclass of people growing, children who were difficult to educate, people damaged by drugs and alcohol, mental illness and the foreclosure problem that just wouldn't go away. Long ago she had shifted her deferred retirement account into a flat percentage. She couldn't trust the stock market. It had cost her, but eventually she knew the fall was coming.

There's an elephant in the house! But try to talk about it? "Pessimist!" They label you. "Is your glass half empty or half full?" someone would ask. The failing American democracy run by millionaires who are more interested in getting elected and catering to special interests than looking after the future of the country. What could she do about any of it?

"Molly! Where are you?" Jane yelled into her ear. "You look like you just lost your best friend."

"Oh. I'm sorry." In her best southern drawl, Molly told Jane, "You do not want to go there." Then she changed the subject, leaving her thoughts of doom far behind. "How far to the gate? Do you think we'll have time for the ceremony?"

"By my calculations we'll be at the train in three minutes. If the golf cart I ordered is on time, we should have 15 minutes to spare. It will be close, but I think we can do it. Get your paperwork out, and we'll be ready to go."

***

By the time Ursula made it to Gate M23, her heart was pumping, and she felt great. And there they were: a circle of women and one familiar face. She made a beeline for her old friend.

"Katharine!" She embraced her college roommate and tears streamed down her face.

"It has been too long! You don't look a day over... 50?"

The others gathered around to meet their leader.

"So, these are the Magnificent MAMs? I've heard so much about you!"

"Yes, ma'am. We are, ma'am. Yes, we are Magnificent And Marvelous... the MAMs. Got that... a little acronym there? And..." Jane sputtered the words, while the others laughed.

Molly took charge.

"You got here just in the nick of time for your induction ceremony! Circle up, now, ladies." She distributed a piece of paper to each of the women. In the center of the huddle she covered the floor with

16

a brightly flowered cloth, then placed a clear plastic bowl in the center. She pulled out a large package of M & M's from her bag, tore off a corner and poured them into the bowl.

"Let us read in unison our welcome to Ursula."

The ladies placed their hands on Ursula. Jane and Katharine stood with their hands on either shoulder. Molly and Sallie held either hand, Emily and Priscilla stood behind with their hands reaching up to rest on her shoulder blades.

"Is this the laying on of the hands?" She asked nervously.

"Yes. Exactly!" Molly agreed.

"Don't worry. We're harmless. We'll grow on you." Sallie Quisenberry's belly shook and she began the laugh that got the rest of the group going, too.

Molly quickly stopped them. "Ladies, your part, please. Let us read in unison."

And then they did. Katharine, Emily, Molly, Sallie, Priscilla, and Jane formally extended the words of welcome to their new leader.

"We the Magnificent and Marvelous, the MAM's, do hereby bequeath upon Ursula Goodtree, the title of Honorary MAM, in recognition for her amazing achievement of obtaining a grant to make the Archaeological Expedition in Search of Thecla possible, and we do also bequeath upon her the highest award possible. We do hereby dub you Super MAM."

Molly unrolled a red cape with "Super MAM" blazing in yellow letters on the back, dancing it at her side, as if ready to take on the bulls of Pamplona. She placed the cape around Ursula's shoulders and fastened the velcro at her neck.

"Now, Ursula, it's time for your part."

Those waiting to board the flight were beginning to form a larger circle around the MAMs. Ursula looked at Katharine with a question in her eye. "You didn't tell me about this!"

"What is life without a few surprises?" Sallie winked, "The fun has just begun."

Ursula laughed, twirled in a circle with her cape flying up, then started to read.

"I, Ursula Goodtree, do solemnly pledge to loyally serve the MAMs. I will lead their archaeological expedition to the best of my ability. I will eat M & M's. I will laugh at the MAMs' jokes. I will not take myself too seriously. I will share my opinions freely and respect those of the other MAMs. As God is my helper, I hereby accept the title of "Super MAM" for the duration of this expedition."

"Eat up ladies. You may now partake of the elements," Molly instructed. She reached down into the bowl and grabbed a handful of M & M's, handing one to each of the women. They each ate the morsel, and then Molly nodded to Priscilla standing beside her, and Priscilla handed several M & M's to Ursula.

"You didn't know what you were in for, did you?" Priscilla laughed.

"Katharine didn't tell me about all of this!" Ursula stuffed some M & M's in her mouth and twirled around again. "What a riot!"

"And now it's your turn, Emily." Molly pulled out another sheet and began to read. "On this auspicious occasion we do hereby solemnly and most reverently admit to our numbers the favorite granddaughter of our esteemed member, Abigail Wesley. Emily Jean Turner, repeat after me."

"I, Emily Jean Turner, do solemnly swear."

Emily laughed and looked nervously about the large crowd gathered.

"Hold your hand up, dear. Like a Girl Scout taking an oath?" Sallie demonstrated and let out a large guffaw.

Emily held up her hand to begin her oath. The loudspeaker interrupted, announcing general boarding.

"Hurry up!" Molly chided and then finished Emily's part. "To faithfully serve the MAMs and to do my best to uncover the truth about Thecla."

Emily giggled.

"This is a very serious ceremony," Jane stated. "You can't laugh yet. Wait two minutes."

The loudspeaker interrupted the MAMs again for final boarding, but Molly went on, "It's almost time to go. Glad we got that chocolate communion in. Thank you, Jesus, for chocolate!" Looking up, she made the sign of the cross with her hand, touching her forehead, her heart, and then each shoulder.

"You're not Catholic," Jane complained.

"But it was a nice touch," Sallie said. "Part of the ceremony, right?"

Molly nodded and continued. "Now, ladies, it's time for the most solemn vow." Fanning astrobright yellow papers out, she walked in front of each woman, letting them each draw a sheet out.

"Did you write this?" Ursula inquired.

"Of course." Molly smiled.

"She's our writer." Sallie chuckled.

"OK, now..." And they began to read.

> *Bring her out into the Light*
> *Who?*
> *The Lady in the shadows!*
> *Bring her back into her fullness!*
> *Thecla!*

The friend of Paul of Taurus
Bring her out into this time
First-century saint!
Dig her up. Uncover truth.
No longer hiding
No longer mystery
No longer myth.
Saved from fire
Saved from the lions
Saved by the female lion
Heroine of all time
The feminine story.
Spirit awakening
We must find her!

The power of the moment caught the group by surprise. Even those watching felt the energy. In the midst of the comings and goings of mundane terminal life, the proclamation drew applause. The MAMs smiled. Sallie took a bow. Jane clapped and gestured toward Molly. Sallie began to laugh, and then they all were giggling and clapping at the same time.

"Yes, we must find her!" Ursula stopped the laughter.

"Yes, we will," Jane flexed her arm like Rosie the Riveter. "Yes, we will dig her up. Ladies, your plane waits."

Molly nodded, but when the group began to pick up their carry-ons, she stopped them. "Just a minute. One more thing. A blessing circle."

"A what?" Jane protested. "Come on, it's time to get on the plane."

"A blessing circle. We'll each offer a blessing."

"We're going to be late." Jane protested.

"Humor her, dear." Sallie laughed. "God knows we need the blessings."

Molly continued, "I will begin, and then we'll go around the circle. God bless our expedition."

"God bless your little hearts," Sallie quipped in a southern drawl. The others broke up.

Katharine called them back. "Blessings on our pilots across the Atlantic!"

"God bless us and keep us and lift his countenance upon us," Priscilla prayed.

"May God be with us as we bravely go where no archaeological expedition has ever gone before, and may God bless us with rich findings." Ursula twirled around and flung her cape again. "Super MAMs, here we come!"

19

"She's good!" Sallie laughed and looked at Katharine. "Where did you pick her up?"

"May God bless each of us in our journey of discovery," Emily said seriously. Sallie looked at Molly with a slight turn of her head, and then nodded in appreciation for Emily's thought.

"Out of the mouth of babes!" Sallie quipped.

"God bless us everyone!" Jane announced and then from her bag she pulled a bundle of red hats. The floppy straw hats sported the MAMs' embroidered names on the front, and on the back, there was a picture of Thecla from the cave painting with the trip title, "The MAMs Archaeological Expedition in Search of Thecla."

Placing them on the women's heads one by one, she announced, "God Bless You, and You, and You, and You, and You, and You! And Me!"

Molly picked up the bowl and the cloth and the group moved toward the plane.

"Why is Emily's hat shocking pink, instead of red? I want pink, too!" Sallie asked.

"You ungrateful twit," Jane retorted. "You receive a beautiful gift and the first thing out of your mouth is a complaint? I think you taught kindergarten too long! Don't you know that women under 50 are to wear pink hats, and only the wise women 50 and over are eligible for the Red Hat Society. And dear, I just signed us all up."

Ursula whispered to Katharine. "Don't tell them I'm only 48."

Katharine whispered back, "Your secret is safe with me; childhood genius skipping grades. My lips are sealed."

"Thank you, Jane! These hats are wonderful," Molly said. "Is there time for a picture?"

"Ladies and Gentleman, we are now completing final boarding for Flight 1923 for Amsterdam. All passengers should proceed to the gate."

Dan Parks stepped up and tapped Jane on the shoulder. "Could I do the honors? Does someone have a camera?"

Molly had already pulled her camera out of her bag. "Here it is!"

The MAMs gathered together. Ursula, Katharine and Jane took the back row, towering over the others by a head. In the front were the shorter ones, Emily, Molly, Sallie and Priscilla.

"I'll take it on three!" Parks yelled.

The MAMs smiled, tilting their heads together, their arms on each other's shoulders.

"One – Two – Three!" Parks snapped the picture. "One more time. One – Two – Three!"

The MAMs posed, the crowd cheered. The flight attendant said, "Please board!"

And they were off, grabbing their carry-on luggage. The MAMs made their way down the corridor toward the plane and the Archaeological Expedition in Search of Thecla was on its way.

3. Thecla at the Window

September 1, 48 A.D.

"Thecla, come away from the window, now." Her mother barked commands, yet Thecla leaned out, reaching her hand through the window bars, her palm open toward the crowd gathering now around the bow-legged man on the street. Straining she could hear him, "The kingdom of heaven is like a pearl..."

Her mother interrupted again. "Stop this, Thecla. We need to plan your wedding. Thymaris doesn't want to wait. A good match, dear. The best we could find. Come away from the window."

Thecla raised her forefinger to her lips. "Quiet, Mama. Quiet. The man speaks."

Theoclia stomped away and Thecla turned once more toward the street. The crowd circled the man, and she couldn't hear. She tapped a young boy she could reach and offered a coin. "Tell me what he says, now." But before the boy could take the coin, her mother appeared, striking the boy and sending him away.

"Mama, no! Mama!" Thecla cried out, but her mother closed the shutters on the window.

Thecla turned from the darkened portal and ran out the front door, dodging her mother and disappearing into the crowd. She stopped in front of the man speaking. Crouching down she hid herself even while she looked up to hear more words of truth. Her mother searched frantically, but could not find her.

When evening came, the crowd began to disperse, and she sought company with the man. "Could I be your disciple, sir?"

"Who are you but a girl? Go home. Does your father know you are here? They will flay me for taking you away. Go home. You are too young, too beautiful."

"I want to learn about Jesus," Thecla said. "Teach me."

22

4. Chicago to Venice

September 9, 2006

The MAMs pulled their carry-on luggage into the large plane, already filled with passengers heading for Amsterdam. Red hats announced their arrival. A rather fat man sitting in first class started chuckling when they began to parade by. He whistled when he saw Priscilla's legs and laughed out loud when Sallie toddled by.

Jane had booked the MAMs into Row 15. Now, she assigned seats.

Molly found herself sandwiched between Priscilla and Jane. "Shouldn't you two be on my right?" Molly quipped. "And shouldn't I be over there on the far left?"

"Probably so," Jane agreed.

"And you put Sallie and Emily on the far right? I don't think so." Molly knew that Sallie and Emily were closer to her own political orientation, and did not belong on the right side of things.

"It's just a seat, not our political assignments. Calm down," Jane ordered.

The MAMs had long spanned the political spectrum. At one group meeting they had placed themselves on an ideological continuum at Abigail's request. Priscilla, a representative of the moral majority, stood on the far right. "Closest to God," she had explained, although there was dissension in the ranks on that one.

Jane stood beside Priscilla. Ideologically, she might have been to the right of Priscilla, but the God thing wasn't her orientation. She looked for little government interference in the affairs of business and appreciated the Bush administration for butting out of the private sector and permitting her stocks to skyrocket with creative financing in the housing market.

Moving closer to the left, Katharine had explained, "I'm somewhat conservative. I've voted for some Republicans in local politics. I've never registered Republican. Only in this group would I be right of center!"

Sallie took the next place. "I've left politics behind as I've gotten older. I don't like many of the politicians any more. I don't agree with any of them."

Abigail, grandmother of Emily stood to the left of Sallie. She once put her arm around Sallie explaining: "We were both political activists in our younger days! We grew up with the Vietnam War. Meet the flower children! I believe Jesus walked with us then and now. I think the Democrats are closer to a path of suffering love than the Republicans."

Molly, the sole African-American in the club, had taken the far left position immediately, but waited patiently to explain. "I'm for Martin Luther King, Gandhi, and the poor all the way. The political system is jacked for the wealthy whites. I'm in solidarity with my people. You won't find me bought off by the Republicans like Colin Powell."

At the time, the group had been reading Jim Wallis' political piece, *God's Politics: Why the Right Gets It Wrong and the Left Doesn't Get It*.[iii] Abigail wanted the group to respect the differences and realize that well-meaning people come down on different sides of the political debate and could interpret the Bible differently. She opened the discussion reminding them, "Variety can be good."

"The spice of life!" Sallie had quipped.

For the most part, the MAMs had been able to listen and learn from each other, although at times the debate became heated. Agreeing to disagree had been their motto. They prided themselves in building friendship across the great divide, even in the midst of a divided country.

"Wine is the great equalizer," Jane Masters announced one night when they were laughing after a difficult political discussion. It did seem when the MAMs relaxed together, they could pretty well accept the differences they knew existed.

In the plane this day, the seating arrangements were of convenience and friendship, not representing the political positions. Tucked into the left side of the plane, the old college roommates Ursula and Katharine were seated together to catch up on life.

The MAMs had come from three states and many different walks of life to reach this place. Now they were irrevocably yoked on a mission, and Molly hoped they would make it through alive. The war in Iraq and terrorist threats had her spooked, and she knew all planes could crash.

Molly kept a prayer chant going quietly in her mind, and only occasionally did she whisper a "Help us, Jesus!" when the plane started shaking.

"I'm praying. I'm praying," Priscilla would reply. "Jesus will take care of us."

Molly retreated back into her silent prayers and threw in a few for Priscilla's naiveté.

Meanwhile, Katharine and Ursula were sorting through the experiences of their teaching careers and wondering where time had dropped them. Next to Katharine, Priscilla had been reading the Bible, but she stopped for a few minutes to reflect and focused in on Katharine's voice just when she began to tell Ursula her latest news.

"Did I tell you that my husband hired a private detective for me last spring?"

Ursula turned in her seat and squeezed Katharine's shoulder. "What?"

"A crazy guy started posting on my web page. Argues with my biblical interpretation of Revelation. Makes threats."

"Is he serious? What kind of threats?" Ursula's mouth dropped open. She pushed her curly hair back out of her face, and put her hand back on Katharine's shoulder in support.

" 'Stop your false teaching, or else.' It's scary."

"Geez. What did you do to bring this on?" Ursula laughed out loud, trying to bring some lightness into the dialogue.

"I think it was a debate with a professor from Word of God College. I was just setting the record straight. That Rapture stuff, the *End Times* books. Debunking with scripture."

"And you're the heretic!"

Katharine laughed again. "I'm afraid so. His name is Moses Sun. It would be funny, but ... "

"Is he hanging around?"

"I don't think so, but John's still paying the detective to keep an eye on him. He's on the plane." Katharine shook her head a few times, grimaced and then managed a smile.

***

Across the aisle, Priscilla had heard enough. Now her thoughts were spinning. Moses Sun threatening Katharine? And she went out with the guy? She had thought there was something about him when he came over last week. She remembered a chill she felt, attributing it to the fall weather. But he had been so nice, giving her his *End Times* DVD, enjoying her cinnamon rolls. She had told him he couldn't come on the trip. He said he'd catch up when she got back. Priscilla closed her eyes, tuned out Katharine and Ursula and began to pray.

***

Katharine changed the subject, deciding to focus on Ursula's life and forget about Moses Sun for awhile. "What about you? What's new in Michigan?"

25

"Not much, until this dig! Oh, but Joe! I got an email from Joe."

"The heartbreaker from California?   The love of your life?" Katharine probed Ursula's face to figure out what was going on. "The one and only Dr. Joseph Cohen, linguist extraordinaire?"

"Yes, that Joe."

Deep in Ursula's eyes, Katharine saw a light flash.

"His wife died of cancer a few weeks ago. He sounded awful."

Katharine raised her eyebrows, a smile danced on her lips. "Super MAM to save the day?"

"Katharine, don't laugh."   Ursula shook her head slowly and looked down at her knees.   "It's hard. I don't know what will happen now, but at least he wrote."

Katharine remembered so well the fire between Ursula and Joe back in the days she thought surely they would be together forever. She'd always thought the joy of that love held up against the anguish of betrayal, had kept Ursula from trusting another man.

"I emailed him back and signed it 'love always' without thinking. Help me!"

Holding her reservations in, Katharine searched for words of encouragement. "Maybe you'll help him.   Stranger things have happened."

Ursula disagreed. "I gave up looking for my knight years ago.   I rely on myself. I'm happier that way."

"You're happy? I thought you were on Prozac."

"I just mean I'm independent. I don't want to rely on a man."

"OK... OK."   Katharine realized Ursula's internal struggle over Joe had resurfaced and would take some time to work out.

Now Ursula changed the subject. "So tell me again, how did you get this idea for the dig? How did you ever get this group of women to read *In Search of Paul*?"[iv] Ursula gestured toward the row of the other MAMs. "That group studying Crossan and Reed? A serious theological view of the Roman Empire? Does not compute."

"I know." Now Katharine was laughing again. "They weren't very excited about the book, but we were taking turns on selections."

"Romance Readers Anonymous?"

Katharine smiled and giggled. "You still don't comprehend how I could get into romance novels, do you?"

Ursula swallowed a laugh, "It's your thing, not mine for sure. But how did you get from romance to Crossan?"

"After our cabin burned down on the Niagara Falls retreat ..."

"Katharine. You were in a fire? Why didn't you tell me?"

"Oh, no one was hurt. It was quite the adventure, actually."

"I guess so!"

"Remind me to get the other MAMs to tell you that story -- a defining moment. They tell it better than me. It's all about transformation. That was the year we left romance behind."

"But Thecla?" Ursula kept digging to get a clear idea of how this wonderful idea had been born.

"Well, after we branched out to new genres, we'd do something different every six months. There are six of us, so we'd take turns getting our choice."

"You left Nora Roberts behind? As long as there are M & M's, you can handle anything, right?"

"Well, not my favorite food, but the chocolate helps."

"Jane had us reading Zig Ziglar."

"Oh my God. Katharine! How long have you been in this club?"

Katharine cringed hearing the familiar academic disdain for chick lit and other less academic reading..

Fortunately for Katharine, Priscilla interrupted. "Do you know where the restrooms are on this plane?"

Katherine answered. "I think you can go either way. We're closer to the front, but they may be reserving those for first class. Better go back to be safe. You can stretch your legs."

Priscilla stood to go, the plane lurched. Losing her balance on her high heels, she grabbed on to Katharine.

"Oh, dear. So sorry." She smoothed Katharine's sweater in apology, steadied herself and walked on back the narrow aisle.

Ursula eyed Priscilla's blonde hair curled into a tight permanent and her decorated face. Red glossy lips and a little too much makeup for Ursula's taste.

Ursula looked back to Katharine with a smile spreading across her face. "And what did SHE have you read?"

"*Seven Minutes in Heaven.* A Texan man died, then came back to life. Have you read it?"

"I don't think so." Katharine could tell by Ursula's face she had no interest in doing so.

"Back to Thecla. How did you get this idea?"

Katharine leaned back in her chair to relax and turned her head toward Ursula. "Well, the night we discussed *In Search of Paul,* Jane hadn't done her homework, according to Sallie. Those two can really go at it."

"So I noticed!"

"Jane treated us to some Funky Llama wine, one of the new Australian varieties. Have you had it?"

"No." Ursula leaned forward. "You drink wine at your book club?"

"Sometimes, wine. Sallie accused Jane of bringing the wine because she hadn't read the book. We didn't complain. Well, Priscilla doesn't drink."

"OK... so wine led to Thecla?" Ursula kept fishing.

"Well, after the wine they started to loosen up a little. I filled their minds with the Crossan and Reed stuff. Jane and Molly barely opened the book. Priscilla may have read a little. Sallie and Abigail loved it. They all listened, but mostly they were getting drunk."

"Am I going to have a problem on my hands with the MAMs on this dig?"

Katharine laughed. "No, they're not that bad. And when I told them about Thecla, they were all ears."

Now Ursula opened up. She'd been waiting for a chance to talk about Thecla. "You know, I had never read Thecla's story before I got your email. That probably went over a little better after a few glasses of wine. What a woman!"

"You'd never read *The Acts of Paul and Thecla*?ᵛ I did a research paper on that in graduate school. I thought I shared it with you."

"Not that one girlfriend. I wouldn't have forgotten Thecla."

Katharine giggled. "Quite a story, isn't it? The MAMs were impressed, too. But it was the picture on the cover that got to Jane."

***

Meanwhile, in the back of the plane, Priscilla finished up in the bathroom and opened the door. A small man stood in the aisle and grinned the moment she stepped out into the cabin. A vaguely familiar face registered in her mind, yet something didn't compute.

"Priscilla!" The man whispered to her and suddenly she knew.

"Moses? What are you doing here? What did you do to your hair?"

Priscilla looked at the blonde pony tail and held her hand over her mouth to suppress a laugh.

"Are you trying to look like me?"

Moses placed his finger over his lips and looked up toward the MAMs row. "Don't say anything, dear. I know you didn't want me to come along, but God told me to come. I won't get in the way. Pretend you didn't see me."

Moses slipped into the restroom stall, leaving Priscilla alone.

Priscilla concentrated on keeping balance on her high heels, making her way back down the aisle and into her seat. She didn't notice Dan Parks watching from Row 25 and tucking his camera away. Looking at the other passengers was the last thing on her mind.

Once safely seated, Moses Sun took front and center in her thoughts. She wondered what he was doing on the plane. What would she tell the MAMs if they found out? Could he really be after Katharine? Should she tell the police? Should she warn Katharine?

***

On the other side of the plane, Emily sat back in her seat and looked at the video monitor at the front of the cabin. The screen registered the airplane's speed at 679 miles per hour. She wondered how the plane could possibly be going that fast, when the cabin seemed stationary. On the screen, the trajectory arc displayed the flight path of the plane. Somewhere over Toronto, she thought. A little airplane indicated their location on the global tracking device. The yellow part of the arc was the path completed, the green part was the part to come. She saw the arc extending over the Atlantic Ocean, crossing south of Greenland and then over the British Isles and eventually reaching the target of Amsterdam. The screen read "4.5 hours to destination." The outside temperature is -54 degrees Celsius.

The atmosphere on the plane was so calm. The food was delicious. Emily had just finished eating her lunch of chicken with orange sauce, mashed potatoes with real potato chunks and had a glass of free red wine! She had turned 21 a couple months ago, and while she didn't drink very often, she thought the wine might help her relax, maybe even sleep before starting a new day in Holland and arriving at the harbor of Venice.

On her headphones, she listened to Rascal Flatts and Me and My Gang. In front of her, a man played Shanghai on his personal video display. This was Emily's first transatlantic flight alone. So peaceful. She wasn't sure what she expected, but it was a nice experience, really, as she thought about it. Scheduled to arrive in Amsterdam at 5:55 a.m., midnight in Indiana. That would be difficult, but the wine was relaxing and she felt at peace as she ate the last mint chocolate chip cookie from her meal.

Could she sleep? The excitement of the days ahead were keeping her thoughts rushing almost as fast as the airplane. The wine found its way into her bloodstream and her mind started to wind down. For a while, she let go of the events of the past two months. She stopped thinking about Josh, the love of her life, who had broken off their engagement when she chose this trip over a fall wedding. She let the wine take her into a soothing suspension. Somewhere between the U.S. and Europe, somewhere between college and graduate school, somewhere over Newfoundland now, Emily smiled, breathed deeply, lay back in her chair and went to sleep.

Across Row 15, the rest of the MAMs followed suit. Priscilla had prayed over her dilemma, turned it over to God and had gone to sleep. Molly, worn out with chanting "Help us, Jesus," slipped into a snoring zone, fortunately after her seat mates were already asleep. Soon the whole row lay quiet, gathering shuteye for the work to come.

***

Four hours later, the loudspeaker blared through the airplane, waking the MAMs from deep sleep. "Good morning. It's 5 a.m. in Amsterdam and time for breakfast. We should be on the ground in 55 minutes."

Katharine opened her eyes as a small man lumbered up the aisle. When he reached her seat, the plane shook briefly. He lost his balance and fell into her arm. He glared at her with dark beady eyes that seemed to bore into her body and warned, "Watch it!"

She wondered why he told her to "Watch it!" when he was the one at fault.

Katharine shook the sleep out of her eyes and took a cup of coffee as the flight attendant passed through the aisle. "Thank you," she murmured absentmindedly as she continued to mull over the strange man.

Where had she seen him before, she pondered. Like a word on the tip of her tongue, his identity was on the edge of her consciousness, but she couldn't quite place him. And as soon as she formed the question in her mind, she knew the answer and could feel the hair standing straight up on the back of her neck. That was Moses Sun!

Before the reality could fully register in her waking mind, Dan Parks appeared at her side. "Don't worry, Katharine. We've got him covered. We're watching him closely."

"What?" Katharine responded. "What is HE doing on the plane?"

"Don't worry," he whispered. "That's why I'm here."

Katharine noticed that Park's hair was now blonde and his familiar face hidden with a mustache, beard and 10-gallon Texan hat. Totally weird, she thought and wished she were still asleep. She never should have taken that coffee. Nevertheless, she reflexively reached over to her tray to finish the coffee off and noticed an envelope. "Directions for the Airport" it read. This is getting stranger by the minute, she thought.

Katharine glanced around to make sure Moses Sun was nowhere in sight and then picked up the envelope and ripped it open. A letter fell out onto her lap.

Dear Katharine,

Moses Sun has your original flight schedule and has booked his flight to mimic yours. He doesn't know that your schedule changed and that you are actually flying directly to Venice and the cruise. When you arrive at the airport, go to Gate 23A departing at 8:00 a.m. for Istanbul. Moses Sun will be plan-

*ning to get on that flight with you. Sit until they call the pas-
sengers, and plan to be toward the end of the line. As you get
close to the entrance for the plane, ask the stewardess if you
can take a quick run for a drink of water. Walk off to the restroom, and when you come back, wait until Moses boards the
plane to show your ticket to the stewardess and get directions
to the proper gate for Venice.*

*Memorize this information, then crumple the note and put it in
the flight attendant's trash bag. Don't worry, I've got your
back.*

*Sincerely,
Dan Parks*

The head flight attendant's voice boomed over the airplane public
address system while the plane came to a stop on the tarmac. "Ladies
and Gentlemen, Welcome to Amsterdam. The local time is 5:57 a.m.
It is 60 degrees outside and lightly raining. Thank you for traveling
Northwest. We hope you have a pleasant visit. If you are continuing
on, please consult the airline representatives inside the terminal for
your connecting gate."

Katharine glanced at her watch and reached up to get her carry-
on luggage out of the overhead bin. Gate 23A was her destination,
but it would take a while for the plane to clear. She sat back down
and closed her eyes in prayer.

Reaching over, she tapped Ursula on the arm. "We're in Amsterdam, dear! I need to make a phone call. Something I forgot about.
I'll meet you at the gate later. Tell the rest of them, OK?"

How on earth would Moses think I was going to Istanbul? This
cruise has been booked for... Istanbul? She fidgeted in her seat and
then she remembered. My website! Before the cruise was booked, I
was scheduled to fly to Istanbul and to go on to Kusadasi from there.
My itinerary – I had posted my travel plans on the university website.

Katharine shivered and wrapped her blanket around her shoulders while the passengers began deboarding. She reread the note,
tore it up into 20 pieces, scattering it between her seat pocket, her
carry-on and the ash tray in her seat arm. Now, she realized she
should have brought John along.

***

In Amsterdam they boarded a plane for Venice. Katharine managed to ditch Moses Sun, who walked into the plane headed for Istanbul, before she made a beeline for her correct gate. The women

31

arrived in Venice at 2 p.m. and a tour bus picked them up at the airport and took them to their cruise liner.

Pulling her bags toward the ship, Sallie said, "It's not as big as I expected." Sallie said.

"Certainly smaller than most of those Royal Caribbean boats I've been on," Jane agreed.

"Just the right size for us, though." Molly said. "Three stories."

Ursula chimed in. "This boat sleeps 500, which is relatively small for a cruise ship. Because it's an educational tour, they generally have a smaller crowd. Quality, though, with a common cause. The larger ships carry several thousand people."

"What's that flag?" Sallie asked

No one answered. The women walked over the plank, onto the ship.

"This is like 'The Love Boat'," Sallie announced. "Look at the crew lined up to greet us."

A group of people in uniforms, smiled and welcomed the MAMs. They checked them in and showed them to their cabins on Deck A.

An hour later, the MAMs were ready for a quick tour of Venice. The boat was scheduled to depart at 5:30 p.m., which allowed them two hours to explore the town. Jane negotiated a water bus ride for them, but Priscilla opted to stay close to the boat and sat down at an open cafe with her Bible. The other MAMs filed after Jane into the little boat.

***

Sun was furious. Pacing in the Istanbul airport, he tried to figure out what to do next. "That damn broad. How could she deceive me? She will pay."

Then he reviewed the plans and realized his error. A cruise to Greece and Turkey wouldn't start in Istanbul. Pulling out his laptop, he reconnected to the website and realized the plans did not mention the cruise. Now, Googling the cruise line, he continued to search for the error.

The man beside him took a little rug out of his bag and knelt in front of his chair. Then he touched his forehead to the floor, bowing in prayer.

"And now I'm in Istanbul with a praying terrorist, probably trying to figure out how to blow me up." Sun continued his search. "The Taliban is following me. Jesus come quickly now." Sun scanned the list of cruises beginning today in the Mediterranean. "Athens.... Venice..."

His eyes focused on the Venice origination. "Venice! That's it." He slapped his laptop shut and walked back to the ticket counter. Pulling out his wallet he asked: "How much is a ticket to Venice?"

***

The MAMs cruised through the waters of Venice. "I'm getting wet!" Sallie called out.

"Well, what did you expect?" Jane said?

"You didn't tell us that this was an amusement park ride, Ms. Know-It-All."

Jane winked at Molly and then spoke to the boat driver. "Could you speed up a little bit? The ladies want to have some fun."

The young Italian smiled at Jane and took off down the channel. Water washed over Sallie seated in the back of the boat, and Jane laughed out loud. The beauty of Venice zipped by and the MAMs felt the cool air whipping around while the sun hovered in the western sky, beginning its journey down to the sea. The sunset reflected off the water and turned the Italian buildings into unusual hues of gold, tan and blue. The boat slowed as they approached a large church.

"Do you want to get off here?" The driver asked Jane.

"No, we need to go back to the boat now. What church is that?" Jane inquired.

"That is the Basilica of St. Mark, one of the largest in Venice. Next time, you must visit." The driver headed the boat around and back toward the cruise ship.

The evening was ablaze with color and Katharine put her arm around Ursula's and said, "How beautiful. I'm so glad we are here!"

Emily shivered, feeling very alone, and for the first time, she wondered if the trip had been a good idea. She could have been married by now. In her mind, she started composing an email to Josh.

Molly looked back across the Aegean Sea, thinking about how long it might take to get to Iraq by boat. The beauty of the evening couldn't erase the pain in her heart and the fears that clenched her stomach every time she thought of Mark.

Sallie took a deep breath, sighed and said out loud, to no one in particular. "Now this is living!" Thousands of miles from Ohio, she enjoyed the beauty of Italy and celebrated inside. "What a trip!"

5. The Cruise

September 11, 2006

Ursula tiptoed out of the cabin quietly, while Katharine slept on. Through the porthole, she had seen the sun hovering on the horizon and had decided to go to the top of the ship to greet the day. Her steps were slow, because she was not sure exactly where she was headed. She found some stairs and started to climb.

She remembered her orientation to fitness on board the night before and the walking track on the top level. She entered the central cabin and took the elevator up. Stepping out onto the swimming deck, she circled the pool and then climbed one more set of stairs to the walking path that skirted the lookout deck.

Her feet felt heavy. She needed the exercise. Once on top of the ship, she felt lighter than usual. She walked the first lap, circling the ship, gazing out over the coastline. On one side, she could see the coast of Italy with little towns and houses dotting the green. On the other, the Balkan coast stood out in dark relief, barren hills creating black triangles against the orange sky. Her feet picked up the pace, and she started to jog. In her mind, thoughts were racing, like the school of fish she could see swirling in the water below.

Self-doubt was planted front and center in her thoughts. "Foolish" was the word that described this expedition. She laughed. How could they fund such a frivolous trip? "The Archaeological Expedition in Search of Thecla." Thecla... a first century woman, a mythological saint with a crazy story that Ursula simply could not believe. A rain storm kept her from being burned at the stake? The lions wouldn't kill her, twice? She spent her life living in a cave back in her home town of Seleucia? Even if there was something to be found, why would it be in Ephesus? The cave where Thecla reportedly lived out her days was on the other side of the Mediterranean.

And then there were the MAMs. How could Katharine actually spend one night a month with this group of romance readers? Priscilla, preparing for the rapture. Molly, a depressed war mother, writer wannabe. Sallie, a chubby kindergarten teacher who couldn't stop laughing. Jane, the Republican spelunking millionaire who was more concerned about the stock market and the U.S. dollar than

34

Thecla or this expedition.   Then there was the young heartbroken Emily who had no clue about her future.

The sweat began to roll off Ursula's brow, yet she picked up her pace and raced herself around the path.   The coast blurred, the morning sun was moving up into the sky and her heartbeat began to set a rhythm.   The thud of her Nikes on the deck punctuated her pounding heart.   She wiped the moisture off her face and began to feel alive.

Now images of successful digs began to dance in her thoughts. The Dead Sea Scrolls. The Titanic. She raced into the morning, and suddenly the light of the new day was shining into the possibilities of this trip.   OK, so it is crazy, she thought, but what harm is there in excavating a little more of a cave that historically has been known as the Cave of Paul, and is also marked with Thecla?   She had spent a lifetime digging up the mysterious past. Why stop now?

She lost count of the laps, but her watch told her she was nearing the three-mile mark. The endorphins had kicked in.   "God, I feel good!" she announced to herself.   From her vantage point on the highest deck, she felt on the top of the world. She raced around the deck several more laps, resting her eyes on the beauty of the morning, the coastlines and the Aegean waters welcoming a new day.

***

Moses Sun walked into the Venice airport at 7 a.m.   He had waited all night for the short flight to Venice.   He knew he was late, but hoped he could charter a small boat to catch up with the larger cruise ship.   Walking toward the ground transportation signs, he plotted out his strategy.

Behind him, the tall man with the cowboy hat hovered and considered his options, too.   Parks shadowed Sun carefully, wondering if he should have continued with his previous plans for the cruise. Stretching his arms and legs, he popped open his cell phone to report back to the Boss.

***

The MAMs gathered for breakfast on the Promenade Deck at 9 a.m. Sallie informed the group, "I've brought you each a present. We have a day at sea and I want you to read a fascinating book. I present to you... *The Rapture Exposed.*"[vi]

Jane laughed. "You have got to be crazy. You think I'm going to spend my cruise reading a rapture book. I didn't come halfway around the world to do that. No thank you."

35

Ursula seemed interested. "Why did you pick this book, Sallie? Have you read it?"

"Yes, actually it's a very good book. Written by a female Lutheran minister, I might add," she said glaring at Jane with bug eyes that quickly transformed into a smile, while a little chuckle emerged from her throat.

"Is she an authority on the rapture?" Priscilla asked. "There's a lot of false teaching out there."

"Authority." Katharine jumped in. "Whew. Heavy breakfast conversation. Barbara Rossing is representative of quite a few authors in recent years who have been revisiting the book of Revelation in light of the renewed interest in end times, the *End Times* series, and a widespread belief that things are getting so bad, we must be ready for Jesus to return. Yet, through history this has happened time and time again. The book makes some good points. Very worthwhile reading."

Molly chipped in, "Honey, I am on the cruise of a lifetime and reading theology is the last thing I want to do. Hell, do you think I ever read *In Search of Paul?* For that matter, did any of you really read that through? I say, let's have some fun. If we want to get intellectual, let's start writing that romance novel we've been planning. This is the perfect setting for romance."

Sallie placed her hand on Molly's arm and with a tilt of her head, she motioned the group's attention toward Emily, whose eyes were tearing as she looked out the window of the Promenade Deck toward the sea.

"Oh, Lordy," Molly responded.

Emily jumped up and ran toward the restroom, behind the breakfast bar.

"Let's get some food, " Jane said. "I'm hungry."

Sallie stood and announced, "Well, you each have a copy of the book, whether you want it or not! Now, I'm going to comfort Emily."

***

And so the MAMs' day at sea had begun. After breakfast they hurried back to their cabins and then headed out for the first lecture of the day, "The Roman Empire," in the Captain's Room on the first level. Jane and Priscilla had wanted to play hooky, but Ursula had convinced them that it would be helpful background information for Thecla, and reminded them that it wasn't every day they could hear a skilled speaker from Harvard bring the first century to life. "I wrote this "Journeys of Paul" cruise into my grant for a reason, and you're along for the ride," Ursula had reminded. The lectures were designed to share historical and Biblical information with cruise participants

as they retraced the travels of Paul, the first-century Christian con-
vert and evangelist who touted the Jesus way.

Emily dried her tears in time to eat a little breakfast and actually
shooed Sallie out of their cabin to get to the lecture on time.

***

Later that afternoon, Molly wrote an email home to her husband.
She was laughing while writing and for a few minutes had forgotten
about her son, Mark. Even while the ship sailed closer to Iraq, her
fingers typed freely, and she loved telling her worried husband she
was safe and sound.

"Honey, I am not the one behind the eight ball here. I'm on the
cruise of a lifetime. If you want to worry, send your prayers up for
Mark. He's the one." Oh, Lordy, she thought. The laughter died in
her throat and she signed off quickly. A euro for each half page of
email, she had to write tight. No more of that, no. On to dinner.

***

On the Promenade Deck the MAMs gathered, waiting for the second seating of the evening. Candles glowed on the linen tablecloths
and Jane led the way to their seating by the window. Pulling out a
chair with a flourish, she motioned to Sallie, "Age before beauty,
dear."

"I beg your pardon?" Sallie laughed. Although she was limping
and actually felt very old at the moment, that didn't prevent her from
arguing with Jane.

"For your information, I was the runner-up in the Ms. Chubby
Ohio pageant last year. Look again before you put down my innate
beauty. But thank you for the chair." Sallie plopped down, and
grabbed her ankle. "OK, I'm not a spring chicken."

The waiter appeared and asked the MAMs for their choice of
courses for the evening.

"We need some more time," Katharine spoke for the group.
"Could you come back in five minutes?"

"Do you have any recommendations?" Jane asked.

"I would recommend the raspberry sherbet for starters to refresh
your palette. Then, the spinach salad with strawberries and shrimp.
If you'd like the soup option, the asparagus cream is delicious with a
hint of garlic. All three of the main entrees are superb."

"Thank you, sir. Yes come back in a few minutes, we have some
slow people here." Jane looked at the MAMs and gestured at Sallie.
Winking at the waiter, she smugly turned her face in the direction of
Mrs. Q.

"We got a cute one there. I'm going to enjoy this week!" Jane smiled.

Sallie rolled her eyes and put her fingers to her lips. She didn't think that Emily would be able to handle Jane coming on to the waiter. "There are children present."

Ursula sat back and watched the ongoing banter between Sallie and Jane. She smiled at Katharine. "They are a riot!"

"Keep us animated, for sure. What did you think of Mr. Harvard?"

"A handsome man." Ursula replied. "I wish we had professors like him at the University of Michigan!"

"I meant, what did you think of the lecture?" Katharine asked.

"That man knows his stuff. And he was funny!"

Molly chuckled and soon they were all smiling and giggling.

"Ah, laughter. The tonic of the gods," Sallie whispered, trying to stop the guffaws. "Let's keep this up, so our bar tab won't be so high."

"Drinks are on me tonight," Jane announced.

"OK, I'm ready for a Guinness," Sally said, folding her hands on the table in front of her. She smiled, bugging her eyes again at Jane.

Priscilla grimaced. "You guys. This is a religious cruise. Really. If I had known you were coming to drink, I would have stayed home."

"What did you think of the lecture today?" Katharine asked Priscilla to change the subject.

"That was really good. I took notes. I want to tell the women in my Bible study about that one when I get home. I didn't realize all that about the Roman Empire."

"Yes, the Pax Romana was unprecedented in their day. They established a firm hold over a great deal of territory, building roads, a water system with aqueducts. They were cruel and they were very successful. They had quite a system of commerce, government and they also supported the arts. You will understand more when we visit some of the ancient ruins. Wait until you see their theaters, and their library."

"And they killed Jesus," Priscilla said. "Why was he a threat?"

Before anyone could answer the waiter was back and Jane was ordering the beer and wine for the MAMs while Priscilla's question dissolved into the night of fine dining. It would be the next day before anyone thought about Mr. Harvard or the Roman Empire again.

***

Priscilla retired to her cabin quickly after dessert. The MAMs were out of control, and she had some Bible reading to get in before bed. Katharine and Ursula left shortly later to catch up some more on their teaching stories. Emily excused herself to go email Josh. She was beginning to realize that she really wanted Josh to be a part of her future, and she hoped it wasn't too late.

She slipped away, just when Sallie, Molly and Jane began a new rendition of the "Magnificent MAM" song that they had begun composing on their first retreat at Niagara Falls several years ago.

"I am so glad you suggested we go find Thecla, Jane." Sallie remarked after chugging her third Guinness.

"There, now that is proper gratitude. Just keep that up." Jane stood and bowed. "At your service, ma'am. Could I help you back to your cabin, dear?"

"At this point, I doubt I'll be able to feel any pain. That's a good thing." Sallie laughed.

"Yes, a very good thing. No pain. Now, I think I'll go back and read that book you gave us for a little night time reading. What was it?"

"Right, you are going to go read *The Rapture Exposed*, and I, too, am a millionaire."

"Quiz me at breakfast. You'll be surprised. I will be an authority by then." Jane burped and then hiccupped. "Ladies? Shall we go?"

Molly stood and put one arm around Sallie and the other around Jane. "You two are the greatest. This is the best time I've had since ..." She looked up to Jane's smiling face and down Sallie's beaming cheeks and didn't have the heart to complete the sentence. For one night, she'd almost forgot to worry about Mark. "Let's go, girlfriends," she said instead. They were off for a stroll in the Mediterranean air on the top deck. For one night, she deserved to be happy.

6. Thamyris Accuses Paul

September 3, 46 A.D.

Theoclia welcomed Thamyris into their home, but Thecla still would not speak. "For three days, she will not move from the window," her mother explained. "She only listens to this foreigner, Paul. You must do something. Bring her back."

Thamyris approached Thecla, reaching for her hand. She held his fingers loosely, continuing to lean into the window, listening outside.

"Thecla! My love!" Thamyris put his arm around his betrothed. "Let's go for a walk."

But Thecla pushed him away. "Shhh! Listen. He speaks truth." She grasped the window bars, straining to hear.

"Thecla! How rude. Speak to your guest," Theoclia pleaded with her daughter.

But Thamyris shook his head, waving his finger back and forth, talking to the mother.

"I will take care of this. I will not let another man steal my wife away." He held Theoclia's shoulders in his hands and gave her a quick kiss on her cheek. "Don't worry, Mama. I will deal with this man Paul."

Thecla didn't even turn when he left the house.

Thamyris went out and engaged two men in the crowd asking them, "Who is this man, Paul? I promise to give you a considerable sum, if you will give me a just account of him; for I am the chief person of this city. Come dine at my house and we will talk."

After the dinner, the man Demas told Thamyris, "Turn Paul in to the governor Castillius, because he tries to win converts for the new religion of Christians. According to the order of Casear, he will be put to death and you will have your wife."

So Thamyris rose early and went to the house of Onesiphorus, at-tended by the magistrates, the jailer, and a great multitude of people with slaves, and said to Paul, "You have perverted the city of Iconium and the woman Thecla, who is betrothed to me, so that now she will not marry me. You must come with us to see the governor Castillius." Paul did not resist, but walked peacefully with him and his entourage to the governor's quarters.

Once inside, the governor asked Paul to give an account for himself.

Paul told him, "God sent his Son, Jesus Christ, whom I preach, and in whom I instruct the people to place their hopes. So if I only teach those things which I have received by revelation from God, where is my crime?"

When the governor heard this, he ordered Paul to be bound, and to be put in prison, until he should be more at leisure to hear him more fully.

7. The Cruise Continues

September 12, 2006

Two days later, three days into the cruise, the MAMs had completed two days of sightseeing on the Greek mainland. They had traipsed by the narrow ancient canal at Corinth and learned to identify Corinthian columns. They had stood overlooking a fairly empty field at Philippi, once the site of battles and intrigue in the ancient world. Their tour guide had been so excited to have them walk on remnants of the Roman road "where the Apostle Paul once walked." The MAMs were more interested in knowing if Thecla walked there, but the tour guide didn't recognize her name.

The highlight for the women came at the Church of Lydia, only a mile west of Philippi. Katharine explained, "Lydia came to Philippi from Thyatira in Asia Minor (now Turkey), one of the seven churches in Revelation. Paul visited her at the river, where she was dyeing purple cloth. She asked Paul to baptize her. Her conversion began Christianity in Europe."

"Now there's a woman for you!" Jane said.

"I always enjoyed teaching the children her story in Sunday School. One of the good woman stories in the Bible about a business woman who welcomed God into her life." For once, Sallie agreed with Jane.

Molly wrote in her journal, "Apart from the picturesque sea towns, the Greek countryside consists of shrubs and fairly barren, though hilly terrain. Among the trees standing near the river at Lydia, I could imagine women coming centuries ago to relax, chat and dye their cloth in a wonderful shady haven, far from the hot and busy marketplace."

To commemorate the story of Lydia, the Greeks had built a nice church at the place. At the entrance to the church was a bowl of sand for placing candles and a money box to pay to light the prayer candles. Molly lit 10 for Mark, and Emily lit one for Josh, before they went outside for a tour talk at a little concrete amphitheater by a small river. The beauty of the area astounded the ladies.

Jane asked Molly to baptize her in the creek by Lydia's church. Molly had declined, so Jane baptized herself in the name of God Herself, the female breath and Lydia, disciple of Jesus.

"Why didn't I turn purple?" she had asked the MAMs. "I thought this was where Lydia dyed the purple cloth for her business."

Priscilla's face lit up like a beet in embarrassment, but the other MAMs laughed and Sallie told Jane she was going to have to quit drinking so much, now that she was tight with Lydia, her business mentor.

***

On the morning of the fourth day, Ursula assembled the MAMs for an orientation to -. After getting to know the women, she was beginning to lose sleep worrying about how they would adapt to life in the field. Mostly she was questioning her sanity in committing to such a ridiculous mission. But at about 4 a.m., deep into a fitful night of tossing and turning, a eureka moment came.

At breakfast she announced, "There will be a mandatory meeting for all those wishing to participate in the Archaeological Expedition in Search of Thecla at 9:00 a.m. on the Captain's Deck."

"But we arrive at Kusadasi at 10:30 a.m. How will I get my hair done in time to disembark?" Jane had whined.

"Since when is your hair a priority? Come on, Jane. Come clean. You just really are dying to get back to your cabin to finish *The Rapture Exposed.*" Sallie countered.

"Speak for yourself, I told you I read that book nights ago. But don't ask me what it was about."

Jane and Sallie fell into their habitual sparring. Ursula looked at Katharine for help.

Katharine asked, "So you think we're teachable then? I wondered how in the world you'd turn us into archaeologists. Teaching, what a novel idea!"

"You are the least of my worries, Katharine. You studied archaeology in college. In four days we are going to be on site, and I know some of you don't have a clue about what we'll be doing."

Emily smiled at Ursula and informed her, "When I was 10, I did my own dig on my grandfather's farm. I opened a square, just like they do at Sun Watch, a Native American site in Dayton."

Molly nudged Sallie, "A child prodigy! I knew she was something special from the moment I laid eyes on her."

"A square? You opened a square? What does that mean?" Sallie asked.

"Well, I don't know if that's how you dig in a cave, but at Sun Watch, they open squares to dig down past the part disturbed by the farmers in the past 300-400 years. Then you create a flat surface, troweling the square to look for discolorations that may indicate trash pits, post holes or even burials." Emily smiled. "Do you want to know what I found?"

"Indiana Jones, I mean Emily, tell us, girlfriend!" Jane said.

"I found a tin, from the original Turner farm. They were planning to sell nuts, but the trees didn't survive, and they raised horses instead."

"Oh, you didn't tell us you were one of those little rich girls," Jane sized her up with new eyes. "We will have to talk.

"My Dad is a Mennonite minister. There's no silver spoon in my mouth."

"What was in the tin you found?" Katharine interrupted.

"It was a diary! My great-great-grandmother's diary. She told all about the failed orchard, and how she began preaching at a young age. At 16 she rode horseback to speak at churches around the area. Those horses were so fast, they got the idea to breed them."

"A woman preacher? Do you think that is biblical?" Priscilla asked.

"Absolutely not. Women are supposed to be barefoot and pregnant and kept under lock and key with their man," Jane announced. "Did they burn her at the stake, Indiana Emily?"

"Stop that, Jane. Have some respect." Sallie looked over her glasses and bugged her eyes out at Jane.

"Well, it happened to Thecla. Women are treated better in 21st century America for the most part, but that came after years of struggle. The Salem Witch Trials, Susan B. Anthony, Elizabeth Cady Stanton, They couldn't even vote until 1920." Jane returned a resolute stare to Sallie.

Molly picked up on the right to vote cue and began singing in her strong alto voice, the women's suffragette song from *Mary Poppins*.[vii]

Sallie let her finish and then broke in. "Finish your story, Emily."

"My grandmother eventually did settle down and raise a family, or I wouldn't be here! On the frontier, things were different in those days. At least that's the story that has been passed down through the family across generations."

"OK. Thanks, Emily. I didn't realize we had an experienced archaeologist along!" Ursula interrupted. "Emily explained well what happens on digs. However, we won't be digging the floor of the cave. We will hope to open some squares, though, on the hillside outside the cave.

"Will we dig into the walls of the cave, too?" Emily asked.

"Sometimes, there are passageways that have been filled in over time. So we will examine the walls carefully. Also, there are already paintings that have been uncovered, so that will make our progress very slow, looking for other paintings that might still be covered." Ursula explained.

"How can you trust us to do this kind of work?" Katharine asked. "Aren't you a little worried we might ruin the evidence?"

Ursula smiled. "Well, I haven't been sleeping very well, actually. But, the Turkish government will be providing one of their experienced archaeologists from the University in Istanbul and some of his students. The Austrians supervise the dig at the Ephesus Site for Turkey, so they are overseeing our work. They've recommended strategies. They'll have the final say on our daily work plans. And, the person in charge of the work at the Grotto of St. Paul is a woman, Sophie Simons. We'll be in communication with her daily by email."

"I've been giving quite a lot of thought to how we can maximize our strengths. Some of you, obviously, aren't physically able to do the more demanding work."

"I bench press 200 pounds," Jane informed her. "I used to explore caves. I brought my old outfit and tools."

"Katharine told me that. I'm planning for you to help open the square, though. The interior of the cave is quite small, so Emily will work in the cave. The two of you have the most physical stamina and will have no problem doing the physical labor. Our archaeologist will also provide some of his students to work along with us in the cave."

"And what about the rest of us? Are we just along for the ride? Do we play tourist while you slave away in the salt mines?" Sallie laughed at herself, somewhat nervously. "You don't really need us, do you?"

"Oh there's plenty of work to spread around. Nobody will be playing hooky."

"Molly, you're the writer in the group?" Ursula asked

"Well, that's my dream. At the moment, I mainly write my journal and government reports, press releases."

Ursula interrupted her. "You have an English degree from Ohio State and have worked as a reporter. You will write our daily dig journal, photographing and chronicling our excavation, techniques, finds. Turkey will be supplying a mapper, a student who will be drawing the pictures that will go along with your text, and another student will translate what you write into Turkish. OK?"

Molly consented. "Yes, ma'am!"

Ursula moved on. "Sallie, you will be our sifter. All of the sand and debris that comes out of the cave must be examined before being discarded. You will work closely with a student who will train you so that you know what you're looking for. Pieces of pottery, tiny pieces of bone, even sometimes jewels and carbon are keys to the past that might be found in the sifting process."

"I can do that!" Sallie exclaimed.

"Exactly," Ursula agreed. "and Priscilla, you are a secretary? I think you will be perfect for cataloging all of our finds. Anything that we remove from the cave must be properly documented, with its location, description and then bagged and preserved for the trip back to the field office."

"Katharine, I'm planning for you to be our online researcher. We have access to most archaeological data online now. Each day there will be questions that arise, and I'm counting on you to answer them so we can proceed. We will also have some researchers at the university in Istanbul, who are fluent in several languages. We'll put you in charge of the daily communications with Sophie. You know German, right?"

"Yes, German and French."

"Good, good. Write Sophie in German, then."

"So we are really going to be archaeologists? I thought this was a joke! I thought we'd arrive in Kusadasi and you'd tell us to get lost!" Sallie looked at Ursula with new respect. "You are going to take a bunch of menopausal crones and turn us into Indiana Johannas!"

"Well, one Indiana Johanna, and five Ohio Johannas!" Jane corrected Sallie. "You're out of our beloved state five days, and already you're a disgrace to the Buckeyes."

Sallie crossed herself, before telling Jane, "And YOU are certified crazy!"

Katharine looked at her watch. "It's 10 a.m., Ursula. Is class over for today?"

Ursula laughed, "You've become like your students!"

"Yes, I'm identifying with them now. We need to get ready for the trip into Kusadasi."

"OK, archaeologists, just one more thing. Today is the most important tour of our trip. We will be touring the site at Ephesus. Our cave is located in the hills above our site. Everything you learn today will help set the stage for our cave excavation. Please listen carefully. There will be a test tonight when we return to the ship."

"You can't do that!" Sallie laughed. "A test? We aren't your students."

"No, you are my apprentices and I'm going to make sure you know as much as possible before the dig begins."

"Will one of us get eliminated?" Jane asked.

"That would be you!" Sallie bantered. "You are the lazy student who doesn't read the book."

Katharine looked at her watch again and looked at Ursula with a shrug and a question.

"Class dismissed. Take good notes."

8. Kusadasi and Ephesus

September 13, 2006

Molly went directly to the Promenade Deck and looked out over the railing. The entrance into the harbor had become one of her favorite cruise experiences. Earlier, she had watched the brightly colored tugboat greet their large ship and lead it in to the wharf area. Now the tugboat was heading back out from the harbor, and she saw another large ship in the distance. Down on the deck, she observed final preparations being made to open the walkway onto the dock.

Little fishing ships lined the harbor's network of docks and bobbed in the crystal blue water. In the distance, shops and a busy city street created a picturesque first impression of this major Turkish seaport, Kusadasi. In the back of her mind, she was thinking about Iraq, but this beautiful town by the sea seemed so far away from anything dangerous. Should she be afraid, she wondered.

Earlier in the summer, a group of terrorists planted a car bomb at a tourist resort farther south on the coast. At the time, her husband had been quick to suggest her trip was too dangerous.

Molly focused on the small boats and then followed a bird winging into the sky. Kusadasi means "Bird island," she remembered from their orientation the day before, because over 200 species of birds make their home in the region. The sun danced on the waves lapping the dock, and the bird soared into a clear blue sky. Within her heart, Molly felt safe. Mark was the one in danger, and her husband knew that, too.

The loudspeaker interrupted her inner dialogue, calling the passengers to disembark.

Now she looked back to the harbor. Behind the dock and ships lining the port, the modern city loomed. Apartment buildings, hotels, restaurants stood, most seven to eight stories high. At 8:30 a.m. the sidewalks teemed with people, the street busy with cars. In the bay, she noticed a walking path and an interesting statue of a hand, holding birds. She wished they weren't going directly to the buses so she could have some time to walk along the water.

***

Moses Sun fumbled with his wallet, standing at the Kusadasi Port Custom's Desk.

"Your passport, sir." The Turkish agent stared at Sun, impatient with his nervous search.

Sun glanced at his watch. Time was running out. Where was the passport?

"Sir, please step aside. Take him back," the agent instructed the female assistant at his side.

"This way, sir," she said to him, motioning him to a small room behind the desk. "Please have a seat."

Sun shuffled through his laptop bag and then realized that the passport was safely tucked away in the backpack that he had left behind in the hotel room that morning. Another delay. Headquarters would not be happy. He flipped open his cell phone and prepared to make the call.

Officer Parks slipped quietly by the Custom's Desk and motioned to the agent. Handing over a 100 Liras, he flipped his security badge and then asked a favor.

"Yes, sir. No problem. The man doesn't have a passport. We will have to keep him here for the rest of the day."

Parks smiled. Every now and then there were aspects of his job that were so easy and sweet. Now, he could join the cruise ship tour and spend some more moments with Jane Masters. She was popping up in every dream, haunting every night since he'd been tracking Sun on this trip. He extended his hand to the agent to express his thanks. Then he slipped away, just as Sun began his conversation in the next room.

***

Emily's eyes scanned the parking lot past the ship. Twelve tour buses were lined up in three columns waiting for passengers. Like the giant in Jack's beanstalk patch, the buses seemed too large for this humble port town. Glancing down at her cruise name tag, she took note of her purple paper and then saw the purple flag in the hand of their bus captain standing in front of the first bus. Fortunately, the MAMs were all in the purple group. First position today, she remembered -- unlike the first day on tour when the purple group had landed in the very last bus.

For a moment, Emily wondered how these buses appeared to the residents of Kusadasi. Do they seem like a foreign invasion? These megabuses stood in stark contrast to the tiny Turkish vehicles on the streets of the town. Gas prices were already high here. Americans may have those little cars soon, too, she thought.

"Let's go, Lambkin!" Sallie nudged Emily out of her thoughts, as the passengers moved down the steps from the boat into the parking lot. "Let's get the front row on the front bus. This is our day! I think Ursula arranged for us to be first on the Ephesus tour. I'm not complaining."

Jane came down the steps next, with Priscilla and Molly close behind. Katharine and Ursula brought up the rear. Before long, the MAMs were stepping up into the purple bus.

Jane grabbed the bus's hand bar to step up when a hand tugged on her arm. She recognized a familiar face. "Officer Parks, sir? What did I do now?"

"It's not what you've already done, but what you might do today that has me worried. I think you need a chaperone so you don't get in trouble. The Turkish government runs a tight ship."

"Oh they do, do they?" Jane smiled. "Do you really think they're going to let you on our bus?"

Parks flashed his purple cruise name tag in Jane's face. "You're holding up the line, dear. Get on the bus."

Jane stepped up into the bus, and Parks was right behind her.

"I like to sit in the front," Parks informed Jane.

"So do we!" Sallie said out loud. "We were last the first day. And you know what they say in the Bible about that."

"The first shall be last." Molly responded.

"And the last shall be first." Jane completed the sentence. "Front row seats in the first bus. Does life get any better?"

"Probably not. I bet you've never been in the front row in the first bus with the most handsome man on the continent before." Parks remarked as he took the window seat.

"Well hello, Mr. Male Ego. I had almost forgotten what it was like to spend time with Egos after being on a Women-Only Expedition." Jane replied.

"I can see I'll have to temper my tongue in your presence. Such delicate ears. The truth is sometimes hard to handle. You'll find me that way quite often." Parks answered.

Katharine and Ursula filed down the aisle and took the seat behind Molly and Sallie. Emily and Priscilla sat behind Jane and Parks.

"How many times have you been to Ephesus, Katharine?" Ursula asked after they sat down.

"Umm... four times, I think." Katharine laughed out loud. "The years are starting to run together. John and I came here first, to scout out a class trip. Then I did bring students here three times. It's a great location to show the locale and the magnificence of the Roman Empire. And the price was right. What about you?"

"I have only been here once, with Joe. We took a week trip to Turkey. Bathed at Pamukkale, stayed in Kusadasi overnight; more occupied with love than archaeology at the time. Good memories." Ursula responded.

"Speaking of Joe, what's he doing?" Katharine asked.

"He's teaching at USC, a linguist, heads a Center for the translation of Biblical Languages. Long-term position." Ursula explained.

"His wife died of cancer? How awful." Katharine put her arm behind Ursula. "Is the flame still there?"

"Scary. I haven't had a date for five years. One email and it all flooded back to me. Bring me back to reality, Kath. I'm obsessing on this man."

The tour bus made its way along the seafront. Emily looked out the window, then asked, "How does he navigate around all of those small cars on this busy road?"

"I have no idea. But I think I'm going to order my next car from Turkey," Priscilla said. "What do you think the gas mileage is on those little cars?"

"Forty to fifty miles to the gallon, I heard," Emily responded. "I think two of those could fit in the parking place for one American compact car! How does this bus driver do it? We need to give this man a good tip today!"

The road carried the women out into the picturesque countryside while it climbed up, away from the port town. The sparkling blue sea greeted the light blue sky, and they could see the cruise ship sitting in the port. It stood large among the smaller boats docked along the catwalks and sidewalks by the water. In between the view of the port and the road were the hills surrounding this little sea town. Olive trees, brown earth and grasses punctuated little white cinder block houses capped with copper-colored ceramic tile roofs.

In the front of the bus, the tour guide took a little microphone off its stand and turned to face the group. The short man with dark brown hair winked when he spoke, and smiled warmly. His English served the MAMs well.

"Good morning, my name is Balaban, and I'll be your guide today. We will be traveling to the ruins at Ephesus, the best archaeological site of the former Roman Empire, but first we are going to the Archaeological Museum."

"The best site. How fortunate!" Sallie explained.

"The Turkish government writes his script. It's all about money." Molly muttered.

"This is a very good site," Katharine added from behind the seat. "Very, very good. If not the best, close to it."

The guide continued his talk. If he heard Molly's comment, he didn't show it. "After the earthquake in the 1960s, building practices

50

have changed in this area. The cinder-block model is built to last. As you see, there are sometimes open structures above the living area. The families often build additional forms, to allow for expansion as their family grows," the tour guide explained. Emily saw a family house, with concrete forms standing open on the second floor. Blue sky filled in the rectangular areas that could be enclosed to make additional living spaces.

"Earthquakes have been very common in this area of the Mediterranean world," he said. "In fact, most of the ancient ruins in this part of the world were long ago toppled and buried by earthquakes, more so than by the destruction of conquerors, although that happened also. Another large earthquake of seven-point magnitude is a certainty in the next 30 years," he continued.

"The Turkish government devotes considerable time and resources to the antiquities sites. Tourism is our number two industry here, and we are working to reconstruct these sites for the many visitors that tour our country each year. Today, we will be visiting the ancient site of Ephesus. Ephesus was originally a seaport. However, the Cayster River has been depositing silt at its mouth for centuries, and the original Ephesus is now six miles inland. Even in ancient times, earthquakes led to reconstruction, and there are four sites of ancient Ephesus. The ancient Roman city of the early centuries fortunately covers an area not currently inhabited, which makes restoration possible. It's now one of the best sites in the Mediterranean."

Molly took in the view of the quiet countryside. Although modern vehicles traveled the roads, she observed workers in the field, plowing with horses. The beauty and peacefulness surprised her. Why did her husband think it would be dangerous to come here, she wondered. The guide interrupted her thoughts.

"Before we go up to the site, we are going to stop at the Archaeological Museum in Seljuk and there you will have a glimpse of early Roman life. Remember, we will go as a group today. Please stay with the group and don't wander off by yourself. You will need a ticket to enter the museum. We'll gather at the gift shop, and wait for those who need to use the restroom before we begin the tour in the museum. Our tour will be brief, so please wait for those going to the facilities," the guide continued.

A half hour later, the guide gathered the group around a replica of the Temple of Artemis. "This temple once stood at the harbor of Ephesus. People came to worship the Goddess Artemis. They had games and many rituals during Roman times. Tourism was a big industry here."

The MAMs stood in front of the glass case enclosing a model of the ancient temple. Huge columns lined all four sides of the recreation, and also ran through the building, in even rows.

51

"One of the seven wonders of the ancient world, writers described this marble structure as 'the most beautiful building in the world.' Built originally in the sixth century B.C., there were 127 columns, each 60 foot high."

The guide moved on to a large statue of a woman with three rows of breasts, a flat turban hat and a body lined with winged creatures. "And here's the Goddess of fertility – Artemis. You notice she's well endowed on the home front!" The guide smiled and winked at Sallie. "This statue was found at Ephesus."

"I'm going to have to get a copy of her to take home!" Sallie laughed. "They'll never believe this if I just try to tell them about it."

Priscilla's eyes brightened. "Is this what Paul was preaching against in Ephesus?"

"Yes, halting worship of Artemis could hurt their business. The merchants wanted to keep Paul quiet. They sold statues to the pilgrims, and also a lot of food. Just like today – tourism brings big business. Ephesus earned a lot from the pilgrims coming to visit the temple." Balaban nodded. "Some things don't change."

"What about male fertility gods?" Parks asked.

Balaban moved across the room to another case, pushed a button, illuminating a small figure with an erect penis as large as the figure itself. "Yes, Priapus. The male God of fertility. Also found at the Ephesus site."

"Now that is what we call mythology," Jane whispered into Parks ear.

"I don't think so," Parks put his hand on Jane's shoulder. "We can measure that up later."

Jane rolled her eyes, but her face flushed beet red. "Men!"

The guide motioned the group toward the corner of the room, where a small replica of a terrace house invited guests to peek back into first-century life.

"This looks like a condo!" Priscilla said.

"Yes, remarkably like condos. The government officials and rich people lived in these houses, three stories high. We call this the 'Socrates Room' because of the frescoes found on the wall with his picture. They painted the walls with frescoes, covered the floor with beautiful mosaics and even decorated the rooms with statues. Did you know that the system of aqueducts even piped in running water?" Balaban stepped back so the group could look more closely at the pictures and displays. "We will not be able to enter the excavation of the terrace houses today, but we will walk by."

Emily felt tired, jet lag predominated her body. She stepped away from the group and pulled the last email from Josh out of her pocket. Her eyes hung on the last sentence. "I miss you, too, Lambkin. We'll talk when you return. Love, Josh." Maybe there was hope. Emily took a deep breath. She had begun to realize all of this didn't really mean anything if she was going to be alone. She wondered whether or not she should have come in the first place and why she had thought it so important to see the world. She knew Josh was more important than digging up old stuff and a ridiculous archaeological expedition in search of some crazy lady of the first century.

"Time to go," the guide instructed. "You can stop at the gift shop, but please be on the bus in 10 minutes. We're on a tight schedule."

Emily dragged her feet out of the museum and looked at the stalls of vendors waiting for tourists to buy. The MAMs hurried toward the shops. Sallie purchased a statue of Artemis. Parks bought one of Priapus and handed it to Jane. Molly gawked at the Roman soldier statues.

Sallie put her arm around Molly as they walked back to the bus. "Men and war. It hasn't changed, has it? They were fighting each other then, and they're still doing it. Doesn't make any sense, does it, dear?"

Molly swallowed and took a deep breath. "No sense at all. But that doesn't keep them from doing it. Why, Sallie? Why?"

Sallie squeezed Molly closer as they neared the bus. "We just have to hope and pray that someday the people will begin to follow Jesus, don't we?"

"Amen, Sistah! I'm glad there's at least one person who thinks like me. Now, if we could just figure out how to convince the others."

***

Back on the bus, the MAMs rested on the way to Ephesus. Jane closed her eyes while Parks was busy with his Blackberry. The tour guide counted heads and went back out to round up a few more purple people.

The sound of galloping horses flooded into Jane's mind. Looking up, she saw them coming, one hundred strong. Bright red capes waving in the wind, armored bodies. The lead man brandished a sword and swiftly dashed it against a poor woman standing close to the path. The woman fell back, the horses pressed on down the marble street toward the harbor. At the end of the horses she saw a chariot, painted brilliant red. When the chariot passed by, a man looked out of drawn curtains, calling out to her, "Et tu, Brute?" Jane shook her head fitfully from side to side, then felt someone shaking her shoulder.

"Jane, wake up. You can't sleep today. Wake up, dear."

Jane jerked up, confused by the images. She wondered what the dream meant. Betrayal?

Once again, the tour guide interrupted her thoughts. "Now, ladies and gentlemen, we are soon to arrive at the best archaeological view of the Roman Empire. We will enter at the top of the site and as you look down the hill, imagine that you are actually heading down to the sea. In the first century, Ephesus was just above the harbor and at the mouth of the Cayster River. Because of silting and earthquakes, this was actually moved three times. The Turkish government, in cooperation with great archaeologists from around the world, is currently reconstructing this site. Come back in two years, and there will be more."

Katharine and Ursula stepped off the bus and looked down. "This is a great site. Maybe not the best, but close to it," Ursula remarked.

"Yes, I love this place." Katharine said. "You can almost feel the Romans walking along the marble road, stopping by the fountain, or taking time to read in the library."

"I love this place, excellent reconstructions. It reminds me why I got excited about archaeology in the first place!" Ursula laughed. "Who woulda thought a trip to Turkey might be the key to unlock my depression. In search of Thecla! Thank you, girlfriend! This is all because of you!"

"Teaching is no picnic, is it? We call ourselves the Cynic Circle at my school. Take brilliant PhDs who want to set the world on fire and put them in front of hormone-crazed 19-year-olds and what do you get?" Katharine asked.

"A bunch of middle-aged women who need a vacation!" Ursula replied. "Thank you for the invitation!"

"Thank you for taking me seriously. It was such a lark." Katharine remembered.

"It was a songbird. Sometimes, life hands you wings." Ursula put her hands up around her face and ran her fingers through her curly hair. "Maybe this is an opportunity to fly?" Raising her arms and flapping them at her sides she twirled around and then looked sheepishly at the tour group forming into a bunch around the guide.

"Chicken little came along?" Parks asked Jane.

"I heard that," Ursula laughed and pointed her finger at Parks. She looked up and imagined soaring over the dusty site, smiling deep within.

The tour guide began. "Now we enter the site of Ephesus. Note that the site slopes down, originally to the harbor. We make it easy on you. You get to walk down the hill. The buses will pick us up at the bottom of the site. From this point you can see the layout of the site."

The September sun warmed the air. The treeless path ahead was covered with marble blocks and brown earth. White columns, pieces of structures once forming this Roman town stood out against the blue sky and dusty ground.

"On the right side, you see the Varius Baths. Built in the 2nd century A.D., and later used as a gymnasium. In the middle, are the toilets."

Reconstructed arches made of stones hinted at the building that once provided a place for the Romans to bathe and clean themselves in pools of warm, hot and cold water. The guide led the ladies on down the main path toward the Agora.

"And this was the shopping area, ladies. Where the Roman men brought their wives! The merchants had stalls here." Now only hints of the foundation and clumps of stones marked the walls of ancient stalls.

"The market is closed! Darn!" Sallie said.

"Oh, but you can shop soon!" Balaban laughed. "Turkish hospitality, we keep ladies happy, even at Ephesus."

Balaban walked on and gathered the group near a little amphitheater. "And here we have the Odeion. Built in 150 A.D., this was a small theater, once covered, and also used for concerts and meetings of the advisory council. It could hold about 1,500 people. You know Ephesus was a very large town, population 250,000. We know there were that many, because the large amphitheater holds 24,000. Generally the Romans built one seat for every 10 people."

He called attention to the pillars standing alongside of the road. "In Roman times, columns lined the street and you can see that there was a walkway for pedestrians on each side of the road. The walkway was covered. In addition to the pillars, statues of famous people also lined the road."

"Wow. This is amazing!" Emily said.

Her youthful enthusiasm contrasted with the older women who were sweating, and ready to sit down for a break. Balaban was careful to lead the women in areas shaded by the ruins for lectures and nearing the bottom of the site, turned the group into the Latrina and encouraged them to sit.

"For men only," Balaban explained. "But today, we let the women sit." The MAMs bottoms rested on a thick marble ledge punctuated with large holes. By their feet a narrow channel remained, and in the center a rectangular pool.

"The Romans moved the waste away through the pipes under the seats, and the water in front of their feet was available, too. Mosaics and a pool of water in the center made it a beautiful place. The men carried a stick, and they would have cloth at the end of it, to dip into the water to wipe themselves. That is why Jesus refused water on the cross; it was a Roman soldier's wiping stick."

Priscilla looked at Balaban with confusion. "Are you sure?"

"The historians tell us," he replied.

"Ah to be a first-century man. Defecating and shooting the breeze together." Katharine laughed.

"Not much different than the modern row of urinals, do you think?" Ursula countered. "And the stadium is coming up."

"Men and boys and their toys. Not much change in 2,000 years, huh?" Katharine agreed. "If only we could keep them at their games, and not let them play with lives. They certainly can make a mess of things."

***

Moses Sun fidgeted in the back room at the port. Would his cell phone battery hold out? Headquarters planned to send some important information today about the latest plans for thwarting those bleeding liberals. His shoulders drooped. Plans were not working out. Not only had he not trailed Professor Long, but he had accomplished almost nothing for the cause since he left the States five days earlier.

The iPhone lit up bright red and he opened the text message, the news bite for the day, "The Liberals are funding the Terrorists." Brilliant, he thought. Absolutely the truth. Destruction loomed if the Liberals take control. "Beware of False Gods. Tell the Muslims to go home." Excellent, yes, he thought. Then he looked around and remembered that Turkey is 97% Muslim and switched to another screen.

"This way, sir." The agent touched his shoulder and motioned him back to the desk. "Your passport?"

"I'm sorry, I left it in my hotel room. But here is a copy, and I do need to go back to my room to get the bag I left with my passport."

"The ship doesn't sail until 4 p.m. That should give you time, sir." The agent looked at the itinerary for the cruise ship and covered the 3 p.m. departure time with his hand. He tapped his wallet with his left hand and smiled.

Sun hailed a taxi. He emptied more out of his wallet when he arrived back at the hotel. Some days he felt like he was on a conveyor belt walking forward while standing still. A few more dollars to the desk clerk brought up his suitcase.

He decided to take in Ephesus. All the hype, the crazy ladies, and false teachings about the book of Revelation. His mouth took a firm grimace. God being his helper, he would press on to stop Professor Long.

Soon he was on his way. As the taxi neared the ruins, he saw a large military compound on the right side of the road. In the courtyard, young men were marching in formation.

"Are you at war, sir?" He asked the taxi driver, motioning to the compound.

"No, we have mandatory military service for all men over 18 years of age. Eighteen months. Important to be prepared. Fighting on the Western border near Iraq, you know."

Sun smiled. He knew soon the Americans would have mandatory military service again, too. The draft was just one more war away. Everything was ticking like clockwork. He couldn't wait until the Republicans sweep the House, Senate and White House again.

Thirty minutes later, his taxi dropped him off at the foot of the Ephesus site. Twelve buses were lined up waiting and he could see groups of tourists standing at different locations up the hill. The buses were marked with the name of the ladies' cruise.

Moses Sun tipped his hat to the bus driver waiting for the tourists. "Good morning, sir." Then he brushed off his pants and strolled toward the amphitheater. He chuckled, then murmured to himself, "Perhaps this trip wasn't a total loss after all."

***

Balaban now led his group to a large two-story facade. "We know that this was the library of Ephesus. Legend has it that the underground tunnel from the library went across the street to the brothel. The men could go into the library, then head underground to the brothel and come back out of the library when they were finished. Their wives didn't need to know."

Officer Parks laughed. Jane reprimanded him with a stern look on her face. "Don't even think about it."

Parks raised his eyebrows. "A little possessiveness coming out, here? Does that mean that you like me?"

"I like to associate with good men. That's all. But I do think you're cute."

Molly and Sallie exchanged glances. Then Molly whispered to Sallie, "I think she's falling hard."

"Stay tuned," Sallie whispered back.

Parks put his arm around Jane's shoulder and turned her away from brothel. "Who needs a brothel when a man has a charming, intelligent, good woman by his side?"

Sallie looked back at Molly. "You may have a point there."

Molly nodded her head in affirmation, "I can spot romance a mile away."

Meanwhile, Ursula was informing Katharine that the brothel story was just that. "They really have no solid information on that one. More recent research has suggested that this building was not a

brothel, but part of their public bath system.   But it's a good story
for the tourists."

Katharine laughed. "Are you going to tell the tour guide?"

Just then the tour guide was telling the group exactly that.

"These Romans weren't quite as exciting as we thought then?"
Jane laughed.

"No, most of the prostitution went on at the temples." Parks explained.

"How do YOU know about that? Jane asked.

"Well, history was my first love. I do have a history degree from
Vanderbilt. What more do you want to know?"

"Did Brutus really betray Julius Caesar? What is that whole story?" Jane asked back.

"Let's save that for the bus, I don't want to miss the tour." Parks
responded.

***

Balaban called the group together and herded them toward the
amphitheater. "Your group's service starts in 10 minutes. Please
take a seat, and I will tell you more about this place later."

Sallie and Emily walked into the large structure and followed
their bus driver's purple paddle toward the middle of the large arena.

"This is fantastic!" Emily exclaimed. "Incredible. It's like going to
a modern outdoor theater. We are just building replicas today!"

"Civilization was quite advanced back then, wasn't it?"   Sallie
agreed.

Emily sat down and looked around the huge stadium. She could
see stone crumbling, but the seats remained solid where they sat.
She scanned the aisles, the steps, a stage where the cruise leaders
were preparing for a service.

"Are we really going to have communion?" Emily asked Sallie.

"Yes, that's the plan. I wonder if Jane will partake. I don't think
she attends church."

"But she's baptized now, like Lydia."

Sallie laughed. "Right. Self-baptism. Only Jane."

Emily began snapping pictures with her digital camera.   "To
think, that Thecla and the Apostle Paul were in this place. It's fantastic! I'm so glad I came!"

"Yes dear, me, too." Sallie nodded.

Ursula and Katharine were sitting behind Sallie and now Ursula
tapped Sallie on her shoulder. "Ladies, the cave where we will be
digging is visible on the hillside over there. Do you see the red flag?"

Emily and Sallie looked across the amphitheater and up the large
hill.

58

"Where?" Emily asked.

"Look beyond those trees, and then a little up to the right. Do you see it?"

"I think so, but I'm not sure." Sallie laughed. "How are we going to get up there?"

"I hope you brought your hiking shoes!" Ursula responded, winking at Katharine.

"So, do ya think Paul sat up there in the cave with Thecla, watching the ceremony going on down here in the amphitheater?" Sallie asked.

Katharine piped in on this one. "We do know that some of the early Christians lived in caves, and that may have been their dwelling. Although you know Paul was also a tentmaker, so he may have had a tent somewhere else in the area."

It was just about that time that Katharine noticed him.

"Ursula, look. Am I seeing things? Is that Moses Sun? Oh my God. What am I going to do?"

Katharine pointed down to the bottom left entrance of the amphitheater where Ursula saw a small man standing scanning the crowd.

"It's him. I know it's him." Katharine said.

"Leave. You can walk out behind the people seated to our right. Just go, Katharine. He won't see you."

"Are you crazy? I'll stick out like a sore thumb and he'll see me."

Katharine shrank back behind Ursula. "I'll just have to hope he doesn't see me."

Ursula pulled a white floppy hat out of her shoulder bag.

"Here, put this on."

Katharine gasped and quickly donned the hat.

Ursula motioned to Sallie. "Could you sit on the edge of your seat? Katharine is trying to hide. Don't look now."

Ursula shook her curls and glanced over to the side of the row where Sun was standing.

"Are you sure it's him?"

Parks overhead the conversation and scoped out the entrance.

"No question about it. Stay put." Turning to Jane, he apologized, "Duty calls, dear. Perhaps we can meet again in Patmos?"

Parks jumped up and told Katharine, "I've got you covered. That's why they pay me the big bucks. Enjoy the rest of the service."

Parks was gone in a flash and when Ursula looked over again he was taking Sun by the arm and ushering him up the hill from the stadium.

"Parks is leading him away. You're OK," Ursula reported.

Katharine held her stomach. Her hand was shaking.

Ursula put her arm around her friend. "You're safe. Parks is the best. He showed me his credentials."

Katharine shook her head. "But that man is crazy. He followed me around the world. God knows what he is capable of."

The rest of the service was a blur for Katharine. Grape juice and wafers, a male quartet punctuated the scripture with music. Katharine yearned to get back on the boat. She wondered how it could be possible to be so full of joy one moment and so full of terror the next.

Ursula tried to distract her as they left the amphitheater for the bus. "Here, let's get our picture taken with the site in the background. When we make our great find, we can email this to our universities to put up on their website media pages. I can almost read it now, 'Old college friends and professors, Katharine Long and Ursula Goodtree, get reacquainted in Ephesus where they made one of the most significant Biblical archaeological finds of the 21st century.' "

"Right," Katharine laughed. "Well, OK. I'd like that picture. Let's ask Emily to take it."

Later, on the way back to the bus, Ursula continued to take Katharine's thoughts away from Moses Sun, starting a new conversation. "Have you read *The Secret*? The law of attraction? Do you stay up on Oprah's Book Club features? You know I have visualized a wonderful outcome for our expedition."

"*The Secret*?" Katharine laughed. "Do you really take that seriously? On my campus when that hit the bookstores they sponsored a debate. On the right, the Christian fundamentalists said it was dangerous New Age witchcraft. Those on the left said it was abundance theology that begs the question of poverty and starvation of millions in the global community. It was a lively debate, I'll say that much. And they made very good points. Do you have your own personal genie, Ursula?"

Ursula looked at Katharine and realized it had been years since they shared their deepest dreams and fears. Would Kath label her crazy if she told her the fantastic pictures she had created at home about her hopes for the dig? She decided to keep quiet.

"Can we go home now?" Katharine asked Balaban, when they approached the bus.

"We have one more stop before we go back to the ship. My friends at the Turkish carpet store will give you free drinks and snacks and show you some beautiful carpets." Balaban replied.

An hour later, the MAMs were back on the ship. They shared lively stories at dinner and the wine flowed freely. Jane bragged about her carpet purchases. "My family will love me at Christmas!"

That night in the cabin, Katharine left to email her husband about Moses Sun, and Ursula pulled out her journal. Thumbing back, she found the entry of visualizing an incredible dig. "Deep in the cave, we will find scrolls telling an incredible story of first-century

Roman and Christian life. The scrolls will change the perceptions of Christians living today, as they begin to understand more about the early church."

Ursula smiled. Not even her therapist knew about this one. But she was visualizing it with all the imagination she could muster, and that was her secret. It was her experiment. She turned on the night light, flipped off the light and pulled the covers back. Sweet, she thought to herself. So sweet.

9. Thecla Escapes

September 4, 46 A.D.

Thecla slipped back into the house after dark, collapsing onto her pallet. Sleep came quickly and she dreamed of Paul. In the shadowy, ephemeral reality, she followed him from town to town, but someone was shaking her.

"Wake up, Thecla! Where have you been? Thamyris comes soon to tell us the fate of your Paul. He's taken the matter into his own hands. Get ready to greet your betrothed. Start behaving like a proper daughter! You will not spend your day at the window again."

Her mother left a pitcher of water and a cloth for her to wash, and placed her best gown out on the table. Thecla's heart raced. Even as she prepared herself for the day, she planned her escape. She would not allow them to hold her against her will. She must find Paul and learn more.

When Thamyris arrived to give the report, Thecla behaved as a dutiful daughter and humble lover. She knew her only chance now would be to play by their rules, until could she find a way to return to Paul.

"He's in prison now," Thamyris bragged. "We took him to the governor. He breaks the law. The governor will put him to death for preaching such blasphemy, tarnishing the Emperor's name. He insists there is only one God, not the Emperor."

Thecla's mother enfolded Thamyris in a warm embrace. "You solved our problem, then. Thank you, for saving my daughter from this man."

Thecla fumed quietly within. How could they plot such evil against a man of God? What had Paul done to offend, other than speaking the truth in love? Her own faith burned brightly. She would follow Paul to death, rather than be subject to Thamyris for the rest of her life.

"Should we set the date for your wedding, now, Thamyris?" Thecla's mother continued, as if the day were like any other. She proceeded with plans to link her daughter to the most eligible, prominent Roman in Iconium and thereby secure her future as well.

Thecla listened while they planned a future she hoped fervently to avoid. They would seal her fate, just one fortnight from now. Her

62

fears tumbled in her stomach. She tried to maintain an outward veneer of enthusiasm, while she plotted her next move.

Later in the evening, after her mother slept soundly, she took her gold earrings and looking glass and slipped way to the governor's quarters to find the prison guard, keeping watch over her holy man, Paul.

10. Patmos

September 14, 2006

At the Kusasdai pier, the boat captain motioned to Parks, then looked at Moses Sun. "In the first century, the trip from Ephesus to Patmos would have taken a day in good sailing weather.   With modern boats, we can make the journey in four or five hours."

Sounds like a good deal to me. What do you say, old chap? $100 a piece? Should we take the ride?" Parks slapped Sun on the back and then tightened his fists with thumbs up and a smile.

Sun smiled back. The light was shining today. A friend, a boat, and a trip to Patmos. What more could he ask? "Count me in."

Parks pulled out his wallet and handed the boat captain 200 liras. "This one is on me." What Sun didn't see was the other 200 he had already given to the captain, to assure that the boat would arrive in Patmos long after the MAMs' cruise ship sailed for other shores.

Parks' phone chimed. Flipping it up to his ear, he listened to the silence of his own call. Responding in kind, he exclaimed "Oh my!" Then turning to the boat captain, he bowed out. "Very sorry, sir, duty calls. Keep the change, and take good care of my friend. No pleasure cruise for me today."

Parks jumped back onto the dock, striding like a man with a mission toward the shore. To lend credibility, he glanced at his watch and took off in a sprint toward the waiting cabs. Then he laughed. He'd nail the departure time for his helicopter lift to the island. The pilot would be waiting, regardless.   He whispered into the morning sun, "Hold on, Jane, here I come!"   Whistling Louis Armstrong, Dan Parks hailed a cab for the short ride to the airport. He saluted back to the boat in the harbor. "Happy Trails, Sun!"

***

On board the cruise ship, the MAMs gathered at the morning Bible Study. Jane sipped her coffee and rolled her eyes. "Got me out of bed early for a reading of the book of Revelation? Pinch me. I can't believe I'm really here."

"Oh, you're here all right," Sallie responded. "You just wish you weren't. But cheer up, you might learn something. You've probably never read the book of Revelation. You're about to learn what all the hullaboo is about! Sit back and relax!"

The MAMs were nearing the end of their "Journeys of Paul" cruise. And although most of the educational programs on board involved explanations and interpretations, on this morning when the boat made its approach into the harbor of Patmos, the plan called for a simple reading of the book that gave Patmos its fame.

The Bible Study leader turned out the lights and projected the night sky over Patmos on to a large screen. Ragged black stones rising out of the dark sea reflected the moonlight. Stars lit the dome of the heavens. Still photos captured views of the Patmos rocks and the sea in the night.

"Wow!" Molly exclaimed. "Patmos is a beautiful place!"

"Yes, many people would agree with you," the leader spoke. "This is the setting in which John wrote the book of Revelation. In a couple hours, you'll see it for yourself. But now, I'd like you to relax, sit back and listen. An inspired work by a man named John, exiled to the island of Patmos from Ephesus circa 94 A.D. Without modern conveniences, food and shelter, John experienced a harsh reality. In this milieu, his vision unfolded. Let it speak to you this morning."

The leader pushed a button on the audio player and the reading began,

> *"The revelation of Jesus Christ, which God gave him to show his servants what must soon take place; he made it known by sending his angel to his servant John, who testified to the word of God and to the testimony of Jesus Christ, even to all that he saw. Blessed is the one who reads aloud the words of the prophecy, and blessed are those who hear and who keep what is written in it; for the time is near. John to the seven churches that are in Asia: Grace to you and peace from him who is and who was and who is to come, and from the seven spirits who are before his throne, and from Jesus Christ, the faithful witness, the firstborn of the dead, and the ruler of the kings of the earth. To him who loves us and freed us from our sins by his blood, and made us to be a kingdom, priests serving his God and Father, to him be glory and dominion forever and ever. Amen. Look! He is coming with the clouds; every eye will see him, even those who pierced him; and on his account all the tribes of the earth will wail. So it is to be. Amen. 'I am the Al-*

65

*pha and the Omega,' says the Lord God, who is and who
was and who is to come, the Almighty."[viii]*

The MAMs quietly absorbed the strange images of life and death,
destruction and hope, worship and mystery. Priscilla's eyes remained round and excited, while Jane seemed to be dozing off. Molly
concentrated and jotted notes while the reader droned on. Emily lay
mesmerized with the vision. Katharine and Ursula whispered to one
another throughout the reading. Sallie for once didn't lead the group
in laughter. "Not a laughing matter," she said out loud when the
horses of the apocalypse materialized in her mind's eye during the
reading.

An hour and a half later, the leader flipped on the lights as the
reader concluded the book,

> "Then the angel showed me the river of the water of
> life, bright as crystal, flowing from the throne of God
> and of the Lamb through the middle of the street of the
> city. On either side of the river is the tree of life with its
> twelve kinds of fruit, producing its fruit each month;
> and the leaves of the tree are for the healing of the na-
> tions. Nothing accursed will be found there anymore.
> But the throne of God and of the Lamb will be in it,
> and his servants will worship him; they will see his
> face, and his name will be on their foreheads. And
> there will be no more night; they need no light of lamp
> or sun, for the Lord God will be their light, and they
> will reign forever and ever."[ix]

On the screen a brilliant sunrise spread over the jagged rocks
earlier covered with night, a lush tree in the center of the screen il-
lustrated the words.

"Whew!" Jane remarked. "What a journey! What a trip! Was the
man high?"

Priscilla shook her head and spoke with a firm voice, "He had a
vision from God!"

The Bible study leader spoke, "And that is the book of Revelation.
More books have been written trying to explain this one book of the
Bible than any other scripture. As many interpretations as stars in
that night sky. Tomorrow, we'll discuss the book, but today, we visit.
Prepare to disembark. Our buses leave in 30 minutes."

The MAMs scattered to their cabins and gathered on Deck 15
minutes later. Their ship sailed into the harbor of Patmos. Molly observed the little boats, the white sandstone buildings and tranquility
of this shore where sea met notorious island. From a distance, the

dark rocks reminded her of the volcanoes that originally formed these Greek islands scattered through the Aegean Sea. She wrote in her journal:

> *"Sailing into Patmos harbor, a calm spirit pervades my consciousness. I know that we are slowing down, leaving the busyness of the larger cities behind. We arrive at a very quiet island, a sacred space, a place of significance that links us to our collective past. The sun dances on the waters, the breeze ripples through my hair. I sense God illuminating, moving and breathing among us."*

"Doesn't look like we're going into exile today!" Jane announced. "In fact, we might even be able to drink a little wine this afternoon if we're lucky."

Katharine and Ursula hooked arms and headed toward the dock. "You'll enjoy the tour of the Cave of St. John," Katharine told Ursula. "Last time I brought the students, our tour guide kept telling us, 'Legend has it...' That upset the dogmatic ones. Priscilla will be livid."

Ursula smiled. "We humans need our legends. But sometimes the truth is stranger than the fictions we create. I have a good feeling about this place. Do you feel it?" Ursula searched for words to explain the feeling that had begun to pervade her being."

"A nice little island, yes. Most travel writers agree with you: Patmos oozes spirituality. I can't say that I feel it, but you know me -- I'm not the touchy-feely type. Wait 'til you see the art objects crowding the Monastery of St. John. People have offered their gifts and creations to this shrine for hundreds of years."

Along the water, a concrete ledge separated the sea from the small port town of Skala. Along the ledge, rubber tires hung, suspended by huge chains and metal bars, ready to cushion ships from the hard concrete. Only 10 feet from the dock, a road carried morning traffic. Katharine observed a taxi stand, a police department, a port authority and little shops already busy with customers. The dock area looked rather ordinary, although she had to admit the picturesque views of the water below and the white stucco houses and blue sky above were quite dramatic.

The MAMs walked up the plank. Sallie yelled. "*Terra Firma!* Ah, sweet land once again." Jane, Emily and Priscilla were close behind.

"Keep moving, ma'am," Jane instructed Sallie. "We've got a bus to catch."

"Like they are going to leave us behind! The fleet has arrived again! I'm beginning to feel like the Ugly American. Don't you think

those huge tour buses look a little out of place on this quaint island?"
Sallie asked.

"You worry too much. Just enjoy the trip. This is your trip of a
lifetime, remember?"

Jane looked up into the small town and saw a familiar figure
strolling toward the dock. She squinted to confirm, but she would
recognize that gait anywhere. An unexpected warmth radiated
through her body. A smile lit her face. Walking forward, she extended her hand, "Well, howdy Mr. Parks. Fancy meeting you here!"

Parks grabbed Jane's hand and then planted a firm kiss on her
cheek. "At last!"

Molly heard his words and launched into a throaty version of the
Etta James jazz tune by the same name.

Parks grabbed Jane's waist and began a little waltz on the dock.
The other MAMs began to heckle, but Molly sang on. Other cruise
members streamed out of the boat, circumventing the dancers. The
people waiting to disembark began cheering and clapping. The dancers continued and Molly sang on.

Parks planted a large grin on his mouth and then told Jane, "Let's
sign her up!"

"For what?" Jane asked. Parks draped his arm around her neck
and dangled his hand on her shoulder.

"Hold that thought." He paused for a moment. "You know, they
say Patmos is a wonderful place for a honeymoon."

Ursula complimented Molly. "Wow! What a voice you have there,
girlfriend. That was beautiful."

Molly grinned sheepishly. "It's just something I do in church.
Since I was a little girl, they've had me singing."

The MAMs filed toward the bus marked for the purple group.
Soon the buses were making their way down the picturesque street of
white sandstone shops and climbing up toward the Monastery of St.
John. Katharine intentionally took a seat across from Parks who was
busy entertaining Jane.

Soon Jane was laughing loud and hard, and Parks looked over to
Katharine and said, "It's good to keep them laughing."

But Katharine wasn't smiling. Her stomach was churning and
her blood pressure felt like it was nearing the top of Everest. Forcing
out a question through her fearful voice, she asked Parks. "Where is
he now?"

Parks continued to laugh and turned to Katharine. "He's on the
slow boat to China. Don't worry, dear. He will be arriving this afternoon when our ship leaves the harbor. I paid the boat captain well.
Enjoy Patmos. I left Sun in the dust this morning when I boarded a
helicopter after paying for his passage to Patmos."

"Oh," Katharine nervously giggled. "Are you sure?"

"Is the Pope Catholic?" Parks asked and turned back to Jane. "You're in good hands, dear." Then he looked over to Katharine. "You, too, dear. Don't worry, be happy." He whispered to Jane, "I haven't been this happy in a long time!"

Katharine turned to Ursula, "Did you hear that? Parks put Sun on a slow boat to Patmos!" Letting out a deep breath, she admitted, "I am really scared, Ursula."

Ursula put her arm around Katharine and said, "We're all here for you. You'll be safe. Parks is the best. He took care of him at Ephesus, and now he's sent him off into the blue. Let's enjoy this place. Look at that postcard view out the window."

Katharine looked past Ursula to the panorama of Patmos harbor. She could see their large cruise ship that dwarfed all the little boats bobbing by the docks. Fluffy white clouds floated above blue water, fishing boats were out on the morning prowl. Looking out of the front of the bus, Katharine saw little shops.

The tour guide began to speak. "We are going to stop here and you can walk the rest of the way to the top and enjoy the view and the shops on the right side of the street. Our tour will continue at the monastery in one hour. Feel free to make some purchases. You'll have a little more time to shop on the way back down."

The MAMs launched into their Patmos shopping opportunity with glee, and when they reached the top, each of them had added a bright shopping bag to her arm.

"This is heavy," Sallie complained. "But my family will be happy at Christmas. Tell me it's worth it!"

"It's worth it, girlfriend," Molly laughed. "How many opportunities are you going to get to shop in Patmos in your lifetime? You did it right. Just a little pain for the rest of the day, carrying your loot." Then she read the sign out loud. "We welcome you to our Holy Monastery. Please be aware that you are in holy place of the worship of God. Proper attitude and dress are therefore requested."

Sallie glared at Jane with bug-eyes. Then she took pointed her index finger toward Jane and started shaking it.

Jane bugged her eyes back and turned toward Dan before Sallie could say anything.

Soon the tour guide ushered them through the monastery, sharing stories of its origin, development and the mysterious way that artists continued to shower their work on the place.

"No cameras, please. Not in the areas of worship." The guide stopped at the entrance. "This is the exonarthex, the entrance to the chapel." Lining the wall were wooden chairs with arm rests. Covering the ceiling and walls were religious paintings. "From the 18th and 20th centuries," he said. "And now we enter the Katholikon, the main sanctuary."

A dome covered the high ceiling, with paintings of religious icons surrounding it.

"12th and 16th century," the guide said.

The MAMs walked quietly through the dark, ornate place of worship.

"A little spooky," Sallie whispered to Molly.

Molly nodded in agreement.

The group walked out of the sanctuary and up through the stairs and arches of the inner courtyard, climbing up to the museum of paintings and artifacts, displayed in glass cases or roped off to keep the public from touching the monuments to John.

Jane stopped in front of a painting of a religious icon. "It's Thecla! Here she is, ladies."

The MAMs crowded around the faded painting of the woman who had brought them half way around the world.

"A moment of silence, please." Sallie chuckled. Then she added with a straight face, "I'm serious."

Molly reached out to hold hands with Sallie, and extended another to Ursula. The rest of the MAMs followed suit, leaving Dan Parks outside their circle, while Molly spoke.

"Thank you, Jesus, for bringing us safely to Patmos. Thank you, Jesus, for Thecla. Thank you, Jesus, for this wonderful group of women. Lead us to Thecla again and again. In the name of Jesus we pray. Amen!"

"Amen!" Sallie echoed.

Dan Parks reached out to grab Jane's hand. She smiled, and moved away from the circle.

"Wow." Emily continued to look at Thecla. "Wow. What a woman." She considered how Thecla had given up her engagement to become a disciple of Paul. Would this be her path, too? A sober thought reverberated in her heart. Perhaps her choice to come on the trip had already echoed Thecla's?

The MAMs moved on to examine the rest of the artifacts.

"These rooms are stuffed!" Ursula exclaimed.

"Reminds me of my attic!" Sallie laughed. "I'm your classic pack rat."

Katharine asked, "Have you ever been to Catholic shrines where people are healed? They tend to be decorated with all kinds of things that people come to leave behind in gratitude. This is a shrine."

Ursula nodded her head, "That's what I'm talking about. This place is holy. I can feel it."

Emily agreed, "I feel it, too."

Katharine could see the blue seascape out the window from their perch at the top of the island. She disagreed. "You are all fanatics. This is just a place." Yet just as she finished her sentence, a white dove glided by, circled and perched on the window ledge. "Look at this!" she motioned to Ursula.

When Ursula came over, another dove circled and landed beside the first.

"It's a sign from heaven!" Ursula announced.

"What's a sign from heaven?" Sallie asked. She saw a third dove circling and landing.

"Spooky!" Katharine said.

Emily and Priscilla crowded in to peek, and Ursula exclaimed, "Look, two more are coming!"

Soon Molly joined the group, with Parks and Jane towering behind the cluster, all looking down at the birds.

"And two more!" Sallie added.

Jane pointed and began to count, "One, two, three, four, five, six, seven."

"Our birds," Ursula decided. "They are a sign from God."

"A blessing, a blessing from God." Molly agreed.

"Wow!" Emily whispered. "I knew this was a holy place."

Katharine grabbed her camera. The doves began flapping their wings and lifted off. "Never can take pictures of birds," she complained.

"Look!" Priscilla yelled. "Look! Do you see that heart?"

The doves flew in formation toward the sea.

Katharine snapped another picture, the white wings framed a heart of deep blue sky. She snapped again before the doves turned into specks flying toward the sea. Stepping back, she captured an incredible view of the peninsula, framed by the window and metal bars.

Ursula smugly looked at Katharine. "You felt it. I know you did."

Glances were exchanged and nobody said a word. Katharine didn't comment. Ursula focused on the goose bumps on Emily's arms.

Katharine pushed "review" on her camera and scrolled through the pictures. She zoomed in and counted them. "Seven," she muttered to herself, then glanced up to the heavens, turned off her camera and slipped it back into her bag.

"The perfect number. Biblical. Holy seven, dear. We are, they were. You got it, girlfriend," Molly laughed and slipped her arm around Katharine's waist. Katharine laughed nervously, and then their guide led the women out of the monastery and down the path toward the cave. The guide put his forefinger over his lips, signaling silence.

Emily looked beyond him to a gathering of some sort in an outdoor amphitheater. Wood benches stretched across tiered steps. A speaker at the lectern spoke to the group of 30 or 40 people, some robed and others in regular dress. She focused on the familiar brown robe of a Franciscan, looking closer and thinking about her father's good friend, Brother Gabriel, from the Catholic church in her home town. Her mother had always told her that it's impolite to stare, so she looked away, but then heard her name.

"Emily!" The Franciscan monk jumped up and ran down the amphitheater steps, toward her. "Emily?"

"Brother Gabriel?" She reached out to him with both arms, and he embraced her with a bear hug. "What are you doing here?"

"I could ask you the same thing!" He bellowed out in his familiar tenor voice. "I'm at a conference, and exploring the island. A vacation of sorts. And you?"

"An archaeological expedition! We are going to Ephesus, to the Grotto of St. Paul to dig. Can you believe it? We'll be there tomorrow. It's my grandmother's book club, with an archaeologist from the University of Michigan," Emily said.

"Tell me more!" Brother Gabriel put his arm around Emily.

The tour guide motioned to her to come. "We don't have much time. We must go on to the cave."

"We're actually on a cruise, and our boat is leaving in 45 minutes. Wow, I can't believe we found each other in Patmos. Dad will never believe this."

"I'll come with you to the cave." Gabriel walked with Emily toward the small house enclosing the Cave of St. John.

The MAMs' group entered into the dark stone room. A small slab of rock protruded from the wall of the cave. "This is where legend has it that the scribe wrote the book of Revelation upon John's dictation," the tour guide explained.

A rectangular block of stone graced the floor of the cave. "This is where legend has it that John rested while writing the book of Revelation."

Katharine laughed and bumped Ursula's arm. "See, I told you!"

A jagged crack extended across the ceiling of the cave. "This is where legend has it the lightning struck when John received the vision." The guide smiled and seemed to be laughing at the thought himself.

"What does he mean 'legend'?" Priscilla asked. "This is the Bible we're talking about. This is truth!"

The archaeologist in Ursula spoke, "You know that 2,000 years later, it's hard to know much about John's life on the island Patmos. To establish as a fact that this was his cave? Impossible. Over the years, the legend tells us this was his cave. The Bible only tells us he was on the island."

"This is a holy place," Emily countered. "Legend or no legend. I feel it. This is an amazing place."

Brother Gabriel agreed. "Yes, the pilgrims have been coming here for hundreds of years, to be in this place, this holy place, where they believe God spoke to John. A very holy place."

Parks placed his arm around Jane's shoulder and pulled her close. "Yes, this place is wonderful, and the company even better."

"Holy smokes!" Sallie yelled at him. "This is a public place. Please save your affection for a private place."

"You're just jealous," Jane smirked at Sallie, then turned her lips to Parks who eagerly met her mouth with a probing kiss.

"You're right, we're jealous," Ursula said, "Come on Sallie, enough of watching this."

Brother Gabriel and Emily sat down on the wooden benches facing the wall of the cave. Emily closed her eyes in prayer. She prayed for Josh, she prayed for the MAMs, she prayed for the archaeological expedition to come and she gave thanks for finding Brother Gabriel in a strange land. She grabbed his big hand, and he held hers firmly.

But soon the tour guide interrupted. "We must go now. Please return to our bus." The MAMs filed out of the cave into waiting buses. Tomorrow they would return to Kusadasi, but today they were absorbing the beauty of Patmos. Emily bid adieu to Brother Gabriel with a promise to visit when she returned home.

"Hey, I'll try to come over to Kusadasi, then, in a few days. Maybe we can meet up again?"

"That would be great! Please come!" Emily waved good-bye again and headed toward the bus.

On the way back to the port, the women sat quietly. Katharine pushed the review button on her digital camera and began clicking through the pictures of the monastery and the Cave of St. John. When she came to the picture of the birds, she paused. Yes, it really was a heart. She counted them again. Seven. The perfect number. Seven churches. Seven MAMs. Seven birds. Seven on a trip to Ephesus, a dig at one of the seven cities of the seven churches.

Ursula looked over her shoulder and put her arm around her friend. "Something important is going to happen. I can feel it."

Katharine shrugged and didn't want to admit that the magic of Patmos was affecting her, too. Realism had been her modus operandi for so long. "Seven is a perfect number." Was all that she could manage?

"Perfect! Right! Maybe there's hope for even you!" Ursula laughed. "Stay tuned!"

An hour later, the boat sailed out of Patmos harbor. Ursula and Katharine were on the Promenade Deck, taking pictures and enjoying the scenery for one last time. Suddenly a small fishing boat passed the cruise ship, heading for the smaller dock.

Katharine saw a man with binoculars pointed up toward the ship. "What is that?" she asked, and before the words were out of her mouth, she knew. She sat down, so the side of the boat hid her figure.

"Ursula. It's him! Where is Parks? I'm going to our cabin." Katharine began to shake.

"It's too late now. We are on our way. You're out of reach. Parks delivered. Let's go have a beer before dinner."

The college roommates locked arms and headed toward the bar on the deck below.

***

Moses Sun put away his binoculars and decided it was time to resort to prayer. She had eluded him for several days, but he knew she'd be in Ephesus for two weeks. The good Lord and time were on his side. Tomorrow, he would enjoy a private tour of the island and then he would finish his assignment. God never promised things would be easy. Men of God must persevere.

11. Orientation at Ephesus

September 15, 2006

The MAMs' ship sailed from Patmos through the Aegean to the official cruise destination, Athens, where most of the passengers disembarked. But Ursula had arranged for an additional leg to Kusadasi. While the women slept, the ship traveled back to Turkey. In the morning, they packed up their suitcases, made their way through customs at the Kusadasi port and checked into their hotel.

Sallie sat on the side of the bed in her new room, lacing her hiking boots. She groaned. "I'm not getting any younger!" The rolls of fat in her midsection presented a barrier to her shoes. She panted and then turned to Emily, who was busy studying a map of the Ephesus site.

"How far are we going to have to hike up that mountain?"

"It's not a mountain, it's a hill, and I think Ursula was trying to spook you." Emily patted Sallie on the back. "You can make it. I have confidence in you."

"Thank you, dear. I'm glad someone does. I've never gone on an archaeological dig before but I have climbed mountains in Colorado – 35 years ago!" Now she remembered panting on the Colorado Wesley Reunion six years ago, trying to retrace her steps there as a college student. But she kept her mouth shut, and listened to Emily's youthful enthusiasm.

"Digging is fun. You get to explore the past through the present. You've got the disposition for this sort of thing. I've seen your house. You love to collect things. You'll be mesmerized by the pieces we pull out of the cave."

"Do you really think there is going to be anything there besides dirt? Don't you think it's already been found? This cave has been used for centuries. How are a bunch of women from a reading group going to find anything more?" Sallie scratched her head. "Now the reality catches up with us. 'In Search of Thecla'? We are out of our minds!" She started laughing. "We are crazy. This is absolutely crazy. We are not going to find anything in that cave."

A knock on the door interrupted Sallie's rave. "Ladies? Are you ready to go? Don't forget your hats! It's a sunny day." Emily opened the door to Ursula, dressed in a traditional archaeological outfit.

"Here's the real Indiana Jones. Look at this lady -- khakis, clipboard, pencil behind the ear. We've got ourselves a real archaeologist, Emily!" Sallie saluted Ursula. "We're coming, we're on our way."

Ursula blushed and then turned away from the door. She looked down and realized that she did indeed look like the typical field archaeologist. After so many years, she was actually returning to the field. Like fitting fingers into old gloves, she felt comfortable the moment she stepped into her khakis. Not only did she feel good, she felt deeply alive. Something started stirring within her, something calling out, something important enough to cause her to look forward to the work ahead. Her hair bounced, and she felt a light spring in her step when she walked on down the hall to summons the rest of the MAMs.

Sallie threw the sunscreen into her backpack and grabbed her hat off the hook on the wall. "After you, my dear. Age follows beauty. Let's go, Indiana Emily. We're off to search for Thecla."

Molly and Jane were already at the van when Sallie and Emily arrived. "At least we traded in our monster bus for a smaller van!" Molly was telling Jane.

"It's still five times bigger than anything else on the road. Conspicuous consuming Americans, here we come!" Sallie said.

"Modern convenience. Would you prefer we each take a private tiny taxi?" Jane asked. "The big vehicle takes more gas, but it also holds more people. It's not necessarily a bad thing, ecologically speaking."

Sallie stopped complaining. "OK, OK. I hate to admit it, but you might be right." She offered Jane a high five and then added, "But don't let it go to your head!"

Katharine and Ursula came out locked arm in arm. Then Priscilla appeared, dressed primly in neat jean capris, a white blouse and her MAM hat.

"The perfect seven present and accounted for! Let's go for it!" Sallie gestured to Ursula. "Lead us on!"

Katharine stepped into the van first, nervously glancing around. She shivered. Parks had been with the group the night before in the hotel and said he had to leave for awhile. Sun arrived in Patmos two days ago, but could be back in Kusadasi by now. The clear blue sky did nothing to calm her.

"Wow! Isn't this the perfect day!" Emily exclaimed. "Look at the harbor. Isn't that a postcard view!" Little boats bobbed on the water, and fluffy white clouds floated in the sky. "It doesn't get any better than this!"

Balaban picked up a little microphone. "It's so good to see you again. Ms. Ursula has arranged for me to be your driver and inter-preter during the dig. Thank you, Ms. Ursula."

"My pleasure," Ursula replied, saluting him with a smile.

"Ladies, welcome back to Kusadasi. Did you sleep well?"

Murmurs of assent floated out of the MAMs' throats. "Very com-fortable on the boat. And we like your town!" Molly told him.

"We aim to please," Balaban responded. "Tourism is our Number Two industry here."

"And what is Number One?" Jane asked.

"Agriculture, of course," Balaban explained. "Now, I want to go over our schedule for the day. This morning – the field headquarters. I will help you get along with Turkish crew." Balaban smiled, "We've heard about American women." Balaban raised his eyebrows. "Yes, we've heard all about you." He laughed.

"Don't believe a thing you've heard," Molly said. "Besides, we're not your average American women."

"You can say that again!" Sallie laughed.

"We're not your average American women!" Molly repeated.

"Don't take me literally!" Sallie bugged her eyes at Molly and con-tinued, "Seriously, what have they told you about us?"

"Let's see," Balaban said. "Beautiful, very friendly. Very, very friendly." Balaban looked at Molly with warm eyes. "Like to shop."

"What do they really tell you?" Sallie wanted to know.

Balaban shook his head. "No more on that right now."

"We're going to meet Halim Mohammed this morning?" Ursula asked. She needed to discuss the dig plans with the head Turkish archaeologist. Although her plans had been approved by Sophie Si-mons, the head Austrian archaeologist for the Grotto of St. Paul, she wanted to connect with Halim, too. The Turkish archaeologists were working for Sophie, who supervised from Vienna most of the year. Ursula had been surprised to learn that the main crew at the cave had been female. An exciting discovery she had yet to share with the MAMs. Unfortunately, none of the Austrian women could come. They would be working with Turkish men for this dig.

"Halim? Who is Halim?" Balaban questioned Ursula. "Should I know him?"

"He's the archaeologist from the University of Istanbul. He's in charge. He will meet us at the field office in Ephesus." Ursula wor-ried that communication had broken down. "We can't do anything without his approval."

Balaban winked at Priscilla, who was sitting quietly in the front row of the van. When he winked, she elbowed Molly sitting beside her and put her hand over her mouth.

"Halim Mohammed," Ursula stated. "You don't know him? We have to see him today. Can you call the University?"

Balaban smiled. "You're in good hands. What do you need this Halim for? Balaban is the best. No competition today."

"But he's the archaeologist," Ursula insisted. She got her papers from her briefcase and handed them to Balaban.

"Hey, I'm driving here. No reading. Just like they told me – those American women, demanding, strong, impossible!" Balaban laughed. "Calm down, ma'am. I'll take care of you."

The van rounded a corner and the MAMs realized they were once again at the Ephesus site. Balaban parked the van in front of a small building and turned off the engine. "We have arrived. The field office for Ephesus. Please enter at the side door. They are expecting us."

***

Halim Mohammed sat in the conference room, looking through the remote control cameras that usually kept him abreast of the current work on site. Now he started to chuckle as the MAMs emerged from the van. He summoned his assistants to watch along. Muttering a few choice words in his Turkish dialect, he switched to English in preparation for the orientation to come. "Here comes our crew. American women. Old American women. What are those red hats? What word is that?"

"M... A... M... MAM?" Karim, the youngest assistant read out loud.

"Look at that big one. Does she think she can fit into the cave?" Abdul laughed.

"They aren't all old! Look at the one in the pink hat. She's mine. Hands off." Akber, the senior member of the student archaeological team claimed his territory. "American women are beautiful."

"E.M.I.L.Y." Karim read the name on the pink hat.

"Which one is your assistant, boss?" Abdul asked Halim.

"I bet the one with the pencil behind her ear," Karim announced. "Looks like an American archaeologist. They all dress the same."

"Look at the one with the camera. As dark as us!" Abdul told the group.

"M.O.L.L.Y." Karim read. "Look more words on the back of the hats."

"Archaeological Expedition in Search of Thecla," Halim reported. "That's name of grant that brought them here. Now be good, boys. We get big American bucks to host the ladies. Make them feel important. We, of course, do work, but pretend they help. Bring them in, Karim."

78

Balaban knocked on the field house door.

Molly snapped picture #20 since stepping off the van. Balaban had taken a group shot for her with the Ephesus amphitheater in the background. Then she had taken individual shots of each of the MAMs with a similar background. "When you're famous, these pictures will be hot items. I'll sell them for $500 apiece to Fox News. They'll be plastered all over the Internet."

"No, don't sell them to Fox, just CNN," Sallie complained.

"I can tell you right now no picture of me is going to be worth $500," Katharine laughed.

Karim opened the door, giving Balaban a hug and welcome. *"Selam! Kim ar insanlar?"*[x]

Balaban laughed and said, "The Amerikan *kadinlar. Dikkat! Insanlar seninki, halen."*[xi]

Then Balaban turned to Ursula, "Here is your man. May I introduce Ursula Goodtree to Halim Mohammed."

Ursula extended her hand and looked into the warm eyes of the lead archaeologist on the site.

"A pleasure to meet you, ma'am." Halim firmly shook her hand. "And this is your crew?"

Ursula laughed at the expression on his face. "An unlikely bunch, I know."

"Bunch?" Halim looked to Balaban for interpretation.

"Demet... grup, a group, right?" Balaban looked to Ursula for confirmation.

"Yes, an unlikely group. Let me introduce them. Professor Katharine Long. She will be our Internet researcher. Jane Masters, our strong woman, a spelunker and general contractor in the States."

"Spelunker?" Halim asked Balaban.

"Mağara kâşif," Balaban reported. *"İnşaatçı, patron."*[xii]

Halim raised his eyebrows at Jane and extended his hand. "Good, good. Very good."

"Emily Turner. She has worked on an American dig."

"Oh? Which one?" Halim spoke directly to Emily as he extended his hand to shake hers.

"Sun Watch, in Ohio. A Native American village. 1600s."

"Very good, very good." Halim answered.

Akber stepped up and offered his hand to Emily when Halim let go. "Akber, senior assistant. Pleased to meet you, ma'am."

His smile lit his face and his eyes probed Emily's when she smiled back and shyly said, *"Selam, Bayim."*[xiii]

"Do you speak Turkish?" Akber asked.

"Bir nebze,"[xiv] Emily held up her Turkish-English dictionary.

"I can teach more," Akber eagerly said.

"Not now," Halim gestured to Akber to be quiet and then looked at Ursula. "Go on, please."

"Priscilla Johnson, a secretary. She'll catalog everything in English if needed."

"Secretary?" Halim asked Balaban.

"*Sekreter*," Balaban explained.

"Yes, yes," Halim went on. "Very good, very good."

"Molly Grinlough, a writer and photographer. She will keep the daily log." Ursula countered.

"Oh, yes, yes." Halim answered. "Welcome, Molly."

"And this is Sallie Quisenberry. She will be our sifter." Ursula smiled. "We are quite a group."

"Very good, very good," Halim answered. "You are good leader. Already jobs assigned. Have seats, ladies. Please, sit down. Karim, get the ladies water, please."

"This morning, we will have an introduction to the site at Ephesus. We are very proud of our work here and happy you join us. First, a documentary by the BBC. Enjoy!"

Akber switched off the lights and directed the MAMs attention to a large screen at the back of the room. The documentary began with a description of the Roman Empire and then a map locating the various sites now open for tourists around the Mediterranean world.

For the first time, Priscilla could get the big picture of what was going on at the time of Jesus in terms of the Romans. Flashing in front of her eyes were frescoes and sculptures of the warriors, the gods and goddesses, and then the huge statue of Domitian towering above the harbor in Ephesus in an artist's rendering of the Roman city-state in the late first century. The narrator began a description of the importance of this port city in the Roman world, the temple worship of the goddess Artemis and briefly mentioned the sojourn of the Christian Saint Paul and the exile of John during the reign of Domitian.

"Domitian." Priscilla thought to herself. "That was the bad man who sent John away. The Romans were very powerful. Was a follower of Jesus going to fight them?"

The documentary continued with a tour of the site at Ephesus, alternating pictures of the rebuilt ruins and an artist's rendering of how the port might have looked in its time.

Molly focused on the armor and the pictures of the Roman army marching down the marble road toward the sea. Brilliant red capes, dazzling silver swords, and large decorated armor created a picture of power against the poor peasants depicted in torn cloth along the side of the roads. "We haven't changed very much as people in 2,000 years, have we?" She murmured out loud.

Then, taking comfort in Jesus' words and the fact that John was in exile because he resisted empire, she fingered her Martin Luther King, Jr. necklace she always kept close. She murmured the words she knew were inscribed there. "Have we not come to such an impasse in the modern world that we must love our enemies – or else? The chain reaction of evil – hate begetting hate, wars producing more wars – must be broken, or else we shall be plunged into the dark abyss of annihilation." It was a present she had given to herself when Mark completed basic training. She tuned out her own thoughts and focused back on the film that was beginning to chronicle the history of archaeological work at the site.

Ursula had viewed the film before. So now, she reviewed her dig plan and mentally rehearsed the questions she had for Halim. But glancing up at the screen, a view of the Roman bath dislodged a memory of Joe from their visit 25 years earlier. Oh, Joe. Her heart warmed. She could see him now, standing at the site, laughing and pulling her into the bath in jest. She smiled and wondered when she could get to the computer to send him an update on the dig.

Emily meticulously recorded notes on the history of the dig.

Sallie's eyelids closed into sleep. She leaned over, bumping into Emily, knocking her pen onto the floor. Emily started to laugh. Akber caught her eye and grinned.

Sallie jerked back, awake again and asked, "Could I have some coffee?"

"No problem, ma'am," Karim jumped up and returned in a minute with a small cup of very dark, concentrated liquid.

"You know Turkish coffee?" he asked.

"A first time for everything. Will it keep me awake?" She replied.

"You may never sleep again. Turkish coffee, the best." Balaban said.

"Strong, very strong." Karim added.

The movie concluded with a summary of the Roman Empire, the progress on the Ephesus site and the plans for the future.

"Thank you very much for coming. The Turkish government – very interested in working with archaeologists from around the world for digging our antiquities." Halim told them at the end of the film. "I know you want to get busy. I have few words of instruction. We run tight ship, you call it?"

An hour later, all the MAMs – except for Ursula – were fighting sleep. She ordered another round of Turkish coffee for the group, but Halim declined, saying it was heating up and the caffeine would make them hotter on the site. Instead, he offered Turkish pastries and water, and then gave each of the MAMs a box lunch to eat on the ride to the site as he concluded, "OK, ladies. Orientation finished. Now, you become archaeologists. We go to the site to begin."

12. Thecla Faces Fire

September 5, 48 A.D.

"Sir, please, I beg of you, take these earrings and let me enter your prison. I must visit your prisoner." Thecla took the gold earrings from her ears and handed them to the man keeping watch over the jail. Inside, she encountered another man guarding the cells. She offered her looking glass to him, "May I visit the man Paul?"

The jailer looked out to the turnkey who shrugged and held up the earrings she'd given him. He took the offering and led her back to Paul.

Through the night, she sat at Paul's feet listening and learning about Jesus of Nazareth, and his loving God, the maker of heaven and earth. She marveled that he would continue to preach, even when they threatened him with death. "And are you not afraid? They could kill you for preaching! Have you no fear?"

The small man smiled. "God has brought me safely this far. There is no fear in love, Thecla. Perfect love casts out fear. For me, to die is gain. If I die, I go to be with God. What can man do to me? Greater faith have no man, than that he lay down his life for his friend. Jesus died, yet he lives. I have no fear, no."

Thecla saw the candlelight reflecting and dancing in his eyes. Overcome with great joy and love for this man Paul, she bent down and kissed his chains, then his feet, and fell asleep there, beside him on the cold floor.

***

In the morning, Thecla was missed. Her family and Thamyris searched every street to find her, and then the porter told them that she had gone to the prison to seek out Paul. So they went to the prison and found her and went to tell the governor.

The governor ordered both she and Paul to be brought before his judgment seat. Thecla went with great joy. But the mob cried out after Paul, "He's a magician. Let him die!"

Yet the governor listened to Paul's preaching on Christ with a smile on his face. Then he asked Thecla, "Why do you not, according to the law of the Iconians, marry Thamyris?"

She stood still, with her eyes fixed upon Paul and did not answer.

Her mother cried out saying, "Let the unjust creature be burnt; let her be burnt in the midst of the theater, for refusing Thamyris, that all women may learn from her to avoid such practices."

So the governor ordered Paul to be whipped out of the city, and Thecla to be burnt. Thecla watched while they brought wood and straw to burn her, remembering the words of Paul. And then in the distance she saw an angel whom she knew to be Jesus, in the likeness of Paul and knew he had come to her in her crisis. When she looked at him closely, he ascended up to heaven. She knew it was a message not to fear because she would follow soon.

They stripped her naked and she cowered to cover herself. The governor cried to see such beauty, but he did not stop the mob. She signed herself with the cross when they lit the straw and tied her down to burn.

But suddenly the heavens opened out, pouring down rain and hail that extinguished the fire. And then the earth rumbled and huge cracks appeared in the ground, swallowing many of the people cheering for her death.

In the bedlam that followed, Thecla ran away, reclaiming her clothes. Because she could not go home, she ran to look for Paul, whom she found praying and fasting for her in a cave saying: "O Holy Father, O Lord Jesus Christ, grant that the fire may not touch Thecla; but be her helper, for she is thy servant."

Thecla cried out: "O sovereign Lord, Creator of heaven and earth, the Father of thy beloved and holy Son, I praise thee that thou hast preserved me from the fire, to see Paul again."

13. The Dig Begins

September 15, 2006

The group filed out of the little building and straggled toward the van. Ursula checked her clipboard as they piled in. Halim directed her to sit with him in the front row. Balaban shifted into reverse and backed out, jerking the van and Ursula's clipboard dropped onto the floor.

"Just making you laugh." He winked at her.

"Now, who will be digging with Jane and Emily?" Ursula turned to Halim.

"Abdul and Akber." Halim replied.

"And that leaves Karim to sift with Sallie?" Ursula responded.

"Yes, he's good boy. He does good job." Halim explained.

"The cave wall? Who does the cave wall?" Ursula asked.

"Akber. That's the most delicate. Emily works with him. OK?" Halim raised his eyebrows for Ursula's assent.

"Yes, then Jane and Abdul will work on the area outside the cave. Did you bring the maps?"

Halim looked across to Balaban. "Serious American woman! Keep you busy, eh?"

Balaban muttered something in Turkish that Ursula couldn't understand and then concluded with a laugh, "Brilliant, beautiful American woman. Your wife knows she's here?"

"My wife no talk about my dig. She just wants me in Istanbul... yesterday."

Halim pulled the maps out of his bag. "The wall work will begin here, a small alcove on the right, just inside the cave entrance. Most of the walls – already excavated. We can't touch frescoes uncovered by the Austrians. If we are lucky, we find more."

Ursula listened without comment. But her thoughts focused on her dream, an enlargement of the cave, a passageway that would lead to a new chamber. Without an opening, it was unlikely the dig would last more than few days.

Halim summoned Akber and Emily up to the seat behind him to talk about the wall excavation. Akber displayed a picture of the layer of fresco, photos from the Austrians' work. He knew the technique well. "You chip carefully, looking for variety. We will remove four inches, you go more slowly. We look for openings. At the side of the cave, a cave-in could cover other parts of cave. Cave of St. Paul – very small. Most caves much bigger. We wonder why – long time. Understand?"

"How do I know if I'm ruining a fresco?" Emily fast-forwarded into her worries.

"I'll show you. I have experience. I won't let you make mistake." Akber tapped Emily's shoulder, with a nod of comfort. "We don't expect more fresco. The wall – very different in the side alcove."

"OK you two, back to your seats. Jane, Abdul! We talk to you now."

In the back, Akber continued explaining the technique to Emily, who became more and more excited as the van neared the site.

Up in the front, Jane asked Halim, "So, boss, what's our job?"

"You dig outside the cave. You will see stone walls. We believe there were houses on the hillside. You look for trash pits, houses, storage areas, artifacts. First, we go down six inches – first week. Maybe six more next week. Traditional archaeological technique. Start with shovel and mattock, remove dirt and dump into buckets for sifting. Trowel the surface. Look for markings to dig further. That ground – packed very solid. You strong?" Halim looked at Jane.

Jane laughed and cocked her arm muscle. "I press 200. Don't worry."

"Press 200?" Halim didn't understand.

Jane flexed her arm again, imitating the Rosie the Riveter poster she kept in her workout room at home. She laughed and bent down in her seat, to pick up an imaginary barbell. Grunting, she lifted it high above her head.

"Ah... female strongman!" Abdul guessed.

"No... strong woman!" Jane replied.

"Watch out!" Balaban laughed. "You be in big trouble soon. American women, strong, brilliant, don't like putdowns!"

Jane laughed again and shrugged her shoulders. "I'm strong." She reached her hand out to Halim, and they each sensed the other's strength when their hands met. "I'll look forward to helping you, sir." Showing respect she had always found was a sure path to good working relationships.

The van lurched to a stop in front of the main gate.

"Checkpoint?" Jane asked.

"No, don't worry."

A group of four soldiers with machine guns approached the van, and Ursula flinched.

Balaban opened the van door and greeted the men in Turkish. Shaking their hands, he welcomed them into the bus and then explained, "Ladies, your protection has arrived!"

Emily nervously eyed the uniformed men who walked down the aisle, taking the open seats among them. Akber noticed her fear.

"Don't worry," he explained. "Grave robbers, big problem in Turkey. We expect no problems, but take no chances. Keep dig peaceful, no problems. Government pays for artifacts now, so people are out looking. They make sure we are the only diggers today. They are rural police, *Gendarme* – soldiers who patrol countryside."

"Gen-dar-may," Molly sounded it out. "The military?"

"Yes, mandatory service in Turkey for young men. They serve the country. Remember, Iraq is our Eastern border."

Molly exchanged a look with Ursula. Neither of them were pleased.

Sallie changed the subject. "We're starting at the bottom this time. It's all uphill from here."

You can say that again," Balaban laughed.

"It's all uphill from here." Sallie's belly laugh punctuated her repetition.

"Don't take him literally," Jane scolded.

Undaunted, Sallie continued. "Most visitors get dropped off at the top, so they can walk down."

"You're a good student," Jane said. "But notice, we're not walking?"

The van slowed, waiting for crowds of tourists to clear. Every 20 feet, a crowd gathered around a guide, conducting a mini-lecture.

The marble road, although smooth, seemed rather bumpy because the blocks had settled again into the earth after being leveled by site restorers. Marble pillars and statues lined the wide road. The amphitheater towered to the left of the van. Turning, the van neared the two-story library facade.

"Are you allowed to drive in here?" Sallie asked.

Balaban laughed. "Only very important people. The MAMs are VIPs, no?"

Ursula explained, "We have to get our equipment close to the dig."

The van pulled to the right, and they could see the protective roof of the terrace houses rising in waves to the top of those ancient condos that the MAMs had visited only a few days earlier. On the edge of the terrace house enclosure, concrete steps led from the lower Ephesus site all the way up to the top of the houses.

Sallie looked up and gulped. "We're going up there? Emily, you told me we were driving up."

Emily sheepishly shrugged. "I guess I was wrong."

Sallie peered out the van window, looking up BûlBûl Dag. Scrubby trees covered the mountain side. No, not a mountain, a hill, Emily had said. For a moment, the scenery felt like southern Ohio, yet she knew she traveled today on the other side of the world, Turkey. She pinched her own hand to make sure she hadn't landed in a dream, then chuckled at herself. The coffee had turned on a light inside her body, and she felt like turning somersaults, realizing she was about to become an archaeologist, in search of Thecla. Smiling inside, she looked forward to the climb.

Halim gestured to Balaban, and the van screeched to a halt. Akber and Abdul jumped out and went to lift the large wooden box carrying the tools. Karim and Halim carried the rest of the supplies.

"Ladies, take your lunches. Jane, can you carry the water jug?" Halim asked.

"No problem, boss." Jane saluted.

The MAMs tumbled out of the van, chattering with excitement. Molly led the motley crew after the men. She turned to announce, "The Archaeological Expedition in Search of Thecla has officially begun! Ladies, start your engines!"

Two of the soldiers stayed at the van, and the other two joined the group heading toward the cave.

Ursula and Katharine walked arm in arm toward the steps. "Can you believe we are actually here?" Ursula asked Katharine. "Did you have any idea when you sent me that email that we would end up on BûlBûl Dag actually looking for Thecla?"

"No, really, I thought it was a joke. But sometimes, menopause makes me a little crazy! You know, I've been thinking about Thecla's story. The historians place her in Seleucia, over in Eastern Turkey. But if she traveled with Paul, he spent a long time in Ephesus. It's certainly possible she spent time here with him. If she lived her life out in a cave, it could have been this cave, don't you think? The frescoes seem to suggest that they were both here. You know, I'm not ruling out the possibility that this expedition will surprise us all." Katharine spoke optimistically and Ursula clapped.

Perhaps a small concession for an academically conservative religion professor, but Ursula knew that statement erupted from a hope that was building inside them all. This little moment in time created an opening for Ursula that she firmly believed could lead the whole expedition into an incredible adventure.

The motley crew began to climb up the concrete steps toward BûlBûl Dag and the Grotto of St. Paul. None of them knew exactly how far they would have to go. Sallie and Molly started panting after the first 20 steps and stopped to catch their breath, while Jane and Emily sprinted by, with the men. Katharine and Ursula continued steadily, but not as quickly.

"We've only just begun..." Molly sang out.

"Oh, you're bringing the Carpenters back? Didn't Karen have a problem with anorexia? I wish I were a little thinner at the moment, but not enough to give up my life for it!" Sallie took a few deep breaths. "The journey of a thousand miles begins with a single step. Onward and upward!"

She began to climb again, and Molly followed behind. The distance grew between them and the rest of the crew. Ahead, they could see the team spilling out onto the hillside at the top of the steps.

"Is the dig up there where that shed is?" Sallie asked Molly.

"I certainly hope so!"

Molly and Sallie doggedly continued up the steps.

"You can do it, Sallie. We didn't come all this way to give up now." Molly patted Sallie's shoulder.

"A good thing I started swimming again this summer! Don't make me laugh."

Molly smiled, conserving her breath without a response. Placing one foot in front of another, she continued to climb.

Sweat gathered beneath their T-shirts. Sallie slipped out of her hoodie and tied it around her waist. Molly mopped her brow. A good 30 steps still separated them from the rest of the crew, taking a break near the shed.

Molly pulled out her camera and turned around, snapping a quick picture. Ephesus spanned the flat plain below. She paused to take it all in, then turned and climbed more quickly. Reaching the top before Sallie, she snapped several more pictures, before walking over to join the rest of the group.

Sallie slowly, but resolutely, climbed onward telling herself she could do it, remembering climbing Colorado mountains many years before. She pulled a water bottle out of her backpack and took a few swigs, then finished the last 10 steps with a surge of energy.

Again, she pulled out her water bottle. "Are we there yet?" She panted out her question and continued to breath heavily.

Halim smiled and pointed up. "We still have long way to go."

Sallie gasped. "Can I make it?"

Ursula stepped in to respond. "You can do it Sallie. You don't have to run to the top. Take your time. We'll go slowly together."

"Could you drive us up?" Sallie asked Halim. "This looks like a road."

"The path narrows. We only drive with very heavy equipment, everyone else walks. If you prefer, you can work in the field office."

Sallie shook her head. "Let's go. I can do this."

So the group began the hike leading up BûlBûl Dag. A small road led up the hillside. Switchbacks eased the climb. Plastic bottles and pieces of plastic hung in the trees, marking the trail. Silence carried the group onward. The MAMs didn't know how far they would be walking, and the climb continued to steepen. Abdul stopped and pulled a small green fruit out of the tree, took a pocket knife out of his pocket, and cut it open handing a piece to Emily.

Emily put it to her mouth, "Mmmm... What is this?"

"Figs," Jane responded.

"That's good! I've never had one fresh before. A great taste.."

Trees punctuated the scrubby scenery, providing some shade. Molly continued to stop to snap pictures of the incredible view of the Ephesus site. The trail took them further west, yet she could see the huge amphitheater below. Sallie and Molly continued to bring up the rear. Molly began to sing, "Climb Every Mountain"[xv] from the *Sound of Music.*

Sallie stopped to pant and then yelled up at Molly who continued resolutely climbing upward. "Julie Andrews! What are you doing here? And how in the heck can you sing and climb at the same time?"

Molly stopped singing. She caught her breath and snapped a few more pictures.

"You better save your energy, Julie Andrews." Sallie told her. "We don't know how far we have to go."

The rest of the group had eased out of sight.

"What if we get lost?" Sallie asked.

"Where else would we go but up?" Molly asked, stopping again to take some pictures of the valley below.

Sallie wiped the sweat off her face and fanned herself with a handkerchief she pulled out of her pocket to pat herself dry. "Never give up. Never give up. Never give up."

"Who are you trying to convince?

"Myself, who did you think!"

Molly put her arm around Sallie and together they continued to climb. Small bushes lined the dusty path. A few trees obscured the view up the hill. It felt like they were walking through a sparse woods.

"Paul and Thecla must have been in better shape than us!"

"That wouldn't take much." Molly patted her belly. "Maybe we'll be in better shape after a few days of this, too! You can do it. Come on, Sallie. I know you can do it."

"We're here!" Sallie yelled out when she and Molly finally arrived at the cave, a half hour later. "Did you think we wouldn't make it?"

"I had my doubts," Katharine replied.

"Don't get too close. Or do you want to smell my sweat?" Sallie held up her arm, showing the wet stain, sniffing it herself.

Molly started right in snapping pictures of the outside view of the cave. She backed up to take in a full view of the front of the cave. An arch of stones covered a brick facade built into the hillside framing the rectangular portal to the cave. Next to the cave, a makeshift canvas roof attached to poles provided shelter for a small table. Although the cave seemed to be carved into the side of the hill, there

89

were some flat areas in front of the cave. She captured the hillside and the spectacular view of the Ephesus site below.

The crew jumped into action, setting up the site. For Sallie and Karim, they erected a little canopy and folding chairs, with a table and two square sifting screens. For Priscilla and Molly, they unfolded two small desks for writing. They unloaded an array of boxes and bags by the sifting table. "For artifacts," Karim explained to Sallie.

Halim gestured toward the cave. "We begin with a cave tour. This way, ladies. See – arched corridor, carved out of hill centuries ago. Now covered with frescoes. The Austrian dig team took many, many pictures. Someday, they publish book."

The MAMs crowded into the small cave, looking at fragments of pictures on the cave walls. Halim offered an explanation. "You see the pictures from many Bible scenes here." He pointed out white etchings in Greek. "These inscriptions are prayers to Paul and Christ. Three hundred of them. Graffiti, you call it. Because they pray to Paul, named the Grotto of St. Paul. Here is the man himself."

"This grotto was rediscovered in 1998. The Austrians took white-wash off these pictures. This depicts the story from the *Acts of Paul and Thecla*. The only ancient picture of Paul at Ephesus, and so well preserved.

"St. Paul!" Jane exclaimed. Plastered on the wall stood a bearded man in a blue robe, holding his right hand up, with two fingers displayed. Two women flanked him, one behind a window inside a house. The other had been defaced with her eyes gouged out and her fingers destroyed.

"There she is! There she is!" Jane stopped, put her hands on her hips and curtsied.

The MAMs gathered around an ancient cave artist's rendering of the woman who had called them halfway around the world.

"We found her, MAMs! We found her!" Jane announced.

"She's already found," Sallie laughed. "Next you're going to tell me Christopher Columbus discovered America!"

"Yes! First Christopher Columbus, now the MAMs. Great explorers of the world. We're going down in the history books, ladies."

The other MAMs smiled at Jane's declaration, looking quietly at the fading colored markings depicting Thecla.

"Hey, are you sure this is right?" Sallie asked. "This isn't the picture in Crossan's book."

"No," Halim explained. "Crossan stretched truth. You see here the picture is not of Paul and Thecla side by side. The picture depicts Thecla's mother refusing to let her go with Paul. Thecla's back there, behind the window."

"And then they tried to burn her at the stake?" Sallie responded.

"Yes, that's the story, " Katharine smiled. "Then Thecla followed Paul, became a disciple. That's why her picture is in his cave."

"Crossan's book identifies the defaced one as Thecla, but that's actually her mother?" Sally asked.

"That's right."

"How can that be? How could he publish that?" Sallie continued to question Halim.

Katharine laughed. "It happens all the time. You can't believe everything you read in books."

"But why would he do that? How could he make such a mistake?" Sallie couldn't let it go.

"Perhaps he came with a guide who didn't explain it well. If you don't read Greek, you might mistake this for Thecla." Ursula pointed to the words clearly identifying Thecla's mother. "But I agree it doesn't make sense. Crossan's a Biblical scholar. He should know Greek. It's very clear here." Ursula stopped to read the Greek letters out loud. "Theta, Epsilon, Omega, Kappa, Lambda, Alpha, Iota. TH-E-O-K-L-I -A. You see, there are extra letters here. Thekla would just be TH-E-K-L-A."

"A very interesting fresco, not a Bible story, but from the apocryphal writings. Thecla's mother is not mentioned elsewhere. We date this fresco to the late fifth century."

The MAMs continued to stare at the cave wall. Jane saluted Thecla's head. Most of her body had disappeared over time, along with most of Paul's lower body and Thecla's mother below her shoulder's.

"We'll find it, Thecla. We'll find it." Jane smiled at the picture. "We'll tell your story."

Sallie shook her head in embarrassment. "Jane, please."

Ursula beamed with joy. "Yes, Thecla. This one is for you."

Halim called the women's attention back to a small room near the entrance. 'This is where you'll dig," he told Emily and Akber. "You handle small, dark places?"

"No problem," Akber replied.

"I'm excited!" Emily announced.

"Look at the small red flowers here." Halim pointed to faded flowers painted on to the archway entrance to the small alcove where they would soon be digging. "Now these flowers match flowers in the terrace houses. May go back to first century, early second century. These flowers are the oldest fresco in the cave."

Ursula smiled. She knew it could happen. They could find something big here.

Halim led the women through the long corridor of the cave. On both sides frescoes told stories that he explained. "Many layers, here. We can't take off a layer without destroying what is on top." At the back of the cave, the corridor opened into a rectangular room. "See the pictures here, layers. On the left, four women. Probably important women in the community, saints perhaps. See the nimbus around the head?"

Halim's finger traced the halo-like ridge covering the heads of the women.

"A cave for women!" Molly said.

Ursula put her arm around Katharine and squeezed. "Wow!"

Katharine laughed. "Women were more prominent in the early Christian community, you know."

Halim continued, "Here you see the Christ, with a large, golden cross nimbus, sitting on a rainbow, flanked by two men in white and blue mantles; suggesting they are prophets, apostles or saints. The other men probably, like the women, are important people – bishops, or local saints.

"Any questions, ladies?" Halim concluded his tour of the cave and led the women back outside. Hearing none, Halim announced, "Well, then, let the dig begin!" Halim said. "Ladies, take your posts."

So Sallie, Priscilla, Katharine and Karim took up their positions on the side of the hill. Katharine opened the laptop and began to read articles about similar digs with cave passageways, cave paintings and excavation techniques. Halim probably knew most of the information, she imagined, but yet he asked for a summary and verbal report back in the field house at the end of the day. She felt like a graduate research assistant once again, helping a major professor with his work.

Inside the dark cave, Ursula inhaled the smell of musky earth. She joined Halim to survey the back wall of the side alcove. They brought Emily and Akber two pails, a large jug of water, and another empty bucket. Halim told them, "No frescoes here, but be careful. Wash the wall See if any cracks off. Have Molly take pictures before you remove more."

Outside, he told Jane and Abdul, "Start here, to the left of the cave entrance. Tomorrow you can do the other side. Remember, six inches and take all dirt over to be sifted. Ursula, you're in charge here, yes? I will help at the wall."

Halim gestured to the crew. "Let's begin!"

"What about tree roots?" Jane asked.

"Work around them," Halim ordered.

Molly began photographing the cave while the others quietly began their work. She focused on the original surfaces and the frescoes, bumping into Ursula in the passage way.

"Have you ever read any Joyce Rupp books, Ursula?" Molly inquired, snapping a picture of Mary, the holy Mother.

"No, I don't believe so. What does she write about?" Ursula asked.

"Well, she's a Catholic nun who writes books on spirituality. Our book club read one a few years ago, *Dear Heart, Come Home.*[xvi] I had forgotten about it, but walking into this dark cave brought it all back. In her work, the cave becomes a metaphor for going deeper into ourselves, for the darkness of life's journey, a discovery process. I wish I had brought that along," Molly said. "Katharine didn't like that book. Navel gazing, she thought."

"Did I hear my name?" Katharine asked, laughing while ducking through the arched entrance to the cave. "Could you come out a minute, Ursula, I want to show you my summary of the articles so far. What was Molly talking about?"

Molly and Ursula followed Katharine out onto the hillside. "*Dear Heart, Come Home;* remember that book you didn't like at all?" Molly asked.

"Actually I brought it with me. I've been rereading it on our trip. I thought I might be able to get into the cave thing now!" Katharine explained.

"That's good. Getting into the cave thing! Me, too." Sallie laughed

Katharine reached into her bag. "Listen, these words are about journey. I wrote them down in my journal this morning. It's from the preface: 'the persistent voice of midlife wooed and wailed, wept and whined, nagged like an endless toothache, seduced like an insistent lover, promised a guide to protect me as I turned intently toward my soul. As I stood at the door of Go Deeper, I heard the ego's howl of resistance, felt the shivers of my false security, but knew there could be no other way. Inward I traveled, down, down, drawn further into the truth than I ever intended to go.'"[xvii] Katharine stopped reading. "This takes on a whole new significance, doesn't it?"

Ursula looked at Katharine and then felt another surge deep within. "Do you feel it, Kath? I think you're beginning to feel it, too?" The afternoon sun cast rays through the trees, and Ursula couldn't help but think that somehow, that light would eventually find them all.

"I finally understand Joyce Rupp and the cave stuff, but do I feel what?"

Ursula shook her head, "I guess I'm projecting my feelings onto you. OK. What did you want to show me?" Katharine opened her file and began to read about passageways in caves.

Sallie and Karim began sifting through dirt in the first bucket carried out by Halim and Ursula. They were on their second bucket when Sallie felt a small shape within her dirt. She picked it up and held it up to Karim and asked, "What is this?"

Karim reached over and took it out of Sallie's fingers. "Pottery, I think. Let's show Halim. Halim!" Karim called, and then stood up and walked over to the cave and walked in and called again, "Halim!"

Halim came out and took the piece from Karim, "Clay pot. Very common on this site. The lab will date it. Where did this come from?"

Sallie answered, "I'm sifting Jane's bucket."

"Good, good," he answered. "Priscilla, your job begins now." Halim instructed Priscilla how to label and package. "Mark the location of each object on this map of the site."

A few minutes later, Sallie felt another small shape in the dirt. "Another find! This is my lucky day!" she told Karim.

"Lucky?" Karim asked.

"Good fortune. Happy. I found something!" She held it up for Karim to see, a small thin object, a little bigger than a toothpick, with a hole in the end.

"What is it?" Sallie asked.

"A bone needle, I think," Karim answered. "Very unusual."

"Priscilla, another find!" Sallie called, getting into the swing of things.

Jane and Abdul made quick work of the first six inches of earth. "A few more shovels and we can start scraping," he told Jane.

Jane took a drink of water from her flask. "Usually I have something stronger in here," she told Abdul.

"Tomorrow, then?" he asked with a smile in his eyes.

"No, I'm going to be good," she said. "For Thecla, only water!" Jane took another sip. "Would you like some?"

"No, no. No thank you," Abdul politely refused. For Thecla, only water? What did she mean, he wondered while he stuck his shovel into the floor of the cave and filled his bucket. He carried it over to Sallie, who was busy admiring her bone needle.

"Look," she said. "Look what I found!"

Abdul took the needle from her hand, "Very nice. Very nice." He wiped the sweat off his brow and returned to the cave. "Now you can sew me a new shirt."

Sallie laughed. "A woman's place is in the house ... and in the Senate!"

"Senate?" Abdul asked. American women... very strange, he thought. He left Sallie and returned to scraping the cave floor. He found Jane talking to herself.

"Thecla, baby, we're here. We've come to find you. We're going to dig you up. You've waited 2,000 years, a few more days and we'll get you out of here." Jane knelt on rough ground, scraping and smoothing the surface with her trowel.

"Who are you talking to?" Abdul asked.

Jane smiled. "Wouldn't you like to know!" She began whistling "She'll be Coming Around the Mountain When She Comes." She pushed the shovel into the hard soil and heaved another load of dirt .

Abdul shook his head again and picked up his trowel.

Meanwhile, Emily and Akber had determined there were no frescoes on the back wall and were beginning to remove the first layer.

"This is like digging rock!" Emily said. "Can we really get anything off?" Although the arched opening to the side alcove seemed to indicate a room, the small space ended in hard rock. "Maybe this was just a closet." Emily chipped at the rock.

Akber asked for a heavy pick and pounded on it with a rock, knocking stone off the wall. In between his pounding, he bumped into Emily, teasing her slow progress. She laughed, enjoying the dig. They had only filled one bucket between them, when Emily found a pocket of sand in the wall where she was carefully removing a two-inch layer.

"Look at this!" she said to Akber, who poked his finger in the hole and gently coaxed the sand out into the bucket. Akber then used the tool to enlarge the opening. Sand began streaming out of the hole. Emily held the empty bucket up to the hole to catch the sand.

"Ursula!" Emily called out. Ursula didn't answer.

"Here, hold the bucket. I'll go get Ursula and Halim," Emily handed the bucket to Akber.

"Wait a minute," Akber said. "Maybe just sand."

But the sand kept coming. Akber handed the second bucket to Emily and grabbed the other bucket from the cave floor. "Take this out. Tell Halim and Ursula to come."

Emily carried the bucket outside and motioned to Halim and Ursula.

"We need you! Come see!" Emily disappeared back into the cave with an empty bucket.

"I think we found something." Akber said.

"Is the sand unusual?" Emily asked.

"I don't know. We ask Halim." Akber answered.

"Ask me what?" Halim stuck his head into the cave.

Akber explained, "Emily found a small opening in the wall under the crust. The sand started flowing. We enlarged the opening, and it continues to stream out. I need more buckets."

"Go get buckets, Emily." Halim instructed.

Then he turned to Ursula, "A sand chamber? In the article, remember? Could be another room. We must have sand tested."

"Would there normally be sand in the cave?" Ursula asked.

"Hard to tell. Yes and no," Halim responded. "Sometimes earthquakes cause shifts that release pockets of sand. But here, maybe carried in -- to fill this hole."

Emily picked up the extra buckets and motioned to Molly to come. Walking back into the cave she explained. "Photo op. I think we've found something! The sand is pouring out of a hole in the back of the cave."

Jane and Abdul continued to work outside, watching the buckets come out.

Hiram motioned to them. "Come help."

"Let's do a bucket brigade," Jane suggested.

"Bucket brigade?" Abdul asked.

"We make a line and pass the buckets. An old-fashioned way to put out fire," Jane explained.

"Itfaiyeci."[xviii] Hiram said. "Good idea."

So Hiram, Ursula, Abdul, Jane, and Emily created the formation and the buckets began flying back and forth through the cave. Molly snapped pictures. Outside, a mound of sand continued to grow next to Sallie's table. They emptied buckets to make room for more sand.

"Slow down!" Sallie told Emily when she dropped off the last bucket. "We can't sift this fast."

Inside, Hiram was trying to plug the hole to stop the flow.

"What does this mean?" Jane asked Ursula. "Was there a beach here?"

"We can't be sure. It will depend on how much sand we find. This is unusual, but Katharine and I were just discussing an article about a sand-filled cave area that turned out to be a storage chamber," Ursula explained.

Hiram successfully plugged the hole and looked at his watch. "We must stop today. Good job, crew! Tomorrow we start, eight hundred sharp."

Emily looked down at her wristwatch. "6 p.m.? Impossible!" She hadn't checked the time for the past four hours.

Akber joked, *"Tempus fugit*, Emily, with handsome man, no?"

Emily laughed. "How many languages do you speak? English, German, Turkish, Latin?"

Akber quipped back, "Only Americans learn one language. Here we learn two or three, scholars more. I learn five. Hiram, seven. Big head, boss man."

Katharine and Ursula chattered away about the sand chamber. "There could actually be something in there, right?" Katharine asked Ursula.

Ursula nodded her head in assent. "We are going to find something big. I can feel it in my bones."

"Right," Katharine said somewhat sarcastically. "I don't remember this mystical side of you, Urs. What's going on?"

"You're right, this isn't like me. But I feel something, I'm expecting something. I think I'm going to be right on this one."

Jane interrupted. "How 'bout we go down to those little restaurants near the port for dinner?"

The group walked out of the cave and Ursula told the others to start packing up.

"No, no." Hiram said. "We leave things here." Pointing to the guards he explained, "Round the clock protection for active digs. Need jobs for military men." He smiled and then instructed. "Only take the specimens and cover all the buckets. Tomorrow we bring more buckets, eh?"

14. A Turkish Dinner and Memories

September 15, 2006

And so the Archaeological Expedition in Search of Thecla had begun. The unlikely crew of American women had completed their inaugural day of digging and were ready for a shower and the luxuries of their hotel rooms down by the port of Kusadasi.

Balaban delivered them back to Hotel Atinc just 30 minutes later. The hotel created an unusual addition to the Kusadasi skyline. Triangular balconies extended from each room, giving a modern look to the 10-story building. To the delight of the women, each room provided a spectacular view of the waterfront. Although the rooms had no bathtubs, the MAMs were happy to have showers.

In the lobby, Jane invited them all to dinner and asked Balaban if he could return in an hour to take them to a good restaurant.

"Ladies, you have 60 minutes to primp up. Please return at 7:30 p.m. sharp!"

Sallie saluted, before grabbing Emily's arm, aiming to be the first on the elevator. The elevators could only hold five people at one time.

One hour later, the refreshed MAMs gathered in the lobby for a night out. Balaban pulled up with the van in front of the hotel. Soon he was driving the women into the heart of Kusadasi. The streets became narrower as they left the port area. Apartment buildings towered over small shops closing for the evening. He stopped at a small building with a bright red awning.

"You always find the best food at the small places," Sallie told the group.

"How do you know that?" Jane asked.

"I don't watch the Travel Channel for nothing!"

"Oh right, Ms. Couch Potato. I should have known."

Priscilla nodded in agreement. "But it is true. On those food shows, they always go to little restaurants, holes in the wall, and that is where they find the best food."

"Best tour guide in Kusadasi take his guests to best restaurants only. Ladies, your meal awaits." Balaban held the door for the seven women who entered the small room. Four small tables filled the front of the restaurant, stools lined a counter that separated the kitchen from the customers.

"*Oğul,*"[xix] a small man with a white apron and short grey hair called out. "*Yardim senin*[xx] Mama."

Jane looked at the MAMs. "Hmm... Now we know. All in the family, eh?"

A small woman waddled out from the kitchen. A scarf framed her wrinkled brown face, and her dark brown eyes twinkled. .

"Bala!" she called and Balaban dutifully leaped up and ran over to hug and kiss her. "Ladies, I present Mrs. Yaseem, and Mr. Yaseem. My Mama and Papa."

The MAMs ate their fill at Balaban's family restaurant that night. Laughing and carrying on, Balaban played interpreter for the group when Mr. and Mrs. Yaseem joined the group for dessert. They sampled the confections, while Balaban translated the ingredients. The MAMs laughed when he poked fun at his Mama's no-nonsense monologue on her baked items.

After dessert they brought out the Turkish liquor, reserved for special occasions, and all of the MAMs, except for Priscilla, started drinking. Mr. Yaseem told stories of Turkey from his younger days, and then Katharine remembered. "You need to tell Ursula how we made it from romance novels into theology!"

"Si, no comprendo." Ursula laughed. "Oops. Slipping into my mother tongue with the spirits."

"Spanish?" Mollie asked.

"Yes, I grew up in San Antonio. My parents were farm workers."

"San Antonio?" Emily broke in. "My parents met in San Antonio. Mennonite volunteers."

"Oh, we were good Catholics."

"Yes, most of the people in San Antonio are, except for the Midwest transplants."

"Small world," Ursula laughed. "I still try to get back home once or twice a year."

Meanwhile, the Turkish liquor made headways into the MAMs bloodstreams, and all but Priscilla relaxed and discovered the delicate feelings caused by the special drink. They laughed and cried. And Katharine asked again for the story.

"Our 10th anniversary! I treated the MAMs to a long weekend at Niagara Falls," Jane began.

"It must be nice to have this wealthy woman in your group. Jane, you are very generous." Ursula looked at Jane. "You really don't have to pay for my dinner tonight. Actually, I have funds in the grant for our evening meals."

Jane shrugged. "I enjoy taking along my friends on vacation. OK, ladies, let's get on with the story."

"In the Butterfly House on the Canadian side – transformative stuff," Molly continued.

Sallie picked up the storyline. "So we began to dwell on butterflies. Molly asked the question that became pivotal."

Molly chimed in. "Yes, my pivotal question. We were talking about the butterfly. Such an incredible, amazing creature. A worm morphing into a cocoon and then an exquisite flying creature. They got it goin' on. Mmm hmm. Butterflies doin' it. Change. So I asked, "If a butterfly can do all that, don't ya think we people can change, too?' "

Jane played narrator and nodded to Sallie. "Your experience, dear?"

"After being a kindergarten teacher for 25 years, I had the parents, and then their children. When those parents walked into my classroom, their personalities were remarkably the same as the five-year-old little whippersnappers I had known 20 years earlier." Sallie bugged her eyes out, pushed her glasses on her forehead and took a deep breath. "I think change is possible, but it doesn't happen very often." Sallie sat back in her chair, put her hands on her belly and laughed.

Jane winked at Ursula. "You can tell we've been through this discussion before! Now Katharine, Ms. Professor?"

"I think you're right," Katharine agreed. "As much as I'd like to think that college is a time for young people to come alive and develop themselves, I see a remarkable similarity between the students when I meet them in common courses their freshmen year and when I have them in the senior religion seminar."

"And now it's my turn." Jane pointed at herself and nodded to Ursula. "Here I go. That is hogwash. You need to read Zig Ziglar. People can change. Look at me. I pulled myself up by my own bootstraps and became a millionaire. That wasn't anything I learned at home. It certainly wasn't in my genes." Jane shook her head, took another drink of wine. "Maybe your problem is that you just haven't had enough Turkish liquor. Want more?" She held the bottle out, and Molly and Sallie offered their glasses for a refill. "Priscilla?"

Priscilla rolled her eyes. "You do not need any more liquor. Of course change is possible. When I accepted Jesus as my personal savior, I became a new person. You didn't know me then, but believe me I was a real party animal. Overnight, I became a disciple of Jesus. I have never been the same. And it's happened again and again. Look at Saul of Tarsus. He was blinded by the light and went from persecuting the Christians to becoming the best preacher Christians ever had."

Then Jane said, "I'll have to fill in for Abigail. 'You can't ignore the fact that people change, and we all have that ability to become better people. God gave us choice. We can choose life or death, good or evil. Every day we must choose. If we follow our inner light, we change into loving creatures.' "

"That's my Granny Abby for you. Doesn't she have a way with words?" Emily nodded her head in affirmation and gave a thumbs up for her absent grandmother.

Jane turned to Molly. "Molly?"

Leaning against the wall, Molly said, "I think you're all right. We can change, but change be hard. People go to counseling for years, no change. But then, you'll see some shift. An 'aha moment,' an 'alleluia, sista,' when all of a sudden the light floods in. Transformation just creeps up on you and turns on all the lights. They've studied that process, trying to figure out why some people change and others don't. Someone discovered it's a physical process, a shift. I went to a workshop once on 'Focusing,' a process to try to help make that shift happen. Change be real. I just wanted to bring this up because..."

Jane broke off Molly mid-sentence. "And it was about that time when thunder rolled in and shook the cabin breaking Molly's sentence in two. A flash of light and a loud crack pierced the night. Sallie yelled out that it was too close, and I still remember Molly screaming 'Oh my, God!' and pointing up to flames leaping on the cabin roof."

"A fire? The fire you started to tell me about on the plane, Kath?"

Katharine nodded in agreement. "Right."

"I had to order them all out of the cabin. They wanted to start packing, but I saved their hides by making them leave," Jane smugly explained to Ursula.

"And then it wasn't until we gathered again at Molly's the next month, that Molly got to finish her sentence." Jane nodded to Molly

Molly picked up her cue. "I think we should try some different genres this year. I think we need to change."

Jane's narrative continued. "Now, I'm an advocate for change, but I had to remind the MAMs that there was a lightning strike in the middle of that sentence. I wasn't so sure that was a message to proceed."

Molly looked at Ursula. "The lightning strike disrupted our weekend. Fortunately we had been able to grab our purses and even some belongings before making it out of the cabin into the night. The insurance covered our loss, refunded our money and they gave us a complimentary weekend in the future for a repeat appearance."

"In the end, we made out like bandits," Sallie explained.

"Granny Abby told us that the Quakers believe God speaks in a still, small voice. And that lightning was too damn loud." Jane slapped her knee laughing.

Sallie looked at Jane with a frown. "She did not say damn! And then I said... 'Thunder is thunder, lightning is lightning. If there was a thunder and lightning storm in the middle of your wedding, would you go through with it?' To which Jane replied..."

"I sure wish it would have burned the church down for mine, then I wouldn't have had to suffer for 10 years."

Ursula laughed, and the MAMs continued laughing with themselves.

"And then Priscilla asked us to take this seriously." Jane pointed to Priscilla.

"Let's hear Molly out. I agree it may be time for a change." Priscilla suggested.

"And Katharine?" Jane pointed to Kath.

"I hate to admit it, but I am ready for something new. I've been a closet romance reader for quite a few years, and I'm ready to shift now." Katharine agreed. "I'm ready for your idea, Molly."

"Praise God!" Ursula yelled.

"Cut her off!" Jane replied.

"She can't believe I'm into romance novels," Katharine explained.

"Just wait until she falls in love!" Jane continued. "After that, Molly explained her idea that in the coming year we would try two new genres, each for six months, so each MAM could pick a selection. After a short discussion, we all agreed to go for it and put the names of different genres into a hat to draw. Historical fiction and mystery books were the winners for the first year."

"At a return visit to Niagara Falls, we had decided to continue the change the following year and drew for a new genre."

"NONFICTION!" Sallie continued. "I drew the genre out of the hat and wanted to put it back in. I didn't believe we were really ready to read the real stuff."

"But," Jane continued, "there were no lightning strikes this time. In fact, there was complete silence. No one else suggested departing from the luck of the draw."

"Nonfiction," Katharine said. "My professional genre. I thought maybe I could get them to read one of the cutting-edge books in my field. To hear how people out of academia react to some of this theological stuff seemed like a good idea."

"I voted for Zig Ziglar!" Jane announced. "Possibility thinking. Today is the first day of the rest of your life, and you need to get on with it! And Priscilla over there asked for the Bible."

"And so it happened that the MAMs continued to venture outside the realm of romantic fiction. After one jaunt through the real stuff, we spent six months on Oprah's books, and then voted *The Secret Life of Bees*[xxi] our all-time favorite. We proceeded to *The New York Times* bestseller list, completing six months of bestseller nonfiction, and six months of bestseller fiction."

"To kick off our 14th year, we agreed that each of us could bring a book of her choice for the six-month cycle. And that was how it happened the MAMs found themselves one January evening, sitting around in Molly's living room, eating M&M's and discussing the theological treatise, *In Search of Paul*."xxii

"Great story!" Ursula patted Jane on her shoulder. "Thank you for sharing it."

Molly yawned. Balaban, who had been helping his parents clean up, reappeared from the kitchen. The MAMs' bellies were full, and they were ready to call it a night.

Balaban deposited them back at the hotel and the MAMs decided to turn in early to get a good night's sleep. They all wanted to be fresh in the morning to explore the sand chamber.

But Katharine took a few minutes to read before turning out the light. She opened Joyce Rupp's book once more and read over the preface. The words jumped out at her, and for the first time, she believed they were written directly to her.

> "*The persistent voice of midlife wooed and wailed, wept and whined, nagged like an endless toothache, seduced like an insistent lover, promised a guide to protect me as I turned intently toward my soul. As I stood at the door of Go Deeper I heard the ego's howl of resistance, felt the shivers of my false security but knew there could be no other way. Inward I traveled, down, down, drawn further into the truth than I ever intended to go. ...I entered the sacred inner room where everything sings of Mystery. No longer could I deny or resist the decay of clenching control and the silent gasps of surrender... Much that I thought to be "me" crept to the corners and died. In its place a Being named Peace slipped beside and softly spoke my name: "Welcome home, True Self, I've been waiting for you. Welcome home, True Self, I've been waiting for you."*xxiii

She focused on the idea of going deep, beyond her fears. She hadn't seen Moses Sun all day and for a few moments she relaxed and realized that perhaps Ursula was right. Something was going to happen. The expedition would uncover something important. Katharine felt excitement stirring and journaled her gratitude. *"Thank you, God, for this incredible trip. Thank you for a funny, engaging tour guide who took us to a good dinner. Thank you for my friend, Ursula, who brought us on this dig. Thank you for the possibility of change, even in old ladies like me. And thank you, dear God, for the possibility of a sand chamber."*

Ursula was sleeping soundly by the time Katherine crawled into bed and switched off the light.

15. Thecla Refuses Alexander

September 15, 48 A.D

So Thecla escaped execution and soon discovered Paul again, in a cave with the family of Onesiphorus. Late into the night, Paul preached and opened new understandings within her heart. She yearned even more to be a disciple and to follow the Way of Christ. Overtaken with the love of God, she told Paul, in the language of Ruth from the Hebrew scripture: "If you be pleased with me, I will follow you where ever you go."

But Paul said, "Ah Thecla, you are so beautiful, I must not marry, I have too much work to do. You will tempt me to give up my ministry."

Thecla replied, "Grant me only the seal of Christ, and no temptation shall affect me."

Paul answered, "Thecla, wait with patience, and you shall receive the gift of Christ."

"But I want to be your disciple, to learn of Jesus, to serve the Lord our God. Please don't make me go home. Now I have no home, my mother sent me to burn. I don't want to marry Thamyris. I want to follow you."

Paul did not agree to take her as his wife, but he sent Onesiphorus and his family home, and took Thecla along with him to Antioch. Now, the beautiful woman provided companionship, and he felt a new joy in his preaching. The lonely itinerant life gave way to a journey of companionship, with her sweetness and devoted ear.

He made sure that neither of them would be tempted beyond what they could resist. He arranged separate quarters for her, with a family whom he had baptized on a previous visit to the town. And he couldn't quite figure out why he became so upset when a man of importance in the town, the Syrian magistrate, Alexander, saw Thecla and fell in love with her, and began to play suitor by bringing expensive gifts to Paul.

Paul actually didn't quite believe his own words, when he told the man, "I don't know the woman of whom you speak, nor does she belong to me." Later he wondered, if he had spoken the truth in love, as he instructed others. True enough, she did not belong to him, and he had no right to give her to Alexander. He knew Thecla would be furious with him if he took a payment for her. Yet, he also knew the right

105

thing to do would be to arrange a suitable match for her, to protect both of them from temptation. Paul knew he was only a man, and it would only be a matter of time, if they traveled together. Yet he never expected the calamity that would greet Thecla because of his denial. When he learned of Thecla's fate, he felt like Peter must have felt when he denied company with the Lord.

Alexander, being a person of great power in Antioch, expected to get what he wanted. He grabbed Thecla in the street and kissed her.

Thecla looked frantically for Paul and yelled, "Don't try to force me to love you! You don't know me. I am a servant of God, one of the principal persons of Iconium. I left that city because I refused marriage. I don't want to marry you either!" Struggling to get loose from his embrace, she tore his coat and threw his crown on the ground.

The people in the street laughed at Alexander, and his face turned beet red. He would not be humiliated by this woman, this beautiful lady whom he wished for his own. He grabbed her by her robe and led her to the governor. When Thecla confessed her action, the governor ordered her to be thrown to the beasts.

16. The Sand Chamber

September 16, 2006

At 8 a.m. sharp the MAMs reported for duty at BûlBûl Dag. Balaban pulled into the lot, squeezing the van between several cars and two pickup trucks. "We're on time, but it looks like the rest of them were early!" Sallie observed.

Hiram greeted Ursula with a handshake. "Welcome back! Today we have students from Istanbul. They help take the sand out."

The dew sparkled on the trees and covered the grass when the MAMs puffed up the steps and began the hike up to the dig site. "I love the smell of early morning," Sallie announced.

"Early morning smells?" Jane asked.

"That fresh dew permeates everything. Can't you feel it? Can't you catch the fragrance?" Sallie plucked a wet leaf off a tree and shoved it near Jane's face.

Jane backed away from the leaf and rolled her eyes. "Can't say that I can."

"You didn't grow up on a farm. Never had the pleasure of doing the early morning chores. Never had time to take in the aroma of a new day."

"But I've been out many mornings working. Remember I did construction before I made my millions."

"OK, you two, enough! Sistas, we've got work to do." Mollie zipped her mouth shut with her forefinger and thumb, then pointed the women on with a jab of her forefinger.

Jane whispered to Emily, "Some folks can't talk when they're exercising." Jane hung her arm around Emily's shoulder to share a private laugh, and they broke into an early morning jog up the mountain.

Katharine and Ursula followed them, walking briskly, but carrying on a conversation, despite Molly's direction.

"I could barely sleep last night," Ursula laughed nervously.

"What are you worried about?" Katharine asked.

"Not worried, just excited. Katharine, can you believe it? Can you believe we really found something in that cave?"

"No, not really. I don't think it's sunk in yet. It's a bit surreal, actually. Look down there, Ursula. Do you see the amphitheater? I keep wondering if Paul really used to be on the side of this mountain, too. Was this his hideout?"

"There's a lot more to discover on this hillside and in this cave. Vastly unexplored territory. Maybe someday we can answer that question. But for today, I'm excited to see what we've found."

Meanwhile, Molly and Sallie were panting on the climb. "I thought this would get easier!" Sallie stopped to catch her breath.

"Maybe after a week or so. We aren't spring chickens, you know." Molly grabbed Sallie's hand and pulled her on up the path.

Sallie laughed out loud and plodded on. "Don't make me laugh. I need my energy for the climb."

Jane and Emily arrived first on the site. The other archaeologists were sitting around the table drinking tea. The men rose quickly to greet the women and poured some tea for Jane and Emily, gesturing them to sit down. A few minutes later, Katharine and Ursula joined them. By the time the other women arrived, the tea had disappeared. Abdul was finishing up an orientation for the four young men from the University at Istanbul. He introduced them to the women. Clad in jeans and T-shirts, the men seemed shy but smiling. "My archaeology students," Hiram laughed. "They dig old stuff."

Sallie sat down on the bench to rest and laughed at Hiram's joke. "Then you'll love us." The MAMs started giggling, but the students were quiet. "Do they speak English?" Sallie looked at Hiram.

"Some. On paper, they know English. In person, not so much. Balaban will stay and translate today." On cue, Balaban translated Sallie's quip into Turkish, and the students laughed and responded in their native tongue.

Balaban looked at Sallie, pointing. "They say, you very funny lady. Smart boys."

By mid-morning the bucket brigade had carried the last container of sand out of the cave. Several students joined Sallie and Karim in the sifting. They continued to pick small pieces of pottery out of the sand, and then Sallie hit the jackpot with a small metal ornament that Hiram liked very much. "Looks very much like Roman armor. We'll analyze in lab, but possibly first century."

Hiram made an executive decision to enlarge the opening into the sand chamber, so someone could actually climb in. He picked Emily and Josef, the smallest people in the group.

When Molly finished taking photos through the opening, Hiram gave her orders. "Describe what you see in your pictures. Molly, write it down."

"Let me get my dig journal. And I'll need a light." Molly ran back out to her desk.

Emily and Josef climbed into the small room. Hiram handed them battery-operated lanterns, and they began to explore.

When Mollie stepped back into the cave, she turned her digital camera on and reviewed the pictures she'd taken of the cave. She zoomed in to take a closer look.

"Hey, there's something in the corner. I can't tell if it's just dirt or something sticking out. See?" She showed them the picture.

"Emily, Josef, start there." Hiram pointed toward the bulge.

Emily crawled over and patted it with her hands. "It's very firm. I don't think it's dirt."

Hiram handed some tools through the opening. "Carefully, dig around the edge. Josef, put dirt in this bucket. Get Priscilla."

Emily began the slow task of digging around the large object. Priscilla came in, and Hiram directed her to map the chamber.

"Take time," Hiram said. "No hurry. Don't damage."

After a half an hour of slow progress, Hiram ordered Josef to begin helping Emily.

Josef dug on one side and Emily on the other. They gradually filled the bucket. Hiram directed a large lantern on their working space.

Emily asked for Molly's camera. "It's beginning to look like a very large clay pot. Like the shards we found in the dirt yesterday, but in one piece," she explained.

She passed the camera out for Hiram and Ursula, who reviewed her pictures.

"Yes, yes! I think you're right, Emily." Hiram's voice quaked with excitement.

"Could we enlarge the opening to the chamber?" Ursula asked.

"Not safe, may collapse. We'll leave it for now, better not to disturb any more than necessary. Go have some water."

Ursula walked out, enjoying the fresh air and looked down at the Ephesus site beginning to swarm with tourists. She plopped down next to Katharine, who was searching for first-century pottery on some artifact discs from the Kusadasi museum

"So, it looks like the MAMs might at least find a pot!" she announced to Katharine.

Katharine laughed and showed Ursula an array of clay pots from Asia, circa first century.

"It's fitting, don't you think, for the women today to find the pot carried by the women of yesterday?" Katharine asked.

"Well, you know that the pots were also used to store things. Perhaps there's something in that pot!" Ursula continued to focus on her desired outcome.

"Why is it that we always want to fill empty spaces?" Katharine asked.

Ursula eyes lighted at Katharine's statement. "You're right. All we have is that empty space called 'now' and that is everything. Have you been reading Tolle?"[xxiv]

"Oh, I read a little of his books. But that isn't what I meant. I just think sometimes we must let life be what it is."

"Exactly. Exactly what Tolle would say," Ursula said.

"No, that's not what I mean." Katharine looked out over the hillside to the ancient ruins of Ephesus, wondering. Actually, she knew exactly what Ursula meant and could feel that truth. Her mind skipped back to Rupp's words. "Entering the sacred inner room where everything sings of Mystery." She couldn't argue. The eternal now made incredible sense.

"You're right, Ursula, absolutely."

***

Not very far away, just down the hillside from BûlBûl Dag, in the ruins of Ephesus, Moses Sun paced back and forth in front of the ancient library. He wondered where the women could be. He knew they were coming to Ephesus to dig, that was on her web site. So why weren't they here?

The terrace house site was buzzing with people. He had paid the special fee to enter, only to find an entourage of Austrian archaeologists. No American women on that job. This was becoming a very expensive excursion.

Sun's thoughts raced on. Fortunately, with Parks out of the picture for awhile, he gained time to get to Katharine. If only he could find her. Tapping his money belt, he considered a bribe. Perhaps the tour guides could find out for him if there were Americans digging this week. Ah, Priscilla. He could tell them he was just looking for his American girlfriend. True enough. Sun stalked with new purpose toward the exit. It wouldn't be long now. He looked up toward the hills, then headed for the information booth. Not too far away, the MAMs' dig continued, but trees and distance obscured his view.

***

At that very moment Katharine stood, staring down at Ephesus. Her thoughts left fears of Sun in the dust of the warming day. Visions of clay vessels, shards of the past occupied her mind now. Gathered together, little remnants pieced together a picture of ancient realities. She'd learned enough on the laptop to know the shards very likely dwelt here with first-century residents. Goosebumps formed when she tried to imagine the Apostle Paul, standing in this very location, gazing at the imposing drama that must have

110

played out in the City of Ephesus back then. Roman soldiers, marching up the hill from the sea with chariots pulled by Arabian horses. Paul preaching in the amphitheater, threatening the livelihood of the large town's dependence on the Temple of Artemis, the Goddess Diana, and all of the money made on those visiting the spiritual mecca. The Emperor Domitian arresting John and banishing him to Patmos. She wondered if Thecla had been here with Paul.

Her musings stopped abruptly when new voices rang out greetings. A small group entered the site. She recognized the familiar cadence of the German tongue. She stole one more glance at the site below and hurried over to offer welcome.

"Guten Tag,"[xxv]

"Guten Tag." A friendly woman with white hair and glasses extended her hand.

"Katharine Long," She smiled into the brown eyes of the newcomer.

"Sophie Simons." The woman introduced herself and turned toward her friend, "Hans Parli."

"You dig Sophie's Cave! She must check up on you! She's boss here 10 years now."

Small crinkles radiated out from Hans' eyes, while he teased his companion.

Undaunted, Sophie explained. "Hiram called us about the sand chamber. So exciting! We caught the next plane."

Hans winked at Katharine.

"Well, then, let's not waste time. Let's go to the cave." Katharine motioned toward the opening, and the trio walked quickly in.

"Sophie! Hans! Welcome! Welcome!" Hiram hugged them. "We have big find here!"

Ursula looked at Katharine with a question in her eyes. "Sophie Simons and Hans Parli from Austria," Katharine filled in her friend. "She's the lead Austrian archaeologist on this site. She approved your digging plan, but wasn't going to come until Hiram called yesterday about the sand chamber."

"Oh! Dr. Simons! So pleased to meet you. I've read your papers. You have done so much work here. How honored we are to have you come!"

Sophie smiled back. "Thank you, Ursula Goodtree. An important day! I wouldn't miss it for the world."

She asked Emily and Josef to climb out, so she could take a closer look.

"She's the boss now!" Hans seemed to jest, but no one defied her orders. Emily and Josef crawled out of the sand chamber, and Hiram helped them down.

Emily decided she needed some light and water and left the cave for the hillside.

Katharine watched Sophie scrunch through the small opening easily. She removed a small camera and light from her pocket and began to examine and photograph the partially uncovered pot.

Katharine talked to her through the hole in German, explaining her research and how the markings matched other first-century pots.

Sophie continued snapping pictures, and then picked up a tool and started to dig around the pot.

Hiram asked her if she wanted Emily and Josef back, but Simons was working in a vacuum. Intently scraping and digging, she switched tools frequently. Her intensity and excitement did not provide time for even a response.

Ursula motioned to Hiram. "The cave is her baby!"

Hiram questioned, "A baby?"

"This is her dig. She wants to do it herself," Ursula explained.

"Right," Hiram said. "Let's take break."

The MAMs picnicked on the hillside, munching their lunches, while Sophie Simons feverishly worked to uncover the pot inside.

"I thought this was the MAMs' expedition," Jane complained.

"Come on, Jane." Sallie laughed. "We are not archaeologists. If there is something really important, you have to expect the real ones to take over."

"We can do this. Look at us. We're a team. An all-woman team," Jane complained some more.

"Buck up, Masters," Sallie retorted. "Take a break. We're on vacation, remember? We've got a very capable woman in there digging for us. She's a real archaeologist."

So the MAMs sat and laughed through the afternoon, chatting and reminiscing, while Simons worked away to free the pot inside. It was 4:45 p.m. when she emerged from the cave. She spoke to Katharine in her native tongue, her smile spreading across her face.

Katharine interpreted for her. "She's freed the pot from the wall. The next step will be to figure out if it can be removed from the cave without breaking."

Hiram offered to go get a padded container from the field office, and Sophie agreed. With the container, they hoped the pot could be lifted from the cave without causing any stress on the ancient piece.

Hiram headed down the mountain with a couple assistants, while the MAMs continued to sit, chatting on the hillside. By 6 p.m. Hiram was back with the container. Josef helped Sophie lift the pot into the container, and then together they hoisted it out of the chamber opening. Hiram and Akber cradled it in their arms and carried it outside the cave.

Molly was busy snapping pictures when they placed the container in the clearing in front of the cave.

"This is like receiving a Christmas present," Sallie said. "You can hardly wait to open it to see what's inside!"

"Don't get too excited," Jane cautioned. "After 2,000 years, whatever is inside is probably just a lot of dirt."

Ursula shook her head. "It is possible that something has been preserved. The sand was very dry and had a high concentration of salt, with very little water. Remember the Dead Sea Scrolls. Occasionally it happens. It's unusual, but the conditions would be exactly what we would use for preservation of artifacts."

The MAMs stood waiting. Simons emerged from the cave to look at the find in the light of day. She motioned to Hiram. They stood the pot back upright and began to remove the plug. Meanwhile, Priscilla was recording the dimensions of the pot.

"A very large pot," Katharine had reported. "For first-century standards, likely a storage pot."

"Wait," Hiram stopped. "An inscription here." He dusted off the ceramic plug covering the hole on the pot. In a dark red ink he read the Greek letters out loud. "Theta, epsilon, kappa, iota, lambda, lambda, alpha."

"Thekla?" Katharine asked.

"Thekilla," Sophie corrected. "Perhaps a variation of Thekla also spelled, Thecla."

"Like the Spanish names?" Sally asked. "They add "illa" on for the children, or for an affectionate name."

Sophie and Hiram looked quizzically at Katharine, who quickly translated into German.

"Yes, yes, possibly," Sophie quickly agreed. "The mother of Thecla was spelled, "T-h-e-o-k-l-a." on the cave painting. Variations were common."

More pictures were snapped and Molly wrote, while Priscilla carefully noted the find, copying the letters on the paper where she was recording the information about the pot specimen.

"Go ahead," Hiram told Sophie, "Your baby!" The men laughed and the women smiled.

Sophie took a pocket knife out of her back pocket and inserted it around the plug, like loosening a cake from the pan. The plug was tight, but not glued shut and popped out abruptly.

The MAMs' mouths popped open in surprise.

Ursula held her breath when Sophie reached into the jar.

"More sand," she reported.

Hiram handed her a bucket, and this time she began to shovel the sand out into the bucket with a small spoon attached to her pocket knife. "My best tool," she said to Hiram.

113

Lifting a pinch of sand to her nose, then licking it with her tongue, she said, "Salty, same sand in chamber. Good preservative."

The bucket filled while the MAMs circled and waited.

"Do you really think this is 2,000 years old?" Sallie asked.

"It's possible." Ursula said. "In the lab they can find out more, but the preliminary results from yesterday suggest it's very likely."

"Wow!" Emily exclaimed. "We didn't find Thecla, but maybe something that belonged to her."

"Or to Thecilla," Jane said. "Little Thecla. Maybe her daughter?"

"There's no evidence Thecla had any children," Katharine laughed. "The virgin saint, remember?"

"How can you really know something like that, though?" Sallie asked. "We don't know if Jesus was married. Actually, they say it's more likely that he was married, or it would have been mentioned in the scripture."

"You're right, Sallie." Katharine replied.

"I'm on a roll now! I'm telling our religion professor the truth!" Sallie laughed.

Shhh," Ursula said. "Pay attention, ladies." Ursula was worried that the MAMs would break into more laughter at an important moment, and she wanted to be taken seriously by these men who seemed to be taking her dig over. Male egos. Some things are the same, in Michigan and in Turkey.

As if he could read her mind, Hiram announced, "We are calling this the Ursula Goodtree dig. Very rare to have a beautiful, intelligent American woman archaeologist in the field."

Ursula blushed and looked again at Sophie who was starting to pull a long object from the jar.

"And a beautiful Austrian woman, too." Hiram winked at Sophie.

"You know, we have a long tradition of women digging in this cave. Even our Italian restorers are women. It's actually unusual to have so many men on site here." Sophie smiled at the group of MAMs. "I'm so happy you came."

Hiram laughed. "Yes, she's our boss."

"Look at this. Wow!" Sophie held the first offering from the pot high, brushing sand off into the bucket.

Priscilla wrote a description on her page, "An oblong object, with a rounded surface, approximately 12 inches long. Appears to be a material rolled onto a long bone."

"A scroll!" Ursula stood up and came closer to look.

"Yes, yes, a scroll!" Sophie agreed.

Katharine stood by smiling. Ursula had been right all along.

Sophie consulted with Hans, and they both agreed, "Do not open here. May be brittle. Will take to the lab." But he reached into the bottle and pulled another one out, and another, and another.

Priscilla scribbled away, measuring each scroll as they placed them on a large cloth beside the pot and noting them on the ledger.

Hiram left to get another box for safe storage.

Molly's camera clicked continually.

Twilight cast shadows over the site, while the sun slipped down behind the trees. The group huddled around the pot watching Sophie pull the last scroll from the pot.

"Seven scrolls!" Priscilla counted. "A perfect seven."

Sophie reached into the pot and felt the bottom once again. But then, she felt something more. "Wait! Wait!" She called out.

She pushed her pocket knife down into the pot and eased a false bottom loose. She pulled a small marble disc out of the pot and then reached back again, pulling out a small scroll that fit in her hand.

"Number eight," she said. Cradling the little scroll with her fingers she showed it around to the group. "Very special, no?"

The sky continued to darken, and Hiram asked the crew to pack up. "Tomorrow, another day. Enough excitement for today!"

The MAMs scurried like little housekeepers sweeping up their house for guests. Within five minutes the site was clean, and all the tools deposited back in tool chests for safekeeping. Sophie and Hiram carried the box with the scrolls between them like a baby in their arms, walking slowly back down the hill.

"Tomorrow, 8 a.m. sharp." Hiram announced. "You come to field office to see the scrolls," he told the MAMs.

The entourage headed back down the hill toward Ephesus. The MAMs chattered away. Downhill went much more quickly. They stayed together through the switchbacks, and enjoyed a few more fresh figs.

What they didn't see was the drama unfolding at the bottom of the steps leading up to the cave. Moses Sun had finally learned about the Cave of St. Paul and was ready to go find Katharine. He wasn't sure exactly where he was going, but the man had told him to go up the hill.

The *Gendarme*, however, had been alerted to a man climbing the steps, off limits to Ephesus tourists. Two soldiers hurried up behind him on the steps, heading him back down to the site.

"No entrance. Not open today," one soldier told his guide.

The guide shrugged and said to Sun, "I sorry, sir. Cannot visit today."

Steam poured off Sun's head. He wiped his brow and sighed with disgust.

"Tomorrow -- another day," Sun's guide suggested. "I bring you back tomorrow?"

Sun shrugged, then nodded his agreement.

"Where now, my friend?"

"Back to my hotel, please."

"Where?"

Sun handed a small card with the hotel address to the driver.

"Yes. Yes. Not far, not far."

Sun began to compose a report to headquarters, then stopped. Nothing to report. Tomorrow would be a better day with some good news to write home. He was sure of it.

By the time the women arrived at the steps, Sun and his guide were long gone, heading toward his hotel.

17. Ursula and Ephesus

September 17, 2006

And so, on the third day of the dig, instead of heading up the mountain, the MAMs were heading to Seljuk and the Austrian archaeologists' home away from home. Just a half hour after leaving their hotel, Balaban passed the Archaeological Museum in downtown Seljuk, which the MAMs recognized from their cruise tour, and headed down a narrow street behind the museum. He passed under a wrought iron gate and pulled into the Austrian compound, where trees sheltered a courtyard enclosed by small buildings.

The MAMs babbled, while Balaban stopped the van and opened the door for the ladies to disembark.

"I haven't been this excited since I got my first teaching job!" Sallie exclaimed.

Ursula laughed, "I haven't been this excited since I was in love 30 years ago!"

"I haven't been this excited since I broke my leg on Mount Everest!" Jane sarcastically added.

"Oh come on, Jane. We know you're excited," Sallie challenged.

"Ursula is right. We did find something. This is incredible," Katharine said.

"Now when Katharine gets excited about something, you have to listen." Sallie pointed her finger at Jane. "You have to admit there is something amazing going on here."

Jane shrugged her shoulders. "Let's go inside and find out."

Priscilla said, "Now the Bible is already written. We can't find any more of God's words, you know."

Ursula and Katharine exchanged glances, but did not speak. Molly did. "There have been a lot of scrolls found that shed much light on the Bible, and perhaps should have been included. *"The Acts of Paul and Thecla*, for example."

"That isn't scripture!" Priscilla disagreed.

Sophie Simons came out one of a buildings with a welcoming smile. "*Guten tag*! Good morning! Welcome. We've been waiting for you!"

The MAMs followed Simons into the small building where the others sat, crowded around a table. Coming closer, they could see the large pot standing tall, and beside it, the scrolls. Several men stood as the women entered the room.

Ursula recognized the crew from the day before, Sophie and Hans, Akber, Abdul, Karim, and then she noticed several new faces. She extended her hand to one of the new men, a short, portly man standing at the table. "Ursula Goodtree, pleased to meet you."

"Akti Sumer," the man shook her hand, and introduced the two other men standing beside him.

Ursula rattled off the names of the MAMs, and the men all nodded.

"This morning, we open the scrolls." Hiram explained. "Our friends from the University of Istanbul have come to join us. They are language specialists. Akti in Ancient Greek, Mustafa in Latin, and Halim in Hebrew. We will open the scrolls, let the language experts look, and photograph the scrolls to send them to several language centers around the world for best translations. We begin."

Molly prepared to take pictures and noticed that Akber also had some sophisticated photographic equipment ready to capture the scrolls.

Akti gently touched the first scroll and tested it, trying to unroll it. Sand and salt were evident on the thick material, and the scroll was somewhat stiff.

Hiram said, "Maybe we send to lab? May break. Maybe not safe to open. Hard."

Katharine looked at the group and explained to the MAMs. "Papyrus doesn't last 2,000 years. The Dead Sea Scrolls were the exception, but even then, they were very fragmented."

The Austrian archaeologists nodded in consent. Sophie looked at Hiram. "May I look?"

Hiram nodded in assent.

Sophie gently touched the scroll open on the table, testing the flexibility of the material.

"Could they be fake?" Sallie laughed.

"Perhaps," Katharine said.

Sophie then demonstrated that the material was flexible enough to bend back and forth. She gently moved the material to begin opening the scroll.

Ursula held her breath. Jane's attention was focused on the scroll. Priscilla placed her hand over her mouth. Mollie snapped pictures as quickly as her Kodak EasyShare would reset. Katharine put her arm around Ursula's shoulder and looked on. Sallie's eyes bugged wide. Emily watched the other archaeologists in the room.

Akti stepped closer to Sophie and watched her unfold the scroll.

"It's opening!" Hiram exclaimed.

"Very unusual," Akti's voice chimed in.

"It's not brittle," Sophie said.

"Oh my God!" Ursula said when the scroll lay open on the table.

Akber took many pictures, while Hiram explained to the group, "These pictures preserve the past, even if the material crumbles."

Molly was amazed that the scroll seemed remarkably sturdy and intact. She snapped pictures, while Priscilla continued her journal, writing the description of the scroll. Halim held a meter stick close to the scroll, so that the pictures would record the size, which appeared to be about 12 inches wide and 40 inches long.

Akti held the scroll open with his hands, while the three linguists examined it.

"Akti's job," Halim announced. "Greek to me!" Laughter erupted. "We know some American jokes," he explained to the group.

Sophie stood behind Akti when he looked more closely and began to read. "It's a letter. She writes to Thecla!"

Sallie poked Jane. A grin spread across Jane's face, and she returned the poke with a thumbs up motion, then extended her hand for a high five slap. Ursula hugged Katharine from the side.

Silence broke when Akti spoke.

"Now I read the best I can, later the experts will find better translation. Excellent Greek. The writer, very well educated. Not all words are clear here."

"A girl?" Hiram asked.

"We'll see, we'll see."

He began to read, pausing after each line to translate into German and then English. Priscilla wrote the English down and the MAMs stood mesmerized when the story began to unfold.

Scroll # 1 Ephesus

Dear Teacher,

Amazing life! Ephesus to Patmos and home [ ]. You [ ] proud of me. Grandmother Priscilla [ ] proud.

Yesterday, I read Uncle John's vision [ ] house church at Eph [ ].

They asked, "We lost our first love? What [   ] do?"

They prayed [ ] night, [ ] filled with joy and God's love [ ]. But they don't understand. They think God calls

119

*them to war. [ ] Jesus won the victory. I explained the
sword is the tongue. They want to battle the Romans.
[ ] the Romans are destroying themselves.*

*Pray [ ] they understand. Pray for Claudius! He [ ]
the May games [ ] Temple of Artemis, [ ] prize. Tells
me [ ] stop preaching. [ ] knows the Romans. [ ] worries about me.*

*I tell him I serve the God of Moses, [ ] waters, the God
of Sarah, [ ] Abraham a baby in old age. I [ ] serve
the God of Jesus whom the Romans killed on a tree... [ ]
resurrected. [ ] the granddaughter of Priscilla and
Aquilla, who preached the Word of God, yet [ ] died at
the hands of Nero. I tell him that I am [ ] of Thecla [ ]
thrown to lions and tied to the stake to burn, but [ ]
lives to a ripe old age [ ] taught me to [ ] faith and be
strong.*

*Pray that Claudius [ ] faith. Dear Teacher, [ ] come to
you soon.*

Your student, Thecilla.

Priscilla glanced up from her journal and looked at her watch. It
was 10 a.m. Everyone stood mesmerized, enthralled, listening.
When the closing lines of the letter were translated into German and
then English, the room was quiet. There were no words.

And then Sallie began to clap. One by one the MAMs stood and
clapped. Ursula beamed at Sophie and embraced her with a warm
hug. The men cheered. Hiram asked Ursula if he could have a hug,
too. Then they all laughed and hugged, caught in the apex of a moment where the first century intersected the twenty-first and an in-
nocuous dig by an unlikely assortment of women had uncovered an
astonishing pot of scrolls, casting new light on the present.

"The vision, Katharine, the vision. What vision?" Ursula
searched her friend's face. "What is this about?"

"Patmos... John... vision... Well, it sounds like..." Katharine
looked back at Ursula.

"Revelation! Oh my God!" Emily blurted out before Katharine
completed the sentence. "The letters to the churches. She took
John's scrolls to Ephesus. To the Christian church."

"Yes, I think Emily's right. If we can believe this is authentic."
Katharine smiled.

"Fantastic. Fantastic. Amazing." Ursula reached out to hug Katharine, and others followed suit.

Soon, Emily broke in. "Is this possible? A girl taking the scrolls to the churches? Could it happen?"

Katharine smiled. "Stranger things have happened. There is much evidence that women were more a part of the early church than the Bible reveals. Certainly Priscilla was a leader, and Thecla became a disciple, traveling with Paul.

"Can we read some more? Let's hear another one." Emily urged.

"One more," Hiram decided. "Then we'll spend the morning photographing the others. We want to make sure we get photographs first. There will always be time for translation."

"Yes," Akti agreed. "We send digital photos to linguistic experts for careful translation. We compare to mine. There will be differences."

"I have a friend in California," Ursula began."

"We have a list. We have a man at the Biblical Languages Research Center in California?" Akti nodded.

"Yes!" Ursula exclaimed. "Yes! Dr. Cohen?"

"Yes. Yes. We have plans to send them there." Akti smiled. "So easy with the Internet, you know?"

"I will email him! Is that all right?"

"Certainly, certainly," Akti replied.

"You can even use my phone," Halim smiled into Ursula's eagerness. "I have international cell phone," he said held it out to her.

"But first, the second scroll." Akti turned to Halim.

Hiram took another scroll up from the table and handed it to Akti. Again, Akti carefully held the scroll dusting off the salt and sand, and then started to unroll the scroll. A piece cracked and he stopped for pictures. Then gently he urged the scroll open, revealing very legible writing. When all the photographers stopped snapping, he began to read again.

Once again the room was quiet. The words echoed in the hearts of the MAMs like a sound reverberating off the walls of a cave. The words were sending out transforming waves into their thoughts and lives.

A thud was heard at the window and turning, Katharine saw a white dove hovering. She elbowed Ursula and pointed at the bird. Ursula and the others looked just as the dove turned and flew off into the new day.

The rest of the morning passed quickly. Molly wrote. Priscilla carefully prepared entries for each of the scrolls in the dig journal. Sallie helped clean the artifacts found in the sifting dirt. Katharine and Hiram began the international communications with translation experts around the world. Jane helped the guys clean the tools.

Emily pulled out her own journal and began to write. She had come a long way in the two weeks since she left home and she needed to collect her thoughts. More than anything, she wanted to tell Josh about their find, but first she needed to spend some time with herself.

Ursula took Hiram's cell phone into a quiet corner, pulled a slip out of her back pack and began to punch Joe's number, then stopped. "Am I crazy?" She wondered, "What will he think? Who am I to think that he may still have feelings for me after all of these years? He's grieving. I should let him alone." But, she argued with herself, "He's an expert. He's just who we need. They are going to contact him anyway, so why shouldn't I call? It's natural. There's nothing wrong with me making this call. It's the most natural thing in the world to call a personal friend, a language expert, someone who definitely could translate these scrolls."

Ursula punched in the last few numbers and waited for the connection. Then, she remembered the time difference. Noon in Kusadasi would be the middle of the night in Michigan and late night in California. Perhaps Joe would still be up. More disturbing to stop a call than to let it go through, she decided. Nothing she hated more than to be awakened by a ringing phone that stopped in its tracks. The phone continued to connect.

A groggy voice answered, "Hello?"

"Joe!" she exclaimed. "Did I wake you up!"

"Ursula? Is that you, Ursula? I thought you were in Turkey. Are you OK?"

Ursula's heart turned a few somersaults when he automatically identified her voice and then expressed a question of concern.

"Are you all right?"

"Yes, yes. Oh, Joe, I'm sorry to call you so late. I forgot about the time difference."

"No problem. I don't get much sleep these nights anyway. Mostly tossing and turning. Thank you for interrupting my nightmares. What's up?"

"Joe, you won't believe this. It's just incredible! We found some intact scrolls in the Cave of St. Paul. They are legible Greek. It's amazing! I can't believe it! You won't believe this! They seem to be first-century letters from a young woman who helped John at Patmos. Joe, I can't believe this. This is...."

"Whoa!" Joe interrupted Ursula's babbling and asked a few questions to orient himself. After several minutes of exchange, he cut the conversation short.

"Ursula, I'm on my way. I'm getting dressed. I'll be there tomorrow."

The phone clicked off and Ursula sat holding the phone. She closed it and held it tight in her palm and then she began to cry. Glancing around the room to avoid others, she rubbed her eyes and managed to get up, put Hiram's phone on a table, and scurry to the restroom without drawing any attention to her face streaming with tears. She closed and locked the door, and then let the tears flow freely. She sat down and bawled. She cried for all the nights she had spent alone. She cried for all the love she had felt for Joe over the years. She cried for Thecla and Thecilla and Emily. She cried and cried and cried. And then she stopped.

A realization began building in her chest and as it grew she began to smile and as she smiled she began to pull toilet paper off the roll and wipe her eyes. She suddenly knew her tears were tears of joy. The vacuum that had been lodged in her chest had been filling ever since she received that first email from Katharine. Now the vacuum was gone, replaced with light overflowing.

"How will I ever explain this one to my shrink?" she thought. "That here on a toilet in Ephesus my depression has rolled away and the light of a new day has started to shine deep within?" Standing up, her smile turned into a laugh and she rushed out of the bathroom to share her good news with Katharine.

***

Moses Sun finished dressing and looked at his watch. The tour guide had promised to pick him up at 10 in the lobby. He shuffled the papers on the dresser and carefully placed his passport where it belonged in the pouch hanging inside his shirt. Clipping his cell phone to his pants, he opened the small refrigerator by his bed and took out a Coke. Nothing like a fresh can of Coke to start the day.

He opened his laptop to surf the net, happy to finally find a hotel with access. He decided to check in with Headquarters. Today was his day. He knew it. Today he would find Katharine and then it would just be a matter of time.

"Orange alert." He read on. God and the President held strong, still keeping the terrorists from blowing up the good U.S. of A, he thought. Buying time until Armageddon was in full swing. He knew. Jesus will come again and rescue all of the good guys from global warming, the food shortages, the fuel shortages, the greed, the lawlessness, the violence, the lack of morality. Whew. What a mess in the United States today. That's what happens to people without God. But the good ones are humbling themselves, getting Jesus and supporting the war effort in Iraq. It won't be long now. Jesus will come in the clouds and then it's all over for you, bad guys.

His thoughts turned to Katharine. Now she was a good example. To some people she might look like a perfectly respectable woman, but he discerned evil. Beware of the wolf in lamb's clothing. She speaks against the truth, against Armageddon, against the big war that will start when Jesus returns. She must be silenced. Headquarters would want him to do whatever it takes. They may say "Monitor her behavior," but he knew they wanted more. He would deliver. All in the name of Jesus. It's all for you, Katharine. He smiled and closed his laptop and headed for the lobby.

***

In the Austrian field office, Hiram told the MAMs to take the afternoon off. "In fact, if you want, I'll send you to Pamukkale."

"What's that?" Emily asked.

"That's an unusual rock formation in west central Turkey," Ursula explained. "It's been a resort for years. You can actually swim in the pools. It looks like ice, but it's really the limestone formations, something like you'd see inside a cave. I've been there. It's an amazing sight." Ursula started daydreaming back 25 years earlier when she and Joe spent the night at a hotel near the cliffs. Her heart drummed with memories. She journeyed deep into her memory of the night of joy at Pamukkale. Images of water and warmth and love swirled around her. That memory lodged in her chest like a permanent resident. The best night of her life.

"How far is it?" Emily was asking. She looked at Ursula, but Ursula didn't respond. She turned to Hiram. "Is it far?"

Hiram looked off to a map on the wall and went to point to Emily. "It's 20 kilometers from Denizli. From here to Denizli -- 200. 220 kilometers total."

"How many miles?" Emily asked

Jane pulled out her blackberry and did a quick calculation, "136 miles, dear."

"Would we spend the night?" Emily asked.

"Your wish is my command," Hiram responded. "I just happen to have some friends in Hierapolis who will welcome you to their house. Turkish hospitality, the best."

"Let's go!" Priscilla enthusiastically nodded. And soon the MAMs were all excited.

Balaban showed up at the door, almost magically and they were off to the hotel to pack overnight bags.

***

Moses Sun smiled to himself. She's not going to be expecting me! His tour guide led Sun toward the steps heading up to Paul's Grotto. Sun tapped the little gun strapped under his shirt. He managed to keep that after he had been ousted from the FBI Academy, but making it through airport security in his suitcase was another feat. He hadn't been able to pass the FBI psychological testing in the end. They couldn't take the Jesus stuff. Persecuted again. The good guys are running the show, but some of the bad guys still keep religion out of the government, he thought. That will change soon. He knew. It was just a matter of time.

The guide stopped at the bottom of the steps. The *Gendarme* stood erect, guarding the steps, machine guns slung across their backs. Sun slinked behind while the guide went up to ask for entrance. Sun looked at his watch: "11 a.m."

They seemed to be arguing. Finally, the tour guide handed over some money, and the soldier stood aside to let the two men pass.

Sun wondered what the women could possibly be doing in this place on the side of the hill. Didn't they know the real chalupa was Ephesus, down below, not some supposed Grotto of St. Paul with pictures of people that weren't even in the Bible? False teachers, you find them everywhere. Speaking of such, he tapped his gun and looked forward to meeting Professor Long for the last time. Through the wooded path, they walked quickly. When they reached the cave, Sun was surprised. There were no voices. He walked further. There were no people. Katharine? Where is that woman? Where did she go now?

The guide shrugged, "The soldiers said the women have not been back today. They have orders to keep the public out."

Sun fumed and then stomped back down the hillside to the car. Foiled again. He knew she was in Kusadasi. He would find her. Then Sun knew he would have the upper hand.

18. Thecilla in Ephesus

September 14, 94 A.D.

The setting sun slipped behind darkening clouds, yet streams of light radiated out into the blue sky now turning gray. Brilliant bands of orange and pink touched the horizon while dusk settled into the nearby hills, casting shadows over her path. Thecilla lingered by the tent, like a child not wanting to come in from play. After four moons, she was home. Yet everything had changed. Her parents were upset. They didn't understand. They were the ones who had sent her to Patmos to care for her uncle. She felt the responsibility of the scrolls, like a mother longing to give birth, she needed to push the news far and wide. She must travel. And Claudius couldn't begin to understand.

Growing shadows danced around the tent, light flickering through the heavy cloth. Now she returned to the family of tentmakers, where she would soon take up her place sewing and helping her father with the craft, a good income for the family. Like Priscilla and Aquilla, the family tradition continued.

Thecilla couldn't wait any longer. She opened the tent flap, and stepped into the familiar gathering, the evening meal. Her family reclined on the tent floor around the long table. She bent to kiss her mother and then her father, then patted the heads of her little brother and sister, before taking her place.

Her mother offered dates and bread and poured a cup of water.

"Now, dear, your father and I want to talk with you about these scrolls."

Thecilla looked at her mother with wary eyes. "Uncle John's scrolls? His Patmos prophecy?"

She looked down, afraid of what her mother might say.

Her father's eyes flashed anger. "You can't take those scrolls to the churches. It's too dangerous."

Yet, her mother smiled. Something about that smile seemed so out of place. Thecilla wished she could flee. Yet she stayed, sitting quietly, her thoughts racing beyond the tent into the night and the mission that called her.

"Your father and I have decided it's time for you to marry. You are of age. You've waited long enough Tomorrow, Jacob of the Silvermakers will visit."

Thecilla closed her eyes to pray. Not only were they going to stop her mission, but they would push Claudius away for a Christian from the house church. She couldn't let them have their way.

"Uncle John may be confused, you can't take the words of an old man too seriously, dear."

"But I promised. He prayed for me. He sent me on a mission. I must go."

Her father stood. "Thecilla, that's impossible. You are a girl. You may not travel to the other churches. Even if we wanted you to go, which we don't, it would be too dangerous. The Romans do not like the Christians. We try to stay out of their way. You would draw too much attention. It's not safe. You cannot travel. Now is your time to be married."

Thecilla looked at the food and around the table. The place of her childhood had become a foreign land. She forced the food down and didn't speak.

"Jacob's a good man," her mother continued. "You know his family. He will treat you well."

Thecilla raised her cup to her lips and swallowed. The water got stuck in her throat. Coughing, she nodded. Then another protest formed.

"But what if Thecla hadn't traveled with Paul? She followed Paul to become a disciple. She chose to follow God over marriage. You've always respected Thecla. Don't you want me to follow God also? Are you really going to be like her parents?"

Her mother gasped.

Her father's anger boiled. "That has absolutely nothing to do with our decision. How dare you suggest that we would have you burned at the stake! You will do as we say."

Thecilla knew better than to argue again. But in the morning, she would go to Claudius. She didn't want to disobey, but she loved her God first. Remembering now the teaching of Jesus, she reviewed the words that she never before understood. The scroll of Matthew opened into her thoughts. "For I have come to turn a man against his father, a daughter against her mother. A man's enemies will be the members of his own household. Anyone who loves his father or mother more than me is not worthy of me."

"I'm sorry, Papa, Mama. Please forgive me. I'm going to bed. I'm very tired. I'll talk to you in the morning."

She carried a candle back to her sleeping tent. She must write Thecla. In the morning, she would pay Thomas to carry her letter to her wise friend. Whatever happened, she would keep Thecla informed.

Thecillla wrote quickly and then let the scroll dry, before rolling it up and tucking it under the mat, in case her mother came looking.

She brushed her long brown hair, working out the knots of the day, mouthing her evening prayers until both her soul and hair were smoothed and soothed and ready for sleep. She cuddled down onto her mat.

In the morning, before the first light she would take the scrolls to Claudius and beg him to take her on to Smyrna. She couldn't let Uncle John down now. She must put God ahead of her parents. She must follow Jesus, as her great teacher Thecla followed Paul, rather than be married to someone she didn't love. She must journey for Uncle John.

19. Thecla in the Lion's Den

September 18, 48 A.D.

"Please, then, I ask that you keep me safe until I meet the beasts."
Thecla pleaded with the governor.

"Bind her to Trifina," the governor told his assistant. He knew the
wealthy widow's daughter had recently died and thought she would
be eager to look after her. Soon he released Thecla into Trifina's custo-
dy.

But after several days passed, Trifina brought Thecla to the amphi-
theater where a multitude of spectators sat waiting for the showdown.
Thecla told Trifina, "Do not worry, the God of Jacob and Sarah goes
with me. I have no fear. If I die, I will be with Jesus soon"

They began to push Thecla into the lion's den, but she walked in
ahead of them and sat down. A fierce she-lion roared, but came to lie
down beside Thecla, beginning to lick her feet. Thecla gently petted
the giant cat. The crowd roared with pleasure.

Trifina called out, "The judgments of this city are unrighteous!
Save this innocent one, God of Abraham and Sarah!"

The lions made peace with Thecla and after several hours, the
guards let Thecla out of the den. Trifina took Thecla home with her,
and they went to bed. During the night, the dead daughter of Trifina,
appeared to her mother in a dream and said; "Mother, let Thecla be
your daughter in my place and ask her to pray for me that I might be
happy that you are not alone and that I will live with God forever."

In the morning, Thecla found Trifina crying in her bed. "What has
happened?" Thecla asked the older woman and sat beside her on her
bed, placing her arm around her with concern.

"My daughter, Falconilla, appeared to me, and asked me to take
you as a daughter in her place, and asked you to pray for her so that
she might be happy and delivered into life eternal."

When Thecla heard this, she immediately prayed to the Lord, "O
Lord God of heaven and earth, Jesus Christ, thou Son of the Most High,
grant that her daughter, Falconilla, may live forever."

Trifina heard the prayer and cried more, calling out in anger, "O
unrighteous judgments! O unreasonable wickedness! That such a crea-
ture should again be cast to the beasts!" Because she knew she

would have to take Thecla back to the arena in the day to come to face more danger.

20. The Vacation

September 17, 2006

The MAMs packed in record time. Thirty-two minutes later they waited in the lobby when Balaban strolled in to pick them up.

"A first for American ladies," he laughed. "I told you 30 minutes and expected to wait another hour. Good for you! You enter that for Guinness Book of yours, no?"

The women laughed and then posed for a splashy picture, courtesy of the desk clerk. Decked out in their floppy red hats, they floated out of the hotel like a group of circus clowns going to the beach. They wore sunglasses, sandals, flip flops and there were even high heels gracing Priscilla's legs.

"Take those shoes off!" Sallie ordered. "You can't go walking on cliffs in those!"

"Let her be a lady," Molly disagreed. "Just because you can't show off your legs with some high steppers don't mean we all have to wear Dr. Scholl's when we're going out."

Balaban laughed. He enjoyed the MAMs.

"Can I drive?" Jane asked when she slipped into the van.

"You have international driver's license and international insurance?"

"Maybe not," Jane admitted.

"Leave the driving to me. You ladies work hard, now you rest."

And so the MAMs, just three days after the launch of the long-awaited dig, were headed off for a sightseeing tour into the heart of Turkey. While they readily agreed to the diversion, they didn't comprehend why they were being whisked away.

Ursula and Katharine sat directly behind Balaban and began to talk.

"Why did they shuttle us away so quickly? I wanted to help with the rest of the scrolls. Do you think they're trying to get rid of us?" Ursula asked.

Katharine raised her eyebrows and shrugged her shoulders. "Very strange. Our dig, a major find, only day three. I don't think it's time for our vacation yet."

Ursula looked out the window while her thoughts strayed to Joe and the pool at Pamukkale. "How long do you think it will take Joe to get here? He didn't tell me."

"At least 24 hours. Maybe when we return tomorrow evening," Katharine decided.

Emily looked out the window, while beside her Sallie dozed off. She focused on the farmland passing by. A man plowing a field with a horse, a women in skirts bending over, weeding, picking or planting? Hard to tell. Her thoughts journeyed beyond the Turkish farmers back to her favorite farmer back home, Josh.

"We will talk," he had said. There was hope. She second-guessed herself once again. Should she have married him last summer? But then she wouldn't be here. Emily took a deep breath and knew that patience was her spiritual practice for this day.

Molly sat by Priscilla and thought about the van taking her closer to Iraq. She had looked on the map. Mark was fighting beyond the next border. Kilometers passing by brought her closer, gave her comfort. She began deep prayers for Mark. Praying without ceasing was her *modus operandi* ever since he left American soil. She prayed for Mark's safety, she prayed for an end to the war, she prayed for sanity among the American leaders, she prayed for an end to the bloodshed, she prayed for forgiveness for the destruction of foreign soil, she prayed on and on and let the love of God bathe her in white light as she looked past the pain lodged in her breast and hoped for a new day.

Priscilla engaged in her own contemplation, wishing she had let Sun come along. Her thoughts rumbled with the wheels bumping over the uneven road. She talked it over with herself. How many more years would she spend alone? She wondered if Moses could be the man that could fill her aching emptiness. While Jesus had brought her much joy, he wasn't the husband she knew God was preparing her for. Had she been too harsh? Had she been too quick to turn him away? Was it her inability to trust? Was she just cooking her own goose?

Moses, a man of God. Even his name was biblical. He knows all about the end times. He knows the Word of God. Priscilla propped her hand under her chin, leaned against the side of the bus and gazed out the window. Her questions met the horizon and bounced back to her with no answers. Was there really something wrong with that man? The bus jostled her body, and the thoughts continued to bounce around inside her mind.

In the front of the bus, Jane bantered with Balaban. Always the life of the party, Jane enjoyed their Turkish driver.

"But the American women are better lovers," Balaban quipped.

"Definitely," Jane agreed. "American women are the best lovers in the world."

"And the best men?" Balaban asked.

"Italians. Definitely the Italians," Jane asserted.

"Turkish men the best."

"Male egos, the same in every country!" Jane laughed.

Balaban continued talking, but Jane had lost the train of conversation when his phone began to toll.

"That sounds like the Mosque prayer bells!" Jane noticed.

"Yes, it is. A call to prayer. Muslims pray at least five times a day. You should do it more often, too."

He stopped the van, opened his phone and answered. "Hiram?"

After a few minutes of silence, Balaban muttered a few words that Jane could not understand, glanced through the rear-view mirror then screeched out, popped a wheelie circling 180 degrees, and headed back toward Kusadasi.

"Hold on to your seats!" Jane yelled

"As if we needed you to tell us that!" Sallie laughed.

The speedometer jerked to the right past the 100 km per hour mark. "What in the hell are you doing?" Jane tapped Balaban on the shoulder. "Slow down!"

Nonplussed, he picked up his small microphone and announced, "Change of plans. Hiram wants you at the field office. The Prime Minister of Turkey has requested a press conference tomorrow morning to announce the archaeological find. The Vatican is participating. You very important ladies, soon to be famous. Sorry, ladies. No vacation today."

Balaban's speed mounted. The fields blurred by the side of the road. The MAMs held on to their seats while the van jumped and bumped down the road. Molly went deeper into her prayers. Jane laughed, crossing herself, the good Catholic girl reverting to prayer the way the nuns had taught. Sallie spoke for them all, yelling: "Hold on MAMs, we're going back!"

***

Meanwhile, Moses Sun's day had started with a stern briefing from headquarters. "No more free vacations on company time." *USA Today* front page announced a huge archaeological find in Kusadasi. Headquarters wanted the scoop. Sun pulled on his khakis and headed for the phone in the lobby to dial up a guide. He'd go back to the field office and find out. Maybe he could score twice.

He tuned in where he left off yesterday, halfway through the seventh book of the *End Times* series. Motivational literature, he called it. Sitting in the lobby chair, his iPhone transported him into a much different reality.

After a nice lunch by the dock, Sun's guide delivered him to the Ephesus field office at 1:30 p.m. He knocked on the door, keeping the guide close to translate, if needed. A tall, dark man came to the door. Sun could see several men behind him, but no evidence of the women.

"I heard there was a find on the dig yesterday? Could I come and see?" Sun asked.

"No, sir. Not open to the public at this time." Hiram tried to dismiss the man. His directions had been clear. No leaks, no promotion until the press conference. This man could be a journalist, they always seemed to materialize out of nowhere and swarm everywhere whenever anything new turned up.

"I'm looking for a friend of mine, Priscilla, she's here on a dig with other women from the States. Is she in?"

"Priscilla?" Hiram asked. Perhaps a journalist who knew about the American women.

"No Priscilla. No women here. I'm sorry, I'm busy, sir."

Hiram closed the door and let out a sigh. Perhaps the little man did know Priscilla. He must remember to ask her later.

Outside, Sun fumbled with his iPhone. Two strikes already and the day had just started. How would he explain? An executive decision came to mind. He'd spend his time wisely, doing some investigative work. That FBI training never failed him on this job.

Sun didn't see the small brown car that had pulled in behind his. Too busy scheming his next move, he stumbled over some stones and headed toward the ancient ruins. Maybe someone on the site will spill the beans, he thought.

***

Dan Parks unfolded his long legs from the brown rental car and put his binoculars back into their pouch. When Sun was safely out of sight, he headed for the field office. When he flashed his badge at the door, he was ushered in without delay.

"I've been waiting for you," Hiram said.

"That man that was just here? Bad news. I'm tailing him. Don't let him near the women." On the subject at hand, he launched into planning. "Now, about security for the press conference, I have three agents coming in tonight. Tell me your plans."

Hiram and Parks worked out the security details, and Hiram dialed up the local base commander. "We have you Americans to watch the American tourists," Hiram explained, "the *Gendarme* do the rest. The Prime Minister insists."

Parks smiled. This was a sweet deal for him. Getting paid handsomely by both sides.

"When did you say the ladies are going to return?" he asked Hiram after the briefing.

"They should be back any time now. Please stay, I'd like you to help with them."

"Yes, sir!"

A smile spread across Parks' face, and this time it was all about Jane. He took a seat by the window where he could see Sun's car and Balaban's van that would be arriving soon. His thoughts lodged in a daydream of the night to come.

At 2:26 p.m. Parks saw the van pulling into the lot, and so did Sun. When Parks walked out of the small building, Sun gasped and started running back toward the ruins. Through the rearview mirror attached to his glasses for situations just like this, he could tell he had not been seen. Parks was too busy ambling toward the van.

Sun chalked up one for himself, at last, and squatted behind a bush, pulling out his binoculars. From his post, he watched the ladies emerge from the van. "Katharine!" He whispered to himself, "Ah .... Priscilla!" Finally after days of disaster his ship had come in. Or would that be his van, he joked with himself. And then he looked at his tour guide standing quizzically beside him.

"Oh, I'm sorry, sir. Beautiful women, no?" Sun handed some dollars to the guide, laughed and then looked again through his binoculars focusing on the backsides of Molly and Sallie, waddling toward the door of the office.

"Beautiful women?" The guide asked.

"You missed the good ones." Sun chuckled. "Come back at 5 to pick me up?"

"Yes, sir. I"ll be back." The guide fingered the bills and figured he could get in a drink or two and headed toward his favorite tavern. "Crazy Americans," he thought.

Sun squatted behind the bush and patted his gun. Perhaps this was his chance. But how would he make his getaway? His iPhone was beeping and he put down his binoculars to answer.

A text message informed him that a press conference had been scheduled for the next morning at 10. He wondered how in God's name they could they have more information than him. He began to doubt his ability to follow through on this assignment. He'd be better off doing the desk research where he started. Sun talked it over with himself and then made a mental note to suggest exactly that to his supervisor when he returned to headquarters. Brains, not field technique was his forte. On second thought, he jumped up and made a beeline for the parking lot to catch a ride back with his guide. Tomorrow would be a better day. In a crowd, he could hide, and no one would notice.

***

In the field house, the women hunched around the small table in the conference room where Hiram briefed them just three days before. Dressed for the beach, instead of an archaeological dig, their outfits made a definite contrast to the dark pants and short sleeve shirts of the men in the room. They placed their red hats in a row, on the table in front of them. Sallie put her arm on the table and propped her head on her hand. The MAMs, like fish out of water, waited patiently for the latest news.

"The prime minister insists that YOU make the announcement."

The MAMs exchanged looks. Emily's eyes opened wide. Ursula and Katharine smiled. Jane gave Sallie a thumbs up sign and patted Priscilla on the back. Only Molly looked wary.

"I will introduce Dr. Simons. She will introduce Dr. Goodtree. Dr. Goodtree will describe the pot and the scrolls. Then, one of you reads the first three scrolls." Hiram's head searched over the group. "Who will it be?"

Jane felt Parks hand on her shoulder, gave it a pat and then removed it with a quick jerk. "I nominate Emily," she offered.

"Me? I'm the youngest one here." Emily's pixie face filled with trepidation.

Sallie aimed to make sure it happened. "Emily is just perfect! A young woman like Thecilla, and she is a wonderful public speaker."

"Will you agree?" Hiram now asked.

Emily looked around the room and felt her heart beating too fast. She stopped and waited on herself to speak. An opportunity. Fear bubbled up, but she felt courage, too. Her college had trained her well for public speaking. "Yes!" she announced. "I'll do it."

The MAMs applauded.

Jane asked, "Can we go back to our hotel now?

Hiram shook his head quickly. "No, no. First we practice."

"Where is this gig going to be?" Jane wondered out loud.

"In the amphitheater," Hiram explained. "We go there now, then you can go to your room."

"The translation." Ursula interrupted. "Have they translated more of the scrolls? Can I read them?"

"Don't worry about that now," Hiram closed her off. "Tomorrow will be soon enough." Hiram looked at his instructions. Tomorrow he would figure out how to put her off again. How could he explain the secrecy that was beginning to shroud the scrolls? How could he tell her that the Vatican had ordered silence? How could he tell her that

136

the words must be protected? How could he explain what he didn't understand himself?

***

Soon the group reassembled at the Ephesus amphitheater. The entryways had been sealed off from the tourists for an hour to give time for rehearsal. The concrete steps rose up to the skyline. On the stage below, the workers placed chairs, and a sound man set up a microphone.

Hiram seated the MAMs in the middle of the huge arena, about midway between the stage and the highest seats. "Perfect acoustics," he told them. "They say you hear pin drop. Maybe. But we know you hear speakers. So, we have microphone. Media insists."

Parks chatted with the guards at the entrances and then sauntered up to the seated MAMs, dropping down next to Jane at the end of the row.

"How have you been?" he asked her.

"OK," she said noncommittally and focused on the deliberations on stage.

Then she turned to Parks. "I have been meaning to ask you something,"

Parks took a deep breath and hoped for the best. An invitation to her room? A quest into his feelings which he had been hoping to unload anyway?

"Brutus," Jane said. "You told me you'd tell me about Brutus. What did he do to Julius Caesar and why?"

Parks didn't skip a beat. Years of training and work in the field paid off. His stone face showed no emotion. Jane would have no idea of the bashing she had just delivered to his ego. He turned toward her to answer her question.

"Brutus had been Julius Caesar's right-hand man. But infighting became commonplace in the late Roman Empire. Brutus and others broke off and formed an opposition group to Caesar. Eventually, Brutus killed Caesar. And that is where we inherited that infamous line, `Et tu, Brute?' "

"What does that mean?" Jane asked.

"'And you, Brutus?' Legend has it that is what Caesar said when Brutus stabbed him."

"Oh," was all that Jane could muster. In her mind she turned over the dreams, the nightmares that had plagued her for so long, wondering what it all meant. Whom was she betraying? Or whom was she about to betray? And how would her subconscious know something about the Roman Empire that she herself had never learned?

137

"So, what was that like? Cheney shooting Bush on a hunting expedition in Texas?"

"Very funny. I thought you told me you were a Republican," Parks laughed. "That was an accident. No, maybe more like if Cheney defected to the Democrats and then beat George W in a general election."

"There's a lot of discussion about what caused the downfall of the Roman Empire. Certainly the infighting was part of it. A lot of people wonder if there is a parallel to the modern era."

Parks stopped the explanation. He felt his frustration mounting and hid his emotions from the woman beside him who had stolen his heart.

Jane quietly mulled it all over in her mind. Resting her chin on her fist she looked down at the circus unfolding below and held the questions in her thoughts. No simple answers today.

Down below, the players for the press conference were trying their turn at the mike. Hiram, Sophie and Ursula tried out the acoustics, then the microphone. Now Emily was coming up. Hiram handed her a document, and Emily began to read.

Katharine looked at Molly with distress. "They changed the name – they didn't refer to her as Thecilla! And they changed Thecla's name. They took it out! What's going on?"

Sallie put her forefinger to her lips in her teacher's pose. "SHHHHH" she whispered. "The show must go on, don't distract Emily."

21. The Press Conference

September 18, 2006

The ancient ruins gleamed in the sunshine against a picture-perfect blue sky filled with puffy white clouds. Molly snapped pictures, walking with the MAMs, making their way into the amphitheater at 9:30 a.m.

"Stop there! Ursula, just you, with the seats in the background," Molly raised her hand up flat toward Ursula. "I"m sending this one to *The New York Times*!"

Ursula laughed, but posed for the picture.

Molly was on a roll. "OK, now I want a group shot for Oprah's web site. Just a minute... Balaban! Could you take this one?"

The MAMs arranged themselves in the familiar pose now showing off their Sunday best. Priscilla, Emily and Sallie took the front, Molly, Jane, Katharine and Ursula were in the back. Priscilla's short-sleeved black dress showed off her slender, but shapely legs that ended in her black high-spiked open heels. Katharine and Ursula had chosen summer suits, Katharine's a pale olive color and Ursula's a light blue. Jane wore khakis and a nice short-sleeved white shirt. Molly modeled a long, gold African-style dress with brilliant blue flowers and sandals. Sallie beamed in her light green silky outfit with short sleeves and capri pants.

"Ah, the beautiful ladies!" Balaban laughed. "Say CHEEZ!"

He snapped the picture. "One more! Say BIG FIND!"

Behind them the members of the press streamed into the amphitheater. One enterprising young photographer came up beside Balaban and snapped a picture of her own. Pulling out her journalist notebook, she asked Balaban, "*İngilizce*?"[xxvi]

"Tell them your names, ladies. You are stars today."

"They are from America," he explained to the journalist.

Hiram sauntered over to the photo op. "Emily and Ursula, come with me. Others, right there, front row. V.I.P. Seats. See gold cord?"

Katharine gave Ursula a hug and then a pat on her back. "Go get 'em Urs! Enjoy!"

Ursula beamed back a wide smile. She practically danced down to the stage, following Hiram.

Sallie hugged Emily and sent her off with encouragement. "Shake a leg! We're proud of you."

Emily shook off the last of her fear and walked confidently down behind Ursula. She could do this. Ever since she was a little girl, her father had depended on her for the morning scripture reading in his services. She wished they had given her the copy for practice, but she remembered the gist of the scrolls. Geez, that was about all she could think of the last two days, along with her growing hunger for Josh and resolve to marry him in the coming year. Strangely, she identified with Thecilla. Although separated by 20 centuries, they were both young women of faith, in love with men connected to the structures of government and empire. They were both on journeys, doing new things. They were both deeply interested in the exiled John on Patmos and what he had to say to the Roman authorities. Emily could not shake a growing realization that there were parallels here, too, between the situation that John and Thecilla shared; the Roman Emperor's disdain for a loving and nonviolent Jesus, and the U.S.A.'s growing infatuation with war and violent strategies and departure from a Savior who taught suffering love.

In the VIP Section, the other MAMs sat watching the stage fill with dignitaries. The machine guns at either side bothered Sallie, who kept asking Katharine question after question about the entourage entering the amphitheater. Katharine couldn't answer all her questions, but easily identified the Turkish Prime Minister and the robes of the cardinal, signaling the Vatican's representative. Hiram rose and shook hands with several men in suits and then showed them to their seats. Priscilla and Jane watched quietly, caught up in their own thoughts.

***

Outside the amphitheater, the predator stalked. He watched the MAMs, although they couldn't see him. Neither could Parks, who had stationed himself by the main entrance to the theater, waiting for Sun to make an appearance.

Parks was ready, but wasn't expecting Sun to grow blonde hair and add a cowboy hat to his repertoire overnight. Parks' gaze focused on Jane. More beautiful than ever, he thought. Last night did not materialize as hoped. For some reason, Jane had turned cold on him. He reviewed his words and actions and couldn't figure out where he went wrong.

Sometimes, it doesn't have anything to do with you, his Dad had always told him. Women. They are caught up in their own game. Don't think it's about you. It's always all about them. Once you play by their rules, you sail smoothly. Parks had found that one of the most helpful pieces of wisdom his father ever offered. Tonight, he thought, I'll get her to open up. I'll listen to her heart.

Right now Jane was laughing, and Park was winking at her. He barely noticed the small man in the cowboy hat slip by him and start the journey up to the nosebleed section in the steeply terraced stone seats. Jane caught the wink and passed it back. Today is going to be a good day, Parks thought.

Meanwhile, Katharine laughed at Sallie's banter about the suits on stage and had forgotten about Sun. She also didn't see the small man slip by and head for the top. But Sun saw Katharine and noted with satisfaction that her back was open to his view. He sat directly behind her, about 50 rows up, conveniently a few rows behind some photographers and a few sightseers that had climbed up before him, and perched slightly to his right. That gave him a direct view and a clear shot. Patting his gun he smiled. Finally, he was going to do his job right.

He pulled out a long spiral pad and placed his journalist identification tag outside his jacket. The perfect cover. Headquarters wanted a report and Sun would deliver.

Settling into his seat, Sun focused on Priscilla from behind enjoying the view. Mighty pretty in that small black dress, he thought. Crossed legs, shapely legs. My goodness, how tall were those heels? Five-inch spikes. Luck be my lady tonight! He smacked his lips and began to decide whether or not he could trust Priscilla to help him on his mission. He knew she was with him. He knew she disagreed with Katharine. But would she keep his cover? Could he take the risk to involve her?

***

Hiram stood at the stroke of 10 and began. He welcomed the audience, speaking first in Turkish and then English. They had decided to go with two languages, but translators were helping the other journalists. Most knew English.

Parks took a seat by the entrance after making sure his two assistants were planted at the exits. A tall man in a monk's robe walked in front of him, blocking his view. Parks stood for a moment, irritated with the latecomer. A Franciscan? Probably just a brother on a spiritual quest to Ephesus.

If Parks had asked, Brother Gabriel would have agreed with him. A spiritual quest to Ephesus was exactly his mission. But beyond that, Gabriel really couldn't articulate the strange prompting the night before that led him to book passage to Kusadasi in the morning. Leaving the International Conference of Mystics on Patmos midstream? A very unexpected change of plans. His community in New

York City had begrudgingly allowed him to make this trip and expected a full report of ALL the sessions. The whole community must reap the benefits of his expensive visit, they insisted. The Abott would never have approved this trip to Kusadasi, much less the use of scarce funds given to expand the monastery library.

Brother Gabriel had no idea a press conference was under way, until he saw a small sign outside the amphitheater. Yet he knew his inner voice rarely led him astray. He wished his superior could hear that voice, too. Oh well. Once inside the amphitheater, Gabriel knew beyond a shadow of a doubt that God had called him there.

***

Moses Sun looked down on the amphitheater filling with tourists and occasional journalists. Most journalists gathered in a special section roped off by the stage, but he saw professional cameras scattered around the stone ledges, where the people sat throughout the ancient theater. Mentally he rehearsed how he would take aim if the time was right. A water jug in his backpack would get its first real life experience, providing a foil for his gun. He'd like to patent this ingenious cover some day, but for now if it got the job done, he would be mighty happy. He settled back, alert and ready. The press conference had begun.

***

Cameras flashed and reporters scribbled away. TV cameramen caught the drama from several locations. The MAMs directed their full attention to the stage, where Hiram stood to begin. He introduced Dr. Sophie Simons, speaking warmly and highly of the Austrian archaeologist who had led excavations in the Cave of St. Paul for several years now, directing the delicate uncovering of centuries of frescoes. Sophie blushed while he read her accomplishments. The small crowd clapped politely when he finished and Sophie approached the microphone.

She gave a brief history of her excavation in the Cave of St. Paul and pointed to the hillside, south of the amphitheater. "If you can see that large red flag, that is where the Grotto of St. Paul sits on the side of BûlBûl Dag. For the last 10 years, we have been digging in that cave and uncovering layers of frescoes on the cave walls. We think that the Apostle Paul may have used the cave during his sojourn in Ephesus. The earliest fresco in the cave may date back to the first or second century." Sophie paused, and the Turkish interpreter quickly repeated her introduction in the native tongue. After a few more details of the Austrians' work at the Grotto, she introduced Ursula.

Ursula's heart fluttered. Strangely, she felt light emanating from deep within when she stood to address the crowd. She briefed the press on her credentials and launched into a technical description of the archaeological techniques used at the grotto. Then she began to build expectations with the practiced flair of a gifted orator, explaining the initial find of the sand springing from the hole in the wall, the discovery of the chamber, the sand bucket brigade, the large pot tucked in the corner. Building to a peak, she explained the examination of the pot in the field office and drama of the moment they removed the plug, and pulled out eight separate scrolls.

Hiram watched her from behind with growing trepidation. Ursula had been given a script, but she gave her own speech. He had impressed upon her the gravity of the situation. Seven scrolls. He told her to say seven. What could he do now? He saw some anger in the eyes of the officials beside him. Better wait until she leaves the lectern to correct the number, he thought. American women will argue in public, don't want to risk her telling the truth against me. He sat tight and hoped she would finish soon. Thankfully, she was using the code name for Thecla, at least she followed some orders.

Ursula concluded her story to thunderous applause before introducing Emily for the reading of the scrolls. Hiram stood to make the correction.

***

The applause gave Sun just the opening he needed. Pulling the jug from his backpack, he lifted it to his lips, slipped the gun through the jug and took aim. He could see Katharine's pale green shirt and zeroed in on her neck. Then he stopped, and pulled out his pen and journalist notebook. He must be ready to write after the shot.

Taking aim again, he took in the stage and surveyed the amphitheater. Emily stood near the tight-lipped archaeologist. Maybe he'd shoot him, too, while he was at it. Some people needed to be taught a lesson. The nerve of him to lie about Priscilla, and not even tell him about this press conference.

Sun prayed to his God of *End Times* and thanked Jesus once more for saving him from the destruction to come. He offered up himself in prayer as God's vigilante, writing wrongs, ridding the world of false teachings. Yes, he thought, two quick shots and then his gun will go back under his shirt, his water jug back in his back pack and he would transform once more into a journalist, frantically writing a breaking story for the international press. Yes.

Sun took a deep breath, aimed and fired. Shot one hit its mark on Katharine's neck, he thought. Without time to spare he fired again toward that stupid archaeologist on the platform. Then he slipped his gun into his shirt and held the water jug to his lips, faking a drink. He looked over the jug, as if surprised by the bedlam that ensued below. A smirk on his face belied his innocence.

***

Parks sprinted to Katharine's side in an instant and summoned a medic on his cell phone.

The *Gendarme* raised their machine guns, pointing them toward people seated in the amphitheater. Down on the stage, the shot intended for Hiram missed its mark.

Hiram approached the microphone. "This press conference is concluded until further notice. Please vacate the amphitheater in an orderly fashion."

Fortunately there were additional troops outside. He notified the commander by cell phone to search parcels of those vacating the premises, while others kept a close look on the remaining people to avoid further violence. The Prime Minister's bodyguards were busy on the job. They were trained to deal with the possible assassin situation.

***

Emily heard one shot and then another and felt a thud on her chest. The thud knocked her backward, and she fell. Crawling behind the men in suits, she approached the side of the stage. Waiting for her was a familiar man in a brown robe.

"Brother Gabriel? What are you doing here?"

"I came to see you! I can help," he said. "Hide under my robe. I'll get you out of here."

Brother Gabriel steered Emily under his robe to the exit. The soldiers had not yet taken their posts and in the confusion of the moment, no one noticed them slipping away to the parking lot where Gabriel's rented scooter provided them transport to the dock.

Emily felt her chest and saw some red spots forming through her pink blouse. "I'm bleeding!" She unbuttoned her top two buttons, fearful of what she might find. She fingered the necklace that Josh had given her for her birthday. "Lambkin" he had always called her. She felt a dent in the small metal lamb. She saw the blood oozing where it had lodged into her skin.

Emily gasped. The small metal necklace deflected the bullet. Did it save her life?

144

Brother Gabriel looked at the blood on her shirt. "Here, let me see what you have there." He took a package of tissues out of his pocket and dabbed at Emily's wound, noting that for some reason the skin had been broken, but very little bleeding was taking place. "Why don't you hold this tissue on here, until I can get you somewhere to clean that up?"

"I'm OK," she told the monk. But she pressed the tissue against the cut and told Gabriel, "Get me out of here." She did not want to wait around and find out if someone was trying to kill her. "Take me away from here as fast as you can!"

"I think we should go to the police, first. You were hit."

"I'm OK. They didn't protect me before. I want to get away from here. I'm OK."

"Do you want to go to Patmos? I'm attending a conference of mystics there. God called me here today, for you, I think. Are you willing to sail the Aegean with a wild monk from New York?" Gabriel was chuckling. "You must think I'm crazy! But it's absolutely true. God sent me to rescue you."

Emily took comfort from his chubby warmth while she hung on to him for her life. The moped sped across the road leading away from the Ephesus ruins. Under normal situations, this would be totally out of the question, but she was in a foreign country and the brown robe somehow felt secure to her, more secure than returning to the open amphitheater where she was an easy target for... Who? She had no idea who might want to kill her, and she wasn't about to stick around and find out. For Brother Gabe to arrive when she needed him most was nothing short of a miracle. She could trust the good monk with her life.

"I'll go!" Emily screamed the words into his ear above the roaring motor and then leaned into his back and buried her face in his robe.

***

In the amphitheater, Sun busily scribbled notes. The audience began to file out. He interviewed those around him, asking if they had seen the gunman. The *Gendarme* stood at the end of each row, dismissing the guests like ushers at a wedding, but their machine guns reminded of possible violence, while the people filed down the narrow aisle to the exit below.

Unabashed, Sun began to interview the soldier when his turn came.

"What happened, sir? Have you found the gunman? Was anyone hurt?" Sun fired off the questions of an overeager journalist, holding his narrow spiral pad up, with his pen posed to capture the answers.

145

The soldier remained mute, shaking his head from side to side. The machine gun nudged Sun's shoulder, and Sun felt the gun slip down toward his pants, lodging between his tucked in shirt and the belt of his pants.

Sun smiled, quietly delighted there were no words to record. He shifted his notebook down, successfully hiding the bulge now evident on his body.

Making his way out of the amphitheater, he used the same technique with the security guards searching the backpacks and purses of exiting people at the exit, asking questions until he was blue in the face. They took a quick look in his backpack, felt around the water jug and sent him on.

Sun held his breath when he saw Parks standing by the ambulance where medics worked on Katharine. But Parks chatted into his cell phone and didn't seem to notice the small blond-haired cowboy walking into the lot and asking his personal guide to take him back to the hotel. Sun's face registered satisfaction at last.

Once safely inside the car, he shuffled his gun back into the holster against his chest and thanked his lucky stars for safe escape. Headquarters didn't need to know the details, he decided. They'd be happy to have Katharine out of commission. He didn't need the praise for his good deed. Sometimes, it was better to do good deeds anonymously. Random acts of kindness. He laughed. He was ready to treat himself to a delicious steak dinner on the company dime.

***

The Archaeological Expedition in Search of Thecla had come to a screeching halt. A sunny day of celebratory disclosure had turned into a nightmare of violence. The MAMs in the stadium circled. Ursula ran off the stage to join the group. They followed the stretcher carrying Katharine out to the ambulance, but were ushered into the field office at Parks' request by the soldiers. Returning to the small conference room where they had begun just four days earlier, they sat down and tried to absorb the reality of their situation. A soldier stood guard at the door.

Molly looked out the windows and shivered at the sight of machine guns posed by both of the portals. Her husband had been right. She should have stayed home.

Sallie looked around the scared group and made a disturbing discovery.

"Emily!" she called out. "Where is Emily?"

The MAMs looked at each other and then behind and beyond one another like mothers looking for a lost child in a room where one obviously didn't exist, but yet the repetitive looking motions continued.

146

"I'll call Parks," Jane decided. Dialing his phone number, Parks answered immediately and told Jane he'd check it out, and assured her, telling her not to worry, Emily would be fine.

Jane informed the MAMs. "Dan's on it. He said Emily's OK. He's going to bring her to us."

"Is Katharine OK?" Ursula began stuttering "K-K-K-K-Katharine? Assssk if, if, if, if Katharine..."

Jane cut Ursula off, "Gotcha."

Jane turned back to her phone. "Dan, how is Katharine? Shouldn't we be with her? Can at least one of us go to the hospital with her?"

Ursula sat fidgeting. She hadn't stuttered since grade school. Suddenly she realized she'd left her Prozac at home. She pulled on Jane's shirt and told her, "Tell him I, I, I w-w-want to go! I want to go to the hospital." There, she had spit it out, and Jane nodded, while continuing to listen to Parks on the phone.

Jane clicked off her phone and put her arm around Ursula, "They are working to stabilize Katharine before they transport her. She's lost a lot of blood. The bullet seems to be lodged on her shoulder blade. They plan to fly her to Istanbul. Parks will accompany her. They notified her husband. He's coming. They will take her to the hospital here, until the helicopter arrives. Surgery better in Istanbul. Parks said that you can stay with her in the Kusadasi hospital, until the helicopter comes. He'll pick you up in a moment."

"What about Emily?" Sallie asked. "Did you see her on the stage, Ursula? What happened?"

Ursula went numb. She couldn't speak. She remembered Emily standing beside Hiram. Then the shot was fired. Or were there two shots? She only remembered seeing Katharine fall and running down to join the MAMs. The conference blurred in her memory.

"Emily was ready to speak. Remember?" Priscilla tried to piece the events together. "Hiram was talking. He had just said that there were seven scrolls, not eight. Why did he say that, anyway? There were eight scrolls. Why would he say seven?"

Sallie shook her head. "Something's rotten in the state of Denmark! It's very scary. Something is very wrong here. Who would be trying to shoot Katharine? What is going on? Why did they change Thecla's name? I think we should go home."

Jane decided to share what she knew. "Parks was tailing Moses Sun. Katharine's husband hired him. Sun posted threats on Katharine's web site. Katharine's been freaked. But Dan swears Sun wasn't in the audience. Fortunately, the various TV and film crews had video cameras focused on almost every space in that place. The Turkish authorities have confiscated the equipment and are reviewing it now."

"It could be terrorists," Molly's voice shook. "They've attacked tourists before just south of here. Americans are targets, you know."

Jane brought a voice of reason and calm to the group. "We just don't know, and it's not going to help worrying about it. Why don't you start praying for Katharine, Ursula? She needs your prayers, she needs all of our prayers right now."

"But Emily. Where is Emily? Abigail will never forgive me if something happened to Emily!" Sallie was beyond calm. Jane may have a cool head in crisis, but Sallie knew she didn't, and she wasn't about to pretend for Jane.

"Pray, Sallie, that's all we can do right now." Jane folded her hands and closed her eyes just as the door to the field office burst open, and Dan Parks came through.

When he rushed into the room, Jane stood and moved toward him. Parks enfolded her with his muscular arms, pulling her against his firm chest. Jane felt the warmth of his strong torso circling her with the support she needed. On the outside, she might appear calm, but inside she was shaking like a leaf.

"OK, OK. We don't have time for this," Sallie interrupted. "Where is Emily?"

Parks looked at her with a blank expression, which turned to puzzlement.

In that instant, Jane realized Parks was scared, like the rest of them. Just a moment of hesitation, but the truth was written all over his face, and strangely, it attracted her to him. A vulnerability poked out of his take-charge personality. On the outside, they were rocks. On the inside, they were both completely human.

"Yes. I'm sure she's OK. I'll have them bring her to you immediately." Parks' moment of hesitation was gone. "Ursula, come with me."

"What about the rest of us?" Jane asked.

"For now, we'd like you to sit tight. Eventually, you'll be able to go back to your hotel." Parks cut the conversation short. Taking Ursula by the arm, he ushered her out of the room.

The MAMs sat and prayed while the morning slipped away. The afternoon brought more fretting, while they picked at the food delivered by a guard. The joy of the Archaeological Expedition in Search of Thecla had dissolved in the dust of the ancient ruins. Violence had struck, and the women felt the wounds deep in their souls.

***

At the dock, Brother Gabriel quickly negotiated passage to Patmos on a ship ready to leave the harbor. Emily watched quietly, still in shock from the events of the morning. There was a surreal quality to her experience. For a moment, she hesitated and thought she should go back to Ephesus. Wouldn't she be safer there? But then, she looked again at Brother Gabriel. His blues eyes were dancing in the sunlight, a smile stretched from one side of his face to the other where little dimples punctuated the jolly expression, all encircled by his bushy brown beard. In her heart she knew he could be trusted. Ever since she was a little girl, she had been able to read people. Her father recognized her ability early and would often ask for help. Her mother got upset with her father for trusting Emily's intuition. Emily was never sure if it was because it scared her or because she was jealous. And her Dad loved Brother Gabe.

Gabriel put his arm around Emily and helped her onto the ship. After shaking hands with the captain, they were ushered to a small suite of rooms. "It's a fast boat," he explained. "Four hours. Make yourself at home."

Emily looked at the comfortable compartment and then turned to Gabriel with a question in her face. "All of this? How did you do it?"

The small apartment had two doors opening to small beds, a sofa and television and a little kitchen on the side, with another door to the bathroom, and a large porthole now framing the harbor.

"When God calls, He delivers. What can I say?" Gabriel closed the door and sat down on a chair. "Maybe you should try to take a nap. You've had quite a day."

"I think I need some water."

"Right."

Gabriel opened the small refrigerator and removed a bottle of water and handed it to Emily, whose legs began to shake.

Gabriel picked her up and carried her into the small bedroom and placed her on the bed. For the first time, he really looked at her, noticing bright red blood soaking through the blouse on her chest. "Emily, you're bleeding!"

"I'm OK." Emily patted her chest, fingered her necklace and looked down. Then she felt blood on her fingers. She jumped up to look in a mirror. "Just a little blood, I'm OK, really." She took some tissues from a box by a little sink and wiped at the blood. She soaked one tissue, then dabbed the rest of the blood off the small wound, which still oozed fresh blood.

"Here, put some antibiotic cream on that." Gabriel had grabbed a first aid kit and already had the tube open. He squeezed a little onto Emily's forefinger, and she spread it on the wound. "And now, a Band-Aid." He peeled open the bandage and handed it to Emily, watching while she pulled off the flaps and pressed it on her chest.

"OK. Good as new. Better rest, princess. You may be in shock. Here." He handed her a velour throw from the chair beside her bed and instructed further, "Cover up and rest."

149

Emily took a few deep breaths and watched Gabriel leave the room and take a seat by the television. But instead of turning it on, he pulled a small book out of his pocket and began to read. On the cover Emily could make out the words, "Franciscan Book of Prayers." She relaxed and soon was fast asleep.

***

When Ursula and Parks reached the ambulance, the driver yelled out directions. "Get in. Quick, please." Ursula and Parks climbed up and squeezed into the small vehicle already holding a medic and a nurse.

"Plenty of room," Parks remarked and then turned to Ursula, "I think you'll have to sit on my lap."

Katharine smiled for the first time and managed a whisper, "Ursula!"

Instead of taking Parks' lap, she climbed over and knelt beside her friend. Katharine's pale face scared Ursula. Her shoulder was bandaged, but blood was seeping through.

"Oh baby, oh baby, I'm so sorry," Ursula cried and kissed Katharine and then placed her hand over Katharine's.

"I'll be OK," Katharine whispered and after taking several more shallow breaths, she continued, "I'm all right."

"Yes, you are. Yes, you are. You're going to be fine. Don't worry. Relax. You're in good hands. John is on the way. Rest, baby, rest."

Katharine didn't have the energy to explain. She wanted to tell Ursula she was ready to meet her Maker, but all she could manage were the more important words, "Tell John I have always loved him." And then Katharine slipped into unconsciousness.

Ursula continued to murmur in Katharine's ear for the 10-minute trip to the Kusadasi hospital and for the next hour while they waited for the helicopter from the hospital in Istanbul. They poured pint after pint of blood into Katharine, replacing what continued to drain from her shoulder now. When Parks came to report the helicopter had arrived, Ursula continued talking and encouraging. She babbled on with positive thoughts and affirmations, hoping to fill Katharine's unconscious head with healing thoughts.

"Your body will make it through that surgery with flying colors, dear." Ursula wiped the tears off her face and kept talking.

When they came to wheel Katharine out of the room, Ursula kissed her for the last time and told her, "You go, girl!"

Ursula collapsed into Parks' arms when he introduced her to a driver that would take her back to the hotel. "Can you go with me?" she asked him.

"I promised John I wouldn't leave her side until he arrives. He's paying me and she needs me. Be strong, Ursula. I know you're a strong woman."

Ursula shook her hair out, massaged her scalp with her fingers and untangled her curls. She dabbed at her cheeks with a tissue from the bed stand. Then she pushed her shoulders back.

"You're right. You're right. I can do this. Thank you for everything."

Ursula turned toward the driver. "Can we go now?"

Joe would be arriving soon. She had done all she could for Katharine and believed in her heart that Katharine would be fine. Parks would protect her, the doctors would mend her, and she would recover. She had to.

22. Thecla Thrown to the Beasts

September 19, 48 A.D.

And so Trifina and Thecla spent a long day together. Trifina gave Falconilla's garments to Thecla, and the old woman began to laugh again, with her new daughter. She had the servants prepare a feast and brought in singers and dancers, and they visited late into the night.

But in the morning, Alexander came to the house of Trifina saying: "The governor and the people are waiting. Bring the criminal forth!"

Trifina ran at him, hitting him with a stick from the fire. Alexander left, unwilling to confront the woman, knowing her to be of royalty. Trifina cried out loud at her plight. "Now my house fills with trouble again. Is there no relief? I lost my daughter, and now who will help me? How can I save Thecla?"

But Thecla calmed the woman and encouraged her to pray. "I'll be all right. I am with God, whatever happens."

So Trifina knelt with Thecla and prayed again and again. "Oh Lord God, help Thecla, your good and faithful servant. Oh Lord, help Thecla."

But then the governor sent one of his own officers to take Thecla. Trifina, taking courage from their prayers and the strength of Thecla, took her by the hand saying, "I went with Falconilla to her grave, and now I must go with Thecla to the beasts."

Thecla prayed while they walked, "Oh God, my confidence and refuge, reward Trifina for her compassion to me."

When they arrived at the amphitheater, they were greeted with great noise. The beasts roared, and the people cried out, "Bring in the criminal!"

Trifina yelled back, "Let the whole city suffer for such crimes and send them, O governor, to the same punishment. O unjust judgment! O cruel sight!"

But they pulled Thecla away from Trifina, stripping her naked, placing a girdle about her, and threw her into the arena. Then they opened the gate and let the bears and lions loose to run in upon her.

The crowd cheered, ready for Thecla's destruction, but the most fierce of all the animals, a she-lion, ran to Thecla, and fell down at her feet. Upon which, the women in the crowd began to cheer for Thecla.

152

And then a she-bear ran toward her, as if to attack, but the she-lion met the bear and tore it to pieces. Again the women in the crowd cheered while the men remained quiet, their jaws dropping in surprise.

Then a he-bear ran fiercely towards her, but again the she-lion intervened and tore the he-bear to pieces. The women were on their feet yelling, "Go Thecla! Thecla! Thecla!"

Alexander let his most ferocious he-lion into the arena. The he-lion had devoured many men. And the he-lion ran toward Thecla, but again the she-lion met the he-lion and they fought each other, until they both were dead.

And the women yelled, "Take her out. Let her go. Thecla! Thecla! Thecla!" And they were concerned that the she-lion no longer could protect her. But Alexander and the governor's men continued to let beasts into the arena.

Yet Thecla stood in the middle of the arena, unafraid, with her hands stretched towards heaven, praying. A hush settled over the entire amphitheater. The animals seemed content. The women sat on the edge of their seats, wondering what would happen to Thecla now.

23. The MAMs Regroup

September 18, 2006

That night, the MAMs gathered in Ursula's room to regroup. The soldiers guarded their door. Parks had reported in from Istanbul that the surgeons were busy with Katharine and no word yet on Emily. Katharine's husband called from Amsterdam and wanted the MAMs to know he'd be at Katharine's side in three hours.

Ursula spoke with a new inner confidence. "Our mission is not over. We are going to complete our expedition. We are going to share Thecla's story with the world."

"How are we going to do that?" Sallie complained. "There are men with machine guns outside our door. They won't let us back at the dig. They shut down the field office and the Ephesus site. They have even closed our cave! And we don't have the story to tell, they took it away from us."

Jane glared at Sallie. The stream of negatives registered, all true. But Jane focused on the possibilities. Zig Ziglar and many other positive thinkers taught her well for many years, and she knew that dwelling on the gloom would get them nowhere.

"When the going gets tough, the tough get going. Buck up, Baby! I'm putting my hat in Ursula's ring." Jane smirked at Sallie.

For once, Sallie held her tongue. She knew Jane was right.

The telephone rang. Ursula jumped, and then headed over to the phone. The MAMs heard her whisper into the phone, "I'll be right there." She skipped toward the door. "Joe has arrived!" She announced before opening the door.

"Don't forget we have a machine gun out there," Jane reminded.

"Right," Ursula said and slowed down. Carefully, she opened the door and told the soldiers, "I have a friend in the lobby."

One motioned her out of the room, "Who?"

"My friend from California," she explained.

"Hollywood?" the soldier asked.

"Not a movie star, but yes, California. Hollywood is in California."

The soldier nodded and smiled, proud of his knowledge.

Ursula felt her heart racing toward the reunion. Twenty five years, yet the flame danced, burned strong. The soldier led her to the lobby with a slow marching gait, glancing from side to side, his gun held firmly across his chest. She bounced back and forth behind him like a downhill skier hoping to catch a glimpse of a dark-haired man in the lobby, a man from her past, the man of her dreams, the only man she had ever loved.

In the lobby, two soldiers were frisking a man. Although the man's back was facing her, even from a distance she would recognize that frame anywhere. Starting to run, she bumped into the soldier in front of her. His hard body stopped her cold. The gun held her back. Ursula gasped.

The soldiers finished their job. Joe turned around. His curly black hair, now graying at the temples, framed a face showing wear. He still wore his clothes well, khakis with fewer wrinkles than his face and a light blue oxford with a button-down collar.   His   eyes scanned the lobby and focused on her.

Ursula leaned to the side, poking her head out from behind the soldier leading her out. A warmth flooded through her body when his face turned into her view. Their eyes locked. An electrical impulse passed from his deep blue eyes into her brown ones. They both felt the connection, standing mesmerized in the moment.

Joe broke the gaze and turned to the officers who had just frisked him.

"May I go now?"

Experience taught him well. He knew that messing with the militia in foreign countries could only bring trouble.

"My friend, Ursula Goodtree," he explained while pointing toward Ursula, still blocked by the soldier.

The soldier in front of Ursula took a cell phone out of his pocket and dialed.

Joe looked back to Ursula and again their eyes were locked.

"Mental massage," Joe had once said, referring to the energy between their eyes. He had claimed it energized and relaxed him when they were young lovers exploring Israel and neighboring lands back in graduate school.

Ursula felt her body awakening. It may be mental massage for Joe, but for her she felt the passion stirring and for the first time in many years she wanted a man. But she could only continue the eye massage and smile. Five minutes they waited, which seemed like an eternity to Ursula. She longed to greet Joe with more than her eyes.

The soldier called his Captain, who eventually connected with Parks, who granted permission for these old friends to cross the gap of the few feet in the lobby and the many years between them to find each other once again. They moved into each other's arms, embracing in a quiet moment of union. Joe held on to Ursula for comfort from the grief of his life. Ursula held on to Joe in reunion with her only love. They were two lonely people brought together once again by discovery and hope.

A few minutes later, Ursula broke the hug and led Joe to the room where the MAMs were deliberating. "Let me introduce you to the MAMs."

***

The next morning, with Emily still missing, hysteria reigned in the MAMs' room. Sallie popped her pills for high blood pressure after spending the night on the phone with Emily's grandmother, parents and finally Josh. Every time she fell sleep, Josh woke her up with frantic calls. Sallie had begged him to stay home, but finally accepted the depth of his young love. By morning, he had purchased a $2,000 plane ticket and called once more from the Chicago airport.

"Call me when you reach Istanbul," she told him this time.

The MAMs sipped their coffee in the lobby waiting for a phone call, for news of any kind. Parks called to say Katharine weathered the surgery well. His resonant voice boomed into the hotel lobby over Jane's cell phone speakers. "Yes, her clavicle stopped the bullet without shattering. The metal in her bra strap probably saved her life, slowing down the bullet."

"Good thing she didn't burn her bra!" Sallie chuckled.

"I'm glad you haven't lost your sense of humor," Parks voice boomed out.

"What about Emily?" Sallie demanded. "Where is Emily?"

"My men are on it. They have been reviewing the footage shot during the event. Quite a lot of information. Eventually, we will know exactly who shot Katharine."

"Emily," Sallie asserted. "We want to know about Emily. Her family is going crazy. I've been up all night taking their calls. Her boyfriend is on the way. Are they holding her hostage?"

"We're working on it. She crawled off the stage and then," Parks hesitated. He wasn't sure if he should explain the rest. The tape wasn't conclusive, but he continued. "There was a man with a brown robe who approached the stage and talked to Emily. The man then walked out an exit before the guards began screening. We didn't actually see Emily on the film, but we think she may have left with him."

"A man in a brown robe? What does that mean?" Sallie's impatience and fear brought a bite to her voice.

"We aren't sure, ma'am. I've got my men working on it. We'll have an answer for you soon."

Ursula interrupted, "Dan, Joe has arrived. He'd like to start translating the scrolls. Can we go to the field house this morning?"

Parks hesitated again. He searched for words to explain to the MAMs the strange developments that didn't make sense, even to him.

"The Turkish government has decided to keep close tabs on the scrolls, er, I mean the photos of the scrolls. At this time, they are not permitting translation or viewing by others. And one more thing, the original scrolls disappeared from the field house over night. We believe they were stolen, but maybe an inside job. No, you may not go to the field house this morning. I'm sorry."

Molly shivered.

"But Joe came to translate the scrolls! He came all the way from California." Ursula cried into the phone. "This is our dig. Why are they taking it away from us?"

"I'm sorry, Ursula. I'm very sorry. The Turkish government calls the shots. They don't like the developments in this situation. The shooting, the theft. They've taken over. Once we find Emily, I'd like all of you to go home. Your safety may be in jeopardy. Katharine will be able to travel in two days."

Sallie interrupted. "Josh is on his way."

"Who is Josh?" Parks asked.

"Emily's boyfriend."

"Can't you stop him? Tell him not to come."

"It's too late. I tried. I need to stay for him." Sallie put her hands on her hips. "We can't leave until we find Emily anyway."

"When are you coming back?" Jane asked Parks.

"I'm in Kusadasi now. Is that an invitation?"

Jane hesitated and then spoke decisively, "Yes. Please come and tell me what the hell is going on."

"I'll be over soon, but first there are a few films I need to review. I'm convinced Moses Sun fired the shots, but they haven't been able to locate him in the audience. See you soon, baby."

Jane didn't see Dan Parks smile to himself and raise his eyebrows, when she told him to come. He loved that direct talk. Jane was certainly his kind of woman.

24. Emily on Patmos

September 18, 2006

Emily rubbed her face, forcing her eyes open to see what kept touching her shoulder. The late afternoon light cast shadows across the small room. Brother Gabriel stood by her bed, tapping her arm. "Emily, Emily. We've arrived. Wake up. Let's go."

"Where am I?" She tossed her head back and forth and fluffed her hair with her fingers until she understood. The press conference, the shots, crawling off the stage and Brother Gabriel. Brother Gabriel – that full, thick, brown monk's robe – the peaceful, happy presence shining on his face.

"Are you for real or am I dreaming?"

Gabriel chuckled. "Pinch me and let me know. In the meantime, we must leave the boat. If we hurry, we can make the Taize service."

"Taize? Taize? Where have I heard that word before?"

"Taize is a form of worship, chanting meditations. We practice the prayer of Taize every day at 4 p.m. at our conference. It's quite beautiful. Come, Emily, let's go."

Brother Gabriel offered his hand, and Emily stood, testing her balance, then followed the good monk out of the compartment and onto the deck.

In the distance she saw the beauty of Patmos rising out of the sea. The afternoon sun hung over the white stucco buildings, and peace flooded into her spirit. Coming here with Brother Gabriel was a good thing. She knew it with all of her heart.

A small car came down the hill to the dock to pick them up. "The conference provides a shuttle," Brother Gabriel explained.

Soon they were traveling through Skala, the small port town. Emily looked up at the monastery towering over Patmos. She marveled at the peacefulness of this little island that held a special place in the history of the Christian church. The quaint shops, the white buildings capped with rust-colored shingles, the crosses reaching into the sky. What a view! She looked back down to the sea.

She knew she should call someone, but for the moment she was caught up in the experience of Patmos and eager to go to Taize. If only she could remember, she knew that word.

A few minutes later, the shuttle pulled up in a gravel lot in front of Hotel Romeos.

"A hotel?" Emily asked.

"The conference I'm attending is here. Come with me." Brother Gabriel took Emily's hand as she stepped out of the van and walked toward the hotel entrance. He led her through the lobby into a courtyard framed with red hibiscus. "Here," Gabe motioned for her to sit.

A chapel? Emily looked at the outdoor, circular meeting room, filled with people sitting in two concentric circles. The music was just beginning. On the far side, behind the circle, she saw a line of musicians with cellos, recorders, and guitars. Candles burned brightly in the center of the group, circling a small altar with what seemed to Emily like a thousand points of light.

Gabriel handed her a small booklet. Emily opened the book and saw the words that the singers were beginning.

"*El Senyor es las meva forca, el meucant. Ell m'ha estat la salvacio. En ell confio I no tinc por, en ell confio I no tinc por.*"[xxvii]

Emily relaxed into the hard seat and leaned back to listen. The repetitive lyrics were soothing. The harmonies of the voices, with the haunting counter melodies of the cello and recorders, along with the constant chording of the guitars created such a warm and holy sound. Emily prayed quietly, feeling God's presence with them. Gratitude flooded into her being. And suddenly she remembered.

When she was in high school, the brothers of Taize had come to her father's church in Indiana for a retreat. They were praying for peace and invited others to join. Josh and Emily had been deeply moved by the brothers and agreed that someday they would go to the Taize community in France together. For a while, they had thought about trying to do fundraising and take the church youth group, but then 9-11 hit and international travel was out of the question. She knew that thousands of young people from around the world flocked to Taize every summer for prayer and spiritual transformation. Now the words of the familiar melody came back to her and she silently prayed along. "In the Lord, I'll be ever thankful, In the Lord, I will rejoice. Look to God, do not be afraid. Lift up your voices, the Lord is near, Lift up your voices, the Lord is near."[xxviii]

Emily gave thanks. Her mind flashed through the events of the past week. The incredible cruise, the archaeological dig, the scrolls, the press conference, Brother Gabriel. She thanked God for her life, for the recent experiences, for her safety, for sending this monk to bring her back to Patmos. A conference of mystics! Emily laughed to herself. How amazing.

And then she remembered. She had left without a word. They would be worried. She tapped Gabriel on the shoulder. "I need to make a phone call." She lifted her cell phone in the air. "I don't think this will work here."

"Come with me," Gabriel said. But the phones were out of order at the hotel and instead Gabriel and Emily returned to the chapel for the conclusion of the service. After Taize, they enjoyed a delicious meal of homemade bread and soup in the hotel dining room, followed by an evening lecture by a Buddhist monk on meditation.

"Is this a Christian conference?" Emily asked when they sat down for the lecture.

Brother Gabriel only laughed. "Ah, little one, "Listen to the words, consider your God and tell me. Reserve judgment. Let the mind of Christ be yours."

Emily didn't understand, but she tried to listen with an open mind. The Buddhist monk had such a peaceful spirit. Once again her intuition told her that he was a good man, and that she could learn something from him.

"Consider the lilies," Brother Gabriel said. "Jesus understood."

They went for a short walk through Skala. Children were out playing. Mopeds sped by. They found a bench and sat by the water, watching the sunset over the Aegean Sea. By the time they walked back to Hotel Romeos, the moon was shining. Emily felt calm.

The phone was still dead at the hotel. Gabriel had found her a little room for the night. He didn't tell her that it was his own.

When Brother Gabriel closed the door on Emily after a long day, he smiled. He prayed his own prayer of thanks for being chosen to be God's instrument to care for Emily. He returned to the circular meeting space and fell on his knees in thanksgiving for being used once more. He prayed and praised his God, the God of Jesus Christ, the God of all the mystics gathered. "There is only one God, one Father of us all." His prayers droned on into the night.

***

Dan Parks entered the police station in Kusadasi and felt like he'd stepped into the set for a circa-1950s crime movie. The large open room held several wooden desks with traditional black phones. At each desk, a uniformed man sat shuffling through papers and some were talking on the phones.

"Parks? We've been waiting for you." A man at the front desk rose and extended a hand. "This way, sir."

He ushered Parks into a small room where two officers had been viewing the films of the day before. "We are ready," one of the men said. "We think we found the gun."

"Can I see?" Parks said.

"Here, right here." The man clicked through the early frames and then froze on a man with a cowboy hat and blonde hair. He seemed to be drinking out of a water jug, but on closer examination there was a gun protruding from the jug. A camera from the top of the stadium had captured it perfectly.

Parks looked at the picture for several seconds and then hit his head in recognition and embarrassment. How had he missed it? How had Sun so easily slipped by?

"That's our man, Moses Sun. He has dark brown hair, and several wigs. I have a profile on him, and I can tell you where he's staying, or where he was staying. When I checked last night, he was still registered." Parks opened his Blackberry and located the file. "Could we hook this up to your computer and print it out?"

"No, I don't think so, sir. Can I take it? Our secretary will type copy. She's very fast."

Parks handed over the small device and turned back to the screen. "That's him. I'm sure of it. Could we look at the pictures of the man in the brown robe?"

Soon they sat together watching the robed man enter the amphitheater, taking a seat near the front. The officer beside him fast forwarded through to the shot. Then they slowed it down and watched the man stand up and approach the back of the stage. He froze the frame and then Parks asked to see one frame at a time.

They could see the man walking behind the row of dignitaries, then crouching down. A minute later he walked off and exited the arena.

"Wait," Parks said. "Let's look at him walking away again."

Together they looked, again pausing after each frame.

"There is a bulge under his robe. Could that be..."

"He didn't have time to drug her. You think he had the girl? Do we have two suspects?"

"I don't know," Parks admitted. "The robe is the kind the Franciscans wear, but it might just be a cover. Do you have the Franciscan order here?

"Order what?" the officer asked.

"Never mind," Parks decided he could find that out later. "Let's go get our man."

"One more thing, sir. There's more. We believe there were two shots, and one hit the woman."

"Which woman?"

"Ameellee."

"Are you sure?"

"I'm sorry, sir." The man then showed the frames from another view.

161

The tape clearly sounded two shots. Katharine fell, the second shot fired, and Emily fell back, then crawled behind the people on the stage. There were no more views of her.

"Could we get a copy of that picture out to the Vatican Embassy in Istanbul? They could find out for us if that was really a monk or an impostor." Parks shuddered to think what it could mean, hoping for the best.

"Yes, sir, I'll take care of that," the officer offered. "And now, they are waiting for you outside."

The Turkish police were mobilizing to go after Sun. Parks walked out of the room and bumped into another uniformed officer.

"Come with me, sir."

Taking Parks' arm, the officer ushered him back through the large room toward the door.

"My Blackberry?" he asked.

"Black berry?" the officer asked.

The secretary walked into the lobby and held it up.

Parks took the small device from the woman, and then held it up and announced, "Blackberry."

"Ah. OK. We go now."

The officer started walking toward the door. "Waste no time now. Sun get away."

The men walked out into the bright morning sun. Three police cars were lined up ready for a mission. Parks asked for an interpreter.

The commander became very impatient. "English not necessary to arrest man," he told Parks several times, but Parks held firm.

Thirty minutes later an interpreter arrived and then Parks recommended a different strategy. "Sun will run if he sees your cars. Let me go first, then you follow, two blocks behind me."

***

Patmos roosters crowed at dawn, waking Emily from a deep sleep. Sun flooded through the window early in Emily's small room. Shaking sleep out of her eyes, she stood to greet the day. The window framed an incredible view down to the sparkling blue water. Emily began to pray. She thanked God for the beautiful space, for her safety and then she realized that she had to get word to someone.

She hurried to the door and realized she had no idea where Brother Gabriel would be, much less where she was. Mentally she reviewed the experiences of the day before; the press conference, the shots. She felt her chest and looked down at her wound. A bruise had formed on her chest, surrounding the small bandage. She felt dull pain. Peeking under the bandage, she noticed the blood had dried. Her mind continued to flip back through the events of the pre-vious day. Brother Gabriel, the moped, the boat and then Patmos. Emily remembered Gabe brought her to a conference of mystics. She remembered Taize, the Buddhist speaker, wonderful homemade bread, and a walk by moonlight.

Opening the door, she looked down the steps and then up to oth-er doors scattered on the hotel grounds. Rather than one building, Hotel Romeos consisted of small buildings connected by stairs and pathways, lined with flower pots. Emily's view took in the circular meeting room while she wondered if she should search for Brother Gabriel or just try to find a phone.

She ventured out. The silence of the white stucco space, arched entryways, and stone floor transformed the September morning into a holy moment for Emily. Peace permeated her being. "I should be afraid, but yet I feel utterly peaceful," Emily's inner dialogue shifted into prayer. "Thank you, Jesus! Somebody tried to kill me yesterday, but I'm alive! God sent Brother Gabriel to save me and here I am in this most beautiful, sacred place and a conference of holy people."

Emily remembered the candles burning brightly the night before and felt her heart glowing. She actually felt like there was a candle burning inside of her.

***

In the chapel at the monastery, Brother Gabriel finished his morning prayers. An orthodox priest had led a traditional matins at 5 a.m., and many of the conference participants had ventured up to this simple, ancient chapel for prayer and meditation. But eventual-ly, most had left for breakfast back at the hotel when Gabriel fell to his knees one more time. The last prayer he offered for Emily. Imag-ining her enfolded in the love and peace of God, in his mind's eye he planted a candle in her heart and imagined God's light shining and illuminating her path.

The events of the previous day confused him. Emily may be in great danger. He asked for guidance. Should he harbor her and give her the secrecy of sanctuary or report her whereabouts to the author-ities? Last night, he had sought cooperation to pretend the phones were not working. He should call Emily's Dad.

Yet now the small voice spoke clearly, "Let Emily guide you."

Gabriel shook out his robe and stood to go. Emily would tell him what to do.

25. The Chase

September 19, 2006

When Balaban came back to take the MAMs to breakfast, he found the group gathered in the lobby with long looks on their faces. "At your service, MAMs." He bowed and held out his hand toward the door. "Our finest protect you where ever you go today." The soldier standing by the door smiled briefly at the gregarious man. The MAMs climbed into the van, with two security guards close behind. Balaban drove a few blocks to a picturesque outdoor café on the side of a hill overlooking the Aegean.

"Are we safe?" Sallie asked. "Maybe we should order in."

Molly shuddered. "Fear is not a good thing. I understand a little more of what it must be like for Mark in Iraq. They don't know from one minute to the next when a bomb might explode, or a suicide bomber might crash into their caravan."

Ursula decided to take the lead. "We have to finish our mission. The soldiers protect us. We must uncover the message in the scrolls."

Jane agreed. "If somebody is trying to kill us, there must be something very important in those scrolls. I'm with you, Ursula. We can't stop now."

"I don't understand. What's going on?" Joe asked. "They agreed I could translate the scrolls, and now they won't let me see them? Maybe I can have my office make an inquiry?"

Ursula nodded. Joe sat so close to her that she could feel his breath on her neck. "Yes, that's a good idea. What else? What else can we do?"

"Stolen? Who would steal the scrolls?" Priscilla asked.

"An inside job; Parks said that they think it's an inside job." Jane reminded.

"Did the Turkish government steal them from themselves?" Sallie laughed. "That's a good one."

"If they don't want anyone to look at them, they might have just taken them elsewhere for safekeeping. If they say they were stolen, that gets them off the hook from showing them to anyone else. It might make sense," Joe thought out loud.

"I keep wondering why Hiram insisted that I lie about how many scrolls there were. And why did they change the names?" Ursula looked at Joe. "Something stinks. The last scroll must have some information."

"I agree." Joe placed his arm around Ursula's shoulder and fought the urge to put his mouth on hers. "We'll see this through."

Molly pondered the situation. The scrolls. Her photographs. She snapped over a hundred pictures of those scrolls. The Turkish archaeologists had very expensive cameras, but she had set her little Kodak Z730 on the text function and snapped away. Later, when she reviewed them and zoomed in, her camera had done the job. Her pictures of the scrolls were as clear as day.

Jane's cell phone rang. "It's Parks," she mouthed to the group. "They're going after Sun! He'll keep us posted."

The food arrived at the table, and the MAMs dined on wonderful Turkish breakfast cuisine. Soon all were flying high on caffeine and sugar, Turkish coffee and pastries.

"We've got to find Emily." Sallie was single-minded. "How could she just disappear? If she were OK, she would have contacted us by now."

"But what can we do?" Molly wondered out loud. "We don't speak the language. It's like looking for a needle in a haystack. She could be anywhere!"

"Parks is working on it," Jane reminded them.

"Parks is chasing Sun!" Sallie stood up and told the group. "I'm going to the police. We need to check the hospital, too." Then she turned to Balaban. "Will you take me?"

***

Moses Sun composed a long email to headquarters telling them that Katharine Long had been wounded, perhaps killed and would be out of commission for a long time to come. He ended the email with, "Mission Complete. I'm coming home." On second thought, he deleted "Complete" and inserted, "Over."

Smugly he eyed the yellow wig that he displayed like a trophy on his bedside table and strutted toward the window to check the weather. Dark clouds hung on the horizon, but blue skies filled the Kusadasi heavens. With any luck, he could make it to the ferry without further problems. But then, his eyes stopped on a more immediate storm brewing - Dan Parks. The large man opened the door of a police cruiser and headed his way.

"I've got to get out of here!" Sun muttered to himself, grabbed his wallet and sunglasses, wrapped a brown sari around his head, tucking it securely into his shirt, and opened his door. It wouldn't be the first time he passed as a woman. Not something he would normally brag about, but if it got him out of this jam he just might. Once outside, he jumped on the little moped he had rented the day before. "I knew I might need this! Praise God for small miracles," he applauded himself and his God. The yellow hair was gone, but the sari was the perfect foil. A biking Bedouin? He laughed to himself. But Sun had no idea that Dan Parks knew exactly which door belonged to him and would not be fooled again. When Sun jumped on his bike, Parks was already ordering the Turkish police to close in.

Sun coasted out of the lot and looked in his rearview mirror to place Parks.

"Oops!" Sun saw the headlights, then the siren. Parks tailed him out of the lot.

"Busted!" Sun shook his head and then hit the gas. "I've always loved a good chase!" At the end of the parking lot, Sun apprised his situation. To the left the road climbed quickly and horseshoed back and forth on the side of the hill leading up from the sea. To the right, a downhill coast would land him in the center of the business district. Not really a choice, Sun banked to the right, and then he saw them.

Three police cars blocked both lanes of traffic.

Again, Sun considered his options. Eying a small path beside the road, he pointed his moped in that direction and gunned it. He left the officers in the dust, when he whizzed by and sailed on down the hill. Parks was close behind, and his interpreter was giving the officers a piece of his mind in Turkish. Parks waved his arms madly, trying to sweep the cruisers out of his way so he could head on after Sun. Parks sped down the hill, with three cruisers behind. Flashing lights alerted those on the street to stay out of the way. The sirens gave Sun a clear idea of how much time he had to make his getaway.

Now Sun eyed the little shops opening for the day. The vendors arranged their stalls with fresh fruits, vegetables, meat and fish. A man leaned against the wall of a small café, sipping a small drink. Ah, he needed some coffee, but not now. The carpet store looked empty. He could head for narrow alleys between the buildings, but then the water seemed like a better idea.

Soon more police cruisers joined the chase. The port authority patrolled the dock. The Turkish police now blocked all roads leading into the business district.

Sun aimed his bike up over the curb to the sidewalk, speeding by the roadblocks, and headed straight down to the bay.

Parks ordered some motorcycle units.

Sun approached the blue water and the fishing wharf. He seemed to be working himself into a corner, speeding along the walk beside the series of docks leading out into Kusadasi bay. He headed away from the big docks and toward the private docks with smaller fishing boats and pleasure cruisers. What they didn't know he hoped would make all the difference.

A policeman on a motorcycle tailed him onto the dock.

At the very last dock, Sun turned out toward the sea, gunned his moped and sped out, past the little dinghies and boats bobbing in the water. At the end of the dock, he aimed his moped between a large sailboat and a cabin cruiser, gunned it full force, sailing up into the air between the boats and toward the water ahead. Behind him, the trailing officer slammed on his brakes, muttering a few choice words.

Sun sailed out, pushing the bike down into the water while he flew up, executed a perfect swan dive and then hit the water with force that helped him in the underwater swim ahead. That stint as a stunt man in Hollywood served its purpose well.

On the dock, Parks and the police cruisers lined up and watched the spectacle with open mouths. Sun swam fast and furiously six feet under. Aimed out a 30 degree angle, he counted 50 strokes, then executed a 90 degree turn and headed toward the shore. He hoped he could make it. A boat heading out to sea provided a cover. Sun surfaced, gobbled fresh air into his lungs and continued his underwater push for a safe landing beyond the eye of the coast guard.

Meanwhile, Parks ordered a boat patrol. The Turkish officers agreed, but it took a few minutes to get the Port Authority involved and then a few more to get their boat headed in the right direction.

Time was on Sun's side. He swam directly toward a small dock he spied earlier about 200 feet to the left of the main wharf. In the past, underwater work had been his forte. He needed all of that experience and more with his out-of- practice lungs. He closed in on the shore but knew now he couldn't make it. The waves battered his body. When a small fishing boat passed, he bobbed up again for one more breath, blocked from view. Up and down quickly, he headed again for the small dock.

Unfortunately, Sun didn't see a speedboat pulling away from that same dock, pointed his way. Just 20 feet short of his destination, Sun heard the noise, but it was too late. The boat plowed into him full force. He felt his head explode. His body went down, and then the back of the boat hit him and lifted him out of the water for a second before he plunged back down.

The speedboat driver felt a thunk and so he changed his course slightly, heading out to sea, steering clear of what he thought was one of the schools of fish that often frequented the waters.

***

On that dock of Sun's destination, three nuns stood waiting for a ride to Patmos.

"Oh dear, do you think we'll be late?" Sister Martha had just looked at her watch and noticed that it was half past ten. "We are supposed to be speaking tonight. What if our boatman doesn't come?"

"Calm down," Sister Mary instructed. "Enshallah. You need to learn something from the Muslims around here. God will provide, Enshallah. God willing. And if we don't make it, it's not the end of the world, either."

Sister Elizabeth tuned out the chatter to watch the speedboat pull away from the dock. She heard a thud.

"Did you hear that?"

Mary and Martha were too busy arguing to hear her question.

"We serve God, not Allah. What do I have to learn from them?" Martha asked.

Elizabeth continued watching and saw a body fly up and then go back down.

"I'm going in!" She flung off her black habit and let it fall onto the wood-slatted dock.

Mary and Martha turned just in time to see an image of their novice flying through the air in her underclothing and then diving into the surf below.

"God have mercy!" Martha yelled.

"Oh my heavens!" Mary gasped. "Mary, mother of God." She pulled the rosary out of the large side pocket of her habit and began fingering the beads while she murmured the rosary.

Out in the water, Elizabeth dove down, searching for her target. Three times she came up and then she felt something in the shallow water. She dove down one more time and found her mark. Circling his neck with her arms, she kicked to the surface and thanked God that his body was limp and not flailing. Good and bad, she thought to herself. Turning onto her back, she let him float slightly above her while kicking her feet, propelling them both toward the dock.

She realized she'd never be able to lift him onto the dock. Instead, she steered them both toward a small beach beyond the dock.

"I'm taking him in. He needs CPR. Please help," she yelled out to her fellow nuns and continued swimming with strong strokes.

Sister Mary held up her full skirt and began to run toward the beach. But Sister Martha nervously glanced about and grabbed Elizabeth's habit, shaking it out and folding it and wondering if anyone else had seen Elizabeth dive in. Out in the harbor, coast guard boats circled. The men aboard seemed to be searching the water, oblivious to the drama unfolding by her dock. Trees blocked the small dock. Perhaps they blocked their view of Elizabeth swimming, too? She certainly hoped so. She headed for the shore with proper attire for the swimmer. What could Elizabeth be thinking? What could be keeping their boat? An hour late. Martha knew coming to Ephesus for a sight-seeing jaunt had been a mistake from the beginning.

Elizabeth struggled to pull Sun onto the small beach. Mary arrived at her side to help. Together, they pulled Sun's limp body several feet up from the water's edge. The sari tucked into his shirt had fallen off his head, but clung to the lifeless form, wrinkles of brown draped against the small man, along with seaweed clinging to his arms and legs.

Sister Mary, Head Nurse of the St. Teresa's Hospital in San Francisco, jumped into action. Rolling the inert body over, she thumped sharply on his back. Water spewed out of his mouth. She thumped again. More water flew out.

She pushed the body back onto its back, pinched his nose closed and began breathing into his mouth. Ten breaths in, five pumps on his chest, ten more breaths in.

Martha ran down from the dock. "Elizabeth! Get your robe on right now!"

"It's not important. We need to save him!"

Elizabeth offered to take over and give Mary a break.

Mary nodded, and Elizabeth slipped in.

"For God's sake, Martha. Could you at least say a few prayers for us? We're trying to save a man's life!"

Martha bowed her head somewhat reluctantly, holding on to Elizabeth's habit.

After a few more minutes, Mary instructed Elizabeth to switch again.

After three Hail Mary's and four Lord's Prayers, Martha put the habit down on the beach and stood in front of Sun and his saviors, with her hands outstretched, looking out to the water. If Elizabeth wouldn't dress properly, she could shield her from view. Her brown robe flailed in the wind that spread dark clouds across the sky.

The port authority ship circled in the waters where Sun had disappeared. A man on the boat saw the nun standing and joked to his comrade.

"Holy lady on the shore. What is she doing?"

"Calling the Pope?"

"Morning prayer. She doesn't want to bow before God like we do, so she acts like a tree instead?"

"Crazy women. Those Catholics."

Behind Martha, Elizabeth and Mary worried. Time was running out.

Mary felt Sun's neck again and detected a small pulse.

"He's alive! Elizabeth! Praise God!"

Elizabeth beamed back. Although she spent her high school years as a lifeguard at the racket club, she'd never saved a life. "Thank you, Jesus!" She shook Mary's hand. "Thank you, Mary."

"You're a hero, dear!"

Meanwhile, Martha busied herself waving to the fast cabin cruiser streaming toward the small dock.

The Port Authority boat headed back to the waters where Sun had gone in. "She's waving at you," one of the crew members told another. "She wants a date."

"You can hide under that robe if you want. Not Me." He yelled back to Sister Martha, "No thanks!"

Martha couldn't hear nor see the Port Authority boat. Years earlier she might have picked up the insult across the waves, but now she needed hearing aids. Her order couldn't afford them. Her glasses were in need of replacement, too. She'd never be in this mess if the Conference of Mystics hadn't offered to pay for their trip. She lifted the folds in her long robe and walked quickly back to the dock to greet the boat.

"Ali's boat is picking up the ladies for a ride to Patmos," the officer in charge of the patrol boat told the crewmen who were still laughing at the funny lady standing erect with arms out.

"Get her out of here, now! Bad for business!"

"She's a holy woman. Better pray for forgiveness at the next call to prayer." The officer shook his head, laughing, and continued to scan the water.

The Port Authority cleared the cabin cruiser, Allah's Ride, to land at the small dock and pick up the ladies for the trip to Patmos. Sometimes money speaks. The richest man in Turkey earned the right to circumvent customs often, even when his boat entered a harbor without him on board.

The fully equipped cruiser came complete with its own physician, visiting celebrities and plenty of room for the three nuns who had no idea what a magnificent boat had been sent to ferry them to the International Conference of Mystics.

Standing at the helm, prepared to secure the boat, stood Allah's Ride first skipper, Miguel. Often known as "Jack of all trades," he spoke 10 languages fluently and could read people better than the written page. The jovial man who never met a stranger got paid well to provide first-class hospitality for Ali's many guests.

Martha greeted him at the dock.

"Just a minute sir, could you wait a moment?"

Martha turned to Elizabeth, trying to block Miguel's view of the women on the beach. She pointed to the neatly folded habit on the beach and then to Elizabeth and made motions to indicate that Elizabeth needed to put it on.

Instead, Elizabeth ran toward the dock in her underclothes. While Martha turned beet red, Elizabeth spoke to Miguel.

"We have a sick man, sir. He almost drowned. We just performed CPR. He's breathing. We must take him to the hospital. Can you help?"

A wide smile grew across Miguel's tanned face, while he scanned Elizabeth's drenched body. The cotton of her one piece undergarment clung to her breasts and hips revealing a quite voluptuous hourglass figure.

Mary yelled, "Can they take him?"

Elizabeth turned toward Mary, put her finger up and yelled back, "I just asked."

Miguel's eyes went down to her full buttocks. Now he had a problem of his own brewing down south, but being a perfect gentleman, he covered the evidence and thanked God for the perfect excuse to go in search of the ship's medical staff, before embarrassing himself in front of the ladies.

"I'll get our Doc," he yelled back. "Yes, we'll take your man. We have a fully equipped emergency room on this boat."

"Do you have a stretcher?"

"Anything for you, dear." Miguel smiled and feasted his eyes one last time on Elizabeth, before heading off to find Dr. Mohammed.

Dr. Mohammed was soaking in the hot tub by the pool when Miguel accosted him.

"I thought this was a vacation cruise!" The good doctor complained.

"You've done absolutely nothing for five days, now you have to earn your keep, sir." Miguel sternly spoke, then yelled and laughed at the soaking physician, "Get out of there!"

Dr. Mohammed often took up his friend Ali on a standing offer to be his doctor in residence on the large cabin cruiser. Ali's wife had several medical problems, and Ali felt more comfortable keeping a doctor on the boat full time for her. She was rarely on the boat, but it also gave him the opportunity to provide free vacations to the overworked staff at the local hospital. Ali's wealth had come through hard work and sweat, and he knew that everybody needed a break from time to time.

Miguel yelled at the crew to get the stretcher. Within minutes, the doctor, Miguel and two small men were off the boat and on the beach where Mary and Elizabeth knelt trying to communicate with the man.

"He can't talk," Mary said. "He was hit by a speed boat. Elizabeth pulled him out."

171

"Good work!" Miguel looked at Elizabeth with admiration, then introduced Dr. Mohammed, who examined Sun and muttered some words to the men with the stretcher, who carefully rolled Sun onto their stretcher and carried him toward the boat.

"Come along, ladies. We have some dry clothes for you on board, ma'am," Miguel told Elizabeth.

Martha, meanwhile still stood on the dock trying to figure out how to discipline Elizabeth.

When Mary and Elizabeth arrived at Martha's side, Martha turned to Mary. "She must be disciplined. Totally unacceptable. Our novices cannot expose themselves to men. I am planning her penance now."

Sister Mary rolled her eyes and winked at Elizabeth. "For God's sake, Martha, she saved a man's life. Would you get off your high horse? I think you're the one who needs some penance. How about reading the story of the Good Samaritan[xxix] 100 times tonight?"

26. The Fast Boat to Patmos

September 19, 2006

Miguel ushered the women up three steps onto the boat and into a corridor with several doors. "This way, ladies. Your suite. Full bath. You'll find some clothes of all sizes in the closet. Help yourself, the captain insists."

"Do you have a washer and dryer on this boat, too?" Elizabeth joked.

"Yes, as a matter of fact," Miguel smiled. "Your wish, my command. Leave wet clothes in this basket. I'll have them ready for you before we reach our destination."

Elizabeth turned toward the bathroom, and Miguel enjoyed one last look at that blossoming behind.

Mary consulted with Miguel. "Should we take him to the Kusadasi hospital? We don't even know his name."

"Let me talk with Doc Mohammed. One moment. "

Miguel left to check with Dr. Mohammed, while the captain sped toward Patmos. Just following orders, aiming to make up for lost time. Although the Patmos ferry took four and a half hours, the captain prided himself in splitting that time in half. Allah's Ride wore its title well.

"How's he's doing, Doc?" Miguel spoke in the doctor's native tongue.

"Regaining consciousness. Quite a large head wound. We've cleaned that and will keep ice on it, but I don't think there are other broken bones. Internal injuries? Hard to say. He doesn't speak Turkish or Arabic. Try English?"

Miguel placed his hand on the man's arm. "Sir, we want to help you. What is your name?"

The man opened his eyes and turned his head toward Miguel, grimacing at the pain the movement caused. He seemed to move his head from side to side, then closed his eyes again.

"Did he mean 'No'?" Miguel picked up a tablet of paper by the bed. "Let's try paper."

He tapped the man's arm again, and handed him a paper and pen.

To the doctor's surprise, the man rolled on his side, and propped himself up so that he could write on the paper. A few minutes later, his head fell back, the pen dropped from his hand and he was snoring soundly.

Miguel reached over and picked up the pad and rescued the pen from the floor. He read: "Take me to Brother Gabriel. An angel rescued me from death. She told me to talk to Gabe." Translating it to Turkish for the good doctor, he laughed. "Looks like we've got a crazy one, Doc. But you know, there is a Brother Gabriel at the conference, we took him to Kusadasi a couple days ago."

"He will speak to Gabriel, then. Enshallah. The man will be fine, the nurse can take over. Can I go back to the hot tub?"

"But could he have internal injuries?"

"I don't think so. If it's his time, then so be it. But if he could write that note and lay on his side? I checked him out. We just don't know about the head injury. Time will tell. There's nothing I can do now but wait. So can I go back to the hot tub?"

Miguel laughed and pushed the doctor out of the room. "Go, Go!"

A Mexican nurse sat beside the man. Miguel pulled up a chair and joined the nurse, putting his arm around her and kissing her cheek. "Muchas gracias," Miguel smiled at his best friend, Anita. Then he jumped up. "Hasta luego, querida."

"Love 'em and leave 'em," Anita answered, but Miguel had already slipped out of the room and was headed off to strike up a conversation with Elizabeth. Could this be the real thing, he wondered for the hundredth time. Love at first sight? Perhaps he could rescue her from the nunnery. A body like hers had no business being hidden away in a convent, much less that awful habit.

***

Meanwhile, the MAMs finished breakfast at their seaside Kusadasi cafe, and at Sallie's urging were headed toward police headquarters. They passed a swarm of police cars near the dock. Jane spotted Dan Parks standing in a Port Authority boat with binoculars, looking out to the sea. She pulled out her cell phone and dialed his number.

"Hello, dear!" Parks answered the moment he saw Jane's number on his cell.

"What are you doing now?"

"Just out for a morning boat ride in the harbor. Want to join me?" Parks waved toward Balaban's van, stopped at a light near the little business district of Kusadasi.

Jane cut to the quick. "Did you catch Sun?"

"Um, er, well, the water did."

174

"What?"

"We were chasing him. He drove his moped off the end of the pier. We've recovered the bike. We haven't recovered his body yet. The Turkish government won't dredge the harbor. They have asked some fishermen to check their nets. The current has probably carried his body out to the sea.

"He's dead?"

"We believe so."

"Call Katharine!"

"Not yet."

"What about Emily?"

"Jane, I have to go. I'll call you later."

Parks snapped shut the phone, and Jane looked at Sallie shaking her head. "We'll have to take this into our own hands. Balaban, we're going to the police."

***

Halim Mohammed paced in his small office, remembering events from the previous day. He'd placated the Austrian archaeologists. Sophie and Hans had left for Vienna, with his promise of first dibs when the scrolls were found. Now he pondered a way to thank the MAMs for their good work, while graciously ushering them out of town. He knew they wouldn't like it one bit. Ursula Goodtree would protest. Holding his face in his hands, he looked out over the towering structures of ancient Ephesus. "Power then, power now," he sighed to himself. "Some things never change."

He heard a knock at the door, then looked out the window. Halim could see Balaban's van in the lot and some familiar figures streaming toward his door. He straightened his shoulders, took a deep breath and prepared to face the MAMs.

When Halim opened the door, he was surprised to see a tall, dark man standing beside Ursula. The man extended his hand to Halim. Halim greeted him with a warm handshake.

"Dr. Joseph Cohen," he introduced himself. "I come from the Center for Biblical Languages in California to translate your scrolls."

"Come in!" Halim raised his eyebrows at Ursula.

Ursula smiled back.

Soon Sallie, Molly, Priscilla, Jane, Ursula and Joe were seated at the conference table with Halim, who was searching for the words to explain the situation, or what he was allowed to tell them, and get them on their way back to the States.

"They haven't found Emily," Sallie complained. "We just went to the police. They have no information. Emily's boyfriend is on the way. Her family called the U.S. Embassy."

175

"Could I get a copy of the scroll pictures?" Joe asked. "I would like to start working on the translations."

"I'm afraid not. I'm sorry, sir. The photographs are in a vault in Istanbul. I have been instructed to work on other things for the moment."

"What is going on here?" Ursula Goodtree put her hands on her hips and faced Halim. "Tell us. We deserve to know. This is our dig."

"I don't know. The danger is great. Two people have been shot. Your country is at war with our neighbor. A dangerous time." Halim shook his head. "Be safe. Go home. In time, the scrolls will be available. Thank you for your work. You did good work. Thank you. I'm sorry."

Ursula looked at Joe. She knew he was simmering under the surface.

Priscilla spoke. "He's right, we should go. It's dangerous here. We did our job, but let's not get too carried away. Look, Katharine was shot. Emily has disappeared. We don't know what will happen next. I'm ready to go home."

"I'm going to talk to Parks first," Jane decided. "Something is wrong here."

"I'm very sorry. There is nothing I can do," Halim shook his head. "Would you like to go on that trip to Pamukkule now before you leave? Beautiful formation."

Molly answered. "If it's not safe here, I'm not about to go on a ride in the countryside. I'm with Priscilla on this one. Let's get out of here."

Joe and Ursula whispered to each other.

"Let's go back to the hotel," Joe announced. "Jane, you can talk with Parks. We can see about getting flights back to the States as soon as Katharine is ready to travel."

"What about Emily?" Sallie asked.

"Yes, and as soon as we find Emily, we can all leave," Joe added.

27. Convergence at Patmos

September 19, 2006

Emily headed down the stairs toward the outdoor chapel. She thought the circular meeting space would be empty, but when she got closer to the small chairs, Brother Gabriel stood to greet her with a smile. She realized he'd been sitting near the candlelit altar in the center of the area.

"Ah! The answer to my prayers. Here you are!" Gabriel greeted Emily with a kiss to her right cheek and then asked, "How did you sleep?"

"Like a log. And this morning, there is a candle inside of me. A holy place!"

"An answer to my prayer!" Gabriel's full beard and mustache framed a large grin. "Let's go get something to eat and talk about our day. Your family and the MAMs must be worried about you."

Over breakfast of fruit, figs, eggs and good bread, Gabriel and Emily discussed the options. "What do you want? You should decide," Gabriel said.

"Could the MAMs come here? This is a beautiful place and so safe. Do you know anybody who could bring them here... secretly? I don't want whoever shot me to get at them."

Gabriel considered her request. "Let me see if Allah's Ride is available. My friend, Miguel, told me to let him know if he could help again. Let me see where the boat is now. Finish your breakfast, and I'll be back."

While Gabriel headed for the conference headquarters, Emily savored her homemade whole wheat bread and sipped on the strong, fresh coffee. The aroma floated on the air, while murmuring mystics filled the hotel dining room with gentle conversation. Emily's thoughts feasted on the events of the past week; the tour of Ephesus, the dig, the sand chamber, the scrolls, the press conference, the shots, Gabriel, this sacred place. Her mind reviewed the press conference and suddenly she heard the shot before the one that knocked her back. Now she wondered what had happened and if someone could be harmed. She realized she never should have left so abruptly. With early morning clarity, she knew the others would be worried sick about her.

Emily felt her cell phone, her artificial appendage, as Josh liked to call it. Remembering she had paid for international calls in advance, she decided to take a chance. It didn't work in Turkey, but maybe here? Dialing Jane's number, she waited for the ring.

Within a minute, she heard the familiar voice and breathed a sigh of relief. "Yes, I'm OK. I'm on Patmos!"

"Patmos! What are you doing on Patmos?" Jane shouted into the phone.

"Shhh!" Emily answered. "Don't tell the authorities, just the MAMs. I'm going to try to get you a ride to come, too."

"Parks. Can I tell Parks?" Jane asked.

"Please don't. Not right now. I'll call back as soon as I know more."

Emily closed her phone, leaving Jane dumbfounded on the other end of the line. Then she dialed Josh. When Josh didn't answer she decided to leave a message. "Josh, it's Em. Call me. I'm safe. I love you. Talk to you soon." Still needing to talk, she dialed home.

"Granny Abby? Is that you?"

Her grandmother sobbed on the other end of the phone. "Emily, Emily! Emily! Let me get your father."

Emily tried to figure out why her Granny had lost it at the sound of her voice. When her Dad got on the line, she understood. The MAMs had called her home and they thought she had been kidnapped, or possibly dead.

"Dad, no. Dad, I'm OK. Brother Gabriel, your friend is here! Can you believe it? He brought me to Patmos. I'm fine. Don't worry."

Then Emily's mouth dropped open as her Dad told her about Josh.

"He's on his way, dear. He wouldn't wait until we heard from you. No one could tell him where you were, or what happened. He was frantic. He spent his savings on a ticket. He's in the air as we speak."

Emily gasped, and then told her Dad she had to go. "I'll call you again, soon, Dad. I've gotta go now."

Gabriel reappeared right after she slipped her phone into her purse. He beamed at her and clapped his hands. "The boat is ready! Let's go pick them up."

***

And so it happened that Ursula and Joe, Sallie and Molly, Jane and Priscilla several hours later, waited on the same dock of Sun's rescue for Allah's Ride to Patmos.

"What did you tell Parks?" Sallie asked Jane.

"I told him I'd see him around, that the MAMs were going to cruise the Greek Islands for a few days. He just laughed and told me we were all crazy. When I told him we were going on Allah's Ride, he raised his eyebrows and said, 'Somebody is trying to get you out of the way.'"

"What did that mean? I don't like the way that sounds." Sallie laughed nervously.

"I'm not sure. He told me Allah's Ride belongs to the richest man in Turkey. I think he thought someone in the government is providing a diversion for us."

"Oh." Sallie laughed again, more wholeheartedly. "And you didn't tell him we're going to Patmos?"

"No, just cruising the islands. I'm afraid that he may be able to get the information, though. I imagine Allah's Ride cruise plans are an open book."

"Maybe not," Sallie shook her head from side to side and rubbed her fingers with her thumb. "Money talks." Laughing again, she propped up her suitcase and sat down on the dock, with her feet dangling over the water.

"Sure is a perfect day." Molly plopped down beside Sallie. "Who could ever imagine that the Archaeological Expedition in Search of Thecla would end up with a vacation on Patmos?"

Behind them, Joe enfolded Ursula in his arms, blocking out the world. He lifted her chin and planted his lips on hers. Slowly savoring the taste of reunion, they feasted on each other.

Ursula broke the kiss and whispered into his ear. "You know, I've never stopped loving you. All these years."

Joe put his forefinger to his lips. "Shh. You don't have to say anything dear. Your face tells me everything I need to know." Returning to the kiss, his hands roamed over her shoulders and into the small of her back. He rocked her in rhythm with the waves and the wind, oblivious to the MAMs and the dock. He bathed in the comfort of familiar arms, soothing his grieving heart. For the first time since his wife died, he was beginning to feel alive again.

Priscilla and Jane looked out across the bay, pointing out boats and wondering which one would be theirs.

Priscilla asked, "Did Emily explain what happened?"

"No, she said she'd tell us later. She said she's at a Conference of Mystics and they want to give us sanctuary."

"Sanctuary? What does that mean?"

Sally explained, "That is a safe haven. I used to be involved in the Sanctuary Movement to provide safety for Salvadoran refugees."

"We're not refugees!" Priscilla yelled.

"Well, maybe we are," Jane said. "They certainly seemed to want us to get out of Turkey fast."

"In the past, during wars, the sanctuaries were safe places; like home base during tag. Like, you can't get me, I'm safe!" Sallie mimicked a five-year-old on the playground.

"You taught kindergarten too long!" Jane complained.

Joe and Ursula rejoined the group, "But what are we going to do about your scrolls? Are you sure you want to leave them behind?"

Molly smiled at Joe and tapped her camera case. "No sir, not at all. I have them all right here. My little Kodak EasyShare Text option saved the day. As plain as day."

"What?" Joe looked like someone had just handed him a million dollars.

"Here, look for yourself!" Molly turned on her camera and zipped through her review function to find the scrolls. "All eight scrolls, as plain as day."

Joe pulled out his Blackberry and asked Molly if he could borrow her photo card for a moment. "I want to get several copies of these before we lose them again. Ursula, can we also put them on your laptop?"

Ursula laughed. "I knew there was a reason I called you. The man is in his element, ladies!"

Ursula opened her laptop case, and soon Joe had copied the pictures there as well.

"They stole the scrolls, locked up the other pictures in a safe in Istanbul, and forgot all about Molly's camera? Somebody's asleep on the job!" Jane shook her head.

"We're not complaining!" Ursula turned to give Joe a quick hug.

"No, ma'am. No complaints out of me, either." Jane smiled.

"A perfect day, don't you think?" Sallie asked. "Look at those fishing boats. They have nets, like the Bible! Two thousand years later, still fishing with small boats and nets."

The group quietly observed the harbor action, boats coming in and out, savoring the blue-green sea. Enjoying the tranquil morning, they relaxed into their wait.

A half hour later, Priscilla was the first to spot Allah's Ride streaming toward the dock. "There she is!"

When the boat got a little closer, they glimpsed a familiar figure waving from the bow.

"It's Emily!" Sallie waved and jumped up. "It's Emily!"

Many hugs later, the MAMs filled Emily in on Katharine and the scrolls, and examined her chest wound. When they were convinced

Emily was really OK, the MAMs enjoyed fresh coffee and Turkish pastries aboard Allah's Ride, streaming toward Patmos.

After a brief powwow, they appointed Ursula to call Katharine's husband, John, at the hospital in Istanbul for an update and to see if they could join the MAMs on Patmos. Ursula took her cell phone aside and made the call. Soon she returned to the group with her thumb jabbed up into the air.

"Some R and R is just what the doctor ordered. John loves the idea. But he needs a doctor to follow Katharine." Ursula's grin communicated her relief to the group.

Miguel overhead the MAMs discussion and suggested, "Dr. Mohammed keeps bugging me to spend a little vacation on Patmos, too. 'Take me to a Greek Island,' he tells me."

"Can we go pick her up?" Sallie asked Miguel.

"Where is she?"

"Istanbul."

"Maybe better to fly her in. That's quite a way by water."

"That will cost an arm and a leg," Sallie worried.

"Let me check on Allah's Flight and Heli," Miguel said.

"On what?" Sallie asked.

"The owner of this boat also has a plane and a helicopter, and Muslims are required to help others, serving the poor and sick. It's one of the pillars of Islam." Miguel said.

"I thought the Muslims are trying to blow up the world," Priscilla looked at Miguel with disbelief.

"Ah, some of you Americans have a distorted view of Islam. Yes, there are violent extremists who think they are Muslim, but they don't follow Mohammed's teachings." Miguel corrected.

"Actually, I heard that Islam means 'Peace,'" Sallie said.

"Are you sure?" Priscilla asked.

Ursula and Joe exchanged knowing glances and then Joe explained, "Not really, no. Islam means submission to God. Some will say it means peace, because the word is similar to *Salam* (Shalom) in Arabic."

Then Ursula added, "My Muslim friend, though, says that Muslims are only permitted to go to war in self-defense. Similar to the Just War Theory of Martin Luther that many Christians believe."

"A true Muslim is a very loving person. Some of my mystical Muslim friends are at this Conference of Mystics. I'll have to introduce you. They're supposed to be dancing tomorrow night," Miguel added. "You'll enjoy them."

"Dancing?" Priscilla asked.

"Yes, the Whirling Dervishes dance as a form of connecting with God."

"Wasn't Rumi one of those?" Sallie asked.

"Who's Rumi?" Priscilla wanted to know.

"Famous poet. Muslim." Sallie explained.

"Yes, he was a Whirling Dervish, too," Miguel smiled. "You will learn much on Patmos."

28. Molly and Smyrna

September 19, 2006

Molly couldn't shake the feeling that she was dreaming. Shortly after Allah's Ride docked at Patmos, the MAMs had been whisked to the conference in two small minivans, then escorted to rooms at Hotel Romeos. Boy, was she out of shape. She panted climbing steps to reach her room, a white stucco cottage on the tiered hillside of Skala, the port town of Patmos. Embarrassing. But what a place, this hotel. Tropical flowers spilled out of pots and grew on the terraces. She pinched herself when she opened a door in her room and found herself standing on a private balcony looking out at the Aegean Sea. Could all this be real, she had wondered more than once. And she didn't understand why the MAMs were now registered at a conference of mystics.

After dinner, she had retired back to her room to rest and try to regain a sense of reality. She'd decided that if she were living a dream, she might as well sleep through it. But just as her head hit the pillow, she heard a knock.

"Molly! Molly! Are you asleep?" She recognized Sally's whispering voice.

In confusion, Molly stood and walked to the door, opening to her friend. "What?"

"Molly, Joe finished translating the second scroll. We've been invited to the Purple Room to listen. Can you come?" Sally tugged at her sleeve.

Molly threw her hands up above her head. "Lordy, Lordy, what next? Yes, I'll come. Turn your head there, dear, while I get out of this night gown."

Molly and Sallie were soon on their way to the reading. When they arrived at the circular meeting place, there was standing room only. Two men offered their seats.

In the middle of the room, Joe sat next to a man in a brown robe. Molly noticed Jane, Emily, Ursula and Priscilla sitting close behind Joe. Candles burned in large candelabras around the perimeter of the room, and several large floor candles illuminated Joe and the robed man. Molly started to ask Sallie where all these people came from, but the man in the brown robe began to speak.

"We are honored with several unexpected guests at our conference this week. Our conference executive committee decided earlier today to provide sanctuary to an archaeologist, a biblical translator and several women who have been working on an archaeological dig in Turkey," he explained to the group. "I must ask that you hold them and this reading in strict confidence. And now, I would like to introduce Dr. Ursula Goodtree."

Molly rubbed the sleep out of her eyes and tried to focus on Ursula's explanation of the dig, the scrolls and first-century dating techniques. Weariness settled into her soul, while she worried once more about Mark in Iraq and the violent eruption at the last reading of a scroll. She looked around the room, wondering if danger lurked in the shadows. The flickering candles created an aura of mystery. Her heart raced with fear, just as it also seemed to be opening into awe. How did the MAMs end up in this circle of mystics? How could Moses Sun translate a gospel of love into a mandate to kill? Ursula's voice became clear, interrupting her confusion.

"While a final translation may take years, through modern technology we've been working with experts around the world to complete a preliminary translation of one of the scrolls. We are all amazed at the condition of the documents. And the version of Greek parallels other New Testament writings.

"We are very fortunate to have a language specialist here from the Center for Biblical Languages in California. I present Dr. Joseph Cohen."

Joe's warm voice filled the room. Molly's fears evaporated into the mystery of the words from the second scroll.

Scroll #2 From Smyrna

Oh, Teacher,

I write from Smyrna, the Jewel Crown of Asia. The buildings [ ] the harbor. What a sight! We stay in the [ ] home of Flavius, a friend of Claudius' father. So many beautiful [ ] here.

The Christians are poor [ ] tents, the children so thin. Yet the love [ ] as big as the love you have for me, the ocean [ ] love. [ ] the truth of John's word was heard.

Their prophetess, Mariah, interpreted [ ] for me. "The Lamb [ ] was slain. Did you hear the vision? The Lamb

184

is Jesus. [ ] died for us. [ ] Victor. The Roman Emperor is the Beast. The Roman Army is not the victor. No, the Son of God, who teaches love, has triumphed over death and the swords of metal. The Roman soldiers can kill the body, but the Word of God lives forever. Therefore, we are not afraid. The 'second death' will not hurt us, because we will be with God. In our baptism, we have already died to ourselves, and we now live with God."

[ ] men thought John means we are to fight the Romans, but Mariah told them, "We are to be faithful to God only, and to Jesus. We follow the Lamb who was slaughtered. They can kill our bodies, but not our souls. We are to follow Jesus and overcome others with love."
When Claudius and Flavius came to take me home, I longed to stay. In the house of Flavius there are fine linens, [ ]. [ ] beautiful garden in the courtyard and the servants are treated kindly, but I would rather live with the poor Christians of Smyrna who radiate the love of God and call me to be a faithful witness.

Molly listened, and then asked Joe, "Could you read that again?"

That hope she had been yearning for, that restlessness that brought her around the world on this crazy expedition, that deep concern for her son and the future of her country and her world, were suddenly eclipsed in the ancient words of Thecilla to her teacher. The simple message from Smyrna, the simple truth that the Lamb calls people to love; that Jesus did not call them to fight the Romans but to overcome the Romans with love. Yes. That was the message of Martin Luther King, Jr. That was the message that she had heard since she was a little girl. That was the truth of God.

Molly looked at the candles again. Now they seemed to dance with joy, reflecting the love in the faces of the people gathered. She saw Ursula's eyes shining and the deep reverence in Joe's voice for the words he read. She noticed Emily's mouth wide open.

When Joe finished reading the scroll a second time, a small woman in the back of the room stood. "I am Grandmother Maria, a Mayan woman born in Central America, now a member of the Grandmothers for Peace. Thecilla speaks truth. Love is the center of who we are called to be. I ask you to stand and feel that love, that nourishing energy of God at the heart of the Earth move through the soles of your feet."

The people in the room obeyed her quiet authoritative voice. She repeated her first request then moved on to another. "Now, ask the heart of the Great Spirit from the heavens to move through the crown of your head. Then let that love meet the energy of God from the heart of the Earth in the center of your being. Feel the great energy of love and God pulsate in your center. And now, allow that love to travel out from you as far as it needs to go."

The candlelight danced on the wall. Molly felt a new candle in her heart. She saw Ursula's face shining. She turned to Sallie to smile and noticed a man in a dark v-neck sweater with a white oxford shirt and jeans stand up, and move to the center of the room, near Joe.

"I am Brother David Merkt," he said. "I have studied the mystical journey through my own Catholic traditions and as a Hindu monk. I meditate, I pray, and I have found that at the center of our spiritual journey is the mystical heart. The reality is that we are all interconnected with everyone and everything; that we are all one. I believe that is the love of which Jesus speaks. He is our leader. This mystical path of love is of deep nonviolence and solidarity with all living things. This is what Jesus preached. This is what John of Patmos and Thecilla remind us. This is what the Grandmothers know. This is what I have experienced in the heart of my mystical journey."

Then the music began. Several monks from Taize began to sing, "Ubi Caritas et amor, Ubi caritas, Deus Ibi Est." ˣˣˣ

Slowly the people gathered joined the song. Harmonies lifted the simple chant into a mighty chorus of love. The candles danced, the faces radiated a deep knowing. Brother David and Grandmother Maria embraced, and then held hands, while around the circle others grasped the hands of those beside them. Joe and Ursula shared a deep hug and then continued in the chorus. Molly circled Sallie's shoulder with her arm, swaying with the music.

Finally the singing stopped. Breaking the silence, Brother Merkt instructed the group: "God is love. Live in love, and God will dwell with you. Let us go to our rooms in silence, and sleep in the love at the heart of God." The people began to file out of the circular chapel.

Molly folded her hands and held them at her waist, waiting for her turn to leave. She replayed the memory in her mind, the words of Thecilla, the prophecy of Maria, the truth of Brother David and the call to love. She noted the shift inside her body. She knew that she would never be the same. Once back in her room, she fell to her knees in prayer. Giving thanks for God's love, she prayed that God's love would be poured out on the Iraqis and the Americans, on the Democrats and the Republicans, on her family and the families of the world. She thanked God for the affirmation that she had received from 2,000-year-old scrolls and from the people gathered at the Conference of Mystics. She prayed long into the night and fell asleep on her knees with a smile on her face.

29. Thecilla in Smyrna

September 15, 94 A.D.

Thecilla joined the family of Flavius at table that night, wondering what the future held.   Flavius prayed in Hebrew to start the meal.   Such a spread of food

"Are guests expected?" *She couldn't imagine such bounty for the small group sitting at the table. She counted them in her mind's eye; Flavius, his wife, Claudius, herself, and one daughter of theirs, still unmarried.*

"We feel very honored to have you as our guests. Flavius misses Claudius' father so much. They grew up together, you know." *The hostess, Jula, poured wine into Thecilla's glass.*

"You are so kind. Thank you," *Thecilla smiled at Claudius, who took her hand.*

The portico of the house offered a view of the harbor. "It's so beautiful here," *she complimented her guests. The wall tapestries, the fine cloth on the floor, and the sturdy walls spoke of wealth she had never encountered among the Christians at Ephesus. Such a stark contrast to the tattered tents she visited earlier among the poor families of the Christian church.*

"Will you marry soon?" *Flavius asked Claudius.* "Your mother must be busy planning! You must invite us."

Thecilla blushed to hear such frank talk. Claudius seemed embarrassed, also.

"We will certainly invite you, if a wedding is planned," *Claudius tried to end the conversation gracefully, sensing Thecilla's unease.*

"And where did you go today, Thecilla?" *Flavius' wife, Jula asked.* "You must be careful. Were you with the Christians? The Romans flog them."

Thecilla wondered how to respond. She knew Claudius would not tell them about the scrolls. Those of the faith of Abraham who did not know Jesus would not understand the importance of the scrolls written by her exiled uncle. How could she explain the warmth and love she felt all afternoon with the poor followers of Jesus?

"Yes, I visited the Christians. Such good people, the real crown jewels of Smyrna, they say. I felt safe. They are very poor, but they serve God with all their hearts."

Claudius raised his eyebrows and shared a smile with Flavius that Thecilla could not see.

"Be careful," Flavius cautioned. "I hear the Romans may clear their tents soon."

Thecilla shivered.

"Stay with Claudius. He knows the Romans. They will not harm you with Claudius at your side. Don't go visit the tent Christians again."

"How long do you stay?" Jula interrupted her husband. There had been enough warning. "Will you go to the market with me in the morning? Have you seen the Street of Gold? You must visit our beautiful city before you leave." She touched Thecilla's hand.

"So kind of you to ask," Thecilla grasped her hand in friendship. "But Claudius and I must move on tomorrow."

"Tomorrow, already? Where now?" Flavius asked. "Could I send my chariot with you?"

A chariot would make the trip so much easier. Thecilla dared a smile. If they were to visit the five remaining churches, they would have many days by foot.

"Are you sure?" Claudius peered into Flavius' gregarious smile. "We travel to Pergamum."

"We have chariots to spare in our household. You would do me great honor to take one."

"Could I carry some mail for the governor? Perhaps I could be paid some for my efforts?"

"Yes, yes. A good idea, indeed. I will check tonight. Jula, could you pack some food for the young ones?"

"Of course." Jula nodded. "Ah, Pergamum. You must visit the great hospital there. The healing center."

"My mother asked for more herbs."

"Your mother the healer, I remember so well."

Thecilla's eyes began to close, and she asked to retire to her mat. "A long day, and a long trip tomorrow. Thank you so much for your generosity."

Jula showed her to her room and left a candle for Thecilla. Thecilla opened the scroll once more and read the message to the church at Smyrna. She realized her Uncle John must've visited here also. He knew the Christians were the real jewels.

She began her prayers. Thanking God for Claudius and asking that her parents would not follow through on their plan to match her with Jacob. Uncle John's words kept playing in her mind. Jesus. Lamb of God. Roma, the beast. Love triumphs over evil. She thanked

God she wouldn't have to share the scrolls with the family of Flavius. They were proud citizens of Smyrna, proud of the temple of Roma, proud of the support they had given to the emperor.

Then she asked God to help her win the people to Jesus, like Paul. In days past, Thecla told many stories of Paul. A great man, a good friend.

Her thoughts rushed on, focusing on the warnings of her father and now Flavius. She asked for God's help, for safety. "Protect me from the the Romans. Help us share the scrolls. Help me fulfill my promise to Uncle John. Help me, God."

She pulled an empty scroll out of her bag to write her teacher, Thecla. Perhaps Flavius would see to its delivery for her. When she finished, she gave thanks once more then blew out the candle. Her body sank into the soft mat and soon she slept soundly.

30. Katharine and Pergamum

September 20, 2006

The small helicopter tilted gently when the pilot began his descent into Patmos. John looked out the window and described the view to Katharine, who couldn't see from the bed. "It's beautiful here, honey, so beautiful. The water is blue. White stucco houses cover the hillside. I see a cross at the highest point on top of what looks like a chapel. Little fishing boats are bobbing at the dock. Honey, we're almost there. Patmos, Patmos. It's so beautiful. Almost as beautiful as you!"

Katharine smiled at John and grasped his hand. She didn't try to answer, but lifted her head from the pillow on the stretcher and strained to look out to see the water and a bit of the view that John described.

"So beautiful, like you," John murmured into her ear and then stroked her head, leaning over to kiss her cheek and then her lips.

"Allah's Heli Flight" made a smooth landing on the helicopter pad. John spotted a small ambulance waiting. He knew arrangements had been made to take Katharine to the island medical center for a few days of observation. When she regained her strength, John had plans to book a honeymoon suite on the water, but for now, he preferred to keep medical care close by.

"What's the weather like?" John asked the pilot.

"Beautiful day, sir. 70 degrees in the shade. Warming up nicely."

The ambulance driver unloaded a small stretcher and wheeled it toward the helicopter. John squeezed Katharine's hand and kissed her cheek one more time, before the men carried her out to the waiting vehicle.

John stayed to thank the pilot and asked for information on the helicopter and plane's owner. Not only had the rich man lent his plane for the flight out of Istanbul, but also his helicopter to complete the journey. "I want to send a thank-you note and an invitation to visit us in the United States," he explained.

"Sir, the owner prefers not to release personal information. I will extend your gratitude to him and if you'd like, I will give him your contact number?"

John reached into his wallet and took out a small business card. "Well, then, tell him thank you very much. Tell him how much we appreciate his generosity during our difficult time. We'd like to return the favor. Thank you so much."

John climbed out of the helicopter, gathered their suitcases and loaded them into the ambulance, climbing in to sit by Katharine.

The driver headed up a curving road toward a higher point on the small island.

"What a view!" John said.

"Yes, so beautiful." Katharine whispered.

"Don't try to talk, dear. Your lungs are getting stronger, but the bullet punctured them. Let them rest. Patmos, a perfect place for healing."

"Where are we going, John?"

John remembered the doctor told him that the strong pain medicine would cause memory lapses. He started to explain the plan again.

"Honey, you're heading to a hospital now, for observation. Your friends were invited to a Conference of Mystics here. A Franciscan priest, a friend of Emily's father, brought Emily to Patmos for protection. Honey, she had been shot also, but just a small abrasion. Once she landed here and realized the safe haven, she asked to invite the rest of you. The MAMs got a free boat ride to the conference, courtesy of the same man who flew us over from Istanbul. Never a dull moment on the Archaeological Expedition in Search of Thecla!"

Katharine smiled and then laughed. "Oh, that hurts," she whispered.

"Who shot me? Do they know who shot me?" Katharine turned to John and then her breathing became labored from the exertion of forming the sentences.

"Rest, dear. Rest, dear. I'll tell you all about it soon. Try to sleep."

***

The ambulance left the Patmos dock behind, but the day buzzed with arrivals. The afternoon ferry from Samos brought quite a group of locals and internationals, along with a few Greeks on a late fall vacation.

Several checked into the Skala Hotel, facing the dock. There a pathway covered with an arched ceiling long overgrown with greenery welcomed guests into the inner courtyard of the prestigious accommodations, a favorite for the wealthy spending a few days on the island.

191

"I like this entrance! Very beautiful!" Brother Leonardo de Chachira walked under the green arch and nodded to his partner. "Thank you for making my reservation."

"We aim to please," Stephan Toflokous replied. "When the Papal See sends his representative to our island, we want to roll out the red carpet. Only the best." He gestured to the Brother to continue on toward the door, while smiling. They both knew relations were actually strained. The talks had begun and stalled out. The Roman Catholics and Eastern Orthodox continued to maintain a distance from each other. Centuries of division could not be erased overnight. But today they united in a common mission. Both churches hoped to preserve orthodoxy and did not want false scrolls confusing their followers.

"I'll give you a chance to freshen up, then we'll have a meeting at the monastery. The Turkish archaeological representative will be meet us there. A most urgent matter." Stephan offered his hand in a warm farewell.

Brother Chachira bowed and kissed his hand, taking a key at the desk for his room. On the way, he unknowingly passed the archaeologist, Halim, who had also been situated at the hotel earlier by Mr. Toflokous. He also passed a ruddy-faced man, headed out to the water front. Smiling, he slipped by into his room.

On a different mission, also checked into the Skala Hotel was George Matthews, a chubby man with a ruddy complexion, who had traveled many miles to do his work. He had begun by establishing a temporary Right Disciples headquarters in his suite at the hotel, with help from his trusted assistant, Mortimer Jacobs. And now, he headed for the cave where John wrote the book of Revelation. He couldn't wait to bow down and worship God there. And then, he'd get down to business.

***

In the small hospital, the nurse worked alone, preparing for Katharine. For years, the clinic had served the island population and their many summer visitors. Most serious cases were transferred to Athens or Kos. Minor cases would occasionally warrant an overnight stay, but many nights the ward remained empty. Now, the unit already housed a man wheeled in a few hours earlier. Samina looked forward to working again. Most years, the summer tourists took the hospital's business along when they left the island for winter. She liked the quiet place, but also preferred the busy days of summer.

The male patient continued to gain strength after a near drowning, but still seemed very confused. He kept asking for Brother Gabriel. His attending physician ordered 24-hour care. Fortunately, the nuns who brought him in volunteered to help with staffing during the night hours. Now one of them, Elizabeth, prepared to leave and gave her a report.

"An ambulance will arrive soon with the patient from Istanbul. An American, shot in Kusadasi. Her friends are attending our conference, so Ali Mohammed offered to fly her also, with her husband. One day post-op, still very weak. A punctured lung. I've been thinking we could move Mr. Jones to the back room and give her the front room. Her name is Dr. Katharine Long."

"Good idea. Two patients, almost a houseful. We transfer most patients to Athens for surgeries and hospital care."

"Sister Mary's on her way. She'll help. At home, we're usually watching at least 12 patients on a shift. Sister Mary is our head nurse. Staffing's a big problem at our hospitals in the States."

"Really?" Samina's Turkish brogue was strong, but she was remarkably fluent in English.

"How do you know English so well?" Elizabeth asked.

"Many people here learn at least three languages. I studied in England for several years during college. In Turkey, English is known by many."

A loud voice interrupted the women. "Get me out of here! Get me out of here! I didn't do anything!"

Samina and Elizabeth rushed into Mr. Jones' room. The small man stood beating on the window. Sweat poured off his face and the bandage on his forehead looked wet.

"Is something amiss, sir?" Samina asked.

"Let me out! Let me out!" He yelled and continued to beat on the windows.

"Would you like to go for a walk?" Elizabeth asked, wondering what challenges she'd bitten off by rescuing this man. Fortunately, he didn't break the windows.

She took his arm and started to guide him out of the clinic. "Come, let's see if you're up for a walk outside. We're not holding you here against your will. We just want you to get better. Come, let's go see what the day looks like." Elizabeth smiled at Samina, and then told her. "Don't worry, I'll take him for a walk. You'll be here for our new patient."

Elizabeth guided Mr. Jones, as they had decided to call him, out the clinic door and down the hall onto a small path. She knew the path provided a nice view of the sea from a previous walk and thought it might be a distraction for Mr. Jones. Perhaps, it would trigger his memory, which seemed to have been washed away in the water off the coast of Kusadasi.

Elizabeth felt a certain responsibility for the man. She hoped his memory would return soon. She knew memory loss could be permanent, but would not give up hope yet. She had never saved a life before and prayed for a full recovery with all her heart. She remembered her mixed feelings on the neonatal rotation when they saved babies' lives, but the children often faced life with such severe disabilities. Then again, perhaps throwing away memories provided a clean slate for some folks. An opportunity to start again.

A beautiful day greeted the unlikely pair. Elizabeth supported the man's arm and they made their way along the path, stopping on a beach to rest and enjoy the blue sky and equally blue water below. Elizabeth still couldn't quite believe the picture-perfect views on this island. Mr. Jones, though quiet, seemed absorbed in the moment and perhaps also enraptured with the panoramic view.

Down on the water below, a small fishing boat bobbed in the water. Elizabeth could make out nets attached to the boat, hanging out the back and over the sides. Like the times of Jesus, she thought. And not too far away, the disciples were fishing some two thousand years ago. She'd like to just stay and watch for awhile, but the morning session at the Conference would start soon. So after a few minutes, she helped Mr. Jones back up, and they started the walk back up to the clinic. He didn't seem to be self-conscious about his bandaged head. She decided that was a good thing, although it could also indicate brain damage. Jones seemed to tire easily, so Elizabeth walked slowly and continued to enjoy the beauty of the day.

***

Soon the driver wheeled their new patient into the small room near the front of the hospital. A tall man followed with their suitcases. Mary and Samina greeted the pair in the room.

The man reached out his hand in greeting to Mary and Samina. "Good morning. I'm John Long, and this is my wife, Dr. Katharine Long."

"A medical doctor?" Mary asked.

"No, a college professor," John smiled. "She won't be telling you how to do your job."

John scanned the view out the window. "Look, dear! A sea view. What a deal!" The window framed an idyllic scene of blue skies, white stucco houses and even some brightly colored fishing boats heading in with their catch.

The ambulance driver lined up the stretcher with the hospital bed and raised it to the same height. Mary and Samina stood on the opposite side of the bed, grabbing the sheet under Katharine, while they worked with the driver to gently slide Katharine onto the bed.

John pulled out several paper bills and handed them to the driver. "Thank you, so much. Thank you, very much."

194

Samina quickly interpreted for John, and the driver smiled. "He thanks you," Samina interpreted. Then he continued to talk to Samina in Greek, handing her the hospital notes he had received from the nurse in the helicopter. Samina read through the notes quickly, asked a few questions and then waved him on before briefing Elizabeth.

"Katharine is doing very well. Her vitals have been strong through the trip. After a few more days of rest, we have every reason to expect she will be ready to go home."

John smiled and stroked Katharine's hair. Katharine had fallen asleep.

Mary opened the small window, letting the sea breeze into the room. John took a seat by Katharine's head. Mary and Samina straightened the sheets and covered Katharine with another sheet and a cotton blanket.

"We'll let her rest for awhile," Mary whispered to John. "We can get the bedclothes arranged properly later." Mary and Samina tip-toed out and closed the door, just as Elizabeth and Mr. Jones were returning from their walk.

"A beautiful place you have here, ma'am," Mr. Jones told Samina as they headed back to his room. "What do you call it?"

"Patmos. The Greek Island of Patmos. You're at our hospital"

"Oh, oh. Patmos." Jones scratched his head looked back out the door. "I have heard that name before. Very familiar. Very familiar. Do you think I've been here before?"

"I don't know, sir. I don't know. It's very possible. Why don't you go and rest for a while and think about that some more. Maybe you will remember more." Mary guided Jones back to his room and waved to Elizabeth who wanted to get away to attend a prayer service at the conference. "I brought you some magazines also. I thought perhaps they would trigger some memories." She placed them down on the table next to Jones' bed.

"Thank you, ma'am. You have all been most kind to me. Some-how, I'm not sure I deserve your kindness. Thank you, anyway." Jones sat down on the bed and picked up a magazine. "*Newsweek*," he said out loud. "Hmm. I know I've seen one of these before."

"Read it. It may trigger something. I'll be back in a while. We have a new patient and I want to attend to her." Mary left the room and went out to the infirmary's nursing desk to consult with Samina about care for Katharine.

***

Brother Gabriel hurried into the monastery library where Joe and Ursula were intently working together on translating Scroll #3.

"She's here! Ursula, your friend has arrived. Katharine's settled in the island's medical center!"

"Wonderful! How is she doing?"

"The nurse says very well. She had no problems with the trip and she is resting."

"Can I go see her?" Ursula asked.

"Yes, yes. I think that would be a good idea. But the nurse suggested you might wait a few hours, because she's sleeping." Gabriel left the room, closing the library door behind him.

Ursula hugged Joe, and then looked up. "Thank you, God! Praise God!" Ursula raised both hands and danced with joy.

Joe chuckled. "Next thing I know I'll have a holy roller on my hands!"

Ursula smiled. "Joe, I have been agnostic most of my life. But I will never be a doubter again. God is with us. God was with Thecilla, Joe. How can anyone doubt the existence of God? How could I for all those years?"

Joe chuckled again. "Who'd of thought Ursula would become a holy roller? Dancing with the Pergamum church. Whirling? Did you just whirl?"

"Joe, let's go read the scroll to Katharine. Let's take it to her."

"Yes, yes. But first let's get this finished." Joe turned back to the computer and looked at the ancient words. Ursula and Joe had been working 20 hours a day on the translation, but they did not work alone. With Internet and email assistance, they communicated freely with other experts and Joe knew the best in the field. "I got another email from John back in the States! Ah, here is one from Berlin. Let's see how their translation agrees with ours."

"Are the Turkish authorities going to find us and put an end to your work?"

"Let's cross that bridge when we get to it. Until now, we're on a roll. It used to take years to translate a scroll, and now you have the assistance of experts around the world at your fingertips! Unreal. 'Circling?'" He told Ursula, "Here look this up in that dictionary you have. I believe this says 'Circling into God.'"

"Let me see, John's translation says 'dancing into God.' And Rudolf from Berlin? Let's see...

He says 'circling,' but then in parentheses has 'dancing.'"

Joe pulled Ursula up. "May I have this dance?"

He bowed to her and then stretched his hands out and touched hers.

He looked into her brown eyes and began to sing. His strong tenor voice filled the room with the Hebrew words of "*Hava Nagila*" and became the accompaniment to the dance. He began to twirl her around the room. They laughed and kicked their legs high in the air.

Their arms locked straight on each other's shoulders. Ursula's hair flew out. Joe began to sweat. Ursula's alto voice provided a harmony to Joe's, and they circled in the small library, dizzy with joy, inebriated with love, feeling a deep connection with the ancient Hebrew people and those followers of Jesus who sang and danced with Thecilla so many years before.

Joe had been raised in a Catholic-Jewish household and had grown up respecting both traditions. He finished singing the Hebrew, and yet they continued to dance. Now, Ursula was sweating also. "Do you know the English version?" Joe asked Ursula.

"No. Do you know it?"

"Sing with me, dear." Joe laughed and frolicked some more. "Let's kick high. Get those legs up!" Then he began to sing in English, "Gather, come gather round me, a joyous sound we will make today!"

After a few more rounds, Joe and Ursula collapsed back into the chairs with laughter. Sweat poured down Joe's face. Ursula took a handkerchief out of her purse and wiped it dry.

After their respirations had slowed down and the endorphin buzz had kicked in, Ursula turned to Joe. "Can you believe it?" she asked. "This is so much more than I ever imagined!"

"Hold that thought," Joe replied. He took the handkerchief from Ursula's hand and wiped her forehead and then her temples. Then he put his hand under her chin and leaned forward covering her mouth with his. Her lips opened, and his tongue gently probed into mouth.

He dropped the handkerchief to the floor and pulled her up, out of the chair, while pressing his body against hers. His mouth was only a little higher than hers, and now he broke the kiss and looked down into her eyes.

"Ursula. Oh, Ursula." He looked deep into her brown eyes and she felt the probing, felt the connection, felt the love. Joe murmured, "Love me, love me, love me."

Ursula responded, "I do, Joe. I do, I do."

But their passion was interrupted by a knock. Joe went to the door, smiling when he saw Sallie standing there with her hands on her hips.

"Yes?"

"Brother Gabriel arranged a driver to take us to Katharine. But somehow I get the feeling I'm interrupting something." Sallie started to laugh. "Should I come back later?" She started to close the door.

"No, no. We'll come. We just finished another scroll. We can read it to Katharine." Ursula pulled Sallie back into the room. "We'll come with you."

When the women walked out of the library into the warm afternoon to the waiting car, none of them noticed the tall man standing just outside the chapel door. But the tall man heard the word "scrolls" and now tried very hard to make himself inconspicuous and contain his excitement. Ever since he left his think tank office in the United States in search of Moses Sun and the newly discovered scrolls he had been running into roadblocks. At last the door had flung wide open and he had hit the jackpot. He watched quietly, holding his Scofield Chain Reference Bible[xxxi] under his arm, and his laptop bag strapped securely over his shoulder. Praying quietly, he noticed a group of people coming down the hall.

They all had on name tags. He didn't.

When the group reached him, a large man in the front of the group extended his hand, "*Guten Tag*. Good morning. *Bonjour?*"

"Yes, Good morning, I speak English," the tall man smiled and met the greeter with a firm hand.

"Are you registered for our conference, sir? I don't believe I remember checking you in?"

"Ah, no, no. Not yet. Could you tell me where the registration desk might be? I arrived rather late last night. You know how international travel can be."

"Come with me, sir. I'll check you in. You are registered, no?"

"Actually, no. Is that a problem? I heard about the conference rather late, after the deadlines had passed. But I just knew I had to come. Is there room?"

"We'll see. We'll see. We've had quite a few unexpected guests. You may have to find your own lodging. Will that be a problem?"

"No, no. In fact, I have a room down by the dock." The tall man was quite well situated, actually, with a suite of rooms. And George would be waiting for him to return soon.

"And what sort of a mystic might you be?" the registrar asked him.

"I am a Pentecostal Holy Roller Mystic. Have you heard of our type?"

The registrar laughed. "A holy roller mystic. That's a new one. But I get it. That is a form of mysticism, isn't it? You dance with God. Hildegaard of Bingen would probably approve."

"Who, sir? Hildegaard? Is he here?"

"No, I don't think so. She died several centuries ago." The registrar laughed and then looked up. "OK, let's get this paper work completed. I don't want to miss our first session this morning. The Muslim Holy Rollers are going to speak."

"Muslim Holy Rollers?" the man asked.

"They call themselves the 'Whirling Dwervishes,' but just like you, they dance with God."

"With all due respect, I don't think it's the same thing. We worship the one true God. They are heathens, worshiping a false God. They are the evil ones."

"Hmm. I think you might have a few things to learn this week, sir. Keep an open mind. Let the Spirit speak to you, OK?"

***

Mary and Samina finished changing Katharine's bed, tucked her in and raised the bed to a sitting position. Snores emanated from Mr. Jones' room, although the door had been shut tight.

"That little walk seems to have worn him out," Mary explained. "We have another patient who is recovering from a water rescue. Amnesia. Earlier he thought he was being held prisoner, so Sister Elizabeth took him for a walk. I hope the snoring doesn't bother you. We do have earplugs."

Mary turned to Katharine who just smiled. "No problem," she said, then added, "What a marvelous view!"

Katharine looked out at the sunny seaside landscape framed by her small window, just as the MAMs walked in.

"Katharine!" Ursula was the first to exclaim.

She ran over to the bedside and kissed her cheek and took her hand. "You're here! You're alive! You look wonderful!"

"Well, I'm not quite wonderful yet, but I'm doing fairly well." Katharine spoke quietly.

"She's still quite weak in her lungs," John explained for her. "We're trying to limit her talking. It's good to see you all again."

John looked with curiosity at the tall man standing beside Ursula.

Ursula explained. "Joe Cohen, John Long. Joe is an old friend who came from California to help translate."

John reached out and extended his hand to Joe. "A very good old friend, I surmise?"

Ursula blushed, and even Katharine laughed. "An old flame, burning brightly again!"

One by one the MAMs gave Katharine a kiss, and Emily introduced Brother Gabriel and Brother David, who had come along to hear the scroll. "Gabriel's a friend of my Dad's. Small world, no? He rescued me from the press conference and brought me here, first! Then he arranged for the other MAMs to come. We owe him, big time."

Katharine extended her hand to shake Gabriel's. "Thank you, so much. And Brother David?" she asked Emily.

"We're at the International Conference of Mystics, Katharine. It is full of people from many different religions who practice meditation, prayer, union with God. Brother David has been on the mystical path for many years. He even wrote a book, *The Mystic Thread.*"

"Oh, yes," Katharine whispered. "I have my students read that in my Contemporary Religious Thought class. Pleased to meet you. Brother Merkt, is it?"

"Yes, thank you, ma'am." Brother David took Katharine's hand and gave it a kiss. "Not many people know my name or have any idea I wrote a book! I'm impressed!"

"Katharine teaches religion at Mainline College back in Riverland, Ohio," Sallie explained to Brother David. "If it weren't for her, none of us would be here now. But that's a long story!"

Ursula interrupted. "We don't want to keep you long, Katharine. We know you need to rest, but we'd like to read you Scroll #3. We just finished translating it this morning. It's wonderful."

Joe opened his laptop and waited for the computer to boot up.

Ursula continued. "Pergamum. It's the letter about Pergamum. You know Pergamum was a hospital at the time. Just what you need Katharine!"

"I think I'd like to avoid any more hospitals for a while," she whispered back.

"Right." Ursula sat on a small chair next to Katharine's bed. Once the computer screen was in view, she took the laptop off the bed where Joe was working, and put it on her lap. "Here, I'll read it, Joe."

Joe crouched down beside Ursula and finished opening the file. "OK, dear. Carry on."

Ursula leaned forward and began to read.

Scroll #3 Pergamum

Teacher, I write from Pergamum. [ ] wish I could carry you here to the healing place for your [ ] and pains. Claudius is learning at the hospital, for his mother [ ] herbs for healing. [ ]

We stay with the Christians in the caves where they are eager to hear the word of John. The scrolls call them to worship [ ] to dance, to praise God.

Teacher, I have never had so much [ ] worship. Have you ever [ ] the Jewish dances? Whirling in circles? Here they sing the words and circle into the night. The candles light the cave walls and their faces when they

200

sing, "Holy, Holy, Holy, the Lord God Almighty, Who was, Who Is and Who is to come."

And yet they said to me, "Read, read some more." When I finally finished, they were not satisfied. They wanted to hear it again.

Their beloved Antipas was killed by the Romans, like Jesus, and so they know that it can be dangerous to love God and defy the Emperor. They understood that John's vision was to bring them hope and faith to persevere.

Their prophet, Jephthut explained, "God is so good to give us this revelation through John, because God knows we love to worship! Thanks be to God for this cave where we can stay up late into the night singing and praising our Lamb who was slain, [ ] loves us and loves the Romans who killed him and seek to persecute us."

Claudius came by late and asked [ ] one more day. He is learning so much from the healers at the hospital, so I promised to read again in the morning.

We started the dance one more time, and Claudius joined us. Circling into God, I thought my heart would explode with the great joy I felt [ ] with God's people and my beloved by my side. I pray that Claudius will listen to the words of John soon.

Then the Romans came to the cave and the people quickly put out the candles and we dropped to the ground [ ] not safe here. We are leaving before morning light. Pray for us.

Ursula stopped reading and looked up.

"Wow! This is amazing. Truly amazing." Sallie poked her glasses up on her nose. "Is this for real?"

Katharine began to speak, then stopped. Her voice was soft and raspy. She began to cough.

Sallie poured her some water from the pitcher by her bed. Katharine took some sips and then began to speak again.

"I had a vision. I had a dancing vision. In a cave. Like the scroll. They danced in the night, laughing, praising God."

"When?" Ursula asked.

"My memory blurs, but I remember the shot, the bright lights. I remember the cave. Everyone dancing and celebrating. I thought perhaps I had... entered heaven. They praised God. And then, when I woke up, I was in Istanbul, in the hospital. No cave. I thought it was a dream."

"Wow!" Sallie exclaimed. "That's amazing!"

Jane raised her eyebrows with suspicion. "Are you guys going crazy on me?"

Ursula looked at Jane. "You don't get it, do you? These scrolls are changing our lives. First me, then Molly, now Katharine. Your turn is coming, girlfriend."

Katharine whispered, her voice fading. "Jane, it's true. I'll never be the same. When we arrived in this room a while ago, I lifted my hands and said 'Praise God!' John thinks I have gone crazy, too. But I'm not. I'm just full of the joy of the Spirit of God. God is with us."

Katharine rested her head on the pillow and smiled. "I'm still very tired," she added.

Ursula shut the laptop and looked at the group. "I think we better let Katharine sleep. Joe and I have more translating to do."

"Sure, guys. Tell us anything," Jane laughed. "I'm sure you're going to head right back to your rooms and translate that spark into something else."

Sallie punched Jane. "You're just jealous because you're not getting any."

"Any what?" Emily asked.

"Never mind," Jane said. "Don't let Sallie corrupt your young innocent ears."

Katharine laughed, and the MAMs headed out of the room.

"The Whirling Dervishes are giving a presentation right now. I want to catch that."

Emily linked arms with Brother Gabriel. "We'll see you all later."

Later, when the van pulled back up to the entrance of Hotel Romeos, Molly told Emily, "I want to go with you to see the Muslim dancers."

"Me, too," Sallie quipped.

"Then we're off." Emily took Molly's hand and Sallie followed close behind into the hotel and then out into the courtyard toward the swimming pool where chairs had been arranged around a small platform for the afternoon session.

"I think I'll pass on this one," Priscilla said. "I'm going back to my room to read my Bible."

"See you all later," Jane announced. "I am going for a walk."

Joe and Ursula headed back to the library, Priscilla and Jane were off their separate ways, while Emily, Molly and Sallie joined the Brothers David and Gabriel to learn more about circling into God, Muslim style.

31. Thecilla in Pergamum

September 16, 94 A.D.

The cave opened into a large, circular room. Niches dug into the cave wall held candles, burning brightly. The shadows danced against the walls and lit the faces of the Christians gathered for evening worship. Thecilla read from the scroll of her uncle's revelation. The people sat quietly listening. From time to time, someone would exclaim. Then Thecilla stopped, while a man or woman discussed the words written.

"Worship, always worship. The theme of the revelation, don't you see?" Jephthut, the elder called the group back into focus. "We must not let the Romans scare us from our faith. Always hope and love triumph over wrong."

Thecilla nodded her agreement. The message of John above all called for worship.

"Shall you join us?" Jepthtut motioned to Thecilla. "It's time to dance. Your uncle always danced with us on his visits."

The people stood, a young man grabbed Thecilla's hand, leading her into the circle.

Thecilla looked to the musicians, who began a lively melody. "Again? You dance every night?"

"Not always," he muttered. "Sometimes we must be very quiet."

Thecilla wondered at his words, but soon she was caught up in the circling dance, laughing, calling out with the rest of them.

The leader sang, "Holy!"

The group responded, "Holy!"

The leader again sang, "Holy!"

The group added, "Holy is our God!" Circling into the night, the dancers moved faster as the musicians picked up the tempo with each repetition. The older ones dropped out laughing, while only the young were left running with feet kicked high. Thecilla laughed along. Her eyes shone with the joy of these holy people circling into love with God and each other. Claudius ducked into the cave in the middle of the dance and took her hand. She felt warm beside him and so happy to have him laughing with her Christian friends.

"Just like our Jewish dances," he said.

Thecilla felt so at home in the cave. A cave had been her second home during her childhood, where she stayed frequently with her dear teacher, Thecla. If only she could talk with her now. She yearned to tell her about the great library she had visited in the afternoon. She longed to return to the library to read. Thecla had instilled in her a love of learning, and how she wished for a way to continue her learning. Claudius had been brought up in the synagogue and even yet spent long hours in instruction. She wished she could go with him, but it was not a place for a girl.

Her family tradition held rare opportunity for women. Mama told her about her grandmother, Priscilla, raised almost like a Jewish boy by her grandfather. She knew the scripture so well. One time she even told Mama she had written the scroll to the Hebrews, although the house church called it Paul's. Grandmother Priscilla taught Mama, then, too. Mama knew the scriptures well. She wished that Grandmother Priscilla hadn't died so young at the hands of Nero in Rome, along with Paul and her grandfather, Aquilla. She wished she could have learned from her, too.

Thecilla wondered now why her parents would not want her to take the scrolls to the churches. To keep the faith, like her grandparents, Priscilla and Aquilla, who preached the good news with Paul in the days of old. That family tradition, she now continued. But Thecla would understand. Thecla, too, had to defy her mother to follow Paul and be his disciple.

Thecilla's thoughts twirled with the dance. Soon she let go of her endless ruminations, allowing the music to transport her into the joy of God. Claudius laughed, his eyes lit bright. Thecilla could not remember a more perfect moment.

But then someone called out. "The Romans come!" The music stopped. Everyone dropped to the floor. Others extinguished all but one candle. In the opening to the circular room, she saw a man with a red tunic and a spear.

"Have you not learned, by now?" He called out into their dark space. No one answered, yet he continued. "You must honor the Emperor! What is this treason that you call this Jesus of Nazareth your Lord? There is only one Lord. Remember Antipas. Remember what happens to those who refuse to serve the Emperor. Quit this foolishness, this worship of your God!"

The Roman backed out of the cave and mounted his horse and rode off into the night.

Thecilla cried. Jephthut looked at her and repeated himself. "Sometimes, we must be very quiet."

Much later, after many quiet prayers and words of hope, Thecilla left the circle and stole away to the small cubicle where they placed a mat for her earlier. She propped a candle close to her writing parch-

ment and began to write again to her dear Thecla. In the morning, Claudius would help her find someone to carry it on its way back to the high cave, overlooking Ephesus.

Then she prayed for Claudius. He had studied at the hospital for two long days, learning about the healing rites to share with his mother, a healer in Ephesus. Once again, he had left when she began to read the scrolls. She so wanted him to hear the news of John. What would he think when he finally listened to the scrolls all the way through? How could he be so content to cart her around from town to town, not even paying attention to the reason for her trip? She knew he was paid well for the items he carried from town to town. She wondered if he could be working for the Romans, but then shook the thought out of her mind and let sleep carry her into a calm and silent night.

32. Jane at Thyatira

September 21, 2006

When Jane left the hotel she needed to run. At first, the situation had been exciting for her, but now she missed the comforts of home. What she wanted bad: Starbucks, *The Wall Street Journal* and some conversations with her stockbroker. But instead, there she stood with a group of crazy women, a conference of religious fanatics, and some very strange scrolls, not to mention Officer Dan Parks camping out in her thoughts.

Jane didn't have any idea where she was headed this particular morning, but she knew she had to get away. Away from the mysterious people populating the hotel and hanging out in her present life. She imagined a little cafe overlooking the water, with some strong Greek coffee. She tucked a recent issue of *Bloomberg*'s under her arm for company. Yet, she felt herself agreeing with Emily and Ursula. Patmos did have some sort of magical, mystical aura. Almost a spiritual aura, she thought now. Could all this talk be rubbing off onto her? Knocking the craziness out of her mind, she started to jog. Her lungs opened up and for the first time in many days, Jane began to feel really good.

She picked up speed on the picturesque street near the hotel, careful to avoid the children playing and the adults standing and chatting by open doors. Soon she noticed another jogger on the other side of the road, almost in step with her open gait. Coincidence, she imagined, but ducked into a shop to be sure and watched him run by.

The tall, lanky man passed the shop, but then slowed to a walk, crossed the street and headed back up toward the hotel, very slowly. He stopped and looked directly at the small shop where she stood, looking right at her.

Her cell phone started to ring, and Parks' number lit on the screen. She considered her options and decided to let it ring. Talking to Parks could only bring more trouble. She'd pledged silence on their whereabouts and Parks could only want one thing. Well, maybe two. He had made his desires quite clear.

That man could not really be after her. Nevertheless, she waited until he walked a block up the hill, then dashed back out of the shop and down toward the water. She turned around to check on him and sure enough, he had changed directions again and was headed her way.

She ran quickly, darting into another shop. Was she losing her mind or he was really tailing her? Then she contemplated calling Parks for help, but resolved instead to take care of herself, like she'd been doing for years. Yet she wondered what the tall man could possibly want with her and why in the hell Sun shot Katharine and Emily. And for that matter, why did the MAMs have to hide out on Patmos right after they found the scrolls and had done absolutely nothing wrong? She sure as hell had no idea what was going on and had no interest in finding out the hard way.

Her stalker walked by the shop, looking carefully, trying to peer through the dark storefront. She doubted he could see her where she hid, behind a glass counter of figurines.

Now totally spooked, she waited a few more minutes, then went back out and headed toward the hotel with a fast sprint. To hell with the cafe and coffee, she thought. Hanging out in a conference of mystical fanatics would be an improvement over being tailed by that strange, spooky man.

Soon panting, her lungs were hurting. Out of shape, from days of traveling, she longed to get back home, back to reality, and back into her daily routine. The trip registered as a freaking lulu in her mind.

When she reached the hotel, she headed toward the dining room for some fresh water and coffee. Looked like she'd be chatting about homemade bread again with Brother Lawrence, who seemed to always be camped out in the hotel dining room

"I practice the presence of God," he had told her the day before. The good brother explained he named himself after a guy who wrote a book by that name. Whatever, Jane had thought. She needed her coffee, he needs his practice. Worked for her.

And so that is how she happened to be sitting there at about 10:30 a.m. when the tall man, whom she had eluded earlier, sauntered in and greeted both her and Brother Lawrence with a wide grin.

"Did you lose this?" He asked Jane, and then held out a copy of the financial magazine that she guessed she must have dropped on the sprint back.

She felt sweat rolling off her face. With a wet T-shirt clinging to her fairly flat chest, especially damp under her arms, she also smelled the rank body odor emanating from her body. She hoped it created enough smell to keep him at a distance.

The man looked very smooth. Too cool, too calm, too collected. No evidence he had just been running or trailing or following the sweating Jane. She wondered now how in hell he could be so composed after fricking messing up her morning. What kind of a jerk was this tall man who had materialized out of nowhere and had become her very own personal nemesis?

"Who are you?" she blurted her words with an edge of anger in her voice.

Mr. Smooth dangled his name tag and spoke with a smile, "I never thought you'd ask."

Brother Lawrence rolled his eyes and went to get some coffee for the man. He left Jane stranded with Mr. Smooth, who proceeded to give his name, address and pedigree and then asked for her number. While Jane stared dumbfounded, he just kept right at it.

"Would you like to check my references?"

He held out a business card and shoved it into her hand. Looking down, she read, "Mortimer Jacobs, The Right Disciples, Denver Colorado." She whispered her favorite profanity under her breath, "Sonofabitch!" .

"Excuse me, sir. I must be going." Jane turned to Brother Lawrence to wave her goodbye. "Great coffee, as usual, Larry. Hey, this is one lonely guy." She pointed to the tall man, whom she now knew to be a co-worker of Moses Sun. "Give him some coffee and help him practice God! Catch you later, Brother Lawrence."

She slipped out of the room quicker than Mr. Jacobs could turn and watch her go. The good brother handed him a cup of coffee, and they both sat down. Mentally she thanked Brother Lawrence for giving her time to make a getaway and call Dan Parks.

Later she had second thoughts, but the moment she was free of Mortimer's advances, she thought of the MAMs, and dammit, herself. They needed protection, and Parks was the best private eye around. She made the call. Later, she'd explain to the MAMs. They would understand. When Parks showed up on Patmos, they wouldn't have any choice.

At just about that time, Jane Masters, who prided herself in just frequenting churches for weddings and funerals, needed some prayer. The place must be getting to her. She hadn't been in a church since – her mother's funeral? But 10 years later, Jane needed some help. The present situation was careening out of control, too far beyond her own sensibilities. Jane made a beeline for the outdoor circular chapel to pray. Fortunately, she looked into an empty space and immediately sauntered into the middle of the chapel, grabbed a pillow she'd seen the people use earlier to cushion their knees, and sunk down on hers. She had some serious talking to do with God and didn't think she could do it standing or even sitting in a pew. The time had come to get down to business.

Unfortunately for Jane, the Conference of Mystics wasn't far behind. Within five minutes the outdoor chapel filled and a service of some sort began to take place. She got up off her knees, sat back in her chair and began to listen.

The people leading the service were setting up a few things on the altar right in front of her, while the music began softly. She recognized the song from her youth catechism activities at church, how many years ago? Even now, her mind mouthed the words so deep in her soul, "And Jesus said 'Come to the water, you won't be denied. I felt every teardrop, when in darkness you cried. And I came to remind you that for those tears, I died.' "

For some reason, Jane began to cry. In the service they were talking about the water, about the living water and about Jesus and about the river of Siddhartha and the oceans of love and after awhile, she thought her tears were right in place because this was one wet meeting.

Right about then, Joe and Ursula came up and began to read Scroll #4. Jane wanted to tell them to sit down, to hide, to get off the stage. She wanted to warn them about Mortimer Jacobs and the Right Disciples, but she had been taught to never to talk in church. So, instead she sat like the obedient Catholic schoolgirl she had once been, scared out of her britches, yet beginning to feel something washing over her that she couldn't even put it into words. Joe's warm voice filled the chapel and soothed her soul. She felt utterly mesmerized.

Scroll # 4 Thyatira

Grace to you, dear teacher, and peace from the valley of the [ ] Rivers in the garrison of Thyatira, where the Roman armies are no match for the love of God in Christ Jesus.

I write this with great joy [ ] visit in this town, where the roads meet and the Christians [ ] meet God. Your prayers are answered [ ]. Claudius stayed near to hear the Revelation of John.

The church here follows in the tradition [ ] and business woman, Lydia, who was baptized by the disciple Paul. We stay in the home of Lycilla, whose grandmother was Lydia. She dyes purple cloth [ ]. The home is adorned with [ ] purple tapestries.

They had a great feast at the [ ]. We ate our fill, and as they reclined at the tables in the [ ], I began to read the message to their church. When [ ], they asked me to stop [ ] they could discuss what the words could mean. The elders prayed for understanding, and suddenly [ ] Chantilla, stood to speak. "You [ ] have become a part of the market and the Roman garrison. You join in the worship of false gods when you eat the meat sacrificed to the Roman emperor and the gods in the temples. You have been corrupted by the whore of Rome. The words of John call us to repent and not serve a false God. [ ] be pure. [ ] worship the one God. We must follow God in all our ways and not participate in sexual relations, unless we lay with our betrothed."

"But, who is the woman Jezebel? We have no woman here [ ]," another said.

"Jezebel is from the ancient scripture, the daughter of Ethbaal, the king of Sidon, and the wife of Ahab. She turned the people away from worship of the one true God. She is a symbol of one who does not follow God. She is all of us; she is the tempter; she is the one who calls us astray. We must repent." Chantilla replied. "Let us go to the river [ ]," the leader, Anias said.

"Yes, let us go and repent!" Lycilla agreed. "The elders will pray for you and baptize you this day!"

One moment we were enjoying a great feast, and the next we were running to the river. "It is our way," Lycilla explained. "My grandmother was baptized in the river by Paul, and our church believes that the river is the place to repent."

At the river they [ ] and prayed. One by one, [ ] confessed their sins and then walked into the water. Anias and the elders prayed over them and told them that their sins were forgiven. There were 10 people [ ] baptized. They confessed their belief in Jesus Christ, and they were in the water [ ] a beautiful sight and as they went under the water, Lycilla explained that they are dying to self and beginning a new life in Jesus. The radiance of their smiles shone brighter than the afternoon sun.

My heart leaped [ ] as Claudius stepped forward and asked Anias, "What must I do to become a Christian?"

"Repent, and be baptized this day, brother. You are a child of God," Anias told him.

They went into the water together and Anias dipped him under the water and then said, "Hear the good news. In Jesus, your sins are forgiven. I baptize you in the name of Lamb, in the name of our God, and in the name of the Holy Spirit. Welcome to the Church, Claudius."

Later, after an evening meal, I began to read again. Claudius held the scrolls for me and listened. [   ].

Chantilla stood again to explain the words. "Do you not hear? We are to resist the empire. We must be faithful to the one True God. We must consider the ways we support the empire and stop. We must be willing to die defending God. The Emperor is not our God."

Claudius was up late into the night praying and asking God to lead him. He has been a staunch supporter of the Romans, and now he wonders what changes he must make. I am not telling him what to do. Pray that God will instruct him on the path of peace.

My heart is filled with so much joy, I feel like a flying bird. Thank you for your prayers for your devoted Thecilla. I love you, dear teacher.

And there in that Patmos chapel, a light went on in Jane's soul. She began to understand something she would never even have considered before this Archaeological Expedition in Search of Thecla. She caught the spirit of Thecilla's life and the truth of God's light and wanted that water to wash over her.

She jumped up, out of her normal reserved character. "Baptism. I want to be baptized again," she yelled out. "I want to have that total cleansing experience. I want the water to wash over me. Like Lycilla, like Claudius, like Lydia, like Jesus of Nazareth. I want the water."

One of the monks from the monastery took the microphone. "On Patmos, we have a long tradition of baptism at the water. There is a beach not far from here. Would you like to go now?"

Propelled by an inner voice, she could only nod in agreement.

"Come this way, then. What's your name?

"Jane? He confirmed her whisper. "Why don't you go change into some light clothes for your baptism. Are there any others?"

And to her surprise, quite a few of the mystics rose to join her, filing out of the chapel, dispersing to their rooms. She noticed Priscilla smiling, sitting with closed eyes and hands held high when she passed by her on the way out. One of the more creative musicians had started a chorus of: "When I went down to the river to pray." And pretty soon the whole congregation of mystics were singing along. The chorus continued with the music following Jane while she climbed the steps to her room. She continued whistling the familiar tune, while changing into a white dress for the occasion.

A short time later, she joined the others back in the chapel. The local monk led their procession streaming out, through the hotel lobby and into the sunny day, heading down toward the sea. Although they looked like an orderly fire drill, the fire raging through Jane's soul told her this was a helluva lot more. Her white sundress was flowing in the light breeze, and the MAMs flanked her in front and behind. She felt special. She couldn't speak. She just let that God presence that Brother Lawrence practiced fill her soul.

Later that night, she tried to explain the joy to Parks, who showed up quicker than she ever thought possible. He didn't get it. She started telling him it was more important than her stocks, and empire was not the thing. Heightened security couldn't hold a candle to the Living Water.

Parks didn't want to listen. He just wanted to jump her bones, which was not at all on her radar screen. He left in frustration, and Jane ended up pouring out her heart to Molly and Sally, pondering her baptism experience.

***

When Dan Parks left Jane's room, wondered if he could have botched the job any worse. First, Sun fired shots right in front of his face, and now his accomplice had closed in. How had the rat smelled out the MAMs and made it to Patmos when he didn't even know where in hell they had gone? Jane's dismissal compounded his unease. On foreign soil, he knew better than to go it alone. He headed toward the police station near the dock. This time he'd have help and he'd be dammed if those Wrong Disciples would hurt any more MAMs. Not Jane, not any of them. He couldn't for the life of him figure out why they would be targeting her.

He parked in front of the police station and took the steps up three at a time. No time to waste with the Right Disciples in town.

Unfortunately, the officer on duty knew very little English, and asked him to be seated to wait for the other officers to return.

Parks fidgeted and pulled out his Blackberry, amusing himself on a game of hearts, trying to calm himself, yet keep the adrenalin flowing for the chase ahead.

***

In the conference room at the Monastery of St. John, Brother Simone offered a full spread of roasted lamb, a traditional Greek salad of cucumbers, olives, tomatoes, with olive oil and slabs of Greek cheese, potatoes and tzatziki sauce with fresh bread for the visiting dignitaries. He sat back and enjoyed a cup of strong coffee, while feasting on the cook's specialty, baklava. He had done his part, as requested by the bishop in Athens. Now he would listen and try to understand what all the hoopla was about.

When the bishop came to the monastery, Simone knew something was up. The bishop often came for ceremonies and feast days, but rarely journeyed to Patmos off season. Simone had been ordered to invite the local orthodox priest, Stephan Toflokous, who managed the Center for Orthodox Spirituality. Joining them at the table were a Roman Catholic official, Brother Leonardo de Cachira from Turkey, an archaeologist from Ephesus, and a representative of the Turkish Prime Minister from Istanbul, Said Ahmed. Sitting in also, at the Bishop's request were the Police Chief of Patmos, Mikel Lagos, and and his assistant, Nicolas Platoniotis.

Over dinner, archaeologist Halim Mohammed, had explained the unusual archaeological find unearthed the previous week in a cave on BûlBûl Dag, overlooking the Ephesus site. "The women from America unearthed scrolls, preserved to such a condition to be legible. It's almost impossible."

Brother Simone knew the Turkish government relied on the economic benefits of tourism to the ancient sites. He himself had enjoyed visiting Ephesus several times. But why scrolls would be of concern to this group, and why the police were called in, continued to baffle him.

"Are the scrolls authentic?" The bishop questioned Halim.

"Yes, we think so. Preliminary lab work establishes them to the first century, plus or minus one hundred years." Halim nodded and remained silent.

"Preposterous! These scrolls are fakes." Brother Leonardo took issue with Halim's remark. "You have no way of authenticating those scrolls. They may very well be plants by these American women, trying to change the course of history."

"That is not our concern." Said Ahmed interrupted the Roman Catholic. "We have reason to believe that the women have taken the scrolls out of the country, and we must retrieve those scrolls. They are the property of the Republic of Turkey."

"I thought you said the scrolls are locked in the presidential vault in Istanbul for safekeeping?" The Bishop showed his confusion.

The Roman Catholic official nodded his head. "Yes, yes. But somehow this woman Ursula Goodtree and her conspirator, Dr. Joseph Cohen, are translating the scrolls. We have a report from our Cardinal in Chicago, Illinois. One of his priests has been consulted for the translation. We must stop them. The scrolls will promote false teaching and lead the people astray."

"How do you know what the scrolls say?" Halim asked. "We haven't translated them."

"I've seen the emails, they have translations for four of the scrolls." Brother Leonardo sat back in his chair with a full stomach and folded his hands over his protruding belly. "They're spreading false teachings. The Holy See wants this stopped immediately."

"The Pope?" Brother Simone spoke out loud. "The Pope is involved?"

Ahmed turned to the police. "We need your help. The women arrived in Patmos yesterday."

Mikel considered the situation carefully. He didn't want to get involved and now looked for a graceful way out. "What do you want us to do sir? This is a peaceful island. We want no problems. The women cause no problem here." He knew the Greek Prime Minister would side with the United States. Greek loyalties would stay with the American women, rather than the Turk. The situation sounded a bit ridiculous to him, also. How could the translation of scrolls, a scholarly matter, be such a cause for concern? Relations between his country and Turkey were strained at best. Although tourist vessels sailed daily between the two countries, the refugees who took to the waters every night were offered asylum on Greek soil. Love between the two countries was unlikely to blossom anytime soon. In the monastery, perhaps, the good brothers offered hospitality to the Muslim Turk, but elsewhere? Unlikely on his island. The officer's thoughts were interrupted by an order from the bishop.

"We must retrieve the laptop and the camera. Too much is at stake. Later, perhaps we find the scrolls are false, or true, whatever, but right now we must honor our Roman Catholic and Turkish brothers and stop unauthorized translations of these scrolls. They have no right to the scrolls, neither by the church, nor Turkey. You must help us, Officer."

"I cannot authorize theft." Mikel shook his head and stared back at the bishop, who was not accustomed to disobedience.

"Thou shalt not steal." Nicolas tried to add some humor. "It's in the good book, sir. We uphold the law in Greece."

"The women are the thieves. We only ask you to recover what does not belong to them. All archaeological finds are property of our country. We send people to prison for stealing our antiquities," Said Ahmed pleaded with the officers.

Mikel looked at his assistant, Nico, shaking his head, and then his cell phone began to vibrate. An American at the station wanted help protecting women? He read the text message, thinking the plot was deepening.

"I'm sorry, I have an emergency at the station. Gentlemen, we will keep peace on our island. Nico, let's go." Mikel stood and shook hands with Brother Simone and bowed out of the room.

The bishop continued to fume. "I will call the Prime Minister! He will put Mr. Lagos in his place. We will show him who is boss."

Brother Leonard sat forward. "No, perhaps there is a better way."

The men put their heads together and worked out the details, while Brother Simone excused himself. It was prayer time. He needed to pray hard for all of these misguided officials. What he really didn't understand was why the bishop would be trying to help the Pope after years of division. The church had started talks, but they were stalled out the last he had heard. And Turkey? Least favored neighbor? Why would the bishop try to forge an alliance now, against the United States' women? Were these women so evil? Certainly, he had some praying to do.

33. Thecilla in Tyratira

September 18, 94 A.D.

Claudius held Thecilla's hand on the walk back to the house of Lycilla. Thecilla's heart filled with joy. At Lycilla's house, while Claudius changed into dry garments, Thecilla sat by a small bush in the court-yard, admiring the beauty of the purple rose. Planted in honor of Lydia, Lycilla had explained. She knew Thecla and Paul had shared company with Lydia in those days. Thecilla bent over to smell the fragrant rose, remembering the stories of her dear teacher. She knew Priscilla and Aquilla, her mother's parents, had spent time here with Paul as well. She once again mourned their untimely death, such an early end to two powerful disciples of Jesus.

She knew it was now her responsibility to pass on the faith and spread the good news. Mama and Thecla taught her well. Somehow, she felt this trip to the seven churches would only be the beginning. And now, Claudius could join her. Would the house church of Ephesus welcome them back when they completed their journey? She won-dered how her uncle fared on Patmos. Would Claudius take her to visit on their return?

Was her father right? Was she in danger? Would the Romans kill a young girl trying to tell the Revelation of John? She must fulfill her promise. The scrolls of Revelation spoke clearly to her, "Do not fear, but love." She served the Risen Lord and not the evil whore of Roma.

Claudius interrupted her reflections, sitting down beside her. "Ex-plain these scrolls to me, Thec. I don't understand the violence. Are we Christians to fight the Romans? Will God destroy them all?"

Thecilla wanted to choose words carefully. Her uncle explained it well, but she knew the images in the scrolls could suffer misinterpreta-tion. Like the disciples of Jesus, so many seek a violent response to the evil leaders of empire. Thecla taught her from an early age, "Only love, my dear. Only love. Jesus refused to kill."

"The people in the churches say the same thing, when I read the scrolls. But no, Uncle John told me the vision is fantastic with plagues and fights and the confusion of evil. But if you read carefully, Claudi-us, you will see there is no violence at the hands of the Lamb, the Christ. Christ is the victor, but not the armored one waging war. The

217

Romans bring destruction on themselves. The only sword of the Lamb is the sword of the tongue. Don't you see, Claudius? Jesus overcame by loving, by suffering love. Do you see his faith shines through the pages of my uncle's scrolls? He writes to the Christians who live in an empire where they face persecution and many false teachings; where they are tempted to follow the trades and stray from worship of the one God."

"Say it, sister!" Claudius clapped. Then his eyes rounded into a penetrating gaze. Sitting close, his arm circled her neck and rested on her shoulder. With his left hand, he turned her face toward him and lowered his lips to hers. Thecilla's stomach fluttered when their lips joined and she felt a powerful energy surge through her body. Claudius' tongue explored her teeth, probed her mouth and he pulled her closer in a deep embrace. Then he pulled back, looked again into her eyes. He caressed her hair and held both cheeks with his hands. "Thecilla, my love."

Lycilla called out of the house, announcing the evening meal. "Do I interrupt?"

Thecilla jumped up, "No, no. I was just explaining the scrolls to Claudius."

Claudius winked at Lycilla. "And I had to explain my love to Thecilla."

Lycilla laughed. "Come along, you two."

Thecilla's face turned beet red. Claudius caught her hand and pulled her toward Lycilla's table. Later that night, Thecilla wrote a long scroll to Thecla to share with her the joy of the day, and tell about Claudius' baptism and their growing love. Thecla always understood. She could almost hear Thecla's prayers echoing into the dark cave. She blew out her candle, falling asleep with a wide smile on her lips, remembering the baptism, that kiss in the courtyard and Claudius.

34. The Baptism of Thecla

September 19, 48 A.D.

Thecla praised God in the arena, twirling with arms extended to the heavens. "I praise the God of Jesus Christ. Alleluia! Alleluia!"

The women in the crowd roared, "Thecla! Thecla! Thecla!"

The men yelled, "Release another beast!"

Alexander and the governor debated what to do about this strange girl who seemed to defy death. The governor wanted to let her out. "Surely she is of God. Can we let her go, Alexander? Surely you've seen enough?"

Alexander stubbornly folded his arms, considering which beast to let loose next.

But Thecla did not know they discussed her fate. Instead she began to focus on a pit of water in the arena – deciding it would be the perfect and most proper place for her baptism. And so she threw herself into the water, and said: "In thy name, O my Lord Jesus Christ, I am baptized on my last day."

The women cried out, "No! Not the water!"

Even the governor himself cried out, "No!"

The heavens roared, and the lightning struck the pond, and the women screamed. They saw fire rising from the pond. But Thecla rose once again with her hands extended into the air. "In the name of the Lord Jesus Christ," she shouted about the din of the crowd. And the people looked down and saw the sea-calves had been killed by the lightning and floated dead on the surface of the water. And a great cloud of fire surrounded Thecla so the beasts could not come near and the people could not see her nakedness.

Yet Alexander persisted and let other wild beasts upon her. But the women in the arena yelled in protest, and this time they scattered herbs and ointment out that the beasts devoured and fell fast asleep and did not touch Thecla. And Alexander became more angry and told the governor, "I have some very terrible bulls; let us bind her to them." The governor reluctantly gave Alexander permission. So Alexander ordered his servants to put a cord round Thecla's waist, binding it to her feet, and then tied her to the bulls. They applied red-hot irons to the bull's privy-parts to torment them so that would violently drive Thecla about and she would be killed.

The bulls charged through the arena making a most hideous noise, but a mysterious flame severed the cords fastening her to the bulls. And soon she stood in the middle of the stage, with her hands once again held high in praise, as unconcerned as if she had not been bound.

Trifina fainted dead away and the whole arena filled with great concern, so that even Alexander became fearful. And the governor told him, "Take compassion on me and the city, and release this woman, who has fought with the beasts; lest both you and I and the whole city be destroyed. For if Caesar finds out that Trifina, his relative of royal blood, is dead at our hands, surely he will destroy our city." And then the governor called out to Thecla who stood among the beasts. "Who are you? Why will none of the beasts touch you?"

Thecla replied, "I am a servant of the living God. I believe in Jesus Christ, his Son, in whom God is well pleased; and for that reason none of the beasts could touch me. He alone is the foundation of eternal life. He is a refuge to those who are in distress; a support to the afflicted, hope and defense to those who are hopeless."

When the governor heard these things, he ordered her clothes to be brought, and told her to dress.

Thecla replied, "May that God who clothed me when I was naked among the beasts, in the day of judgment clothe your soul with the robe of salvation." Then she took her clothes, and put them on.

The governor then published an order saying, "I release to you Thecla, the servant of God."

And the women cried out together with a loud voice, and with one accord gave praise unto God, and said: "There is but one God, who is the God of Thecla; the one God who hath delivered Thecla."

Their loud voices seemed to shake the whole city and woke Trifina, who rose and ran with the others to meet Thecla and embraced her, saying, "Now I believe there shall be a resurrection of the dead. Now I know my daughter is alive. Come home with me, my daughter Thecla, and I will give all that I have to you."

So Thecla went with Trifina, and taught the word of the Lord, whereby many young women were converted; and there was great joy in the family of Trifina. But Thecla longed to see Paul and continued to send inquiries out to find him.

35. Emily and Sardis

September 21, 2006

When the MAMs gathered for lunch that day, Emily thought Jane glowed like the morning sun hovering above the horizon ready to set the world on fire. She kept talking about her baptism experience, with Priscilla chiming in. Emily smiled along with their stories. Transformation rocks.

Then she decided to share her good news. "Josh called. He's coming this evening."

"You go, girl!" Molly punched her fist into the air.

"Couldn't keep him away if you tried, and believe me I did!" Sallie confessed. "Do you have any idea how much he paid for his ticket?"

"I know! Do you think he still loves me?" Emily blushed.

Sallie took a deep breath and sang in her best off key voice, "If that's not love, what is?"

Emily took the bait, singing an answer that she supposed she loved him, too.

Sallie laughed and croaked out, "It doesn't mean a thing, but even so, after all of these years…"

Emily joined her for the conclusion, singing an alto harmony that got lost somewhere among Sallie's off-key notes, "It's nice to know."

"Look out Broadway!" Mollie yelled.

"Does anybody have a cane to pull Quisenberry off the stage?" Jane asked.

Sallie chuckled, and then a shadow crept over her face. "We were all very worried about you, Emily."

Emily nodded, and then withdrew into her own thoughts. She hoped to reinstate her engagement with Josh by nightfall. Being so far away from home, being in danger, being in the path of the Spirit caused change, and for Emily those changes were deep within.

Ursula broke in. "I can't find my laptop. I know I had it in my room before the service this morning. Joe and I took a break from translating, so I thought I'd pick it up later. When I went in to freshen up before lunch it was gone."

Joe tapped his laptop case beside him, and then put the strap around his leg. "I've got mine. Are you sure you didn't leave it in the library?"

221

"That's strange, my camera is missing, too," Molly said. "I might have left it somewhere. Is there a lost and found at this conference?"

Sallie laughed. "Memory lapses. Very common among our age group. I have them all the time."

Ursula and Molly did not laugh.

Jane began to tell of her saga of Mortimer Jacobs.

What had started as a sunshiny day, morphed into gloom. Brother Lawrence turned the lights on in the dining room, but the clouds kept getting darker.

Right about then, John Long showed up from the hospital to get a box lunch and tapped Emily on the shoulder. "Katharine wants to talk to you."

Emily took the last bites of her sandwich and bid adieu to the MAMs. "Catch up with you later!"

She scuttled along the streets of Patmos beside John, wondering what Dr. Long wanted now. She felt a connection with her favorite college professor, like a thread participating in a tapestry. First, studying under her brilliant mind for four good years, and now yoked by a gunman targeting them both. John's long strides kept Emily jogging to keep pace. The exercise felt good, reminding her to go for a jog soon.

"Remember, she's very weak," John reminded, when he opened the door to Katharine's room.

"Yes, sir." Emily saluted with a smile. John often entertained students with Dr. Long in their country home. She liked to think of him as a favorite uncle.

Emily peeked into the room. "You wanted to talk to me, Dr. Long?"

"Yes."

Katharine smiled. Emily approached the bed, kissing her teacher on her cheek

Katharine wasted no time. "I need a mediator."

"A mediator? You need a mediator?" Emily's voice held disbelief.

"Aren't you a mediator, Emily? Didn't you tell me you were a volunteer mediator on campus and that you have also been trained to do Victim-Offender mediation with the Mennonites?"

"Yes, ma'am."

"Sit down, dear."

Katharine talked quietly, with great effort. "I want you to mediate between me and Moses Sun."

Emily's mouth dropped open. Then she tried to bring Dr. Long up to date. "Moses Sun is dead! He drowned off the coast of Kusadasi. Didn't you hear?"

"Emily, sit down."

Emily thought about arguing some more, but could tell Katharine's weakness, coupled with her great resolve should be taken seriously. Emily pulled up a chair and leaned toward her good professor.

"Emily, Moses Sun is in the next room right now. He wants to ask for forgiveness."

Emily pulled her chair closer to Dr. Long's bed. "Are you hallucinating?"

"No, Emily. I'm fine."

"How did he here? Are you sure? He's crazy. Dr. Long, he tried to kill us!"

"Emily, please. I need to talk to him. Will you mediate?"

Sister Elizabeth stepped into the room. Dr. Long asked her to explain.

"I saved his life in Kusadasi harbor. He almost drowned."

Emily started to realize that as impossible as this story seemed, perhaps Katharine actually knew what she was talking about.

Elizabeth continued. "We brought him to Patmos because the boat that brought us here had a doctor on board. He lost his memory, but today it's coming back. He feels terrible. He keeps saying he is like Paul on the road to Damascus. He wants to ask for forgiveness. He won't tell me the story, but when he saw Katharine, he immediately wanted to talk with her."

"Oh my God!" Emily sat back and began to pray. With God all things were possible, but did that include a tall order like this? She countered Dr. Long again. "Shouldn't we be calling the police?"

"Emily, I feel strongly about this. Please help me."

Emily knew she shouldn't do it. Every bone in her body told her to run out of that room and call the police, but Dr. Long called her back.

"You can do it, Emily. I know you can."

"Are you out of your mind? With all due respect, Dr. Long, I don't think so."

But then Emily's Mennonite upbringing kicked in, along with her victim-offender training. She had always been taught that second chances and forgiveness are part and parcel of the Christian way.

"But Dr. Long, I'm not exactly a neutral party. He tried to kill me, too! Mediators are supposed to be neutral." Emily tried to talk some sense into her, but the professor could not be moved.

"I know, dear. Not really a mediation, but you know the process and can guide us. I don't want a cheap apology, but God is telling me to hear him out."

Emily looked at Dr. Long in disbelief. "God told you?"

And then, a smile spread across the good professor's cheeks and her eyes shared light, beaming into Emily's spirit in a way that made

Emily realize without a doubt, something incredible had indeed happened.

"Yes, God told me to listen to him. We're on Patmos and the Spirit is moving. Can you feel it?"

"Jane got baptized! Molly is praising God like there's no tomorrow, and God is talking to you? Yes, something's going on here. You're right about that, but Dr. Long..."

The shadows of midday faded into the sun, which was again shining out from around the clouds. The sunlight cast a shaft of light into the room, illuminating the doorway into the corridor. And suddenly Emily felt that magical, mystical Patmos glow. If Dr. Long wanted her to help, she better report for duty. "OK, let's do it," she said.

Dr. Long motioned to Sister Elizabeth, who knocked on Sun's door and called him in. The diminutive man dwarfed further by a fluffy, thick brown robe, shuffled slowly into the room, his head down. Emily pulled another chair over near the bed, placing him in Dr. Long's line of vision, and motioned to Elizabeth. "Could you guard the door please? I don't want anyone disturbing our discussion. If any one comes, tell them that Dr. Long is changing and ask them to come back."

Katharine's smile continued to light her face. The pale tinge had disappeared. Emily began to feel better. Perhaps she had made the right decision. Sun looked duly repentant. She looked from one to the other, and began.

"I have been trained in mediation, and victim-offender mediation. Dr. Long has requested my assistance in helping you discuss the situation between you. Are you both willing to participate?"

Katharine nodded. "I requested this session, Emily."

Moses Sun nodded his head also. "Yes, thank you so much, ma'am. Thank you for giving me a chance to apologize. Thank you so much."

"Where's John?" Emily wondered, realizing he must have left.

"I sent him for a jog. He doesn't need to know about this."

Again, Emily hesitated, but then forged ahead to give them what they asked for, what she could never be sure Dr. Long could really want.

"OK, we begin with your stories. What brought you to this point? What do you want to accomplish in this session? I want each of you to listen carefully to the other. You'll each have a chance to speak, so I ask you not to interrupt each other. After the opening statements, I'll try to identify the issues that you'd like to resolve and then we'll address each of them, looking for solutions."

The issues of confidentiality and legalities of mediation raced through Emily's head, but then she remembered she was far from the reach of the Uniform Mediation Act of Ohio. She doubted Greece had any mediation legislation. As a servant of God, she would provide a chance for conversation, for reconciliation. Following the path of Jesus Christ, she prepared to begin.

"Who goes first?" Dr. Long asked.

"I think you should start." Emily gestured to Dr. Long and then turned to Moses Sun, "Is that OK with you, Mr. Sun?"

"Yes, yes. Please tell me," Sun said.`

Dr. Long began, "Mr. Sun, I want to tell you this has been the most terrible experience of my life. For 30 years, I've taught the Bible to students from all walks of life, all religious perspectives. In my class, I work hard to create a climate of respect and honest dialogue. We have hearty discussions and often must agree to disagree. I had never been physically threatened for my beliefs and Biblical interpretations."

"When Word of God College invited me to debate the book of Revelation, I welcomed the chance to exchange ideas and perspectives. The debate went well. We discussed the issues respectfully. But then, your posts started showing up on my web site and then you began following me. My husband hired a private detective. I was terrified."

"I believe in academic and religious freedom, but I began to believe that you would do whatever necessary to silence me. That's why the private detective came on this trip. I know now that I was right to be so afraid."

She laid back and Emily noticed sweat on her forehead. Emily mopped off the perspiration, handed her a glass of ice water and noticed her respirations were picking up. She said, "Dr. Long, I don't think you're ready for this yet." Then she asked to Elizabeth to check on her.

Dr. Long's eyes were closed, and Sun's head was bowed. Emily wondered if he was praying.

While Elizabeth checked her patient, Emily looked out the window to the sea. So many problems caused by the night hallucination of the exiled John on Patmos. She wondered who would have thought that 2,000 years later, his bold words to the early Christians of the Roman Empire would be causing such havoc on the late great planet Earth. Taking a deep breath, she gathered her resolve to continue.

"She's fine," Elizabeth reported. "But don't be too long."

Emily began to summarize, "So, Dr. Long. You were very scared by Mr. Sun. In fact, you view this as the most terrible experience in your life. In your classroom and on the debate floor, your goal has always been respectful discussion and agreeing to disagree. But when Mr. Sun began to threaten you, you felt physically threatened, and your husband hired a private detective."

"That's right," she responded. "Sun works for a conservative religious think tank and they spend time building a case for religious views that support the right-wing agenda. In this case, I find the views very dangerous. Not only are they bad Biblical interpretation, but they are supporting a political platform of violence that I do not think Jesus of Nazareth would begin to support. Yet, millions of Americans have been duped into believing."

Emily looked at Sun. No longer praying, he held his forehead with his hands, looking down at the wooden floor. Shaking his head from side to side, Emily sensed great turmoil in his body movements.

"I knew he had gone over the deep edge when he started to write threats, and then when he followed me around the world, I was scared out of my mind. My colleagues and I detest these think tanks, but we had no idea they were this bad!" Dr. Long laughed and then stopped herself. "It's not funny."

"The only reason I am talking so openly with you, Mr. Sun, is because I believe that you have had a change of heart and I want to hear you out. I, too, have had a change. After you shot me, I encountered the light of God in a powerful way. I almost died, but instead, I came back. I have seen God. I will never be the same. I want to hear about your change, because I have changed, too."

"In my dreams, in the hospital, I saw people dancing in a cave praising God. Then the scroll from Pergamum recounted my dream. The Spirit of God was there, with them, is here, with us ... the Spirit of Love. I must listen to you. God tells me to listen to you and give you a chance."

Goosebumps popped up on Emily's arms. The mystical light of Patmos cast a halo of sun glow about Dr. Long's head. Would her scholarly professor be preaching at the International Conference of Mystics soon?

Sun stopped clenching his forehead and met the warmth of Dr. Long's smile with a gaze that seemed to be an equal mix of fear and surprise.

Emily underscored the sanctity of the moment. "Wow. You encountered God, and you want to hear about Sun's encounter, too? This blows me away. You had a dream, that later was revealed in the scrolls, but you hadn't read them yet, when you had the dream? You believe God is calling you to hear Sun out?"

Dr. Long nodded her head and again reclined back on her pillow.

Emily looked at her watch. She knew she couldn't rush the Spirit, but Dr. Long would tire soon. She asked, "What would you like to accomplish in this session, Dr. Long?"

"I want to hear Sun out. If we could reconcile, that would be wonderful. Later, if we could have a respectful discussion about the Rapture Theory, I'd be content."

"So you come to listen, to reconcile and to openly share your own beliefs?"

If only every mediation were so simple, Emily thought to herself. Dr. Long could give people lessons on how to work things out. Yet Emily couldn't understand why the good professor didn't seem to have the anger that would be natural in a victim-offender situation. The man tried to kill her, tried to kill them both. Emily couldn't figure her out, but then she'd never seen God face to face either. Perhaps that created a whole new ball game.

"Yes, Emily. Thank you so much. Now, I'd like to listen." She folded her hands across her lap and there was a knock at the door.

Elizabeth poked her head in. "There's a man here to see you, Mr. Sun."

Sun looked up and shook his head. "Tell him I'm not up for visitors right now."

"Who is it?" Emily asked.

Elizabeth poked her head back out the door, clearly blocking the view of the room. A moment later she stepped back into the room, closing the door behind her. "Mortimer Jacobs from the Right Disciples?" She handed the business card to Sun.

"Oh my God. They've found me already. Now we all need to be afraid. Katharine, you've got to get out of here, now!"

Another knock on the door, and Emily began to shake.

John came in this time.

Sun wasted no time. "Sir, you need to get your wife out of here. It's not safe. One of my associates has arrived. None of you are safe."

"Who are you?" John asked.

Emily looked at Sun and saw perspiration forming on his bruised forehead, around the bandage covering a rather large wound.

Katharine looked at Emily. Neither wanted to answer the question, and Sun remained mute.

John saved them with more news. "Dan Parks is here. Jane freaked out when she met Mortimer Jacobs, so she called him in."

"Sir, none of you are safe. I think you need to leave. I can turn myself in and help them stop Jacobs from doing any harm." Sun offered to go willingly.

"Katharine, who is this man?" John asked again.

Emily held her breath. Katharine told him. "Honey, we need to leave. I'll explain later."

Sun kept sweating. He really didn't want to see Jacobs.

Emily began to see what Dr. Long knew. Something major had happened to Moses Sun and the man with them now was a whole new ball game.

"Could we finish the mediation, first?" Emily asked

"Not here. Get Katharine out of here. Now!" Sun insisted. "Tell Jacobs there's no one here."

Samina closed the door behind her, telling Jacobs, "Sir, we have only sick people here. Please leave the hospital, now."

When she came back into the room, John asked if she could recommend a hotel, and soon they were planning to take everyone away. An ambulance for Dr. Long, a van for the rest of the group. John went back to Hotel Romeos to round up the MAMs. Parks would stay to tail Jacobs, and for the time, no one wanted to risk letting him know about Moses Sun. Sister Elizabeth offered to come along to care for Katharine.

Dr. Long insisted that Sun wait to turn himself in. She wanted to hear him out.

Emily couldn't quite wrap her mind around the reality of this most peculiar situation. In the four years that she had known Dr. Long, never once did she talk about her own experience of God. Moses Sun tried to kill, but now wanted to save? Although the MAMs wanted to turn him in, Dr. Long continued to argue and her voice was weak.

A few minutes later, John returned with the MAMs in various states of alarm, but Katharine seemed calm. She told them, "Let Sun ride with you in the van,"

John heard. "Moses Sun? That is Moses Sun?"

"It's OK, dear. Not now. I'll explain later. It's OK."

John fumed, then argued loudly about Sun. After discussion, the MAMs gave in to the Katharine, but quietly promised John they'd turn him in before the end of the day.

Within the hour, they were headed for a new residence, a small hotel on the water's edge.

Jane explained, "I gave Parks the slip. He's stuck in a session on the music of the mystics tailing Mortimer Jacobs, also stuck at the back of the room. Serves him right for tailing me."

Soon the crew arrived at the small hotel and checked into their rooms.

Dr. Long wanted to finish the mediation. So after leaving her bags in her room, Emily headed for her suite, where she found her waiting with Sun to continue the mediation.

"Are we really safe here?" Emily asked Sun. "If Jacobs found us, don't you think they could find us here, too?"

Sun shrugged his shoulders. "I doubt they sent more than Jacobs. He won't know you left the clinic for a while. When I turn myself in, they can pick him up for questioning."

Dr. Long interrupted. "Could we continue, please? I'm tired, but I want to hear Moses out."

Emily recapped the conversation again and then turned to Sun.

"Now, it's your turn. Tell us your story."

Sun scratched the bandage on his forehead and then sat back in the padded chair near Dr. Long's bed and began to explain.

"I'll try to be brief. My parents worked in Hollywood. I got jobs in high school doing stunt work on the sets. Nothing major, but I got good enough that I worked on some major movie productions. Helped me earn my way through college. That's where I got the idea of riding off that pier in Kusadasi harbor. Just so you know. Now, I can see my judgment was flawed in more ways than one." Sun smirked and then laughed out loud. "I guess God showed me!"

"What do you mean?" Emily asked for clarification.

"God showed me. The Right Disciples follow the Word of God. We believe in the infallible truth of the Bible, which I still do. And one of our goals is to preserve that truth at all costs, because if the Truth of God is profaned it will lead to the destruction of souls. That is why I was trying to stop you, Dr. Long. You speak against the Truth of God."

"My life flashed before me in the water. I scrolled through it all and when I saw myself shooting at you, I heard a voice saying, 'Love your enemies. Love your enemies.' An angel came to me in the water. I knew I was going to die, but then the light came and the angel pulled me out of the water. The angel saved me. She saved my life!"

"When I woke up, I couldn't remember anything but the words, which I heard over and over again, 'Love your enemies.' It all started to come back to me when I saw Dr. Long in her bed at the clinic. I recognized her, but couldn't place her. Sister Elizabeth took me for a walk, and suddenly the images began to roll through my mind. And the mantra that had been playing in my mind since I was pulled from the water continued. 'Love your enemies.' "

"What does that mean to you? 'Love your enemies'?" Emily asked.

"Hit me like a ton of bricks, or I guess like a speedboat! I went down into the water and then I heard. Don't you see? I wasn't following the Word of God at all. I was trying to kill my enemy. I was trying to kill the enemy of the Word of God. God told me that was wrong."

Emily looked at Dr. Long and raised her eyebrows. Sun still seemed delusional. She was tempted to inquire about his mental health history, but then her mediation training brought her back to a neutral stance. She couldn't really argue with what he was saying about loving your enemies.

"So you now believe that you were wrong, and that God told you to love, rather than to kill?"

Sun smiled. "I know it sounds strange. Or it must sound strange to you. But I thought I was doing God's will. That is all I ever wanted to do. That is why I was working for the Right Disciples. Since an early age, I have only wanted to follow Jesus Christ, my savior. Now I am beginning to see, I was going about it in the wrong way. I'm sorry, Katharine. I'm so sorry. I'm sorry for threatening you. I'm sorry for following you. I'm sorry for shooting you. I'm sorry for wanting to kill you. I was wrong. I am so sorry. I deserve to go to jail. Thank you for listening to me. Thank you for talking with me. Can you ever forgive me? Probably not."

Sun hung his head down then and began to play with his thumbs.

Emily took over from there to summarize and catch the emotions in his apology. "So you are apologizing to Dr. Long? You are embarrassed. You feel great shame for what you did. You realize you were very wrong. You are asking for forgiveness?"

Sun simply looked at Dr. Long and said, "Yes." Then he put his eyes back down to the floor and folded his hands over his stomach.

Tears streamed down Dr. Long's face. Emily began to cry herself. Mediators are supposed to be neutral, but she hadn't been neutral to begin with and now the moment overwhelmed them all. The love of God had touched the Right Disciple crazy man, and he had apologized.

Emily's heart filled with an incredible joy.

Dr. Long talked through her tears. "I forgive you. Yes, I forgive you," She reached out to touch Sun's hand. "Thank you." Then she looked at Emily and said, "I think I need to sleep now."

Emily had lost track of time, but now realized Josh should be arriving soon.

"I need to go!" she told them both. And she remembered she harbored a criminal. "What do we do with you now?"

"Turn me in. Turn me in to the authorities."

Emily instead decided to call Jane and Priscilla in to deal with Sun. Jane could talk it over with Parks. A few minutes later, she left Sun in the lobby to Jane's safekeeping and turned to the task of arranging a ride for Josh.

A familiar face stood chatting with the manager at the front desk.

"Balaban? How did you get here?"

"At your service, ma'am. Some things are meant to be. MAMs need me, I come to Patmos, too."

"But how did you even know we came here?" Emily could not figure this out.

"Ms. Sallie tells me you need to pick up important man at the dock?" His eyes twinkled and he cocked his head waiting for Emily's response.

"Yes. My friend should be on the ferry from Athens. You'll take me there?"

Balaban swept his arm in front of him with a slight bow, encouraging Emily to board the bus first.

Grateful for his help, Emily decided not to worry about how he happened to show up in Patmos. "You spoil us! What will we do without you?"

"Good question. MAMs will miss their Balaban when they go home. Good man."

Balaban's chuckle brought a smile to Emily's face, and then she sat back in her seat on the van and began to compose herself, while her thoughts raced ahead, down the hill toward the water.

The dark clouds gathering earlier had evaporated into blue skies. The idyllic atmosphere of Patmos once again created a tranquil environment that helped Emily ponder the upcoming reunion with Josh.

In the past few days her world had been turned upside down and inside out. Would Josh understand? Could they make peace? If Moses Sun and Dr. Long could reconcile, anything is possible, she thought. With God all things are possible. Josh paid $2,000 for a ticket to come halfway around the world to find her. She figured that must mean something. Slipping into prayer, Emily sought God's help for the situation, until Balaban pulled into the parking lot for the dock.

"We arrive at the ferry. Prepare to meet important man," Balaban kept his voice light and winked again.

Blues skies were fading into dusk. The sinking sun reflected off the Aegean, casting a shaft of light over the water. The waves sparkled under the light, while the sky lit with orange and pink hues in celebration of another completed day. The sunset signaled for Emily a new day soon to come. She hoped with all her heart that could include a new beginning with Josh.

She jumped out of the car and headed down to the dock. Her heart seemed to be running ahead of her to get to Josh first. Little fishing boats bobbed in the gently rocking water. A large cruise ship docked farther out. Then she spotted a large ship, smaller than the giant cruise ship, but much larger than the other fishing boats scattered around the bay

Balaban stood behind her, far enough to keep the smoke from his cigarette downwind from her.

Emily turned to him now. "Do you see the ferry?"

Balaban pointed at the large ship she had spotted. "Thar she sails!" Emily jumped up and down, like a child excited about a birthday present. Now she could see the crew on deck scurrying around, readying the ship for docking.

"Where will they walk off the boat?"

"You want to get very close?" Balaban smiled and threw his cigarette down onto the concrete, smashed it with his foot, then picked it up and placed it in the trash receptacle. "Come with me."

He held out his arm, and Emily grabbed it, feeling a little like a prom queen walking up for the crowning dance. Or did she feel like a bride walking down the aisle with her father, about to be given away?

A woman walked out of the galley and now a small boy. Behind them, Emily glimpsed a familiar figure. She watched while he ducked out of the small door and then straightened up to his full six feet. She rushed up to the swinging walkway connecting the boat to the dock.

Josh saw Emily running and a smile spread across his face. After 24 hours of travel and a week of sleepless nights, there she was. He reached down and picked her up, hugging her tight and then twirling her in circles on the dock.

Josh lowered Emily down, took her hand and led her up past the dock, beyond the others.

He stopped and leaned down, taking her head in his hands. He covered her lips with his mouth and began to kiss her deeply. Her body responded with all of the passion that had been pent up within her since Josh had told her it was over. There were no words, just a kiss that went on and on.

Balaban lit another cigarette and chuckled. He found a bench and decided to take in the sunset and wait for the lovers to finish their reunion. Although it had been many years now that he had been married, he could remember that early love like the back of his hand. He knew those sweet moments were the stuff that made a life worthwhile. He could wait. The sunset was particularly beautiful, and he savored his smoke, remembering the beauty of his own lady, his wife back in Kusadasi. And then he saw a dark cloud on the horizon and remembered why he had been summoned to Patmos. The Prime Minister called. He couldn't really refuse. He awaited further directions. While he sat wondering his cell phone rang. Now it became obvious, they had another job for him to do and he didn't like the sounds of this one. But he had no choice. He couldn't refuse the Prime Minister.

After a while, Emily pulled away. "Josh, our driver is waiting to take us to the hotel."

Later at the hotel, Josh came into her room and sat on her bed. "I'm not staying long. I need sleep, and I don't think I could resist temptation very long. But there's something I want to say."

Emily grabbed his his hand and caressed his head with her other hand.

Josh leaned over and kissed Emily briefly and then looked into her eyes. "I love you so much. Will you marry me Emily?"

"Yes! Yes! Yes! I want to be your wife." Emily jumped up and danced around the room. "Yes, Josh! I'm sorry for leaving you. I'm glad I came, but I never dreamed it would mean you'd break up with me. I love you so much."

She came back to Josh and he said, "One more kiss." They sat on the bed and his urge was too strong to pull her down. "I have to go, dear."

"You can stay." Emily said.

"No, I'm not going to screw this up now. I love you. I'll see you in the morning." He jumped up off the bed, kissed her cheek and headed for the door.

But before he made it to the door, someone starting knocking. "Josh! Emily! Are you in there?" The knocking continued. Josh opened the door to Ursula and Joe. "Sorry to bother you. But we just finished translating another scroll, and we're going to read it in Katharine's room in about five minutes."

"We'll be there. OK. We'll be there. But, do you have any coffee for Josh? I don't think he's had much sleep."

"Sure, one pot of coffee coming up," Joe laughed. He hooked his arm around Ursula and winked, and they were off down the hall.

A few minutes later Josh and Emily arrived at Katharine's room to listen. She looked around and saw that everyone was ready. Priscilla and Sallie sat on one bed. Jane and Molly were sitting cross-legged on the floor. Joe's laptop was on the table, where he and Ursula sat in the chairs. John sat on the bed by Katharine, with his arm around her shoulders.

Emily introduced Josh to the group, and then they sat down on the floor, propping their backs against the bed.

"We're glad you made it safely, Josh," Ursula smiled. "I know we haven't given you much time to rest, but we're all excited about these scrolls!"

Joe handed them both a cup of coffee which smelled like hazelnut and cinnamon. Emily enjoyed the smell, the warmth and sipped the delicious coffee. Her whole body felt warm and loved. But then she noticed someone was missing and she asked, "Hey, what did you do with Moses Sun?"

"Sun?" Molly asked.

"I left him with Jane." Emily turned toward Jane with a question on her face.

Jane raised her hands in innocence. "I turned him over to Priscilla when I had to go to the bathroom."

Everybody's head turned toward Priscilla, and she looked nervously at Emily. "I left him in my room when we came over here. He was sleeping."

"Priscilla, you can't do that. Let's go get him. We'll wake him up." Jane jumped up off the floor and headed toward the door, gesturing for Priscilla to join her.

"I'll come along," Joe offered.

The group of three headed down the hall on a mission. Priscilla turned the key in the lock and quietly opened the door. She entered the room first, then turned toward the others with concern. The bed was empty.

"Oh my God!" Jane yelled, "I'm calling Parks."

Joe remained calm. "Check your bathroom, Priscilla."

Priscilla ran to the closed door, knocked, waited, then opened it, peering into the room, and the shower stall, pulling the curtain back and came back out with her report, "Not there."

"OK, I think we need to call the police," Joe said. "Let's go back to consult with the MAMs."

By the time they returned to the group, Dan Parks had agreed to come. They asked Balaban to double as a security guard for the women in the interim. When Parks arrived, they'd call the police.

"Where could he go?" Emily asked.

"Where do you think? Now that Mortimer Jacobs is in town. Don't you think he's joining up with his job? Do you really believe he would change? Now look at we've done." Jane said.

John looked at Katharine and then the other women, "Why in God's name didn't you turn him in immediately?"

Emily looked rather sheepishly at John. But Katharine smiled. "He did change. He wants to protect us. Maybe he was taken against his will."

"Katharine, what kind of drugs do they have you on? Are you crazy? That man has a serious mental health problem. We knew that. How could we have been so stupid?" Jane asked.

"But he told us to run. He tried to help us. I know the man has changed," Katharine insisted.

Joe interrupted. "How soon can Parks get here?"

Jane looked at her watch. "Ten minutes."

"OK, then, let's listen to the scroll and put Katharine to bed. Then we'll have a meeting back in our room to plan from here." Jane took charge.

"I'm fine," Katharine smiled and shook her head. "God is with us, no need for concern. On with the scroll."

Ursula began to read.

Scroll #5 Sardis

Dear Teacher, I write [ ] Sardis, [ ] Cogamus River. Sending my love with prayers [ ] for you. We traveled over the inland [ ] to reach this place. In the lower City, we stay again with friends of Claudius, [ ] restless. He completed his business [ ] joined me at the house church as I read the scrolls.

The church [ ] much wealth, but they also love God. They want to do God's will. I read the message to their church [ ]. They asked me to stop and the elders prayed over the words to their church for a long time, asking God to speak [ ].

Demetrius [ ] nephew of our hosts, began to speak. "Let us don white robes tonight, confess our sins and recommit [ ] to the God, the one who was, and who is and who is to come. [ ] wear the white robes of celebration and have a feast and celebrate the victory of Jesus."

"Yes," the elders agreed. "The boy speaks for us all. But read on, 'Cilla, [ ]."

So I read on [ ] through the day. Many times [ ] to stop, so [ ] they could discuss. They debated the meaning of the Beast and of the Lamb. They wondered if Jesus was to lead a war, and they had me read some of the sections over and over. The women left to prepare the feast, [ ].

"[ ] the beast is the Roman Empire?" one man asked. "The horses of conquest, war, famine and death: they are the mark of the Romans. They conquer, they wage war, they starve the people and bring death. They have destroyed the Temple in Jerusalem. They have burned Alexandria and slaughtered the people. They deny food to those who fight them. The power of Satan is unleashed in the world through those who do not serve God."

Another man [ ], "Yes, but the Lamb is the victor. In the scrolls, the people worship the Lamb, who is covered in blood. The Lamb was slaughtered, and yet he lives [ ] is the victor through his love. God's ways are not our ways. The 144,000 signifies [ ], those of the 12 tribes and those of us who join with the chosen through the blood of the Lamb. The Lamb leads us to victory, not with conquest, war, famine and death, but with the word of testimony and the blood of the Lamb. It is the sword of the tongue and the power of truth that defeats the rich and powerful."

I told them [ ] to be true, indeed, for this is what John had explained to me.

Socrolates, [ ] used to write plays in Athens, asked to borrow the scrolls for the night to create a drama. I invited him to come [ ] in the home where I stay. [ ] his friend is a director at the theater [ ] could get permission to perform. He asked for help in staging the play, [ ] group agreed to meet with him in the morning [ ]. Claudius volunteered and said we could use his horse.

Claudius [ ] excited to join in the feast of purification and rededication. He spent the night up late talking [ ] whether he could continue to serve the Romans and serve the Lamb at the same time. He told me this morning that he thinks he must only serve Jesus.

Yesterday, before dusk, the "Revelation of John by Socrolates" was performed in the great theater of Sardis. The people of the city came. The four horses of the Roman Army brought conquest, war, famine and death, but the slaughtered Lamb spoke the Word of Truth. The horse bowed in the end, and the red of the Roman robes were flung on the ground. The blood of the Lamb was a cloak of love. Claudius exchanged his Red cloak for the lamb's wool and the audience murmured and tried to understand what the story meant.

[ ] cries that we were against the Emperor.

Pray for the church [ ]. Pray for our safety. We will leave town [ ] morning for Philadelphia. Claudius [ ] travel before dawn.

When they finished reading, the MAMS were very quiet. Emily looked at Josh. Her heart filled with love, but her head worried that he would be angry. The scrolls and his reading of Revelation did not jive. She worried that he would begin to argue. She looked at Katharine. Her smile filled the room with a warmth that seemed almost supernatural.

Before she could try to cut him off at the pass, Josh spoke. "What is this scroll? What is this about? Where did you get this? Is this real?"

Ursula filled him in. She told him about the dig, the sand chamber and the scrolls. She told him about the press conference and the shooting. She told him about the disappearance of the scrolls and then she told them about the authenticity of the find. Emily sat mesmerized not only by her account, but by Josh's quiet acceptance of her words.

"We have every reason to believe that the scrolls are authentic from the late first century. They appear to have been written by a young woman who acted as a scribe to John who wrote the book of Revelation, and who later took the scrolls to the seven churches to be read. This sheds new light on all of our reading of the book of Revelation."

Josh looked confused and asked, "What do you mean?"

Then it was Emily's turn. She explained about Sun. She explained about him following the MAMS to Turkey because he disagreed with Dr. Long's perspective. She stopped short of telling Josh that it was actually Sun who shot them. "Josh, this is explaining anew the meaning of revelation. Not about the Rapture Theory – about suffering love and worship."

"The Rapture Theory? How could we be wrong about that?" Josh asked.

Katharine smiled and then began to recite her lecture on how the Rapture Theory was pieced together by an 19th-century cleric from Ireland. She explained how it made it into the Scofield Chain Reference Bible,[xxxii] which became very popular in the United States. Emily knew the lecture well. She had written her senior thesis on the topic, and Josh had argued with her every step of the way. Now she turned to watch his reaction.

"Could you read that again, Joe?" Josh asked. "The part about the Beast, the 144,000. Did she leave out Armageddon?"

Ursula began to read again, and they listened, hearing more than they heard the first time around.

When she finished, Josh had more questions. "What about Armageddon? Won't Jesus return to lead the final battle?"

Katharine smiled. "Actually, if you read Revelation, it's just not there. The only war Christians are to fight is with the tongue. The

237

role of the Christians in the book of Revelation is martyrdom. Jesus is the lamb and also their savior. If you read the book carefully, you will see that the blood spilled is the blood of the Christians. You have to remember that Revelation was written by a man in exile, banished from Ephesus because he was a Christian. The Roman emperor did not want anyone to challenge his authority. In that era, the emperor was God. The Romans pledged complete allegiance to their Lord, the emperor. The warfare imagery is really about a cosmic battle in heaven. The negative images have a direct connection to the Romans. The book is really somewhat like A Christmas Carol. Remember when Scrooge had the dreams of what could happen? The book threatens the Romans with doom if they don't turn from their evil. The book promises the Christians the City of God."

Josh put his forehead in his hands and bowed his head. Emily could tell he needed time to process what Dr. Long said. They had spent so many hours arguing this information. She was amazed that he didn't argue now. Maybe he was just too tired.

"But could half of America be wrong? How?" Josh asked. No one answered.

Jane broke the silence. "The Roman Empire destroyed themselves from within. Political infighting. They didn't get it. They couldn't hear it then."

Joe said, "Well, history tells us there were many factors leading to their demise."

Jane looked at the computer and then began to explain. "I haven't told you guys about this. But I've had this dream. Even before we came here. I mean even before we left Ohio. In my dream, well there have been variations of the dream, but always I stab a man in the back and then he turns to me and says, *'Et tu, Brute?'*"

"I don't even know Latin. Parks explained this to me last week. When Julius Caesar served as emperor, his best friend, Brutus, became part of an opposition party that organized against Julius. The Roman Empire borders extended far and wide. They were at the height of their power. Their ruling assemblies governed the entire empire. Their power was unprecedented in history of the world. The road system, the commerce, the buildings, the aqueducts. Magnificent. *Pax Romana* – Roman Peace – they called it, because they were really able to create quite a civilization. But they killed the Christians, and their internal disputes were the beginning of their decline. Or at least that's what Parks told me," Jane finished and asked, "Do you think my dreams are related to this? Do you think it all connects?"

Goosebumps popped up on Emily's arms. She looked at Josh, and his eyes were open wide. She didn't want to fight. She had no idea how Josh was taking it all.

Jane asked one more question, "Do you think we're doing it again? Isn't our government bogged down with infighting? We've become a nation divided. We haven't killed each other, but don't you think maybe the Democrats and Republicans are destroying our civilization, too?"

Sallie bugged out her eyes and quoted Pogo, "We have met the enemy, and he is us."

Nobody laughed. The quiet filled up all the nooks and crannies of the little room. Joe's computer blinked onto the screen saver, and Emily sat there wondering. She wondered about Jesus, who tried to teach the Romans how to love. She wondered about the early Christians who were martyred for their faith. She wondered about the parallels between the Roman Empire and the U.S. Empire. And she wondered about the love she felt for Josh that had to transcend the differences between them. Surely a Republican and a Democrat could marry and love each other for life? Perhaps the future of their country depended on it. She looked forward to a long talk with Josh. But first she knew he needed to sleep.

She pulled him up and announced to the group, "I need to put Josh to bed."

The group laughed.

Jane replied, "Right. Now you come right back, Emily."

Emily smiled back and mimicked her, "Right. Be right back." Then she looked around the room and laughed. Quickly, she grabbed Josh's hand and hurried him out of the room. She would certainly put him to bed, and she planned to stay right there beside him for the rest of her life.

36. Thecilla in Sardis

September 19, 94 A.D.

The fire burned brightly in the stone hearth of a home in the lower city of Sardis. Claudius talked late into the night with old friends of his family, sharing the revelation from John, and discussing his new life in Jesus Christ. Some Christian men, dressed in white robes from the play, sat with him.

"Don't you understand?" Claudius kept trying to explain Uncle John's vision.

"You fight the emperor! You risk arrest!" The Romans told him.

"Christians serve Jesus. You can serve him, too. We bring no sword"

"But in the play, you brought their horses down. The Roman's power of conquest, war, famine, and death are all nothing in the light of the lamb. You let the lamb walk over their red cloak. Blasphemy! Claudius, they will kill you! They killed Jesus."

In two days time, he had become a strong defender of the faith. Thecilla listened proudly while he testified to the power of God. But now she beckoned to Claudius to leave. She knew Claudius planned for them to ride on to Philadephia by early morning light.

"Ah, the little lady calls you, cousin!" His friend poked fun, but he did not care.

"Thecilla, my love. I will take you on my horse."

Claudius told his friends: "Consider my words, I will return and tell you more, but now I must bid you good day." He hoisted Thecilla up onto the back of his steed, before swinging his own leg up and over and galloping toward their lodging for the evening.

"Socrolates bids us to stage the play again in Philadelphia."

Thecilla held on to Claudius, her arms wrapped firmly around his his waist. "Is it safe?"

"You worry about safety, now? We follow the Christ. Of course we may find danger, but we must spread John's message. Should we only be concerned for ourselves? Now you sound like your father."

Thecilla shivered in the night. She leaned into the warmth of Claudius' cloak. Her courage faltered. Images of Thecla at the stake and in the den of lions haunted her still. Thecla had been spared, but

240

many Christians died.   What did the Lord require of her?   God answered her prayers too well.   Claudius served Jesus with all his heart
now.   She remembered John's admonition to the people of Sardis:
"Watch!"

When Claudius dropped her off at her room, he took her into his
arms. "I will protect you little one. I come for you at early light." Then
he embraced her and kissed her cheek, before jumping back on his
horse and leaving her unblemished for the time to come.

Thecilla's body responded to his so strongly, she wanted to run after him. Yet she knew she needed rest. She also needed someone to
talk with, someone to explain what was happening.   The best she
could do now would be to write once again to her teacher. She filled
the scroll with the day's events. The candle reminded her of Thecla's
comforting words, "In love, there is no fear. Beloved, love is of God.
You who love, know God."

Two more churches. Soon she must return to Uncle John to tell him
of her travels. Soon she would be back home. She prayed then for her
parents and considered writing a scroll to them. But could they understand? Would they send Jacob to take her home? She decided to wait.
She missed them, and most of all she missed dear Thecla. She knew
Thecla and her Uncle John would be overcome with happiness at what
she had done. On that thought she blew out the candle and snuggled
into her sleeping mat, dreaming of Claudius and imagining riding on
with him into the night.

37. Priscilla and Philadelphia

September 22, 2006

The next morning, Priscilla opened her Bible and tried to pray. She knew if she spent some time with God, she would calm down and be in His will. The MAMs weren't exactly the type of Christians she usually hung out with. She disagreed with many of the things they said and with the drinking. Ever since she'd found Jesus, she followed the straight and narrow. She'd traveled that wide path enough for a lifetime in her first 30 years.

Yet something was happening. First Ursula, then Molly, Katharine, Jane and Emily. God touched each of them in some powerful ways. She couldn't deny that God was moving among them. The black and white lines blurred into her present reality. Usually her pastor helped her focus and keep her mind straight. Now she wasn't sure. The guilt she felt for Sun's disappearance threatened to undo her, and yet part of her was glad he got away. The MAMs had prayed over it the night before, and she knew Dan Parks would be involving the police. She hoped they found him. A knock at the door interrupted her tumbling thoughts.

"Who's there?" She asked, then shivered, feeling rather spooked by everything going on.

"Mr. George Matthews, ma'am. May I have a word with you, please?"

Priscilla cracked open her door to a red-faced man, somewhat overweight, yet dressed in a nice black suit with a blue tie that matched the color of his eyes. He wanted to come into her room? The clouds outside cast shadows in her small room. She stood now in gray light, wondering what to do. She hesitated.

"Just a word, please." The man opened her door all the way, and before she could protest, closed it behind him and walked into the small room.

Priscilla backed away from the man, considering her options. Could she run around him and get out of the room? Before she could figure that out, he began to speak.

"Please come with me, Priscilla Johnson, you must help us."

"How do you know my name? Help you with what?" Priscilla managed to question the stranger, but her hands started shaking.

"You are a follower of Jesus. We need you now."

She continued shaking, but found her voice. "Need me for what?"

"Followers of Jesus in all times have dropped what they are doing to follow. The disciples dropped their nets and followed Him. Just come with me, ma'am. I'll explain."

"But I don't know you." Priscilla moved toward the door.

"Moses Sun asked to see you. Will you come with me?"

"Moses Sun?" Priscilla stopped with her hand on the door knob. "Where is he?"

"Come with me. I'll take you to him."

The man didn't offer any answers. Priscilla navigated unfamiliar waters. In a minute she could open the door and head for the safety of her friends' rooms. Or, she could go with the man and find Moses Sun. The guilt of losing him weighed heavy on her heart. Perhaps she could find him and bring him back to rectify the wrong. Yet her internal warning system flashed danger.

"Come quickly. I'll have you back within the hour. Your friends won't know you've left. Follow me."

Priscilla opened the door and let him leave the room first. She looked both ways, hoping perhaps someone would see them leave. But George Matthews headed toward the nearest exit, and they were in the parking lot in a few seconds, undetected by the other MAMs. The man led her toward a compact Fiat. When he opened the door, she got in and soon they were heading into a parking lot near the waterfront.

She read the sign, "Hotel Skala." They walked under a long trellis covered with vines, leading into the courtyard of the three-story hotel. She felt the beauty of the green light above, yet it seemed eerie at the same time. They passed the front desk and climbed the steps to the second floor, before stopping in front of a door – Room Number 215, her detail-oriented mind noted.

He held the door open, and then she saw him. Moses Sun sat at the desk, his hands behind his back. She walked toward him, then saw the handcuffs around his wrists. She froze.

Moses Sun turned his head from side to side. Then he firmly pressed his lips together. "No?" She looked at him with a question mark plastered on her face.

Mr. Matthews interrupted, "We need your help."

The door opened and the tall man Jane had complained about walked in. "Ah, Mortimer, there you are. Meet Priscilla Johnson."

Mortimer stepped up to Priscilla, eying her over his horn-rimmed glasses, and then extended his long, skinny arm. Priscilla offered a lady's handshake, laughing nervously, then turning white as the reality of the situation settled in.

"What is this about? Moses, what are they doing with you? What is going on here?" Priscilla's words tumbled out without restraint.

"I can explain everything," Matthews pulled out the seat by Sun at the table. "Sit down, Priscilla."

Priscilla scanned the room, looking for a second pair of handcuffs. Then she plopped down into the chair, putting her hands in her lap while sending a silent prayer up for help.

***

Dan Parks shuffled up the stairs to the Patmos Police Department and hoped he could get some help this time. A man had disappeared; the laptop and camera had been stolen. The day before, he'd been summarily dismissed. They had said, "Patmos is a peaceful island, no problems." Perhaps they wished for only peaceful things, but they had a problem. He didn't want any more shootings under his watch.

Fortunately for him, the man at the desk today spoke English well. They took his statement, said they'd be on the look out for Moses Sun and would see what they could do. Parks left the office, frustrated. He didn't have a lot to go on, but he had to do his job. He could check out the Conference of Mystics and look for suspicious behavior. With a little luck, he'd scope the criminals out. Mortimer Jacobs shouldn't be too hard to find. A man that tall couldn't hide in a crowd and certainly not in the sparse autumn population of Patmos.

Parks hurried down the steps of the police station and paused. Fishing boats were heading out for a morning catch. Just a few people stood on the dock. But then a tall man walked by. Parks looked once, looked again, and then duty kicked in. Mortimer Jacob had presented himself front and center. Could it get any easier than this, he wondered. Finally, the gods were smiling on him. Perhaps Holy Patmos had turned his luck.

Parks tailed the man. When the thin man turned into Hotel Skala, just a few buildings down from the police station, Parks kicked up his feet into a light jog and managed to get to the trellised entrance before Jacobs disappeared into the hotel lobby. He waited out of sight, until Jacobs started up the stairs, before entering. Within a moment, he climbed the steps, and like a good tail, managed to stay far enough behind to be invisible, yet close enough to watch the man knock and enter Room 215.

Now he needed reinforcement. Once the room door closed, Parks sauntered back down the steps, tipped his hat to the lady at the desk and begin to sprint back to the police station. Hopefully he could get those peace-loving Greek police to come along, question the man and nip any potential for more violence in the bud.

***

In the lobby of Hotel Skala, four men enjoyed a drink at the bar and some fine cigars. If Parks hadn't been in such a hurry when he hurried by, he might have recognized Balaban. Balaban certainly recognized him, but kept his mouth shut.

"We've got two of three now. Balaban, if you could be so kind, we'll have all three and then we can pack up and go home." The priest laughed out loud.

"But perhaps we should stay longer. Such a wonderful place, this island. Why leave right after we've accomplished our goal?"

The other men nodded in agreement, and then the tall one said, "The next round's on me!"

***

Back in Room 215, George Matthews and Mortimer Jacobs began their sales job. They knew they had taken a sizable risk in inviting Priscilla to their room. They had prayed long and hard before bringing her over. Now they stopped to pray again, out loud, for her benefit.

"Almighty God," Matthews began, "we seek to exalt your Word above the false teachings of this age. Thank you for your servant, Priscilla, who came to help us. Bless our work to blot out the evil one and lift high the cross of Jesus who comes to judge and separate the sheep from the goats. We pray in the name of Jesus the Christ who will come soon in the clouds and usher in the golden age. Amen."

Priscilla didn't appreciate the lofty language of the prayer. "What is going on here?" She heard the anger in her voice. She didn't think these men were of God at all. She wondered if they were crazy or just plain evil.

George Matthews handed her a card. "Right Disciples, ma'am. We're with one of the largest Christian think tanks, out of Colorado Springs, Colorado. Have you heard of us?"

"Only through Moses Sun," she said. "Did you tell him to kill Katharine Long?"

Mortimer Jacobs shook his head. "No, no. No killing. We serve Jesus. We are the good guys. Katharine Long, the evil one. But no, we're not trying to kill her. Moses Sun got a little carried away there. We didn't ask him to do that."

245

Priscilla looked at Sun and then at Matthews and back at Jacobs. "Then what are you hoping to accomplish? Why did you both come all the way to Patmos?"

"We want to destroy those scrolls. False teaching. We don't need them muddying the truth. They distract the people from the Word of God. You can help us," Matthews said.

"But we don't even have the scrolls. They disappeared long before we left Kusadasi."

Jacobs and Matthews exchanged looks. Sun nodded. "She's telling the truth. The women don't know where the scrolls are."

Now Priscilla understood Sun's earlier message. He didn't want her to go along with the men. But how could she get out of there? Would they even let her go? They held Moses against his will. How could she call the police when Sun was a wanted man? Her deliberations were interrupted by a knock at the door. She heard a foreign language, sounded like Greek to her. She laughed to herself. Yes, they were in Greece. But then a clear voice sounded in English. "Police, open the door, please."

Matthews whispered to Sun and Priscilla, "Into the bathroom, please, and lock the door."

Priscilla began to walk toward the door instead, and Jacobs pulled out a gun. "Into the bathroom, ma'am." Sun shuffled toward the bathroom, while Jacobs held the gun on Priscilla to make her follow suit.

Matthews shut the door and waited to hear the lock. Hearing none, he opened the door and pointed the gun at Priscilla. "Lock the door, now, ma'am. I wouldn't want to hurt you. And keep your mouth shut!" He pushed the door shut again, and this time heard the click on the inside.

Once inside the door, Sun started whispering to Priscilla. "You've got to get me out of here. These guys are crazy. I'll turn myself in. I wanted to do it before. Get Parks. Get the MAMs. Get help. Leave, now. I don't want them to hurt you. Priscilla, get out of here, and come back with the authorities."

Priscilla started shaking. Her face turned white. She felt her stomach gurgling. She looked at the toilet, wondering if she would begin to vomit in front of Sun. Embarrassed, she tried to calm herself down, taking deep breaths.

"You can do it. Calm down. Easy does it. You can do this, Priscilla," Sun smiled gently at her. She felt the intensity of her eyes and felt the attraction that hadn't gone away.

Then they both went quiet, listening through the door. What seemed like an eternity passed, with only muddled voices making it through the door into the bathroom. Priscilla was quite sure that she heard Dan Parks, and one of the others spoke English. After a few minutes, they heard a door open, then close, and suddenly the room was quiet.

Priscilla started to unlock the door.

"No! Don't! They could be out there!" Sun warned.

"Let me just look. I don't think there's anyone in the room. Maybe they took them down to the police station for questioning."

Sun held Priscilla back. "Impossible. What proof would they have of anything at this point? Remember, they have a gun."

Priscilla looked at her watch. It was only 9:00 a.m. She'd left the hotel at 8:30. If the men had left the room, they had a chance. She put her hand on the door again. "This may be our only chance to escape. If they took Matthews and Jacobs away for questioning, they could be back soon. Let me just check."

"Wait a few more minutes. If they're gone, they'll be gone for awhile."

"OK, five minutes, tops." Priscilla showed her watch to Moses Sun, and they began to wait.

***

The men in the lobby continued to party. Another round of drinks, a few more jokes. Balaban, a good Muslim who didn't drink, felt uncomfortable. He didn't understand how men of the cloth could tie on so many so early in the morning. And now the Greek priest started harping on additional laptops. "Are there any more laptops? Doesn't the translator have one? We need to get that one, too."

"Let's send Balaban in. They trust him," The Turkish official decided.

Balaban looked at his watch. "9:05 a.m." He wished he never would have left Kusadasi. He liked the MAMs. He didn't want to steal. He knew what happened in these situations. The powerful ones order the crimes, but he'd be the one to pay. He slipped away to go to the bathroom, and no one noticed. They also didn't notice when he walked out of the hotel. He made it to his car and no one seemed to be following. But then, he saw two familiar faces coming out of the hotel. He opened his window, and leaned out with a big smile, "Need a ride?"

He jumped out of his van, opening his door to Priscilla, who looked as white as a ghost, and there was the little fugitive right behind her. Darned if she didn't round up none other than Moses Sun.

"At your service, ma'am. Where to?" Balaban didn't waste any time turning out of the lot.

"Back to the hotel, please," Priscilla directed. Balaban detected the fear in her voice, but he let it go. He'd learned long ago women would talk when they were good and ready and prodding them could only make them mad.

Neither Moses nor Priscilla said a word all the way back to the hotel. Balaban opened the door, took a bow. They thanked him, before scurrying into their hotel. Balaban headed off for a smoke. Priscilla ushered Sun back to her room, locked the door and then sat on the bed in shock.

"I can't believe you found the key to the handcuffs in that drawer. God must be looking over us, Moses! But what now? What are we going to do now?" She asked Sun.

"Turn me in. Turn me in now. I can help the police stop Matthews and Jacobs. You can't hide me. They may kidnap me again. Then I'd be no help to anyone." Sun paced in front of the window.

Priscilla deliberated and then decided to call in the MAMs. Together, they'd figure this out. She looked out at the black clouds in the sky. "Looks like a storm brewing. I'm not surprised. I'm going to go get the MAMs. They'll know what to do. Stay here. Don't go anywhere! Keep the door locked until I get back!"

"Yes, ma'am." Sun saluted and waved goodbye, enjoying the back view of Prisicilla heading out the door. He still felt that attraction to the lady, although he knew any future between them dissolved in the seconds of those shots he fired in Kusadasi. He'd take his punishment. He knew he deserved it.

***

Priscilla found Jane in her room and told her: "Jane, we need to have a meeting. Need to decide about Moses Sun. In my room in five minutes. Can you come?"

"Well, OK. What's your room number?"

"Room 5. Hurry, OK?"

"Moses Sun? I thought he disappeared?"

"I know, I'll explain. Just come."

Priscilla made the circuit to the other rooms and headed back to her own in record time. She went into the bathroom to compose herself. She looked into the mirror and decided to add a little blush to her cheeks. If she ever made it home, she'd call her Mary Kay consultant and ask for a makeover. For now, the blush covered her pale fear. She reached into her makeup bag and pulled out some Juicy Fruit Doublemint gum. The familiar wrapper somehow gave her a feeling of home. In the midst of the crazy trip, she needed the comfort of something she knew. And then she collapsed onto the toilet seat and began to pray. God would know what to do. She got off the seat, knelt down and prayed hard, silently. She prayed for wisdom. She prayed for safety. She even prayed for the MAMs and, God help him, Moses Sun. Fortified, she left the solitude of the bathroom to meet the MAMs.

Within 10 minutes they were all sitting in her room, and Priscilla explained the situation. "So, you see, it's not just Mortimer Jacobs, but also George Matthews, and they held a gun on me. They said they don't believe in killing, but then he pulled the gun."

Moses Sun interrupted. "So the time has come to turn me in. I can help the police. I committed a crime. I appreciate your hospitality, you've been most kind. But take me to the police now. If I stay here, they could kidnap me again, and then what help would I be?"

Emily spoke. "My Granny Abby grew up as a Quaker. They believe in listening to God in silence. They have unprogrammed meetings, where they just sit and listen. Sometimes God speaks, and then someone will explain what they heard. "Let's listen to God now. Let's all just listen. Maybe God will tell us what to do."

Very unusual to see the MAMs at a loss for words, but now they all clammed up.

"Are we waiting for something?" Priscilla asked.

"Waiting on God," Molly answered. "We're listening."

"Oh," Priscilla said. "How do you do that?"

Emily put her forefinger up to her mouth. Then she put her hand up to her ear and cupped it. Then again her forefinger to her mouth.

Priscilla got the message. She became very quiet and tried to hear God speaking to her. Sure wasn't anybody else talking in the room.

Emily handed Priscilla a notebook and a pen. She mimicked writing. Priscilla figured they wanted her to write down any messages God delivered. They'd really lost it now, she thought.

But Priscilla tried to be a good girl. She listened. For a long time, she heard the silence filling up the room and her head. She argued with the MAMs in her head. God speaks in scripture, through the pastor, but not necessarily here. But then she thought again and thought, why not? Why wouldn't God speak to the MAMs? Of course God is speaking to them. They just need to listen. Back to square one. She sat quietly, with her pen posed on her notebook paper ready for an earth-shattering message that didn't come.

And then something very strange began to happen. She heard a voice. She picked up the pen and wrote down every word. She stopped to glance nervously around and to her surprise, saw everybody writing. The words were coming faster than she could get them down. She pleaded with God to slow down. He did not.

What was that saying she'd heard more than a few times, "Be careful what you ask for. You just might get it."

"OK, OK, OK, God. I'm writing," Priscilla muttered out loud.

And then as quickly as it all started, it stopped. Dead silence. No more words. Priscilla lifted her pen and looked around the room. They all had stopped writing. Spooky.

"What the hell is going on?" Jane broke the silence first.

"Let's see what God had to say, before we make any judgments!" Sallie laughed. Somehow they needed the kindergarten teacher to call them back to reality and the simplicity of the moment.

Emily began to read. "I love Moses Sun. He sinned. He fell short of my glory. He was wrong, he was misguided. But look at him. He apologized, he asked for forgiveness, he's trying to save you. Do you believe anything about my Son? Don't you understand I am the God of second chances? You need to forgive him and let him work for you."

Now again, silence stopped the MAMs. Priscilla's tongue seemed lost down her throat. She glanced at her page and then again let Emily's words linger. She knew she must read hers, and so she began, "'Moses Sun is my child. He made a mistake. So have you. He asked for forgiveness. I have forgiven him. You must too. It is my way.' ...I missed a sentence here. 'He will not hurt you. Love him.'"

Molly shook her head from side to side. "Mmm, mmm, mmm, when the Lord decides to speak, the waters part! Look out, baby! Bet you didn't know the MAN has got jive dialect down pat. Here's what he told me: 'You think you're without sin, sista? Since when? You think YOU ain't deserving of my forgiveness? You think any of my children are so bad that I quit loving them? You gotta try to be like me. Sometimes it's hard, but that's what I've been sayin' all along. Give the man a second chance. Just like I gave to you, sista.'"

Priscilla knew she didn't trust Sun, even back in Ohio. But now God was asking her to trust, no, to love him? Trusting men was not something she did easily. She took a deep breath. "Looks like God doesn't want us to turn him in."

"Now God didn't say that," Jane protested. "The man almost killed Katharine. Just because we're supposed to forgive him, doesn't mean that we should let him go free."

Ursula passed her paper to Jane. Jane held the paper up and began to read. "Some of you might think Moses Sun deserves to suffer in a Turkish prison for the rest of his life. That is not my way. I forgave him when he asked. You must forgive him, too. If Katharine and Emily can forgive him, there is no need to turn him in to the authorities. You will all be set free when you choose to love."

"God didn't write that." Jane looked at Ursula. "You did. What makes you think the guy has actually changed? He might try to kill us all!"

"What did you write, Jane?" Katharine asked.

"That's beside the point." Jane crunched her own paper in to a ball. "Get serious."

"Turn it over!" Sallie reached over and took the scrunched up ball out of Jane's hand. "That's a good girl."

Then Sallie smoothed out the paper and began to read, "Remember Paul? He was out persecuting my disciples and he went blind. When he got his sight back, he was a new man. It happened then. It happened now. Moses Sun is a new man. The old has passed away. All things have become new."

"Hey! This is scriptural. Jane! You're quoting scripture now!" Sallie laughed.

"That's not in the Bible. What are you talking about?" Jane shook her head and frowned at Sallie.

"II Corinthians 5:17. So if anyone is in Christ, there is a new creation: everything old has passed away; see, everything has become new!" Priscilla quoted the scripture for Sallie. "And the first part, Paul's Damascus Road experience."

Sallie poked her glasses down on her nose, gazed over them and told Jane, "I think it's time to open your Bible, dear."

"I don't even have a Bible," Jane replied.

"I'll buy you one!" Sallie laughed.

Then Katharine looked up from the bed and said, "I have forgiven Moses. I told you that I trust him now. I have felt that forgiveness flooding through my being." Katharine took a deep breath. Her words were whispered, labored, yet she went on. "Deep in my heart, I know what you have heard is the truth. I have no doubt about it. And, he is trying to help us, protect us from Mortimer Jacobs. There is no reason to turn him in."

"There is no way in hell that Dan Parks is going along with you on this." Jane said.

"What about you, Jane? Will you agree?" Katharine laid her head back down on the pillow and closed her eyes, yet she continued speaking. "It's basic Christianity. Forgive us our debts, as we forgive our debtors."

Jane looked at Katharine. Her lips were pressed together and her face seemed to be glaring. Then she looked at each of the MAMs, one at a time. The glare turned into a question mark and by the time she focused on Katharine again, the question had morphed into a smile.

"You all want to keep him as our buddy, don't you? What do I tell Parks?"

"Why does he have to know?" Ursula asked.

"He's a private detective, for God's sake. He's out searching for him, even as we speak. Keeping a secret from him is like trying to tell Santa Claus you've been a good girl all year when you slept with your boyfriend when your parents were out of town."

"The voice of experience!" Sallie laughed. "You are a trip, Jane Masters."

"At least I'm the one sane person in the room."

"Let's take a vote on that one," Sallie said.

But Ursula broke in with a question. "Can we try it for now? If he tries anything, we'll call Parks right away. And until then, Parks doesn't need to know we have him."

"It may be too late," Jane said. "I think you're all crazy."

But in the end, Jane went along with the group. At this point, all bets were off. Priscilla had no idea what would happen next, but knew she needed to trust the process and trust God.

Later that morning, Joe and Ursula called the group back together for the reading of Scroll #6. Somehow, Priscilla winded up sitting by Moses Sun when Ursula began to read. Priscilla felt more than a little nervous, sitting right beside him. She believed God had spoken, that Sun had changed, but wasn't sure that meant she needed to personally trust the man. She still cringed when she remembered she had dated the man. Once was enough.

Joe interrupted her inner thoughts. "We've finished the sixth scroll. It's rather amazing how quickly the translations are coming along. Of course, remember these are very preliminary. Also, there are some gaps. We have a linguist helping out from Colorado who is turning the translations into very readable text. I'm sure the translation will be debated and improved for many years to come, but with our modern technology and links in cyberspace we are able to accomplish very difficult translations in a short amount of time. And now, Ursula will read. 'Scroll #6. Philadelphia.'"

Ursula began to read, and again Priscilla felt amazed, transported back to a different time. She felt like Thecilla was sitting in the room with them.

Scroll # 6 Philadelphia

Greetings [ ] city of brotherly love in the fertile plain of Philadelphia. I write [ ] with great joy, [ ].

Claudius [ ] asked me to be his wife. [ ] seek the blessing of my parents, Joseph and Anna. We plan a Christian ceremony [ ] in Ephesus. Then, Claudius will travel with me [ ] for Jesus Christ. We will come to see you and speak the scrolls [ ].
The church received us with love and an open door. This morning, I read the scrolls [ ].

One of the elders fell down and cried out, "Jesus is the door. The open door is before us. Others will enter because of our faithfulness."

Another said, "We must be strong [ ]. God will test us."

Theocolus, a Greek artist said, "They have changed the name of this city two times, NeoCaesar and Flavia, but God will give us a new name, the New Jerusalem and God's name will be written on us. Let me design a door [ ] to remind you that Jesus is the door and we enter the New Jerusalem through him. "

[ ], they were [ ] interested in the plagues in the scrolls. The [ ] images scare me when I read them, but their rabbi explained them [ ]. He said, "This is the exodus for the people of God from the Roman empire. [ ] a warning to the Romans, if they do not change their ways, evil will befall them, like the plagues visited on the Pharaoh in Egypt [ ]. Yahweh led the people out of Egypt in those days, as the Red Sea parted and the people sang and worshipped. See, [ ] a song of victory and deliverance as they worship the Lamb by the sea of glass. God hears our cries. God cries with us, "Alas! Alas! Alas!" The white-robed martyrs walk out and God will dry their tears away. The whore is Roma, the evil empire who is idolatrous and leads the people astray. They destroyed the temple in Jerusalem. They have massacred Christians in Rome. Domitian has exiled our brother John to Patmos, but even now they can turn from their sins to the Lamb, who does not kill, but leads us out into love and the New Jerusalem where all are one.

They call their growing fields "the burned land," where the fire of the mountain spread many generations past. Now their harvest is plentiful, and they had a feast to celebrate the Victory of the Lamb and our betrothal. The wine flowed into [ ] we danced with great joy.

Grace and peace to you dear teacher. I send all my love and prayers to you.

Ursula stopped reading. Silence filled the room.

Emily announced, "Thecilla's getting married!"

"And so are you!" Josh added, while putting his arm around Emily and looking at her with a smile.

"What?" Sallie nearly yelled at her. "Why am I the last to know?"

Emily held her left hand up for all of us to see a diamond ring shining there.

"We set a date! We're going to get married at Christmas!"

Bedlam broke loose for the next few minutes while everybody congratulated the couple. Emily's grin kept spreading. The corners of her smile seemed ready to jump off her face.

But Priscilla's thoughts were still firmly entrenched in the Red Sea and the plagues. What did the scrolls mean about the plagues in the book of Revelation, she wondered. She had always been taught that those plagues described the tribulation to come. She didn't believe it had anything to do with the Roman Empire.

She waited until the noise died down a little to ask a question.

"That can't be right. That's not true. The plagues are something that will come in the future." She told them.

"You don't agree with Thecilla?" Ursula asked.

"It's wrong. It's simply wrong." Priscilla told her.

"That's certainly not what I've believed for many years," Sun agreed.

Katharine sat up a little. "But that's not a new interpretation."

"No, it's 2,000 years old!" Joe laughed.

"Well, I mean that there are quite a few modern theologians who agree with Thecilla."

"Are you sure? A few weeks ago, I would have never believed this. But look how misguided I was. I thought I was killing in the name of God to protect my own interpretation of Revelation. I thought I was serving God and the United States of America."

"Not the first time Christians have killed in the name of God," Sallie reminded.

"Not the first time Christians have been dead wrong," Molly added. "Quite a few Christians in the USA believe God led us into Iraq. But God is not a killing God, is He? How can He be?"

"Aren't the plagues a form of killing, punishing those who disobey?" Priscilla asked them.

Katharine sat up in bed and began to speak. "You have to see that there are many interpretations of the book of Revelation. But the one that is popular in the USA today, like I said before, is the one that interprets the book of Revelation to be about this day, rather than the Roman Empire. This is a theory concocted by a cleric in Ireland back in the 1800s. He put together pieces of scripture from Daniel, Matthew, II Thessalonians, and Revelation and cooked up a theory that many people hold up as truth in the USA today, but it's really one of the most convoluted interpretations of the Bible I've ever seen. So far away from a literal interpretation, so very far." Katharine lay back on her pillow and took a deep breath.

Then Emily started in. "You know, this is the very topic I chose for my senior thesis. I did the research. Just like Katharine told us yesterday, the only reason that theory made it into the American consciousness was because it was in a footnote of the Scofield Chain Reference Bible.xxxiii And now you have Americans insisting it's a literal interpretation of the Bible. So far from literal. Maybe Thecilla's scroll will help them understand. *End Times* is a perversion of the Bible and the Gospel and of everything Jesus stood for."

Moses Sun bowed his head and covered the back of his head with his hands. The MAMs all quit talking for a while. Priscilla wasn't sure she knew the truth any more. She wished she were back at home where her pastor could explain the Rapture Theory again so that she would know the truth. But then again, the Spirit was here, moving among them. She could feel that with all he being. She found herself putting her arm around Moses Sun and telling him, "God loves you. So do we."

Molly smiled. "Amen, Sister. And don't you forget it! The gospel in one word is love, and we better get busy loving each other, and loving our enemies, too, I might add."

Josh turned to Emily with a gleam in his eye. "Amen, Sister!" he yelled, and then pulled Emily into a deep embrace, and planted his lips on hers.

"Hey!" Sallie yelled. "Love, but don't get carried away, Joshua Turner. Slow down, sir! Your wedding isn't until Christmas."

Josh started laughing and broke the kiss. "Yes, ma'am. I guess I have a few too many chaperones on this trip."

"What do you expect when you try to crash the MAMs Expedition?" Jane asked.

Moses Sun raised his head and looked at Priscilla.

"I'm sorry, Priscilla. I'm so sorry. Can you ever forgive me? I have sinned. I don't deserve to be your friend."

Priscilla looked at Sun and mouthed the words that God had given her earlier during the listening prayer. "All have sinned and fallen short. I have sinned, too. God forgave me. God forgives you. We must forgive each other. I forgive you."

Then Sun took her right hand and raised it to his lips and kissed it gently, while tears were streaming from his eyes.

"Thank you, Priscilla," he said. "I don't deserve this. Thank you for your forgiveness."

Inside Priscilla's heart a light began to shine. She had no idea where that light would end up, but for the moment she was in the presence of God and His children, and she decided to bask in the light. "Amen!" she announced. This expedition had turned out to be so much more than she ever imagined.

38. Thecla in Love

September 24, 48 A.D.

Although Trifina lavished upon Thecla garments and jewels of every kind, Thecla longed to listen to Paul again. She promised herself that she would find him and become his best disciple. She had risked everything for him and his God, and she sought to follow him now.

Finally, her inquiries brought back word that Paul was preaching in Myra and Lycia. So she took along her new friends, both men and women, and dressed as a man to go to Paul where he was preaching the word of God. When she found him, she stood close to him in the midst of the crowd.

Paul recognized her through her disguise and spoke out. "What calamity will come upon us now? Thecla has returned!" He laughed and asked, "Why do you dress as a man?"

And Thecla kissed his cheek and told him, "I am baptized, Paul. The God who helps you preach helped me baptize myself."

The people marveled at the young woman who seemed so familiar with Paul, the preacher. And Paul continued to preach, speaking of her loyalty to God and of her escape from death and the triumph of her faith from the fire at the stake.

Thecla smiled, finding Paul finally accepting her as a woman of God and perhaps even as his disciple. Paul took her with him to the house of Hermes. Thecla explained everything that had happened in Antioch. Paul and all who heard were strengthened in their faith and they prayed for Trifina's happiness.

Paul found himself once again attracted to Thecla. He wanted her to stay as much as he knew he should send her away. Fortunately, she resolved the dilemma for him when she told him the next morning, "Paul, I am going to Iconium."

He replied, "Go. Teach the word of the Lord."

So Thecla left Paul for home, where she stopped first at the house of Onesiphorus and preached. Mixing tears with her prayers, she prayed and glorified God, "O Lord the God of this house, in which I was first enlightened by you; O Jesus, son of the living God, my helper before the governor, my helper in the fire, and my helper among the beasts; You alone are God forever and ever. Amen."

And then she went home and tried to teach her mother what she had learned, but her mother refused to hear the word of God. So Thecla signed her whole body with the sign of the cross and went on to the cave, where she had found Paul with Onesiphorus and fell down on the ground and wept before God.

Meanwhile, Paul could not stop thinking about Thecla. It didn't help when Trifina sent large sums of money and also clothing by the hands of Thecla, for the relief of the poor. He decided that he must travel to Iconium to find Thecla and thank her. If he were completely honest with himself, it would be Trifina whom he should thank. He prayed for strength to resist temptation even as he longed after this beautiful young woman who had given everything for God.

When a friend came and asked him to make the journey, he decided that perhaps God nudged him toward Thecla, so he did indeed travel to Iconium. He visited the cave where they had met in the past and found her there. She welcomed him and together they found an uncommon love that enfolded them both in the heart of God.

Later it would be a night that she would remember and hold in her heart after she went on to Seleucia, and Paul continued on his separate missionary journeys. One night of love that still shined like a beacon of hope, a union of two servants of God. A night she would hold secret, so that Paul's preaching could continue to spread the good news of Jesus far and abroad.

39. Thecilla in Philadelphia

September 20, 94 A.D.

Claudius stopped the chariot by the white cliffs on the trip into Phila-delphia. The unusual pools covered the side of the mountain, with great formations similar to those in an underground cave.

"My mother tells me these are healing waters. People come from many lands to be healed here. She asked me to bring some water back to her."

"And how will you do that, Claudius?"

"I have some empty flasks she gave me. She thinks of everything, you know." Claudius pulled the wineskins out of his bag. "Come, Thecilla, let's bathe in the pools."

"But where will we dry ourselves?" Thecilla worried about riding on in the cool day with wet clothes.

"Can you see the huts in the field below? The keeper of the pool allows the guests to change there. I have been here many times. There are special robes we can wear."

Claudius grew up in a family of privilege, compared to Thecilla's more humble beginnings in the Christian family, where there was just enough to go around most days and not enough on others when her father could not sell the tents.

When they finished changing, they held hands, walking toward the pools. Thecilla pulled up her robe and stepped into the water. "It's so warm! Even with the cold in the air?"

"The water comes from warm springs in the earth. Always warm."

Claudius stepped into the water beside her and then sat down in the shallow pool. "Sit with me." He toyed with her hand, half-expecting Thecilla to jump back out. To his surprise, Thecilla plumped down in the water beside him, robe and all.

Claudius took the opportunity to pull her close again, circling her with his right arm.

Thecilla laughed. "How fun! How soothing." Her bottom felt bruised from long hours in the chariot over rough roads. The warm water and smooth sand brought welcome relief.

Claudius enjoyed her laughter, so thankful for a break from the serious business of visiting the churches. While he promised Thecilla to

259

take care of her, he also knew the Romans could take that protection away at the drop of a sword.

In one pool, Claudius kneeled before Thecilla and lifted his hand to hers. "My lady, my love, would you do me the honor of becoming my wife?"

"Your wife?" Startled by his abrupt request, she questioned his eyes. "Do you jest?"

"Thecilla, I am a man in love. I will ask permission of your parents when we return to Ephesus. Will you say yes, if they should agree?"

Thecilla pulled him up. "Claudius, my love, I would be happy for the rest of my life, to be your wife. Yes! Yes! A hundred times yes!"

Claudius covered Thecilla's lips with his and twirled her around in the pool. Their bodies clung to each other, like the wet material of their robes clung to their skin. They danced, they laughed, they kissed and then laughed some more. Jumping from pool to pool, they made their way up the mountain and then back down. By late afternoon they found the changing hut and dried themselves to continue on to the church in Philadelphia.

The city had become a town of huts. The leader of the church explained that after the great earthquake and countless aftershocks, the people had vacated the inner city. Yet, they were a happy people and long ago had been established as a center of Greek culture. Volcanic ash led to fertile fields and a lush wine industry.

That night, their new friends at the Christian church offered wine to Claudius and Thecilla,

Claudius proposed a toast to their upcoming marriage. They drank quite a lot of wine that night. Thecilla fell asleep, reclining at the table, and Claudius had to carry her to her hut where she slept soundly.

The next day, Thecilla read the scrolls to the church. A warm reception made Thecilla happy. More than any of the other churches, they seemed to understand. The plagues would come, if Roma continued on her evil path. Yet, for whoever opens the door, Jesus will come in.

Thecilla loved the image of Jesus standing at the door knocking.

That night she gave thanks that Claudius had opened that door and wrote another letter to Thecla to share her good news. On a difficult journey, with danger always near, Philadelphia had brought fun and relief. She found a carrier, sending the scroll on the way to Thecla and fell asleep content at the end of the day.

40. Sallie and Laodicea

September 23, 2006

The sun warmed the room by the time Sallie brushed sleep out of her eyes and oriented herself to the day. Her 60-year-old self applauded, remembering that after some wine and laughter the night before, the MAMs voted to take the morning off. She opened her curtains to spend a little time enjoying the beauty of the morning and the foaming blue-green sea below. Her mind raced back through the fantastic events of the past several days. Patmos, Greece. Quite a long way from the farming community in Ohio where she had lived and worked most of her life. She placed her hand on her belly and moved it around in a circle. Menopause made her extra fat respectable at last. She chuckled.

Her mind continued to roam back through the frames of the past days. Greece. Kusadasi, Turkey. The Grotto of St. Paul. An archaeological expedition with an unlikely group of old women who actually found something. Being stalked by a Rapture enthusiast who tried to kill a few off and now had converted? Now a new stalker on the scene. She wondered, not for the first time, if she had morphed into some sort of crazy woman in an adventure film. Ms. Quisenberry, formerly the River City's Kindergarten Institution, also known as Mrs. Q, now exploring intrigue and drama in Greece? Who would ever cast her for the part? "Don't they know that I'm a retired teacher and avid book collector who dotes on my adopted nieces and enjoys a quiet life in rural Ohio?" She asked out loud, then laughed. "And now I'm talking to myself. Definitely deranged."

She stretched her stiff limbs, reaching her hands up over her head. Then bending at the waist, she hung her head down toward the floor, trying to get that yoga feeling again. Out of the corner of her eye, she spotted the little brown chair at the desk, the only chair in her home away from home. She pulled the chair over by the window and sat. Folding her hands over her belly, she assumed a contemplative pose. The fat smiling Buddha, one of her friends had once suggested. "Except the Buddha would put his hands on his knees," she had protested.

"Close enough," her friend had had replied. And ever since she liked to think that this posture took her to that river the Buddha contemplated in Siddhartha. Now the sea was the river; not flowing, but lapping. She waited for silence to slow her racing thoughts.

How could she ever go back to Ohio and return to an ordinary life after this trip? The scrolls were unsettling and exciting at the same time. In the back of her mind, she kept thinking they must be a hoax. They were too good, too close to her Brethren interpretation of reality which was such an unpopular view, yet still the truth she had believed all her life. Long ago, she resigned herself to the reality that the American way was not the path of peace. Once again she wondered how could she grow up believing that the U.S. of A. stood for only good things in the world, when they were the ones who built so many weapons. Now she knew that her country armed the world.

She sighed, then wondered. Was it resignation or relief she felt? Her mind raced on, turning somersaults and she remembered the Buddhist monk telling her they called it "monkey mind." Too many ideas trying to swing around in her consciousness. She watched the thoughts tumbling and playing, then she tried to let go. "Observe and let them go, don't strive," she could still remember his instruction. She focused on her breath, letting it keep time with the gentle waves lapping the shore. Her body relaxed. She absorbed the scene outside the window, letting it flow deep within. Gradually a deep peace radiated through her body.

But then, a knock at the door pulled her back from the Buddhist moment. Pulled her from the present into a very different now. She yelled out through the closed door. "Yes?" Then, looking down at her pajamas, wondered if she should open the door with her general state of disarray.

"Sallie! It's Molly. My camera is back, and Ursula's laptop, too."

"What?" Sallie opened the door to the informant. The peace of the moment dissolved into the chaos of yet another chapter of the MAMs' expedition. "That's good, very good. Right?"

Somehow Molly didn't seem to be very happy. She stood there with her hands planted on her hips and a look that told Sallie someone had better be sorry they were messing with her. Then she explained. "My pictures are erased, along with Ursula's files about the scrolls! Now Joe's laptop has been taken. Ursula and Joe are on the warpath!"

"Come in, sit down!" Sallie laughed, because she had found over the years humor often eased tension. "And you think I can solve this problem? I'm a schoolteacher, not James Bond. This is way out of my league!"

Molly laughed, too, and plopped down on the bed. "Emily's with Josh. Ursula and Joe are off to the police station with Dan and Jane to report the theft. Priscilla is in charge of Sun this morning. It's you and me, girlfriend."

"God help us now!" Sallie laughed again.

"Sister, this situation calls for prayer."

"Only God can help us now. That's for sure!" Sallie kept trying to keep Molly light.

"I want to go up to the Cave of St. John to pray!"

"Can't we pray here? I thought this was our morning off!"

"That cave, it's the place. Look what it did for John. Come on, Sallie, humor me. It can't hurt. I think we might find God there, too."

"Look, I'm no spring chicken, you know. I got my beauty sleep, but I haven't had my bath yet." Sallie ruffled her hair and looked at herself in the mirror. "Look at me! Do I look like I'm ready to go out on the town?"

"Not the town, the prayer cave. I'll give you 30 minutes. You can take a bath, pull on some clothes. You don't do makeup, girlfriend. And I don't think you're the type to spend hours talking to your mirror."

"Can't we go this afternoon? I need some time to collect myself. I mean look what we've been through in the last week! This old lady needs a break."

"I'm not any younger than you. No, let me correct that. You're my baby sister. Now you should be taking care of your elder. I need you to protect me if Mortimer Jacobs shows up."

"And you think I can save you? A 200-pound fat lady? Super Ma'am at your service. I think you need a knight, not a retired schoolteacher from rural Ohio." Sallie started laughing.

"Knights went out with the middle ages. You're all I got, girlfriend, and you're coming with me. Now, are you going to take that bath, or do I have to take you out in your pajamas?"

"OK, OK. Give me some time. I'm getting up. I'll take my bath. At least I got to sleep in."

And that is how it happened that in the middle of her morning off, Sallie joined Molly in Balaban's van to revisit the Cave of St. John. The ladies sat in the first row behind their driver, who chatted amiably while the car sped up the hill toward the stucco monastery on the top. The daunting, quaint beauty of Patmos filled her eyes. Even in the midst of the confusion, she focused on the white buildings, the blue skies, the narrow streets, the feeling of peace the place oozed into her being. The meditation seemed to be doing its work. On a morning like this, she could almost morph into the fat Buddha's double. She took back her pose, folding her hands over her belly, leaned back against the upholstered seat chair and smiled.

Molly looked over at her with a frown. "What you smiling about, girlfriend? I thought I ruined your morning off. We need to figure what's goin' on here. That's why we're headed to the holy place to pray. Who could be taking our stuff and erasing the scroll information?"

Sallie uncrossed her hand and leaned forward. "You know Parks told me last night that back in Turkey he became convinced the Vatican was involved in the scroll's disappearance. He couldn't get Halim to admit it. Halim wouldn't tell. But you remember how the Vatican had a representative there when we read the first scroll?"

"Of course, they were interested. I mean, first century, the Cave of St. Paul. They have been involved in funding the archaeological sites there, from what Ursula told us," Molly said.

"Yes, they have an interest. But were they trying to stop the information from getting out to the public? That is my question."

Balaban pulled the van into the parking lot below the cave, but Molly and Sallie continued to talk.

"They didn't even know what the scrolls said. Why would they stop the translation, before they knew?" Molly asked.

"Did they stop the translation?" Sallie asked back. "Did they stop the translation or did they just move it in-house?"

"Those scrolls are property of the Turkish government, not the Vatican. A very Muslim country," Molly added.

"Yes, and the Muslims respect the Christian scriptures, you know," Sallie reminded. "Would they entrust the scrolls to the Vatican's scholars? The Vatican would be much more well-informed on the intricacies of the early Christian church. It's their thing."

"Hmm..." Molly pulled out her knowledge of modern-day politics. "You know, the Turkish government is trying very hard for entrance into the European Union. Making friends with Italy might be in their interest. It's not out of the question, Sallie."

"OK, OK. Ladies, I present the Cave of St. John." Balaban interrupted the women, pretending not to hear their conversation, which only agitated him. "When do you want me to pick you up?"

"Oh, we're not staying long. Are we?" Sallie looked at Molly. "How long are you praying? This isn't going to be one of your two-hour services is it?"

Molly put her hands on her hips and looked back at Sallie with indignation. "What are you trying to say, girlfriend? Just because your white worship ends at the stroke of noon, you think you done prayin'?" Then she winked at Balaban. "Come back in half and hour."

"Whew!" Sallie wiped imaginary sweat off her brow. "Thank you, Jesus!"

"Quit mocking me, or I'll add an hour. Now let's get in there and get down on our knees. We're going to have to pray fast if we've only got a little time." Molly led Sallie across the concrete walkway toward the small building enclosing the cave.

"Wait, let me take a picture!" Sallie planted her feet firmly, like a tree. "You know I lost all my pictures and now I need to make up for lost time. "Look at the view! It doesn't get any better than this." Sallie pointed down toward the valley and the crystal blue water below. White stucco houses covered the hills, small boats bobbed in the water.

"You got me there. That's beauty at its best, girlfriend. Snap away and then let's get to our prayers."

A few minutes later, Molly and Sallie sat down on the high-backed wooden chairs within the Cave of St. John, looking at the altar and the rock where John's scribe wrote the book of Revelation.

"Can you imagine Thecilla in here?" Sallie asked.

"Um-hm. Sure can. I bet she'd be a-prayin' hard. Now let's get down to work."

Fortunately for Sallie, Molly decided to pray silently. So Sallie followed suit. Once Sallie got beyond the Greek orthodox trappings and stuff that would never grace a Brethren meeting place, she didn't feel the chair worked for her. Eventually, she decided to go up to the front and sit cross-legged on the bench in the lotus position, with hands open, despite a few frowns from Molly. Now she focused again on her breath and tried to get back to that centered spot she'd left when Molly knocked on her door more than an hour ago now. Her monkey mind didn't cooperate very well. It had her swinging from the chandeliers and hanging from the ceiling in the strange building, where an old cave had been glorified into a shrine for pilgrims from around the world. She tried to visualize Joe's laptop reappearing and her pictures being retrieved from some mysterious computer belonging to the thief that took them in the first place. She could see it all coming back and asked for God's blessing once again on the MAMs mission. Perhaps they needed a second blessing ceremony. Seemed like they'd been overly blessed at first, but now look at the mess. Just when she felt her mind was as quiet as the candle burning in front of her and just when she finally let her breath carry her again into that place of wholeness, a burly monk with a full gray beard and a belly to match, sat down on the bench beside her. Although he didn't draw his legs up cross-legged like hers, he did place his hands in a receiving pose, palms up on his knees. She felt a little bit like he was playing follow the leader, although he hadn't bothered to tell her he'd decided she was his leader.

Her slightly open eyes strayed over to the right, taking in the good monk while she turned his image over in her mind. Although he spooked her a little because he mimicked her pose, she decided that she'd try to make a friend, rather than demonize a stranger. Turning to the chubby monk, she asked, "Will you pray for me?" She figured a man of the cloth couldn't turn down a request for prayer.

To her surprise, he extended his hand and shook hers warmly with a laugh that emanated from deep within his diaphragm and then headed up into his throat, coming out with almost a chiming giggle that seemed to set the chandelier swaying above in the dim light of the cave space.

"I'm Brother Simone, and you?"

She chuckled back, returning the introduction. "Sallie Quisenberry, from Ohio in the United States. I thought from your outfit there you might be a monk. Can you help me out?"

"Yes, yes. What kind of prayer would you like?"

"A prayer to catch a thief? My friends' camera and laptop were stolen, then returned, minus some important information. Now another laptop is missing. We don't know what's going on."

Brother Simone raised his eyebrows in consternation, even while his guilty conscience began doing a number on his stomach. "Oh. I'm sorry. Did this happen on Patmos? We don't usually have many problems here."

"Yes, on Patmos. First we had trouble in Turkey. Then we escaped to Patmos for a rest, and now this. All we're trying to do is complete our mission. Doesn't add up."

"Yes, I'll pray for you, Sallie." Brother Simone closed his eyes and soon carried on in a silent prayer. Once again, Sallie found herself wrestling with a swinging monkey, wondering how to quiet her thoughts and let God's light and peace flood her inmost being.

Twenty minutes later, Balaban came into the small room and tapped Sallie on the shoulder. Before leaving, she thanked Brother Simone and told him he could keep up the prayers, saying they had to be off to attend the Conference of Mystics at Hotel Romeos for a session with Abdul Wase.

After Molly and Sallie left the small room, Brother Simone fell to his knees. He had some serious reckoning to do with God, and then he would decide how to proceed.

Molly and Sallie were whisked back to the Hotel Romeos for a quick lunch and an afternoon session at the International Conference of Mystics. Molly wanted to go back to her room, but after dragging Sallie out in the morning, she didn't have much choice but to accompany Sallie on to the circular chapel. They left their missing property concerns at the door, being drawn in to another conference session.

Sallie scanned the gathering. Thirty years of teaching school taught her well in checking out a class room for delinquency. Of course, with retirement she'd relinquished the control over wayward entities. If Jacobs showed up, she might do a disappearing act. Then again, he'd keep the excitement flowing. The MAMs expedition had certainly added some flair to her otherwise boring retirement.

Now she wondered if she hoped for drama. "Do you think?" She chuckled. Molly grabbed her arm and pulled her down into a seat by the door in the second row, just as the speaker stood up to begin.

"Today, I'd like to introduce a good friend of mine," the mystical interfaith guy said.

What's that guy's name? Sallie wondered and then threw some daggers at her aging brain. I hate my mind. David ... David ... Merkt. Yes. David Merkt. Then she remembered to listen, just as he finished the introduction. Oh well.

"Please welcome to the Conference of Mystics, my very good friend and colleague, brother in the faith, Abdul Wase."

Gentle applause rippled through the room. The mostly male audience politely clapped, but looking at the faces she saw genuine delight in the room, such welcoming spirits. She could only get those kinds of looks on her little kindergartners when she was doling out ice cream or Christmas presents.

She sat back, retreating into her hands-on-belly Buddha pose to listen. She considered herself a contemplative, of sorts. Most farmers had the Spirit in them. But that was another topic and now she'd missed this guy's introduction. She opened her ears just as he asked a big question.

"What makes it possible for some deranged men to convince young teenagers to become suicide bombers? What is it about the situation of life for these teenagers that they could allow a stranger to convince them that they should kill themselves and others? How could they believe that is what God would want them to do?"

"In my work with the International Young Spiritual Volunteers, our goal is to give young people meaningful opportunities for service so that they are so busy and engaged in using their gifts and following their faith traditions to help others, they have no time or inclination to fall prey to those who would indoctrinate them with hate and use them to kill."

"For Brother David, the interfaith mystical thread that brings us all together at this conference, is a journey of peace and enlightenment into the heart of God. In my Islamic tradition, the call to service is an integral part of the faith journey. And I know in each religion, the path of service draws believers to good work. Have you read Thomas Merton? If so, you know that he found the life of contemplation intimately wed with the life of action as a man of faith. I believe it is crucial for our young people – and all of us, really – to have opportunities to take positive actions to help grow the ability to flourish as people of peace, as people of faith, as healers in our world."

"My father required that I do act of services when I was in high school. It transformed my understanding of myself in relationship to my world. Now, I want to give other young people a chance to make a difference also."

Wase bowed his head, then raised it again. "Will you join me in prayer? It is time."

He knelt on the floor, and Brother David joined him. They bowed their heads down to the floor, on a little carpet. Sallie closed her eyes and prayed silently. They were saying some words she couldn't understand. Perhaps Arabic, she thought. In a few moments, she peeked to see what they were doing. Fortunately, she wasn't at the dinner table, and her Mother wasn't there to catch her peeking.

She saw the candles flickering over their prostrate bodies, a picture of humility and waiting on God. Part of her wanted to join them, but then she thought about the pain that would cause in her knees, not to mention the thought of lifting her backside to the audience. She smiled, careful to keep the chuckle to herself for a change, remembering her Muslim friend who explained this was why the women prayed behind the men, in a separate place in the mosque.

But at the same time, she knew this was a very holy moment. God had arrived. She used to have this feeling in the morning when she went out to do the chores with the cows in the barn at sunrise. She would see the sun spreading color around the fields, and the promise of a new day filled her lungs with a joy she could not contain.

Now she felt that joy. Deep within, something started stirring. All through retirement, she'd felt content, but also often stressed and overly busy doing not much of anything. Sure she helped out the pastor and visited friends, but she missed having a mission of shaping the little ones into good students and good people. She often wondered what her retirement mission could be. Here she had heard something that called her. The International Young Spiritual Volunteers Organization – she liked this idea. She felt like she was being sucked into a bright light of promise, mesmerized in the moment of prayer.

When the chanting began, she chanted along. "Allah, Allah, Allah."

Molly elbowed her. "Shut up! Just pretend you're singing."

"Just because I can't carry a tune doesn't mean I can't sing to God." Sallie protested, but sang more quietly.

And then, for the second time today, Molly jabbed Sallie in the ribs, interrupted her meditation. She was ready to lay her out. Molly pointed to the brown robe on the periphery of the circle. Sallie took it in and saw Brother Simone, motioning to her. She pointed at herself and looked at the good brother with a question forming on her face.

Then she turned to her right and left, wondering if there were some-one else he could be calling out. But seeing no other person looking at Simone, she looked again, and he nodded and pointed again at her then, motioned for her to come.

Sometimes surprise happens in the middle of an alleluia moment. Sallie stood and told Molly, "Come with me, girlfriend."

A few minutes later, over some of Brother Lawrence's homemade bread and tea in the hotel dining room, Brother Simone offered assis-tance to the MAMs. While Sallie still wanted his prayers, she didn't really have any other ideas, until Joe and Ursula returned from the police station to join them at the table. "Yes," Joe said, "We could certainly use your help. Do you have a computer at the monastery with Internet access? We've lost our work, but I can access it online."

Brother Simone's face lit up and he laughed. "Yes, Yes. You can come use our library and our computer. I'll let you use my desk. Do you want to come now?"

Joe nodded. "Let's round up the MAMs. Ursula and I finished Scroll #7 before my laptop disappeared. I can get it out of my email account. We'd like to read it to you."

Sallie asked, "But do you think we're being followed? Somebody must be watching us. If we go to the monastery, won't they follow us there?"

Jane and Dan showed up about the time Sallie asked the ques-tion, and the good detective offered to give Jane, Sallie and Molly a ride to the monastery. Brother Simone offered to take Ursula, Joe, Emily and Josh.

"What about Priscilla and Moses Sun?" Sallie asked.

Parks balked at that. "Moses Sun?"

"Oops," Sallie laughed. "I forgot."

"Forgot what?" Parks bellowed.

Emily filled in. "We'll go get Priscilla." Behind Dan's back she put her finger to her lips. She didn't want to create a scene. She thought they could pile Sun in and hide him at the monastery, if need be.

Catastrophe averted, Sallie and Molly headed out of the room and within moments the ladies were back outside. Parks seemed to be pushing the women, shooing them like flies toward the car.

Sallie didn't like it. "What's the hurry? I am on vacation!"

"Just get in," he said with an urgency she did not like at all. Jane sat up front. Molly and Sallie climbed in the back seat, and be-fore they could fasten their seat belts, Parks tore out of the parking space.

Jane laughed and yelled back to them, "Hold on, ladies! We're in for a ride."

"What the hell is going on?" Sallie yelled. Parks didn't answer. So she looked at Molly, who was holding on to the grab handle above her window. She felt that fear deep in her gut. For some reason, they had to get out of this place, and Parks was not about to spill the beans. Maybe he didn't have time.

"What is going on?" Sallie asked again.

"I thought you were worried about being followed." Parks laughed out loud. "I'm going to make sure that doesn't happen."

***

Poolside at Hotel Romeos the international delegation considered their options. The three men huddled at a plastic table. None of them were actually swimming, and they kept an eye on the gathering at the circular outdoor meeting space of the Conference of Mystics across the way. Earlier they sat in on the sessions, but after a while they decided sitting at a distance suited them better. They planned to keep the ladies over there under close tabs from here on out. Unfortunately, they sipped some drinks and someone forgot to monitor the group while they shared stories of Turkish nights and Italian days.

Said Ahmed, appointed watchman of the hour, stood when the good Catholic Brother finished yet another joke and strolled over toward the conference gathering, drink in hand. On second thought, he returned the drink to the table, remembering an American Muslim took center stage for this afternoon session. Muslims don't drink, or at least not according to the Quran, and he knew the American Muslims took that edict seriously. Anxious to return to the entertaining poolside gathering, he eyed the area where he knew the women were sitting. He looked and looked again to confirm his fear that the chairs once holding the two heavier women now appeared empty. He scanned the terrace and steps and then headed for the hotel dining room and main desk. There he saw the women, with their friends, slipping out the main entrance. He headed back to alert his comrades.

"Said summoned the group who then walked briskly toward the hotel entrance. They tried to be discreet, so they didn't run.

"These women move slowly, don't worry. I've been watching them. They won't get away." Said Ahmed laughed and moved his hands in a wide hourglass figure.

But once outside, the women had scurried. Parks' car had already pulled out of the lot, and the monastery vehicle followed closely.

Stephan Toflokous recognized a car with monastery plates and then saw a familiar face behind the wheel. "Brother Simone! What was he doing at the Conference?   Perhaps we should go pay him a visit again."

"We left our drinks!" Brother Leonardo complained. "I don't think we need to worry anyway. Let's enjoy the afternoon sun."

The group returned poolside for another hour of laughter and storytelling. They knew where the women were staying, so they decided they could check up on them later after a good Greek dinner by the seafront. "I have a friend, a musician," Toflokous suggested. "His wife runs a good little restaurant down by the water. He plays, sings, also makes balalaikas. A good guy. You'll enjoy his music."

***

Meanwhile, the MAMs sped toward the monastery. The detective aimed to give the ladies the ride of their life. Parks gunned the gas, dashing down the narrow street leading toward the business district and their hotel. Jane grabbed at the passenger seat handle, and the MAMs in the back held on to each other. Instead of heading directly up the hill, Parks left and went out another street taking them back into a different area of Skala that Sallie had never seen before. Parks kept checking the rear view mirror, making frequent turns. Finally, after several minutes of jerking and turning, he told the ladies, "I think we can go to the monastery now."

A few minutes later they pulled into the monastery parking lot, and Brother Simone stood waiting to show them where to park. He ushered the group up to the monks' private library. Although he brought Moses Sun along, he'd already shown him to his bedroom, where he'd signed Sun onto his personal computer. At Joe's urging and Sun's agreement, he'd locked the door from the outside, for safekeeping. The arrangement would keep intruders out and keep Sun in, until the MAMs could decide what to do with him next. For now, they didn't want to upset Parks any more than necessary.

"What do we do now?" Sallie addressed Brother Simone and the group as a whole. "Are we in hiding?"

Dan Parks laughed. "Well, it depends on whether or not Joe and Ursula want to risk being found. They'll have to give you permission to leave. They might want you here for a while."

Ursula interrupted. "First, we'd like to get on the computer and print out our translations. We've already finished the seventh scroll. We thought you might like to hear it. There's only one more to go, you know. And we've made headway on that one, too. They can steal our laptops and erase our material, but Joe tucked the information safely away on his work web site."

"What does that word mean?" Sallie asked.

"What word?" Molly replied.

271

"Safe," Sallie completed her thought. "What does 'safe' mean in this context? They tried to kill Katharine and Emily, they've stolen our laptops and camera, erased information. Do you think information on the web could be safer than us?"

Joe laughed. "You have a point there. Computer hackers are good these days, and we don't know who we're dealing with. I suspect there's some money behind our opponents. Nevertheless, the pictures of the scrolls and translations have been shared widely. At this point, there are too many copies out there, even for experienced hackers. My personal assistant in California backed up the photos in several ways, and she's got our back. I can promise that her strategies have insured the scrolls and translations will outlive all of us."

So the MAMs gathered together in the cozy library sitting on stuffed chairs and some on a bench, waiting for yet one more revelation. Brother Simone offered them tea and Greek pastries. Sallie began to relax in the sanctuary of the thousand-year-old walls. The late September afternoon carried a chill, that Sallie thought might be a product of fear, more than the weather. She realized the good monk must be sensing it, too, when he brought in some logs, starting a small warming blaze in the library fireplace. Now she considered the events of the day, realizing that their earlier prayers had been answered. Brother Simone answered the prayer himself.

"How did you find us?" she asked him now.

"You told me you were attending the conference at the Hotel Romeos. I kept thinking maybe there would be a way to help you. God's nudging, I'd say." The good brother smiled, while he used an iron stick to poke the fire and move the logs to keep them burning.

"Oh," Sallie replied.

"Where did you find him?" Emily asked. "I met him at the monastery when we took our tour."

"While you all were catching up on your beauty sleep, I got Sallie up early to go pray at the Cave of St. John. I knew we needed some divine intervention," Molly explained. "Brother Simone just happened to be there making his prayers, too."

"A holy coincidence?" Ursula asked.

Jane and Parks raised their eyebrows, and Brother Simone chuckled. "Sometimes, God does move us, you know. When you spend every day in prayer, you pay attention to the nudges. Sometimes it feels more like a shove. I felt a shove of sorts today. I had to follow God's lead."

"Mmm, hmmm," Molly agreed. "God answers prayer, and that's a fact."

The noise of the printer stopping turned their heads. Joe held the paper up and flashed it around the room. "The Scrolls of Thecilla, alive and well! Thank you, Brother Simone."

272

Simone took a bow, and Ursula took the papers out of Joe's hands and began to read.

Scroll # 7: A letter from Thecilla in Laodicea.

Greetings to my [ ] from the inn on [ ] road from Laodicea to Ephesus.

[ ], I sit by the candle to write [ ]. [ ] reminds [ ] nights [ ] in your cave with the candles dancing [ ] you taught me of God's love. Today, [ ] began the long journey home to Ephesus. My heart is filled with love for Claudius and joy that I have completed the journey to the seven churches. I have been a faithful witness and now I [ ] prepare for my marriage and [ ] follow where God leads us. Claudius [ ] will bring me to visit you.

Our friends at Philadelphia traveled with us to [ ] Hierapolis, where the Bishop Papias greeted us [ ] asks me to send his love to you. They took us [ ] mountainside pools for a blessing of our betrothal. The mountain looks like snow and ice, but [ ] hard, clear rock with pools of warm water [ ] bathed and enjoyed the day. The Bishop performed the blessing, and we dedicated our future to the service of the Lamb.

I read the scrolls to the church in the evening [ ] impressed with the City of God. The beauty of that place [ ] easy to imagine. The Bishop told the people, "Ah, the New Jerusalem. [ ] at last. Do you see? The fruit of the tree is for good; and the leaves for the healing of the nation. [ ] City of God. [ ] all around us. The Lamb rules. [ ] follow as disciples of love."

The next day, [ ] traveled [ ] to the house of Nympha in Laodicea, the seventh [ ] church [ ]. The church men were busy at the stadium and in the marketplace. The women took us to the shops to see [ ] garments and special black wool [ ]. For Claudius' mother, [ ] to the medical center to hear about the healing measures for eyes, [ ] tablets of eye powder that they sell [ ]. We visited friends of Claudius' parents, [ ] Jewish community. They gave money to Claudius to [ ] for the rebuilding of the temple.

273

So much wealth [ ]. Nympha planned a banquet for the evening at her home. The church members came [ ] asked me to read, [ ] reclined with wine and full bellies. Nympha asked them to be quiet [ ] but they were happy with their wine, and they talked over me. I stopped [ ]. [ ] elders were laughing.

They ordered the slave to pack our bags. Nympha [ ] best to leave before they became more upset, so [ ] traveled by moonlight to the nearest inn.

We know the power of God is foolishness to those who don't believe, but [ ] with faith, it can move mountains.

Pray for us dear Teacher. I write with all my love.

The MAMs clapped. Ursula smiled. Joe put his arm around her and gave her a kiss on the cheek.

"It's getting a little scary, isn't it?" Sallie asked. "Is Thecilla in trouble?"

"We may never know," Joe answered. "This is the last scroll from Thecilla. A few years later, Domitian was murdered, and then in the second century many Christians were martyred by the Romans. But there is one more scroll. Quite a gem, we believe."

Sallie pulled her chair closer to the fire. "What now? What do we do now?"

Brother Simone joined the group huddled by the fire. "What do you want to do?"

Ursula stepped away from Joe and addressed the group. "We have been thinking we'd like to hold another press conference. Reveal the eighth scroll, before we go home."

Molly shook her head. "Another press conference? Are you crazy? Somebody's after us. If we want to release the information, let's wait until we're back home on American soil. I can get the River City police to protect us. I'd feel safer at home."

"But the eighth scroll, it's different. We would like to do it here," Joe interrupted.

Sallie scratched her head. "Do you think they'll run us out of town like they did Thecilla?"

"What's different about this scroll?" Dan Parks wanted to know.

"It's about Thecla," Ursula said.

"What about her?" Jane asked.

"We're not sure, but we think..." Joe cut Ursula off.

"Not yet, not yet. We can't tell you yet."

Brother Simone raised his eyebrows, and then went over to stoke the fire.

Sallie could feel the heat of the flames now. The light created shadows on the wall, and suddenly she wanted to stand up. The chill she'd felt earlier had been eclipsed by warmth and now she began to sweat. She stood up and announced: "Nothing lukewarm about Laodicea for Thecilla!"

"The message upset them because they were too comfortable, lukewarm," Molly explained.

"Right, but for Thecilla, definitely hot, on fire. Is history repeating itself?" Sallie asked the question out loud, but really she talked to herself. If anyone had been comfortable lately, it would be her retired self. But now, sweating with the heat of the afternoon blaze, she felt caught up in the drama and the possibilities of her own life. She knew beyond a shadow of doubt that her days of lukewarm had just come to a screeching halt.

Sallie turned to Molly. "Looks like Thecilla was on the run, just like us!"

"You tell it, girlfriend." Molly smacked her lips together and then just let out that sound of generations, "Mmm, mmm, mmm."

"Yes, sister," Sallie said. "Let's pray again!"

So Brother Simone invited the group to the monastery chapel for prayer. Later, he arranged accommodations and dinner for the women and their male friends at a small hotel owned by a friend. They'd all forgotten about Moses Sun, still locked in Simone's room for safekeeping.

Joe and Ursula asked Simone for a few minutes before he left for the night. They showed him the translation of the eighth scroll and explained the importance of its message.

Brother Simone knew he could be in serious trouble if he helped them, yet he still felt God's nudge, along with guilt from his earlier meeting with the Roman Catholic and the Turks. He trusted these Americans for some reason, even though he knew his bishop did not. Stephen had been a friend, in the past. He hated crossing him. "Let me pray over this tonight. We do have an amphitheater, down toward the Cave of St. John. We've had many gatherings there, celebrations in the past. Perhaps, Thecla, you say?" He stopped to look at the church calendar hanging by the door. "Thecla's Name Day will be Tuesday, September 24 – tomorrow. Perhaps, I could invite the Church of Thecla to hold their celebration here. The timing, incredible. Let me pray on it."

"What's a Name Day?" Ursula asked.

"Oh, we Greeks love an excuse to party. On our island, we have over 400 churches. Each church is named after a saint, and every saint has a day. We call it their Name Day. The church holds a cele-

275

bration with food and music and dancing for the saint of their name. All of us confirmed in the Greek Orthodox church also have a saint name, a name day to celebrate. Here on Patmos, the St. Thecla church is a small church on an island. One family takes care of it, and every year on September 24 they have a Name Day celebration."

"Thecla's Name Day is tomorrow?" Ursula's face beamed.

"That's amazing," Joe agreed.

When Brother Simone returned to the monastery, he checked the calendar for the next day and made a call to his friend, who happened to be part of the family planning the St. Thecla celebration the next day. A promise of a surprise for the Church of St. Thecla and a free party at the monastery sealed the deal. The church would process up to the amphitheater for a short service. Simone cleared it with the abbot, leaving out a few choice details about the scroll and press conference, then headed for late-night prayers with his fellow monks.

When he returned to his room, he was alarmed to discover a man snoring in his bed. Then he remembered who they'd all forgotten earlier. But Simone needed some sleep, so he pulled a cushion off his small couch and slept on the floor. In the morning he'd decide what to do with the MAMs' hostage.

41. Thecilla in Laodicea

September 21, 94 A.D.

The scribe, Plutonius, handed the large bag of scrolls to Claudius. Thecilla climbed up into the chariot beside him, and he secured the bag on the seat beside her. Then Thecilla leaned over to offer her hand to the scribe. "Thank you so much. We have so very little money to pay you for your work, but your reward will be great in the kingdom of heaven!" Her long brown hair fell off her shoulders and draped outside the chariot.

"You will make more copies, then, and deliver them to the library at Pergamum? And to the churches?"

"Yes, my plan will be to send one to the library at Alexandria and one to Pergamum. Then I will make one for each of the seven churches. With your money I have bought enough for at least nine copies."

"I shall tell my uncle of your great work on his behalf. You will make this book famous for years to come. We are indebted to you, dear brother in Christ. We thank you for your service to us."

"When I heard the revelation, I knew I wanted to copy it for you. The City of God shines in the midst of evil. This is the gospel that we have from Jesus, brought to fullness with the river of life and the trees for the healing of the nation. Our Savior knocks at the doors of our lives and then comes in to dwell with us. Although the Romans have built a great empire, they can not hold a candle to the Lamb who reigns with love in our hearts. The Kingdom of God has come to earth. We are rich beyond measure."

"You are a good man, Plutonius. We hope to travel this way again, until then we will take your greetings to the church at Ephesus. We bid you a good day, friend of God."

Claudius and Thecilla were so happy to visit the close-knit Christian community at Hierapolis who offered a warm welcome, a blessing of their betrothal at the beautiful mountain and the service of a scribe who had stayed up all night copying the revelation so that he could publish the story far and wide. "What a gift, our sojourn here," Thecilla said to Claudius while he took the reigns of his black Arabian horse to begin the ride. Then Thecilla held on to the chariot, preparing for yet another day of bumpy roads and jolting moments. "We will be home soon! But first we're on to Laodicea. One more church," she added.

Claudius patted her knee, while keeping control of the horse. "Yes, dear. Soon we will be with our families again."

They reached the house of Nympha by dinner time. The church gathered for their weekly banquet. They found the men and women reclining by large tables overflowing with fruit and lamb, and many cakes. Thecilla worried the laughter and merriment would not suit the reading of the scrolls, but she had no choice because Nympha insisted. And although Nympha asked for silence before Thecilla began, the banqueters only talked louder.

Those who listened argued with the message in the scrolls to their church. A man with a big belly held a jug of wine out to Thecilla and bragged about his town. "We have the finest garments, we produce fine wool. Our medical center works miracles with people's eyes, and we have wealth beyond measure. What does this John of Patmos know?" A church elder complained boldly, "Who would spit us out? Girl, who are you to tell us these lies? You should be on your way."

Claudius rose to defend Thecilla, but she pulled him down. "Do not meet evil with evil. Have you not learned anything from the scrolls? Have you not learned yet the way of the Lamb?"

"I will not stay in this place and allow them to humiliate you in this way!"

But then Nympha appeared with their bags at the doorway. She whispered, "Go quickly. There are some who wish you harm. I will give them more wine."

Thecilla hastily rolled the scrolls and packed them into her bag for the trip. Soon Claudius' black steed carried them through the moonlight, along the wide Roman road toward home. "Are we safe?" Thecilla asked.

Claudius answered, "I will protect you, dear."

Yet soon Thecilla could hear voices and horses behind them on the road. For the first time they traveled at night. She knew Claudius was strong, but he traveled without sword and armor. She worried. The voices became louder, the horses gained on them, and soon they were flanked by two men in red tunics and shining armor. They held their swords out in front of Claudius' horse and ordered him to halt. Claudius reigned in his horse, stopping in the middle of the road, surrounded by the Roman soldiers.

"We hear you create problems in Laodicea!" The soldier poked his sword into the bag by Thecilla's side. "You have scrolls from the man John, banished to Patmos? Domitian ordered him out of our empire. You bring his word back?"

"Sir, it's late, and I beg passage to an inn to take my lady for the night." Claudius hoped they would let them go on. "I carry letters to

the governor at Ephesus. They must arrive tomorrow. Could you guide us to an inn?"

The Roman soldier flipped his sword back into its cover by his waist.

"Give me the scrolls!"

Claudius spoke again. "They do no harm. A vision from the exiled John holds no power over your Emperor. She takes the message from her uncle to her parents at Ephesus. We do no harm."

The Roman soldier pulled his sword back out and jabbed it into the bag by Thecilla's side.

"Scrolls from a blasphemer are not permitted in the empire." He lifted his sword in a giant swoop, flinging the bag into the field beside the road.

Thecilla watched the scrolls arc up into the night and then drop into the darkness. She grabbed Claudius in fear.

The soldier barked his order. "You may go, but leave the scrolls. Do not read them again. Follow us to the next inn." The Romans' horses galloped off, and Claudius sped behind.

"The scrolls, we must get the scrolls." Thecilla begged Claudius to stop.

"No my love, not now." Claudius fought to keep up with the racing horses ahead. "I dropped my cloak by the road to mark the spot. In the morning, we will return."

Thecilla hung on to Claudius and started to pray. The danger of the night closed in around them. She clung to her faith and her hope in her God while they streamed through the darkness.

42. Thecilla & Claudius return to Ephesus

September 23, 94 A.D.

In the morning, Claudius woke Thecilla before the sunrise. "We will leave before the Romans wake." Claudius handed a satchel to Thecilla for the trip. "We must find the scrolls before daylight."

They traveled back on the dark road searching for Claudius' cloak and the field where the soldier had flung the scrolls. The moonlight seemed to guide them to the place where the cloak fell, partially covering the road. Claudius offered his hand to help Thecilla down from the chariot, and continued to hold it while they searched the nearby field together. Suddenly, Thecilla tripped and there she fell down upon the very bag for which they searched.

"Are you all right?" Claudius stooped to help her.

"The scrolls! I tripped on the scrolls!"

Thecilla lifted the large bag, holding it close to her heart while they ran back through the field and into the chariot to begin the journey to Ephesus.

Dawn brought an orange hue to the horizon. Suspended between night and day, Thecilla felt the great fear of the night before but also the deep joy and satisfaction of completing her mission. The sun soon sat like a ball on the horizon, and for a while created a dazzling display of color, which mirrored the growing love Thecilla felt for Claudius. His body warmed her while the chariot flew through the cool morning air. She knew he hoped to avoid more soldiers, and so they traveled fast. She could handle the extra bumps and jostling because she knew they were headed home.

"I doubt we will be safe in Ephesus," Claudius said. "Keep the scrolls hidden."

"They're under my robe. Can you notice them?"

"No, no, they're well hidden. Check in my bag, Thecilly. The cook gave me some bread for our journey. The road to Ephesus lies far ahead."

Thecilla opened the bag beside her on the seat of the chariot. "More than just bread! Dates and cheese. Figs and lamb. She must have liked you, Claudius!" Thecilla offered a fig to Claudius and smiled. "We won't go hungry today!" Thecilla's thoughts raced on to-

280

ward home faster than the horse could gallop. She began to worry about their future. "What should we do when we get home? When can we marry? My parents want me to marry someone else, you know. What are we going to do?" The noisy chariot drowned out her questions. She wondered if Claudius even heard.

His silence gave space for her fears to grow. Not only did they need to watch out for the Romans, but what must she fear in her own home? Her mother and father had chosen her husband, and now she wished to defy them. She wondered if they would even listen to her plans. She thought about Thecla, being burned at the stake for refusing to marry her betrothed. Certainly her parents would not go to that extreme, but banishing her would be painful enough. Would they require her to marry their friend from the house church? What could she do?

And then Claudius had the solution. He must have heard after all. "We will go to your house, and I will tell your father that we must marry. We can invite them to the wedding the next day at my house. My parents will not turn us away. We will have a small wedding and then leave right away. A small trip to celebrate the wedding will not raise suspicion among the Romans. I will invite friends who play with me in the May games. They will speak for me to the Romans. We can slip out unnoticed. That is my plan."

"Travel again? I want to stay home and rest!" After many days on the road, Thecilla longed for home. The thought of more travel rested heavy in her heart. But then she remembered how she had run away, really, against her father's demand. Perhaps she could never return. She asked, "Must we go?" The thought of leaving Ephesus caused her great pain.

"Our experience last night tells us we can't stay. Not now. Maybe things will improve, and we can come back, but now, no. It's not safe for us here. We will travel to Jerusalem and to the places where Jesus preached. We can share John's message there, far from Ephesus, where no one knows of us. God will protect us. Have faith."

Thecilla whimpered and snuggled closer to Claudius. She prayed into the morning for their safe journey and for more opportunities to share the good news in lands afar.

By nightfall, they arrived at the home of Claudius, where his parents welcomed them both with open arms, thankful for their safe arrival. They set a large table with much food, then showed Thecilla to a comfortable pallet for the night. After she fell asleep, Claudius and his mother stayed up late into the night, making plans for the wedding ahead. They decided to invite Thecilla's parents to dinner in the day to come and give Claudius the opportunity to request permission to wed their daughter. His good Jewish parents couldn't understand his deci-

sion to follow Jesus, but his mother welcomed the herbs and information Claudius shared from the hospital in Pergamum.

To Thecilla's surprise, her parents accepted the marriage plan without protest and three days later, Claudius and Thecilla joined their lives at a traditional Jewish wedding ceremony. The toasts at the wedding feast droned into the wee hours of the night. Claudius' Roman friends came to enjoy the wine and after drinking more than enough, kept offering laughing toasts to the marital bed. Thecilla's parents welcomed Claudius into the family. Her father, Joseph, made a touching toast to his daughter and new son and their great faith that caused them to follow Jesus to share his message of love. The House Church members, like a second family to Thecilla, came out in full force and showered the couple with love and prayers for a long life together. Thecilla's mother gave the couple a present of the holy scrolls that her mother, Priscilla, had given her as a young girl. The dancing began when the meal ended. Thecilla and Claudius led the circling group, kicking high and laughing in their celebration. Even Jacob, the one her parents had picked for her to marry, attended the feast and seemed very happy, dancing with some of the young girls.

The celebration erased her fears from the days before, until Thecilla's parents prepared to leave at the end of the evening.

"You must leave Uncle John's scrolls here when you go to Jerusalem," her father had warned. "Don't create more trouble for yourself."

Thecilla looked to her father and then to Claudius.

"I will take care of her, sir. We will take great caution on our trip. I will bring your daughter back to you, I solemnly vow." Claudius embraced Joseph in farewell.

Thecilla hugged her mother and then her father. She wiped the tears out of her eyes. "I love you, Mama and Papa. Thank you for your blessings upon us."

Thecilla regretted that her good teacher's health had been precarious of late, and she couldn't make the journey down the mountain to attend the wedding. The next day, Thecilla took Claudius up to the cave to seek her blessing on their union before their departure. The old woman did not disappoint her dear student. She embraced the newly married couple and offered lavish blessings upon them. Then Claudius left to prepare supplies for their voyage, while Thecilla spent a precious last morning sharing stories and love with her teacher.

As Thecilla tearfully prepared to leave, Thecla led her to a side alcove where a large brightly decorated storage vessel stood. "Here are your scrolls, dear. All safely stored in this large pot. Thank you so much for sending them to me. I will save them here, and hide them for you. Someday, after I am gone, you can bring them out and show them to your children. And now, take this scroll from me. You write me so much love, I had to write you back."

Thecla's arthritic hand clutched a small scroll. She cradled it in both of her hands like a precious jewel, pressed it close to her heart, then touched it to her lips before offering it to Thecilla.

"Know that I love you with all my heart and my prayers go with you. If we do not meet again in this world, my dear, know that you are always close to my heart. Claudius waits for you, you must not be late. God will go with you, along with my prayers. Read the scroll when you are alone, just for you dear. Just for you. Just between us, understood?"

Thecilla nodded and brushed tears off her cheek before she hugged her beloved teacher. "I will be back, teacher. Don't say that. I will be back soon. I love you."

The young woman headed out the cave entrance. She paused for a moment to look down at the amphitheater and saw the streets and marketplace bustling with activity. She cradled the scroll in her hands. Then she heard a snort and looked toward the clearing where a Roman soldier perched on a large black Arabian horse, angrily staring at her, his spear pointed directly at her. The sun reflected off his armor, and the red cloak reminded her of the blood of martyrs. The Romans kill Christians, she knew.

Her heart quickened, and she took off on light feet through the woods, down the mountain and across familiar paths not safe for a horse. By the time she reached Claudius' house, her dress was soiled, her face wet, and her heart still racing with fear. Yet she had beaten the Roman, and soon they would be on their way, off to new lands where Domitian did not reign. She sighed. Claudius' family servant offered her water to clean and freshen up. Now she could prepare for her wedding voyage.

Soon she redressed and waited for Claudius. Only then did she remember the scroll, the parting gift from her teacher, but it was no longer in her hand. She tried to figure out where it had gone. Did she place it on the table by her soiled clothes? She held it in her hand, right before the soldier appeared. But when she started to run down the hillside, did she drop it? Where could it be?

43. Press Conference on Patmos

September 24, 2006

Early the next morning, Brother Simone dressed quietly and left for first prayers, leaving Sun still dead to the world, snoring in the bed. Simone locked him in, but did go to the kitchen to fetch him some bread, cheese, olives and juice, leaving the food for Sun's breakfast.

Brother Simone had a lot to accomplish in a short amount of time. Yet he dropped the day's agenda from his thoughts once in the chapel, letting the familiar cadence of prayer fill his spirit. The connection with God soothed and relaxed him and would provide him strength to face the challenges ahead. On the last "Amen" he slipped out of the chapel, grabbed a bagel and cup of coffee from the kitchen and headed up to his office in the library to get to work. First, he put in a call to Joe Cohen and Ursula Goodtree to share the good news about the press conference. Next, he summoned a driver to go pick them up. Then he dusted off his writing skills to compose a quick press release and sent it out to a couple of friends in the news media in Athens. Offering an exclusive, he tacked onto the end "κρατήσει ήουχο."xxxiv He knew he could depend on them to show up in the early afternoon to cover the event and enjoy one last holiday before winter. Finally, he paid a visit to the monastery cook and put in an order for an afternoon reception. Kristos grumbled, but Simone knew he enjoyed showing off his culinary skills at events. Life in the monastery could be mundane, but when there were guests, Kristos liked to shine. When he left Kristos, the cook was already busy whistling, beginning preparations. He then hurried out to the garden to arrange details with the groundskeeper. "Open the amphitheater by 2:00 p.m. We're expecting a crowd."

Brother Simone felt the excitement building. It had been a long time since he'd been involved in anything of this magnitude. When Ursula and Joe arrived, Brother Simone asked his driver to take the three of them out for a ride. He figured the ride would give them privacy to talk about the agenda for the event.   And Simone also planned to bring them along to Thecla's Name Day Service at the Church of St. Thecla, on a little island in the heart of Patmos.

284

"We need to make sure the MAMs will be on hand for this event. Simone handed his cell phone to Ursula. "Can you call them?"

So Ursula called Jane. "Make sure the MAMs arrive at the amphitheater at 1:45 p.m. Another press conference, but no violence this time." Ursula laughed. "Yes, I promise. And Jane, you know we found her. We really did."

On the other end of the phone, Jane asked, "Found who?"

"Found Thecla. In Scroll #8, Thecla speaks. We really found her. We really did dig her up." Ursula laughed into the phone. "Have the MAMs wear their red hats. Can you also invite Katharine? I hope she can come. If Balaban takes her up to the Cave of St. John, it won't be a long walk for her. The amphitheater is just up past the cave on the right."

***

Back in the hotel, Jane broke the news to the MAMs at breakfast. "We found her, ladies. Press conference at 2:00 p.m. at the monastery."

"Found who?" Sallie asked.

"We dug her up. Remember, that's why we came here in the first place. I said we needed to go dig her up." Jane planted her hands on her hips with a smug grin on her face. "Thecla! The Archaeological Expedition in Search of Thecla, remember?"

"We didn't find any bones," Sallie said.

"No, but the scrolls. We found her scroll." Jane became impatient with Sallie. "The press conference this afternoon will reveal Thecla's scroll."

"Thecilla wrote her letters, they were hers, but Thecla didn't write them," Sallie corrected Jane.

"Scroll Number Eight is different. Thecla wrote it." Jane smiled. "Mission accomplished. Who woulda thought that my little jab into the air on a red wine high would produce such results?"

"What jab?" Sallie asked.

"Remember when I said, 'Ladies, we have to go dig her up!' " Jane smiled again. "Mission accomplished. Sallie, you need coffee. And pack your bags, we're leaving on the ferry for Athens tonight, and we'll fly back to the States in the morning."

"Wait a minute. Who's packing our bags and shipping us out of town?" Sallie asked. "Just when we can start to relax and enjoy Patmos, we have to go home?"

"Dan Parks doesn't want any more mayhem. Disturbing things are happening on this not-so-peaceful little island, if you remember." Jane didn't really want to share Parks' concerns, but she knew it was time to go home and get the ladies out of any further danger.

"What is it about the scrolls that has someone so upset?" Sallie asked. "I understand the Romans were threatened by Christianity, sort of. I mean Jesus preached love and allegiance to God, and the emperor didn't like anybody else to be in charge, but why is someone so upset about our scrolls? Why are the Right Disciples here? And why did the Turkish officials close us out? Do we really know what's going on here? Are we safe?"

"Hell no!" Molly answered. "Don't you understand that love is a threat to empire anywhere? 'Love your enemies?' Hell no! Do you think Mark is allowed to love the Iraqis? Do you think the U.S. military considers letting their men and women have feelings for the people they might have to kill?"

"But these scrolls, are they really all that revolutionary?" Sallie continued to question.

Katharine had joined the MAMs for breakfast and surprised the group with her good energy. Now her scholarship brought light on the discussion. "It depends on your perspective," she said. "Think about Moses Sun. Before his accident and change of heart, he was determined to silence me, because I tried to prove the *End Times* mania to be false. The scrolls say the same thing."

"There are powerful people who have a stake in keeping the Rapture Theory alive. If Armageddon is inevitable, they believe bringing it on may be preferable to more suffering before Jesus returns. So rather than searching for international peace and cooperation, they prepare for war. It fits in well with a militaristic national agenda."

"Rather than focusing our vast intelligence and human resources on our shared problems of sustainable futures, feeding the world, reversing global warming and building bridges of peace, they focus on the end times, keeping the voting populace cheering on their violent efforts. Why do you think Mortimer Jacobs and George Matthews showed up? This is serious business to the Christian think tanks in the States. They don't want people to question the Rapture Theory. And believe me, there are quite a few political strategists that have their back on that."

"But the Vatican, are they behind the Rapture, too?" Sallie asked.

Katharine laughed. "I doubt that, but we think they may just want to control the information more carefully. They aim to preserve orthodoxy, so authentic first-century scrolls could present problems for their carefully crafted theology."

"And the Turkish government? Why did they stop us?" Sallie asked.

"We don't know what the hell is going on, when you get right down to it!" Jane said. "And ladies, that's why tonight, we're getting you out of here and heading home. The scrolls have been preserved through emails and have traveled around the world and back and nobody's going to squelch the truth in them, so our mission is complete and we can go home."

Balaban, a silent observer at the MAMs' breakfast meeting, cleared his throat and stood to leave. "So what time do you need me back?"

"Press conference at 2:00 p.m. How about 1:15?" Jane checked her watch. "That gives you four hours to enjoy Patmos, and then we need a ride to the ferry at 7:00 p.m. tonight."

Balaban saluted Jane with a smile and headed out for the Hotel Skala. He knew his sponsors would be interested in the latest turn of events.

"What about lunch?" Sallie asked.

"We can eat here," Jane decided. "We can pay for the full meal combo for the final day They call it 'FB'."

And so soon the MAMs were packing and preparing for the press conference, the culmination of their expedition, oblivious to events unfolding elsewhere on the island that threatened their afternoon plans.

But Emily called Brother Gabriel at Hotel Romeos to ask for prayer. She felt a sense of foreboding about the press conference. Perhaps her jitters came from their experience in Ephesus, but she knew it wouldn't hurt to have a conference of mystics putting in some pleas on their behalf.

***

Back at the Hotel Skala, Balaban reported to Brother Leonardo and Stephan Toflokous all that he had heard at breakfast with the MAMs.

"Are you sure?" Brother Leonardo asked. "A press conference on the scrolls?"

"That's what they said." Balaban repeated it again. "Two o'clock at the amphitheater by the Cave of St. John. A reading of Scroll Number Eight, written by Thecla."

"You mean Thecilla," Stephan corrected Balaban.

"No, they said, 'Thecla,'" Balaban countered. "The Archaeological Expedition in Search of Thecla. Jane said they had found her. Mission complete. The last scroll, written by Thecla."

Leonardo and Stephan exchanged startled glances.

"We must stop the press conference. I'll call the bishop," Stephan offered.

"I'll call the Pope," Leonardo said.

"I'll the call the Turkish Prime Minister," Said Ahmed shook his head. "Surely one of us will be able to call it off."

They scattered to separate corners of the hotel lobby with cell phones humming, oblivious to George Matthews and Mortimer Jacobs sitting nearby and hanging on their every word.

"We can't take any chances," Matthews told Jacobs. "We can stop this ourselves. I've got the perfect foil. Let's get to work."

***

Meanwhile, at the Church of Thecla, Urusla and Joe enjoyed the music at the Name Day celebration, although neither could understand the colloquial Greek in which the service was performed. They honored an old woman, Thecla Michelopolous, a grandmother who had lived on the island all her life and had come to the church on each of her name days for as long as she could remember. Following the service, a Greek buffet offered an ample spread for the 50-some people gathered. A fiddler played lively folk tunes. Circling line dances weaved around the small church on the little island. Joe and Ursula knew the language of dance and kicked up their heels to the tunes accompanied also by a balalaika and guitar.

Brother Simone hated to cut off the merriment, but knew they needed to get on the road. During a break in the music, he informed the group that the taxis would arrive in 15 minutes for the ride to the monastery.

The women jumped into action, clearing the food, bundling the leftovers into baskets and within 10 minutes, you could barely tell there had been a fiesta. The crowd left the little island by small boats, ferrying a few minutes over to the mainland. Soon they were boarding the taxis, heading into town.

Simone led the taxis in his private car. Once at the monastery, he would make sure that arrangements were finalized. The rest of the group would be dropped off at the bottom of the hill, so that they could weave their way up the monastery on foot in a traditional musical caravan familiar on the little island for wedding celebrations. Joe and Ursula followed in a car with the grandmother Thecla. They discovered the older woman had taught English at the island school in younger years. Ursula invited the woman to read Thecla's scroll at the press conference.

***

Meanwhile, back at the Hotel, Brother Leonardo encountered difficulties. The Pope was traveling in South America, and no one had authority to act on his behalf. Father Toklofolus learned the Greek bishop in Athens had taken a holiday in France, and although he continued to try to reach him, he hadn't been able to connect. The

Turkish Prime Minister was willing and able to lend a hand, but the Greek government tended to side with the Americans. Nevertheless, he put in a call to the Greek Prime Minister and asked for help. Regrouping, the international delegation decided to go back to the police chief. Perhaps they could convince him to stop the press conference, and avert any more violence. They left Hotel Skala and walked down the waterfront toward the police station.

***

Back at the monastery, the groundskeeper kept his workers busy all morning, freshening up the amphitheater. They cleaned the benches, drenched from the rains of the past week. They arranged reception tables between the Cave and the Monastery. A messenger handed the foreman a note, which he put in his back pocket while in the midst of giving some directions to the monastery cook, on the catering event. Later, he headed up to the monastery kitchen for a break with some coffee and baklava.

While enjoying fresh aromatic coffee, he remembered the note, and pulled it out of his pocket.

> *I will explode myself & the St. John Monastery amphitheater at 2 p.m. May Allah be praised.*

He wasted no time in calling Brother Simone, who notified his friend, Mikel Lagos, Patmos Chief of Police and began pacing. He wasn't sure what to do now, but certainly the press conference would have to be canceled or moved to a safer location.

***

In Brother Simone's room, Moses Sun finished up his breakfast and signed on to the computer. Cyberspace helped him deal with his confinement, expanding his borders way beyond the good monk's cell. Yesterday, he'd realized that the Right Disciples hadn't had the foresight to close him out of their system. Now, he discovered that not only could he still get into the system, he could follow Matthews and Jacobs and track their progress in Patmos. If they only knew. He read their account of his kidnapping and escape. Fortunately, they seemed to have lost his tail.

And then he found a new entry, a posting about a press conference scheduled for today. Obviously, he had been locked out of the planning, even while he had been locked in. Moses Sun understood. He didn't deserve to be included in another press conference. He read on. "We will stop them in their tracks..." Following were some affirmations and hallelujahs on George Matthew's Patmos blog. Sun knew he had to get out of there fast and alert the authorities. Would they believe him? If necessary, he could show them the truth on the screen. While picking the lock, Sun wondered what the final scroll would reveal.

***

Chief Police Mikel Lagos sped up the hill toward the monastery, realizing he should have listened to that American, Dan Parks. He took great pride in keeping peace on the island. In the past 10 years, his record stood untarnished. No international incidents, no bomb threats, hell he hadn't even had a murder for three years.

Brother Simone met him at the gates and took the note from his hand to see it for himself. He knew now he'd have to get the military involved, but first he needed to keep the people safe.

"Better call off your meeting, Brother. I don't want anybody getting hurt up here. We're not taking any chances on this one. Call it off." Mikel Lagos looked at his watch, just as Brother Simone looked at his.

Simone thought fast. He wanted the MAMs to get their press conference. "They're on the way up the hill, dancing. A procession for Thecla's Name Day. Could we change the location?"

"But we don't know what we're dealing with here. A bomb in the amphitheater? How far could destruction spew? Depending on the bomb, could be quite a distance."

"If it's safety we're seeking, the people are headed up here now, how about if I head them over to the cave? That's far enough from the amphitheater, and safe in its own right. Stood the test of time. Covered St. John in his day, it can cover the multitude now. It'll be crowded in there, but I think we can fit. About 30 people coming up, along with the MAMs and the press. How many does that room hold?"

"You're asking me?" Mikel laughed. "That's your place, brother. I just keep the peace, not your monastery."

"If I close it to the public, I think we can squeeze them all in," Brother Simone extended his hand to Lagos. "We've got a deal?"

"But close the monastery for the rest of the day. We don't want anybody getting hurt." Lagos let go of Simone's hand and slapped him on the back. "Now, we need to find that bomb."

Brother Simone called the groundskeeper on his cell phone and announced the change of plans, then he called the monastery to shut it down for the day. While the groundskeeper headed down the hill to redirect the procession, Simone headed over to clear out the Cave of St. John and make arrangements for the press conference to come.

***

Moses Sun cracked the lock and pushed open the door. A stranger to the monastery, he had no clue where to find Simone, much less the amphitheater. He darted through the monastery corridors, searching for an exit. Seemed there were steps every few paces. His head throbbed, and he was panting when he finally encountered someone.

"We're closing early today, sir. You'll have to leave." A monastery guard informed Sun.

"Which way out? Where do I go from here?"

"The exit is out the door and to the left. Here, I'll show you." The guard knew he had to clear out the monastery quickly, and if he ushered Sun out, he'd be that much closer to his goal.

"Could you tell me where the amphitheater would be?" Sun asked.

The guard looked at Sun with concern. "That's closed, also, sir. It's on down the hill before you get to cave." The guard decided to tell Sun the truth. "We've had a bomb threat, sir. Best to clear the premises quickly."

Sun walked quickly toward the exit and headed down the hill, jogging. When he approached the amphitheater, he recognized Dan Parks, with a policeman. Hoping to win their trust, he headed toward them to explain his news.

But Dan Parks had other intentions, yelling at Lagos, "Arrest him!"

"For what?" Lagos yelled back.

"That's our man. He shot the women at the press conference."

"What press conference?" Lagos yelled.

"The one in Turkey!" Parks responded.

***

Brother Leonardo, Stephan Toklokfolous and Said Ahmed with Halim Mohammed in tow climbed the steps to the police office in Skala and asked for Chief Lagos.

"He's not here," the officer at the desk reported.

Toklokfolous muttered a few choice words and then pumped the uniformed sergeant for information. Pulling out some bills, he slipped them on the table.

The officer waved the money away and offered information freely. "Bomb threat at the monastery. A press conference being planned. The chief is looking for the bomb. He won't be back soon."

"They called the press conference off then?"

"No, no. They moved it to the cave. Will begin soon."

Brother Leonardo looked at his watch. "If you can't beat them, join them? Shall we?"

The group nodded in agreement and headed down the steps to grab a taxi and head up the hill to the cave. On the way up, the good brother received a message from the pope encouraging him to go listen and report back on the news.

***

Not far away, in the amphitheater, Mortimer Jacobs and George Matthews argued over the placement of their bomb. Matthews wanted to make sure the bomb could be seen. Jacobs wanted to hide it.

"They're going to be on to us if we leave it out in the open. A suicide bomber doesn't plant a bomb, they come in and blow themselves up." Jacob continued to argue with his boss. "You need to go back to the room, dress like a Muslim and come in with a backpack."

"Very funny. Moses Sun tried the Muslim look and look where it got him," Matthews reminded Jacobs.

***

At the Conference of Mystics, a late-morning session gave way to a late lunch where Brother Gabriel made an announcement, asking for prayer for the MAMs and the afternoon press conference. After some deliberation, the group decided to cancel the afternoon session and attend the press conference also. It gave them an opportunity to practice a walking meditation, in the tradition of a Vietnamese Buddhist, Thich Thanh Nanh, the subject of the previous session. So they walked slowly and mindfully in silence up the hill to the Cave of St. John, until they encountered a group of musicians and dancers. Then, they fell in behind the celebratory procession also headed to the press conference.

***

Balaban dropped the MAMs at the Cave of St. John at 1:45 p.m. Right behind their car, he recognized his sponsors and stepped back to fill them in on the latest. The procession of people from the Church of Thecla, the Conference of Mystics and Joe and Ursula neared the chapel, too.

The MAMs watched the celebration. "What's going on?" Sallie asked. Then she spotted Joe and Ursula and repeated her question again. "What is going on here?"

292

"The Church of Thecla had their Name Day celebration today! Can you believe it? September 24. This is Thecla's Name Day. They're coming to hear Thecla's scroll." Ursula laughed.

"And let me introduce to you Thecla Michelopolous. She will be reading the eighth scroll, written by our first-century Thecla."

A small, thin woman with a big smile and wrinkled face extended her hand to Sallie. "Good afternoon, ma'am."

Sallie shook her hand and laughed out loud. "How amazing!"

Brother Simone emerged from the door to the small building enclosing the cave. "Come, come. Come in, all of you. Let's get this show under way."

So the MAMs entered the small building. Not far behind were the people in the procession from the Church of Thecla, followed by the participants of the Conference of Mystics, and then the international delegation.

The MAMs, Thecla and Joe were given seats at the front. The others sat on benches, and some stood in the small room with the cave where John allegedly wrote the book of Revelation. Two thousand years later, the people waited now for a new revelation. Lighted candles flickered on the stone ceiling. In this place where ornate orthodox trappings surrounded the stark gray rock and where pilgrims had visited for centuries, the MAMs waited for the culmination of their expedition.

***

Down in the amphitheater, Sun spotted Jacobs and Matthews fiddling in the trees on the side of gathering place. He pointed them out to Parks and Lagos, just as the "bomb planters" looked up and spotted the police. Jacobs dropped something into the bushes and then he grabbed his partner, pulling him out of the amphitheater and they headed down the hill.

Mikel Lagos considered pulling his gun, but before he could decide, the two men were halfway down the hill. Head throbbing, Moses Sun sprinted after them. His short legs couldn't hold a candle to Jacob's long spindly ones, but Matthews' belly slowed them down, and Jacobs didn't try to break away. Sun reached Matthews and grabbed him from behind. Lagos pulled his gun now, and sent Parks back up to get his car. "Now, you're going to take your bomb and throw it in the ocean, " Lagos informed the two men.

"What bomb?" Matthews tried the clueless approach.

Lagos held up the suicide bomb note. Matthews looked it over, and while astonishment registered on his face, he managed a monotone response, "That's a Muslim note. We're Christians. We believe in the real God. What are you talking about?"

293

"They're lying," Moses Sun said. "I can show you proof they wrote that note."

"Get the bomb. What were you doing in the trees by the amphitheater if this isn't your note? You have two choices. Either go dismantle your bomb now, or you can spend the rest of your life in a Greek prison. If that bomb goes off, your freedom will be over."

"It's not a bomb," Matthews confessed. "It's a fake, we were just trying to stop the press conference. We're not criminals, just trying to promote the truth."

"Get the bomb, now." Lagos had heard enough. He pointed the men back up the hill toward the monastery and saw Dan Parks on his way down.

***

Once again, a press conference began, but this time Dr. Cohen and Dr. Goodtree ruled the day. Joe distributed papers to the MAMs. "We'd like each of you to read one scroll," he said while handing them out.

Ursula began to address to the crowd, "Thank you for coming today. Today we reveal the discoveries of the Archaeological Expedition in Search of Thecla. I am Dr. Ursula Goodtree, on the faculty of the Department of Archaeology at the University of Michigan, in the United States of America, and with me this afternoon is Dr. Joseph Cohen with the Center for Biblical Languages in California. The group of women speaking today are members of a reading club in Riverside, Ohio, who participated in the expedition. They call themselves "The MAMs." At this point, Ursula smiled, laughed briefly. "They are Magnificent and Marvelous."

The MAMs sat quietly in the front row of the cave, resplendent in their red hats, and Emily in her pink one. Ursula didn't wear hers, nor her cape. Instead, she wore her field khakis with a blue blouse and brown sweater, and Joe wore matching khakis with a button-down blue shirt and matching tie.

Joe continued. "The expedition excavated in the Grotto of St. Paul, located on BûlBûl Dag, above the ruins of Ephesus near Kusadasi, Turkey. The Grotto has been popularized for its frescoes dating back to the first century, excavated extensively in the past 10 years, under the direction of Austrian archaeologist Sophie Simons."

Ursula said, "One of the frescoes shows a scene of Thecla in her house, with her mother talking with the Apostle Paul outside the house, a familiar story recorded in the 'Acts of Paul and Thecla.'"

A Greek translator whispered to the group from the Church of St. Thecla and they nodded their heads, having heard about the fresco in the past.

"In our excavations, we discovered a sand chamber in the cave, and within this small room, a large storage pot with scrolls. An unusual mixture of sand and salt, coupled with the conditions in the cave, managed to preserve the scrolls. Archaeological dating techniques suggest these scrolls could be authentic from the late first century."

At this point, Brother Leonardo rose in protest, "You don't know that. It's possible these scrolls are fakes."

Brother Simone looked at Leonardo and considered options. He knew that dissenters could create havoc in the press conference, but before he stepped in, Halim Mohammed stood beside him.

"Greetings. I am Halim Mohammed, chief archaeologist with the site of Ephesus. These scrolls are very unusual. Our labs conducted the dating tests. Quite remarkable, but yes, Dr. Goodtree is correct. We believe these scrolls are from the first century. We have no reason to believe they are fake."

Ursula and Joe exchanged glances and wondered how Halim had arrived at the press conference.

"Let's listen to the scrolls," he told his Catholic friend. "There will be time to debate later."

He began to sat down, and kept his hand on Leonardo's arm, gently pushing him down also.

"Thank you, Mr. Mohammed," Ursula acknowledged her colleague. "I know it's crowded in here, and we'll proceed without delay."

"The scrolls are written to Thecla from Thecilla, a young woman from the house church of Ephesus, we believe the granddaughter of Priscilla and Aquila, the daughter of Joseph and Anna. Her family sent her to care for her Uncle John, exiled to Patmos. While there, she helped him record his fantastic vision, now known as the book of Revelation, the last book in the canonized Christian Bible."

"Thecilla left Patmos to take her uncle's vision to the churches in the region neighborhing Ephesus. The drama unfolds through the seven letters she writes home to Thecla, whom we believe taught Thecilla in the cave in the previous years."

"Today, we will read through the seven scrolls Thecilla wrote, and an eighth scroll also found. If you've read the book of Revelation, you'll know it was written to the seven churches, then located in Asia Minor, in present-day Turkey. The scrolls explain that Thecilla traveled to each of these churches with a friend, Claudius, "

Ursula read the first scroll from Ephesus and then told the group. "Like the Ephesians, I had lost my first love, but have reclaimed my love in this process and have found a new passion for life." She squeezed Joe's hand, and then nodded to Molly. "From Ephesus, Thecilla and Claudius traveled to Smyrna."

Molly stood and began to read. The candlelight flickered on the wall, and the crowd sat quietly; mesmerized as the saga of Thecilla and her journeys to the seven churches unfolded in the small cave. "Do you hear the story of the Lamb? The way of Jesus is the way of suffering love. We are taught to love our enemies. This scroll reminds me of the teachings of Martin Luther King, Jr., who led my people in a nonviolent revolution. It encourages me to follow Jesus to the cross, refusing to take up violence, only to love."

Katharine read the next scroll concerning the Pergamum visit and concluded by telling a bit of her own story. "This scroll was written from the town of Pergamum, a place of healing in the Roman empire. I had no way of knowing when we started this trip, that I would end up in a hospital in Turkey with a serious wound requiring surgery. And if you told me that I'd dream about the early Christians dancing in a cave, like the account in this scroll, I probably would have told you that you were crazy. And yet, I was shot in Ephesus, flown to surgery in Istanbul, where I witnessed the scene Thecilla describes here. These scrolls have awakened a new joy deep within me. I have forgiven the man who shot me. I will never be the same."

Jane stood to share the scroll from Thyatira. "You know, these scrolls do something to you. I'm the last person you'd think would be a religious fanatic, but I was moved. I got baptized, but more than that, I'm aware of God moving me back into the church to serve and celebrate."

The words from the first century hung in the air in the crowded space. No one wanted to leave as the MAMs revealed the history, silenced for centuries. The sacred space once again brought the mysteries of the ages alive to those fortunate enough to attend.

"Wow. All I can say is Wow!" Emily said, when she stood to read Thecilla's letter from Sardis. "John called on the Christians in Sardis to wake up. I did, I did. Like Thecilla, I got engaged! But what really blows me away is the teaching of John brought alive by these scrolls. I wrote my senior thesis on this topic, and it confirms what I wrote last Spring! Jesus is the lamb. Do you get it? Jesus calls us to love, not fight. Wow!"

Priscilla nervously stood to read the scroll about Philadelphia. A stranger to public speaking, yet she wanted to do her part. "You know, a lot has happened for all of us in the past seven days. I'm still processing it all, but the one thing I can agree with, is that Jesus is calling us to love. Only love." Then her shaking stopped, and she read the account from Philadelphia with that love shining through her heart into the room.

Finally, Sallie wound up with the Laodicea scroll. She laughed to start. "Lukewarm Christians. Laodicea fame. Yep, that was me, too. But you can see these scrolls have changed all of us. I'm not sure what I'm doing next, but I know I'll be coming out of retirement when I go home. God calls me to be a little more involved!." The scrolls transported the gathering back in time, as they relived the journey of a young woman and her lover, bringing a story of hope to the struggling Christians in Asia Minor.

When Sallie finished the harrowing account of Claudius and Thecilla's encounter with a Roman soldier in the seventh scroll, Ursula stood to explain. "At first we thought there were only seven scrolls. Seven churches, seven scrolls, considered a perfect number in holy times. But then we discovered a false bottom in the pot. A plate had been wedged into the bottom. When we took it out, we found one more small scroll. Perfectly preserved, this scroll is not from Thecilla to Thecla, but to Thecilla from Thecla herself."

Several people gasped and whispers of surprise were heard in the tightly packed room.

"Thecla? Really? I find that very hard to believe," Stephan Toklofolous shook his head. "This is preposterous."

"Not necessarily," Ursula responded. "Let's hear it out. I'd like to present, from the Church of St. Thecla on Patmos, Thecla Michelopolis who has agreed to read this small, last scroll.

The small woman stood by the cleft in the rock, where a scribe once "allegedly" wrote the book of Revelation. Her head barely came up to the ledge, and her hands shook slightly as she held the paper with the words of Thecla. She smiled and spoke quietly, but with an authoritative voice of a schoolteacher used to keeping her class's attention.

"On the Name Day of St. Thecla, I will read a letter she once wrote to her dear Thecilla, the young woman who made such a remarkable journey so many years ago. As we honor her today, I am so honored to share her words with you." Thecla paused and then repeated her introduction in Greek, before proceeding with the translation.

Scroll #8 From Thecla

My dear Thecilla,

My greatest joy, grand daughter of Priscilla and Aquilla. You are good, prophet, love. Disciple of Jesus, continue his journey. Take the good news. Preach peace. Tell them Jesus is knocking. Tell them the leaves of the tree are for the healing of the nations. Tell them about the living water. Preach hope and love to empire. Be our future.

I could not tell them. I promised Paul, I would hide in the cave. But I never told him I would not tell you."

A commotion outside caused Thecla to stop reading. Mortimer Jacobs and George Matthews burst into the small room. Jacobs held the bomb in his hands, close behind them were the Chief of Police with two assistants and Dan Parks. Moses Sun remained outside the cave, not sure what to do.

Jacobs placed the bomb in the front of the small room by the concrete slab, where John had been purported to sleep. "False teaching must be stopped, at all costs!"

Mikel Lagos yelled at the people, "Clear the room." Then turning to Brother Simone he directed, "Lead them to the amphitheater!"

The people streamed out of the room, heading up to the amphitheater, while Lagos and Parks considered their options. Lagos and his men kept their guns pointed at Jacobs and Matthews, while Parks decided he'd take matters into his own hands. He picked up the bomb and informed Lagos, "I'm going to take my chances and throw this into the sea. Why don't you arrest these men? I'll meet you back down at the police station in a few minutes, if fate is on my side."

While Mikel and his assistants handcuffed the men, the press conference relocated to the amphitheater. Some of the people headed on down the hill, but most remained to hear the final scroll. Once everyone was situated, Thecla began to read again. "And so to continue, I will start over on this very short scroll. Thecla began to read again."

"My dear Thecilla,

My greatest joy, granddaughter of Priscilla and Aquilla. You are good, prophet, love. Disciple of Jesus, continue his journey. Take the good news. Preach peace. Tell them Jesus is knocking. Tell them the leaves of the tree are for the healing of the nations. Tell them about the living water. Preach hope and love to empire. Be our future.

I could not tell them. I promised Paul, I would hide in the cave. But I never told him I would not tell you. You are my granddaughter, offspring of Paul of Tarsus. Your father, Joseph, was our son. You are my beloved.

Keep my secret in your heart. Little one, it is time for me to go. Hold me in your heart. God is with you. Do not fear, only love.

With all my love, dear granddaughter,

Your grandmother, Thecla."

Thecla smiled, and began to repeat the message of the scroll, this time in Greek.

The MAMs sat silently, watching the light of the candles dance on the walls. The Greek words filled the cave while they contemplated the significance of their find. Later, they would discuss and analyze and digest, but for now they had no words. The moment belonged to Thecla.

44. Thecla Speaks

September 24, 94 A.D.

The old woman watched Thecilla run down the hillside, while she hid in the shadows. The Roman soldier hesitated briefly, then charged after her, down the mountain. Thecla didn't fear for her student. She knew Thecilla's swift feet would carry her across the secret trail to safety. She only feared now for her own loneliness, hoping the end would come soon, without too much pain.

Once they had both disappeared, Thecla ventured outside the cave to pick up the scroll that Thecilla had dropped in the flurry of her escape. A tear ran down her cheek. How she wished she could return the scroll to its rightful owner. After all these years, Thecla longed to share the truth. She had chosen wisely, carefully, lovingly the time and place to reveal her secret. She knew Thecilla would have guarded her truth and that it could have warmed her heart and cushioned her loss for years to come. She knew that it would have meant as much to Thecilla, as it did to her. But fate intervened, and now, her gnarled hands closed about the rolled parchment. Tears streamed down her wrinkled face and she let them fall.

She looked down the mountain, past the trees and remembered. Memories of her dear friend danced across the horizon. She could almost see him standing there, once again sharing stories about preaching at the Agora far below. Such special times, then, when they worked together to teach and convince others that Jesus was truly the Son of God. She remembered their travels and their sojourn here, the nights they enjoyed friendship with Priscilla and Aquilla, the tents they made together.

Memories that she had held and cherished for so many years raced through her thoughts. Those memories were all she had after word came from Rome of the great fires and the death of the Christians. Nero, the evil one had killed so many, so many good people. And eventually, word came that the Romans had beheaded the one love of her life, the beloved servant of God, her dear friend, Paul.

The tears continued to flow She remembered sheltering him here and hiding him from the Romans when the store owners were upset

300

with his preaching; because he taught about a God who does not require idols. So misunderstood, her man.

Once again, she pondered the one night when they held each other
against the pain of the Romans and he needed her. Even now, after
all these years, she had no regrets that she had taken him in and
eased his pain and given him deep satisfaction. She knew he regretted his weakness that night, and never quite forgave himself – the
thorn in his flesh – as he called it, but she never could regret that she
had given him all her love. In return, he had given her a gift of incredible measure.

But no one would ever know. For years, she had kept the secret
from the church. She treasured her child in Seleucia, and when the
right time came, she brought her "orphan" to the house church at
Ephesus to be raised in the good home of Michael and Blantas. She
returned to the cave in Seleucia to live and teach other women about
Jesus. The cave gave her freedom to teach, apart from the traditional
society, she could focus on the girls. She spread the good news, quietly, while teaching girls to read and love God.

She knew that among the Christians, she had been known as the
Virgin, and sometimes she was embarrassed about the way they told
her story, encouraging the young girls to follow her path to God. But
she had protected her great teacher and friend, Paul, against any gos-
sip or blots on his character. He was the greatest follower of Jesus she
had ever known, and she would not allow them to put him down, because he shared his humanity with her that one night many years ago.

So many blessings in her long life. She sat down on her thinking
stone and continued to reminisce. When the house church at Ephesus
had invited her to their cave at Ephesus to instruct their children, she
thought her heart would burst with joy. They entrusted to her the
daughter of Joseph and Anna. Anna, the daughter of Priscilla and
Aquilla, had married that child she had borne of Paul. They had en-
listed her to teach Thecilla, her very own granddaughter. She wiped
her tears and smiled. Out of her great loss, came such great love and
such a wonderful young woman. God had been good to her. Her life
overflowed with love. She could not ask for more.

"Ah, well," she sighed to herself and spoke, even though no one
else could hear. "Perhaps it's best that she dropped the scroll. I gave
her all I had, and she is such an incredible woman now. God will
watch over her, she doesn't need my truth to make her whole." Her
heart swelled with pride when she considered the brave girl, her student, her granddaughter continuing the family legacy of preaching the
gospel of love, resisting hate, resisting empire, only serving God. She
treasured the scrolls, and the journey of Thecilla, and those memories
on top of her older ones would ease any pain she might experience as
she prepared to leave this world for the next.

Now she took the small scroll back into the cave and entered the alcove where the large storage pot stood. She took a plug off the top and carefully removed the seven wonderful scrolls she'd received from Thecilla. She placed them down on the cave floor, one at a time, until they rested like long candles, so full of light, laying quietly now on a shared brown bed. Then she tucked her own scroll deep into the large pot, wiping tears from her face. Somewhere along the path of memories this day, her sadness had turned to joy. She laughed and wiped away some more of her happy tears.

She gave thanks for the goodness of God, for the God who had saved her so many years earlier from the fire, from men who would use her, from the lions and the lightening. She gave thanks for the years of learning and teaching, for the freedom she had known as a cave hermit and for the many girls her life had touched, who had loved her. She gave thanks for the love of God that taught a good way of life, an alternative to the ways of evil empire.

She took a round plate off the shelf above her that Paul had once brought to her after his traveling, her precious plate. She pushed it deep down into the pot now, providing a cover for her very own scroll. Knowing she would never see it again, she replaced the seven scrolls on top of the others. Filling in the extra space with salty sand, she began a process that took several days, to fill in the area around the pot. Later, she would have her friend fill in the wall.

She slept soundly that night, realizing that she had never been alone, after all.

Historical Note: On September 18, 96 C.E. members of the Roman Senate assassinated the Emperor Domitian, ending the reign of the Flavian Dynasty. The Emperor had accomplished significant military victories and historians later attributed his reign to creating stability, leading to a relatively peaceful second century for the Romans. But at the time, historians vilified the man, portraying him as the tyrant who became a spokesman for a return to public morality, while killing his wife's lover. His own lover reportedly died in a botched abortion. He had long insisted on being called "Dominus et Deus" (Lord and God), erecting a temple to his own honor and huge statues of himself in his provinces, including a larger than life monument in Ephesus. Following his death, the Senators smashed his statues to bits.

Political changes meant liberation for some. The Senators freed many of Domitian's prisoners. A decree of September 19 ordered John on Patmos to be released from exile. After five years on the island, the old man could come home.

5. Thecilla and Claudius Come Home

September 24, 96 A.D.

The cooling breezes of autumn scattered leaves along the road, and ushered in a new era for the Christians in Ephesus. Anna sent Joseph to Patmos to bring Uncle John home and through the traders, she passed along a letter to Claudius and Thecilla in Jerusalem, encouraging them to return as well.

On a late September afternoon, the House Church at Ephesus gathered for a welcome feast for their old friend, John. They devoured a meal fit for a king, then reclined in the large gathering tent, to listen. The thin, weathered man spoke with spiritual clarity about his vision and communion with God on the island. "Late at night, the heavens opened and the messages streamed down. My scribe wrote for me, and Thecilla helped also. The vision poured out like a heavy rain that would not stop. So much love. God loves us all so much. Keep faith. Don't be discouraged."

"The girl, the young woman, Thecilla, such a treasure. Thank you for sending her to me." John stroked his chin, and then looked with concern. "Where is she now? Where did she go?"

303

Anna looked at Joseph. The candlelight flickered against the tent wall. She turned to her uncle and smiled into his worried eyes. "Thecilla served you well. She left with the scrolls the night after she returned from the island, taking them to all seven churches, as you asked. We would not let her go, but she slipped out into the night."

Joseph glared at John. "How could you ask her do such a thing? A young woman, traveling out to the seven churches? You know the Romans do not like the Christians. Domitian banished you. Didn't you think about what he could do to a mere girl?"

John traced a circle in the dirt with his stick, avoiding Joseph's eyes.

Anna recognized his pain. "Thecilla's friend, Claudius, traveled with her to the churches. Claudius plays in the games. He's from a good Jewish family. His Roman friends loaned him a chariot for their travels. Together, they took your scrolls to the seven churches."

"Did she lose the faith?" John's eyes darted around the circle, searching the faces of the house church for the truth. "What happened?"

"She followed in the tradition of my mother, Priscilla." Anna smiled and began the familiar story. "You know Thecla taught her well. She knows the the scripture as well as a boy, even better than Claudius, who chose to be baptized in Christ during their trip."

Joseph interrupted. "The Romans accosted them on the night road during their return from Laodicea. A soldier stuck his sword into the bag with the scrolls and flung them into a field. When they came home, Thecilla went to visit Thecla and a Roman sentry followed her and chased her down the hill."

"They're OK," Anna interrupted again. "After the journey to the seven churches, they came home to marry, then left for Jerusalem. They follow in the family tradition of my mother and father, Priscilla and Aquilla. They go to preach and teach to the church and make converts in Jerusalem."

Joseph stopped Anna. "They escaped the reach of the tyrant Domitian, they sought safety. They didn't even have time for a proper wedding celebration. Too much fear, too much danger." Joseph glared at John.

Anna turned away from Joseph and put her hand on John's shoulder and looked kindly at the old man.

"Ah, so my scrolls are gone, then. But she continues to spread the news, for that I am grateful."

He had looked forward to reading the scrolls again and explaining the vision.

"But no, they did bring them home. The last morning of their trip, they left the inn before dawn to retrieve the scrolls from the field, and they have carried them along to Jerusalem. They paid a man in Per-

304

gamum to make several copies of the scrolls. We have a copy here. Wait, I'll fetch it for you." Anna left the tent to get the scrolls.

The night shadows lifted from John's face and the candlelight illuminated a bright smile. He followed Anna out of the tent, eager to see his scrolls again.

Soon they came back to the gathering tent, with John clutching the scrolls to his breast. He opened the scrolls, one by one. Then he read and preached long into the night.

"Do you not see? Jesus calls all Christians to love and to keep the faith; to resist the terrible violence of the Romans, the anti-Christ Nero, the whore Roma? Do you not see? The Romans shed the blood of the Christians, but we should not fight back. Do you see? We Christians should not take up the sword, but only the Word of the Lord, which is like a sword which cuts through the lies, immorality and greed. We look to the Tree of Life, the healing leaves, the River of Living Water that flows out through the City of our God. Our Savior has come, he knocks at the doors of our lives and seeks entrance. Now is the day of salvation, now is the day to take up our cross, to follow Jesus in praise and by loving all of God's children."

In the morning, Joseph and John set out on a journey to the seven churches, so that John could teach and preach and share the good news for all Christians that God had given to him on Patmos.

***

A month later in Jerusalem Thecilla and Claudius opened the letter from home.

"Ah, Claudius! Can we go? I want to see Mama and Papa again with my brother and sister."

"Let's pray and listen to our God, then we will know what to do," Claudius said.

So they prayed together for guidance and soon they both felt led to go back to Ephesus. They began the journey home, even though they knew the trip would be difficult for Thecilla, whose belly again swelled, heavy with child. She struggled with constant upset sailing on the rough waters of late autumn, through the storms and gales of the Mediterranean Sea. Nevertheless she felt great joy, anticipating home.

On a bright, calm November morning, their boat sailed into the harbor at Ephesus. They stopped to pray and give thanks for arriving safely. Claudius knelt by the side of the boat, while Thecilla stood, holding the hand of their son.

Claudius prayed out loud, "God of love, you have carried us to preach your good news in the West. Now we humbly thank you for allowing us to return to the land of our parents. Thank you for safe *travel.   Bless our homecoming. Use us to continue to share your love. We remain your servants, in the name of your son, Jesus."*

"Amen and Amen!" Thecilla closed the prayer with a smile and a laugh. She turned to her son, "You will meet my Mama and Papa, and Papa's parents, too. You will meet my brother and sister."

For their son, Paulos, everything was new and he looked with wonder at the large temple of white marble towering over the harbor. Claudius took some coins from his bag to hire a chariot to take his young family home.

"We'll go to my house, first. We can send word to have your parents join us. We have plenty room for all. Tomorrow we'll invite the house church to hear our missionary stories."

"But can we go first to the Cave of Thecla? Please? I need to go." As much as she longed to see her parents, Thecilla most wanted to first run up the hill to the Cave of Thecla.

"It's a long climb, are you sure?" Claudius asked. He knew his wife did not sleep well on the boat, and her pregnancy made any travel difficult.

"Yes, I can do this. I know I must." Thecilla took the hand of her little boy, while Claudius asked the driver to deliver them to the bottom of BulBul Dag.

The steep climb indeed challenged her bulging body, and they stopped frequently. Claudius carried their son most of the way. By the time they reached the top, Paulos slept soundly. They found the door to the cave closed, with a large boulder in front. Outside a stone marked a mound of earth. Thecilla stooped to read out loud. "'Thecla, Servant of Jesus.' Claudius, look!"

Claudius fell down beside Thecilla and wrapped his arm around her, saying, "She's with God now." Then he held her while she wept the loss of her great teacher and friend. She remembered the scroll, which she had pledged to find, even as she remembered she had promised to keep it secret.

"Can we go in the cave and see if she left anything?"

"After four years? Everything will be gone," Claudius told her what she already knew, yet he pushed until the boulder rolled away, and then pushed to open the door. Together, they peered into the small corridor, full of cobwebs. A rat scurried out and Thecilla screamed. She searched the alcove, near the entrance, remembering Thecla removed the pot with her scrolls from the area, but the wall was completely enclosed now. She wondered where Thecla placed her scroll.

Claudius reached out to enclose Thecilla in his embrace. "We must go. You need to rest. Let us go to my parents. They will tell us about Thecla. I'm so sorry. I know this is very hard for you. She goes to be with God, some day we will meet her again."

"We must take her home, back to Seleucia. Will you go with me? Let us go to the market and buy an ossuary, a box for her remains, so she can be buried with her mother and father and her mother's father. Yes. She told me that someday she must return to her home."

And so, after the baby came, and the winter passed, the young family journeyed to Seleuica in eastern Asia to take the bones of their beloved teacher home. There she would find her final resting place, and there for years to come pilgrims would flock to honor the holy woman of the early church, St. Thecla.

***

Editorial Note: In the years ahead, the Cave where Thecla completed her life's journey would become a shrine of the Christians. Known even today as the Cave of St. Paul, early Christians scratched prayers to Paul, and over the years, artists journeyed high up Bulbul Dag to paint pictures depicting the saints of the church, and stories in the the Bible. Layers of frescoes mark this holy place. In the back, Christians carved out a large room for worship.

Several centuries later, an artist climbed up to the Cave of St. Paul to paint Thecla's story. There, the bright colors memorialized that fateful day when Paul stood at the door of the House of Thecla, talking with her mother, while Thecla waited behind the bars covering the window, yearning to become a disciple, when they sent her to be burned instead. Even now, the fresco stands, telling a story of faith and perseverance. Not only did the virgin saint defy death, but she gave life to a son and a granddaughter who helped build the church and taught more about how all are called to love one another.

46. The Revelation – To Be Continued

January, 2007

Jane lifted her wine glass. "A toast. Ladies, pick up your glasses! To Thecla! To Thecilla! To the mystics at Patmos! To Lydia! Hear, Hear!"

The glasses clinked around the table at the party Abigail Wesley hosted for the MAMs a year later in Ann Arbor. The women gathered to attend Ursula's archeological convention entitled, "Thecla's Scrolls."

"I'm so sorry I couldn't go on your expedition!" Abigail said. "Sometimes I feel as if I was there, with all the stories and pictures you've shared. But I'm wondering now that the dust has settled on your dig, did this amazing adventure make any difference in your lives?"

Jane lifted her glass again. "Thank you, Thecla! After I baptized myself in Lydia's river in the tradition of Thecla, those crazy mystics in Patmos led me down to the waters of the Aegean for my third baptism and I will never be the same!"

The women knocked their glasses together and laughed. When the silence descended once more, Abigail looked at Jane. "And?"

Jane smiled and began to talk seriously. "Well, I found a spiritual program to explore mysticism some more. Shalem Institute in Washington, DC. Pretty soon, I'll be able to teach you all how to become mystics. For now, I start each day with a silent meditation. You may find it hard to believe, but I am changing deep within and finding that holy, sacred space close to God where we are all one."

For once, Sallie didn't banter back, but just said "Wow!"

And then a curious spacious silence seemed to fill the room. And without exchanging words, the group members all turned to face Katharine. She laughed nervously at their sudden attention, but wasted no time with her response. "Abigail, this trip changed me, too. I came so close to death. You know people say these near encounters change them. It's true. My dreams carried me into a cave of early Christians dancing into the night by candle light. I felt called first to forgive Moses Sun, and now to focus on dance and spirituality; a totally new undertaking for me in my research and writing."

"You can say that again!" Ursula responded. "The serious, scholarly Dr. Long focusing on dance?" Ursula said.

"Are you going to teach a dance class?" Sallie asked.

"You know I am not a dancer, but I am actually partnering with a dance instructor to teach a class on Spirituality and Dance in the fall. And John and I have been taking ballroom dancing lessons."

Once more a sacred spaciousness filled the circle, uniting the women gathered. This time, Molly broke the silence. "Katharine's near encounter reminded me that life is short and how important it is to embrace adventure. A part of me died when my son went to war. But finding these scrolls that underscored the nonviolence inherent in Jesus' message has stirred something deep within me. I believe God is calling me to do something more with my life. My husband and I want to start a triple bottom line factory to put people back to work in Riverside."

"Triple Bottom Line?" Priscilla asked.

"People, planet, profit. We won't do anything unless it's good for the people we employ and the people of the earth. We will consider the planet and our carbon imprint in all our work. And we will try to make profit, to help better the lives of people in Riverside."

"Wow!" Sallie exclaimed again and this time everyone looked at the large candle flickering on the centerpiece. The light reflected onto the faces of those around the table.

Then Emily took up the baton. "Well, Granny Abby, you know what happened to me. After Josh spent his savings coming to rescue me, he popped the question again and the rest is history. He's still a Republican and I'm still a Democrat, but we're finding a bridge between us and who knows perhaps we'll lead the country in reuniting some day."

"I loved that party you had for the Republicans and Democrats before your wedding," Sallie interrupted. "The bridging exercises, and having purple as your wedding color – such a brilliant idea! You'll bring us together, yet, Emily! Keep it up." Sallie raised her glass, "To Emily and Josh and the future of our country! May they lead us into love and working together across the aisle!"

After the MAMs placed their glasses back down, Emily continued. "Sometimes, when I think about it all, I get goose bumps. Brother Gabriel, the Conference of Mystics, Thecla, and then Thecilla, who could've written my senior thesis better than me. So much mystery, so much hope."

Ursula smiled. "I loved your wedding, Emily, too. Joe proposed to me that night. We still haven't figured out the details, but you'll all be invited when we do. Thank you so much for coming to my conference so I can show you off to the archaeologists. This has opened up a huge new door in my career and my life. I don't know how to thank you all."

Ursula's eyes began to tear up and Katharine reached over to hug her, while Emily offered a clean napkin.

Sallie waited until everyone's faces were wet with common tears before sharing her story. "Abigail, you see? This trip changed us all, even me." She paused to laugh and chuckle at herself this time. "Laodicea -- lukewarm Christians? That was me. Well, I've always enjoyed life and done my best, but my flame seemed to be burning low in retirement. Now? I'm listening for God each day and you know I've gotten involved in a program called 'Circles' helping people get out of poverty through building community. I have no idea where God is leading me, but I'm on the path."

"Me, too," Priscilla answered. "No dramatic changes yet, but Moses and I are considering our future. We've been putting together a presentation on Revelation to take to the churches. Moses suggested a seven city tour! We're going slow. Moses may attend seminary first. We'll see. I'm just praying for God to lead us."

Abigail's silver hair shone in the candle light as once more the women embraced the silence and the wonder seeping into the space that connected them all.

"You know I've been working with 'Grandmothers for Peace' for a long time. I have an idea that I could ask them to help me with a project to build a shrine to St. Thecla in Seljuk, a place for grandmothers from all spiritual traditions to come together to pray for international and interfaith understanding. What do you think?"

"Well, that's the virgin saint you're messing with, you know? You might encounter some resistance." Katharine said. "But it's a wonderful idea."

"Even virgins have grandmothers," Sallie said.

"But virgins are not grandmothers," Jane added.

"Only Thecla!" Emily raised her glass. "To Thecilla's awesome grandmother! To Thecla! Hear, Hear!"

The women laughed and Abigail thanked them for sharing. "Your experiences are quite wonderful, quite amazing. What an expedition. You found Thecla, and so much more!"

***

The next day, the MAMs showed up early for Ursula's convention. They drank coffee to stay awake through the technical lectures and rose to the occasion in the afternoon when they donned their red hats for Ursula's presentation on the dig and the findings, providing some levity in the midst of the academic papers.

To the MAMs surprise, Sophie Simons had flown in from Vienna, Brother Gabriel drove over from Chicago, and Joe Cohen came from California. Ursula had also managed to bring in Dan Parks and Moses Sun. Even Halim Mohammed, the head archaeologist from Turkey, came and brought along Balaban and his wife.

Halim Mohammed presented an overview of the excavations at Ephesus, and Sophie Simons presented a paper on her work with the frescoes in the Cave of St. Paul. A professor at the University of Chicago placed the scrolls within the context of other archaeological finds illuminating the early church, explaining the new information that the scrolls provide, particularly on the role of women in the early church and Thecla.

The second day of the conference, the MAMs were back on stage reading the seven scrolls. Abigail read Thecla's. Then a panel of several theologians responded. Emily's religion professor from the University of Chicago debunked the Rapture Theory. But Ursula had also invited a respected scholar from the other tradition, who explained the Rapture Theory as a plausible scriptural interpretation. A lively discussion followed. The progressive scholars picked apart the Rapture Theory, but everyone had a chance to speak. Emily presented a paper, "Nonviolence, Worship and Faith" that she had prepared in a class during the year, explaining the teachings in the scrolls.

But the highlight of the day came when Moses Sun gave a personal testimony on his own experience in the Right Disciples, and how the message of the scrolls and his experience on the dig had transformed his own thinking on the end times. "You know, Jesus told us we wouldn't know when he'd come again. His teachings were focused on loving those around us. He told us to share what we have with others. He taught an upside down kind of living. I have come to believe that the church should not focus on an end times theology that downplays the importance of loving in the present. I don't think that Jesus wanted us to put all our focus on the afterlife."

"The *End Times* books glorify violence. The book of Revelation and Thecilla's scrolls show a very different picture. The Lamb of God certainly was sacrificed. But you see that the blood that sanctifies was from the suffering servant of Jesus. In Revelation, the Romans were the violent ones. The Christians were called to keep faith and to love. I do believe that the focus that many in the Christian church place on a violent end does a disservice to Jesus. Armageddon is not prescribed by Jesus. As Christians, it is time for us to step out and leave war behind. For 2000 years, we have worshiped the Prince of Peace while supporting war in infinite varieties. The time has come for us to return to the love of Jesus which takes no prisoners."

Another speaker, Donald Yoder, came from the Associated Mennonite Biblical Seminaries in Elkhart. He gave a quick overview of the historical Mennonite theology, and then shared his own work of study looking at the book of Revelation, interpreting it as a call for nonviolence, also. "The scrolls confirm my work in this field. We Mennonites have taken a course of following the teachings of Jesus seriously when he says to love your enemies and we believe that this clearly calls all Christians to take a path of nonviolence. Ours is not a popular stance, but then we know they killed Jesus, too."

***

Before the MAMs left for home, they met together one more time. Jane had brought a surprise from home. "This is the Living Vine Labyrinth," she told the MAMs. "It's a place for quiet reflection and prayer. Some friends of mine created this last summer."

"I drew the flowers!" Sallie bragged.

"Yes, Sallie came in the last night and helped get all the flowers drawn. A big help. I smile every time I come to the flowers, thinking of you, Sallie."

"Aw, that's the nicest thing you've ever said to me, Jane." Sallie replied. Sallie's laughter infected the group with smiles.

"If you've never walked a labyrinth before, take some time to read this informational sheet. There's no right or wrong way to do this. Just be quiet; listen; pray. An ancient archetype, used by spiritual pilgrims in many traditions. Let go. Walk into the center, pray, and then walk back out. Take all the time you need." Jane told them.

She turned on quiet instrumental music. The women sat to read and then began to walk. The spacious silence of the night before once more descended among and within the MAMs. They walked alone, yet together, spiraling into God. The green vines lining the labyrinth path led each of them into the center and at each turn, one of Sallie's flowers greeted them – with the colors of the rainbow; the chakras, "de colores" Ursula called them. In the center of the labyrinth seven small flowers grew from a common seed. Soon the women formed a circle in the center. They paused to pray and then locked arms in a tight group hug, their eyes focused on the seven flowers without a word.

Katharine led the group out, twirling and dancing and the others followed behind. They raised their hands, spinning, following, and moving out of the circle, along the meandering path; back out into their lives, into the mystery of God and the possibilities to come.

Look for the MAMs next adventure, coming soon in:

Revelation at the Labyrinth
The MAMs: In Search of Green

END NOTES

[i]Sheldon, Charles. *In His Steps.* 1897. Find in the public domain at http://www.ssnet.org/bsc/ihs/ihs.html.

[ii]Crossan, John Dominic and Jonathon Reed. *In Search of Paul: How Jesus's Apostle Opposed Rome's Empire with God's Kingdom. A New Vision of Paul's Words and World.* San Francisco: HarperCollins, 2004.

[iii]Wallis, Jim. *God's Politics: Why the Right Gets It Wrong and the Left Doesn't Get It.* New York: HarperCollins, 2006.

[iv]Crossan, op. cit.

[v]*The Acts of Paul and Thecla* is an apocryphal story of St. Paul's influence on a young woman named Thecla now in the public domain. View at: http://www.christianscience.org/thecla.htm." The story of Thecla in this book is a fictitious adaptation.

[vi]Rossing, Barbara. *The Rapture Exposed: The Message of Hope in the Book of Revelation.* Boulder, Colorado: Westview Press, 2004.

[vii]Sherman, Richard B. and Sherman, Robert M., lyrics and music for "Sister Suffragette" in *Mary Poppins,* 1964.

[viii]Revelation 1: 1-20, NSRV.

[ix]Revelation 22:1-5, NSRV.

[x]Hello (Shalom). Who are they? (Turkish)

[xi]American women. Watch out! They're yours, now! (Turkish)

[xii]Cave explorer... Builder, boss. (Turkish)

[xiii]Hello (Shalom), Sir. (Turkish)

[xiv]A little bit. (Turkish)

[xv]"Climb Every Mountain," Rodgers, Richard and Oscar Hammerstein III, *Sound of Music,* 1965.

[xvi]Rupp, Joy. Dear Heart, Come Home. New York: Crossroads Publishing, 1996.

[xvii]Rupp, op.cit. Page 9.

[xviii]Fireman. (Turkish)

[xix]Son. (Turkish)

[xx]Help your mother. (Turkish)

[xxi]Kidd, Sue Monk, *The Secret Life of Bees.* Crossroads Press; New York, 2002.

[xxii]Crosson. op. cit.

[xxiii]Rupp, op. cit. Page 9.

[xxiv]Tolle, Eckhart. *The Power of Now*. Vancouver, B.C., Canada: Namaste Publishing, 1999.

[xxv]Good day. (German)

[xxvi]Who? (Turkish)

[xxvii]*Songs of Prayer and Praise*. Brothers of Taize. "El Senyor" Latin version. English translation: "In the Lord, I'll be ever thankful, In the Lord, I will rejoice! Look to God, do not be afraid. Lift up your voices, the Lord is near, lift up your voices, the Lord is near." Copyright © Ateliers et Presses de Taizé, 71250 Taizé, France. Used with permission.

[xxviii]*Songs of Prayer and Praise*. Brothers of Taize. "El Senyor" English translation. Copyright © Ateliers et Presses de Taizé, 71250 Taizé, France. Used with permission.

[xxix]The parable of the Good Samaritan is a parable told by Jesus recorded in Luke 10:25-37. A traveler (who may or may not be Jewish) is beaten, robbed, and left half dead along the road. First a priest and then a Levite come by, but both avoid the man. Finally, a Samaritan comes by. Samaritans and Jews generally despised each other, but the Samaritan helps the injured man. Jesus is described as telling the parable in response to a question regarding the identity of the "neighbor" which Leviticus 19:18 says should be loved. Portraying a Samaritan in positive light would have come as a shock to Jesus' audience. It is typical of his provocative speech in which conventional expectations are inverted.

[xxx]Songs of Prayer and Praise. Brothers of Taize. English translation: "Where charity and love are, God is there." Copyright © Ateliers et Presses de Taizé, 71250 Taizé, France. Used with permission.

[xxxi]Scofield Reference Bible. Oxford, United Kingdom: Oxford University Press, 1917.

[xxxii]Scofield, op. cit.

[xxxiii]Scofield, op. cit.

[xxxiv]"Keep it quiet."